"VICTORY! VICTORY!" SHOUTED HAROLD FORRESTER.

THE
HEADSMAN OF OLD LONDON BRIDGE.

𝕮omplete in 𝕺ne 𝕭olume.

BEAUTIFULLY ILLUSTRATED.

LONDON :
"BOYS OF ENGLAND" OFFICE, 173, FLEET STREET, E.C.,
AND ALL BOOKSELLERS.

THE HEADSMAN OF OLD LONDON BRIDGE:

"THE HEADSMAN'S VISION."

No. 1

THE HEADSMAN OF OLD LONDON BRIDGE.

CHAPTER I.

AT THE SIGN OF THE "RED CROSS."

IT was about eleven o'clock at night, on the 12th of July, 15—, that a light skiff shot, arrowlike, through one of the narrow arches of old London Bridge, and whirled round and round in the eddying foam.

Its occupant, whom, in the gloom, it would have been difficult to distinguish from a dark, inanimate mass, had the honour, apparently, of having the river to himself.

Not a living being seemed moving anywhere; and out on the broad, rushing waters, nothing could be heard but the clash of the impatient stream against the bridge works, the bumping of ill-moored barges against each other.

The rower, however, knew well, apparently, that though man had done with Father Thames for the night, there were those near at hand who would afford him a hearty welcome.

He glanced rapidly and eagerly around him as if once more to assure himself that no one was on the watch, and then raising his hand to his mouth, he gave a loud, prolonged whistle.

The result was miraculous.

The whole bridge, with its huge, looming buildings, had appeared, until now, in the grey night, nothing but an indistinct and shapeless mass.

But no sooner had the whistle echoed over the river than there was seen on the wall, not far above the daring rower's head, a bright red cross standing out in fiery radiance from a black background.

"Good," muttered the stranger; "they have not forgotten me."

And a second whistle rang out on the night air.

Then, as he rowed gently back, a window was thrown open and a ladder was let down, so that it rested upon one of the projecting buttresses.

The passage of the stream at this point was a feat attended with the utmost danger when the tide was rushing up or down; for at such times the waters were fully six feet higher on one side than on the other, and, pent up in narrow channels, dashed through with the roar and force of a torrent.

The occupant of the skiff, however, seemed not only fully alive to the perils of the situation, but also quite ready to protect himself against them; for, by a skilful manœuvre, he brought the light boat against the wedge-like end of the buttress, and, leaping upon the rough stone-work, moored his boat by a strong rope to an iron ring fixed for this purpose among the stones.

Then he nimbly ascended the ladder, passed through the window beneath the fiery cross, and entered a room which was enveloped in complete gloom.

The person who received him was a stout, ill-looking person, between forty and fifty years of age, and his voice as he spoke was harsh and horrid, like the croaking of a raven.

"Well, you've come somewhat late, Master Alsdon," he said. "The boys were beginning to complain and think that ——"

"Let them cease from thinking, and do what they are paid to do," exclaimed the other, haughtily. "They would so the better assure the safety of their ears, and mayhap their heads. But tell me, Master Wormer, are they all here?"

"Aye, Master Alsdon," said Wormer, in a cringing voice; "they are here as you expected—four as strong and willing birds as ever plumed their pinions in Alsatia. Let me conduct you, sir. There

—mind that step; you know of old that it is scarcely safe footing."

The stranger scowled angrily as he placed his foot on the first step to descend the winding staircase, but the reminiscence--whatever it was—that was called up by Wormer's simple words, had another effect besides that of causing anger.

A cold sweat rushed upon the surface of his body, and his heart leaped violently.

"Mark me, Wormer," he said, in a low voice, "you are getting insolent of late. Take care that a new landlord has not soon to take your place in the 'Red Cross.' *Your* footsteps may slip, as others have done. Lead on then, and keep a civil and a cautious tongue between your teeth, lest my dagger search for its roots."

The words were said in such a cold, cruel voice, that the landlord said no more; but, slipping by his guest, led the way down into a large room where a number of men were carousing.

The entrance of Alsdon was greeted by a cheer, and, with a proud nod of the head, he seated himself by the chimney corner near the fire, which, in spite of its being a July night, was blazing on the hearth.

Here you could see his features, at least such of them as could be distinguished among the forest of wildly luxuriant locks that clustered over his brow and waved round his mouth and over his cheeks and chin.

From out this forest of hair gleamed two piercing black eyes, whose glance, once observed, would never be forgotten.

Sinister would scarcely be the term to apply to their expression.

They were the eyes of a fiend: eyes to crush, to horrify, to annihilate: eyes to soften and melt into serpent-like gentleness."

"Well, Master Alsdon," said one of the men, in a familiar voice--he was a ruffian noticeable among the others as having a huge scar on his forehead, and a flat, broken nose—"we've been expecting you some time, and had almost feared that our noble patron had forgotten us."

Alsdon threw off at once his punctiliousness.

"You need not fear that," he said, in a voice which he endeavoured to make as hearty as possible. "His lordship has not forgotten the services you have already rendered him. But come, Wormer, fill up those empty flagons and we'll to business."

"In the first place, Sharpley," he added, addressing the ruffian who had spoken to him, "you know well Master Launcelot Duke, the diamond merchant ? '

"What, the man who lord's it at Duke's Palace, as the people nickname it, on the bridge here ? " returned Sharpley. "Aye, I should be a senseless loon indeed did I not know him and his pretty daughter, and the two upstart fellows he calls his apprentices. What of them ?"

"It is of all of them," said Alsdon, sinking his voice, as if even in this den of infamy his words could be overheard, "that I have to speak. You say you know the daughter, Eveline ?"

"Aye, well do I know her bright face. She is the only one of all the crew that I would wish no harm to come to."

"You must put your scruples in your pocket then," returned Alsdon, frowning. "It is with her that our business lies. To-morrow, as you well know, is the fair of St. Christopher, which will be held on the green beyond the bridge gates. The merchant, his daughter, and his two apprentices will be there; and when the fun is at its height, when the evening shades begin to fall, then your business begins. A carriage will be in waiting near the dark lane that leads to Ettersly's Farm. To this you must carry Eveline; and as for Edwin Archer—well, he is a thorn in your patron's side, and should he resist the abduction of the fair one, why to kill a man in fair fight is no harm."

The four men listened imperturbably to this harangue, smoking and looking into the fire stolidly, but in reality taking in every word let fall by the speaker, and framing their plans for the future.

"Well," said Sharpley, when Alsdon had finished speaking, "this is a dangerous task you have set us. There will be broken heads over it *I* can see. But as for Edwin Archer, why, he's the white-faced fool that struck me, and brought the ridicule of the mob upon me last May Day. If he but comes within reach of my arm, it will be odd if he lives to insult mortal man again. But for the other one, Harold Forrester; you speak not of him, who is, after all, the more dangerous of the two."

Alsdon laughed.

"He's a brave youth enough, in truth," he said. "But there is no use in wasting time in slaying without necessity. If he resists over much, cut him down, but delay not in doing so. My lord has fixed his eye on him to do great things in the future, and if he but minds his doings, he will live to lord it over many of you. But come, Redlock, you do not speak. Where is the letter which I bade you bring me?"

The man thus addressed growled out something about waiting till he was spoken to, and, taking a note from his doublet, handed it to Alsdon.

The latter seized it eagerly, and tore it open.

His face as he read it brightened and glowed with pleasure.

"Good, good," he said; "this Edwin Archer is the one. I knew it, I knew it. And now let the 'Golden Fleece' spread its sails when it will from the Far West, and bring a host of Don Fernandos—I care not for them."

And with these mysterious words, whose meaning will be unfolded as our story progresses, he sprang to his feet.

"At five o'clock I will be near the old gibbet on the edge of Grantly's Green," he said; "be there to the moment, and before to-morrow night Launcelot Duke's house shall be full of sorrow, and your purses full of gold."

And with the words he threw some money on the table to pay for more liquor, and made his way up the ladder-like staircase to the room above.

"Have a care of these fellows, Wormer," he said to the landlord, who followed him obsequiously. "See that they drink not overmuch, or if they do, see that they mix not too much with other folks, for wine sets loose the tongue."

"I will obey your orders in all things," said Wormer; "but tell me, sir, is it true that his lordship will pass here to-morrow in the queen's train?"

Had Wormer been able to distinguish the features of his guest in the gloom of the old bedchamber, he would have seen that they were suddenly overclouded by a storm of intense fury.

But for some reason or another Alsdon restrained his feelings.

"Again I say, meddle not with what does not concern you," he said. "Some of these days you will cease to wag that tongue of yours at all."

With this injunction he made his way through the window, and, descending by the ladder, without another word entered his skiff, and pushed off upon the now high-tided and quiet river.

Hardly had he quitted the four traitors, than from out an obscure recess in one corner of the room there arose a dark form—the form of a man with a large cloak enveloping him, and a mask shrouding his face.

He said not a word to anyone, but slowly passed to the opposite door, and made his way towards the front gate.

The four ruffians spoke not a syllable; but the glasses trembled in their hands, and their countenances fell, and a chill seemed to seize upon their hearts as if some spirit was amongst them.

Wormer, returning, found them staring at the door.

"What ails you?" he cried, in surprise and fear. "Are you all struck dumb?"

"The Headsman! The Headsman of the Bridge!" said Sharpley, in an awe-stricken voice. "How came he here?"

"I know not," returned Wormer, shrugging his shoulders, "he goes and comes when he likes. I knew not even that he was here."

"He has heard all, then, depend upon it," said Sharpley, with white lips, "and before to-morrow's sunset we shall be in gaol."

Wormer laughed.

"Fear not," he said; "he troubles himself not with such atoms as you. Abduct, murder, do as you please. He takes no heed. He flies at higher game."

But the landlord's words had no power to re-enliven them.

They drank up their ale, bade him adieu, and retired hastily to the rooms they were to occupy for the night, each one imagining as he mounted the dark staircase that the black form of the terrible Headsman was looming up above him as he went.

CHAPTER II.

"DUKE'S PALACE."

"I FEEL an unaccountable gloom over me to-day," said Edwin Archer to Harold Forrester, as they lounged out on a terrace at the rear of "Duke's Palace" not long after sunrise on the morning following the meeting at the "Red Cross." "I have not been able to sleep all night for fearful visions that have beset me. I am glad you have turned out early."

The speaker was a youth about nineteen years of age ; but to a careless observer he would have seemed much younger.

His features were handsome and well-cut, but his complexion was pale and painfully delicate—a quality rendered more observable from the intense brilliancy of his eyes.

His form was slim and graceful, and his voice gentle as a woman's.

His companion, though one year younger, was of a different build and stamp altogether.

His face was a handsome one, but it was bold and healthful, while his form, though without any clumsiness, was built in a mould which spoke of immense strength.

They were, as has been before said, apprentices of Launcelot Duke, and were foster brothers, brought up from the earliest moment together, and bearing towards each an affection which nothing seemed capable of undermining.

We will not pause in our story to say more of them here, or to describe the place where they stood.

Suffice it to say that the house of Launcelot Duke, the diamond merchant, was the handsomest on the bridge, and that, in consequence of its splendour, it was nicknamed by the jealous public "Duke's Palace."

It was on a terrace of this house, then, they met ; a spot where they could see the whole expanse of the fine old Thames, far away towards Westminster, glittering and glistening in a thousand wavelets beneath the bright beams of the rising sun, which danced, too, on the houses of the city and the tree-covered slopes on the Surrey side.

Harold clapped his friend heartily on the back.

"Dreams go by contraries, my friend," he said. "If you have dreamed of horrors, why, then, look out for joy. Depend on it."

"Nay, Harold," returned the other, sadly ; "remember the prophecy of the old witch on the heath, when you and I were but children : 'Beware of the month of July!'"

"I do remember it, and scorn it," cried Harold. "See through how many Julys we have passed in safety. There —remember what fun there will be to-day. A royal holiday, recollect ; the queen and her favourites will pass by at three, and then, hey! for the fair of St. Christopher."

A visible shudder passed through the frame of Edwin Archer.

Then he seized his friend's hands.

"Harold," he said, "I have trusted you always. I will trust you again, with more than ever before. But you must make me a sacred promise—nay, be not angry. I have a reason for this—a great reason, or I would not demand it."

"What, then, is the promise ?" asked Harold.

"First, then, you must preserve strict secrecy ; second, you must not seek in any way to prevent my exercising my free will to-day. That is all."

"I promise, then, with all my heart," said Harold.

Edwin at once, with a stealthy glance round him, drew him away from the open doorway behind him to the extreme end of the terrace.

Then he drew from the breast of his doublet a letter and a knife.

"Last night," he said, "I retired early, if you remember, for I felt ill at ease, and had a headache, which prevented my enduring society.

"I undressed, and threw myself into bed.

"But not to sleep.

"I fell into a doze between unconsciousness and wakefulness ; and while in this condition I saw what I imagined to be a vision, and what threw me into terror and consternation.

"A tall, ghost-like figure, deeply masked, noiselessly entered my room, and, placing a letter on the table, fixed it there with a knife.

"It was so spirit-like, its steps so slow and so noiseless, that I feared to challenge it, and lay there trembling and in wonder, until it departed, as it had come, by the window.

"Then I sprang up, secured the casement, and hurrying to the table, took the paper and read these words —

"*On your life go not to-morrow to the fair of St. Christopher.*

"A FRIEND."

Harold took the paper and glanced over it, and the knife, and examined it.

But he could make no more of it than his companion had done.

"Well," he said, "I confess this is very mysterious, and very suggestive of danger. It is so vague, however, that you can make nothing of it. Stay, here is a motto on the knife. What says it ? ·

"'*A friende to ye goode ; a thorne to ye eville.*'

"Why, that is as mysterious as the other."

"Not so," said Edwin Archer; "I take its meaning plainly. It tells me that, if I persist in going to the fair, I am to take this, my faithful companion, with me—that it will defend *me* and destroy my enemies."

"Then you still intend to go, in spite of all warnings?" said Forrester.

"I do, indeed. Why, Harold," cried the other, his face suddenly brightening, and a bright flush overspreading his usually pallid features, "is not our Eveline—our bright and beautiful Eveline—to be there, for one of whose smiles I would risk death a hundred times. I'd rather even cast aside a thousand such mysterious warnings than let her think I slighted her."

A slight spasm of pain crossed Harold's face as his friend spoke.

But Edwin did not observe it.

"You are a brave fellow," cried Harold, "and this evening at the fair we shall be side by side. Unless from an assassin's knife, there can be no danger for you in such a crowd. So, since I have given my promise, I will not endeavour to dissuade you from going. Hark ! there is Eveline's voice. Conceal that knife and paper ; let her not see that you are concerned about anything, or her gentle heart would be wounded."

Edwin had scarcely time to hide them ere the young girl glided up to them.

She was a beautiful creature, not more than sixteen, with deep blue eyes and long golden hair falling over her rounded shoulders in an exquisite glory, partly shrouding the soft outlines of a form of perfect and bewitching symmetry.

"We are all up with the sun, it seems, this morning," she said, laughingly, as she gave a hand to both. "My father is at the breakfast table; and when he thought to catch you napping in your rooms, you were here. Will you enter with me ?"

A careful observer would have told much from the manner in which her words and gestures were received by the two friends.

Edwin listened and gazed, with a kind of rapture—a kind of dreamy, satisfied delight.

Harold's face became crimson with the quick flowing of the rich blood : his heart thumped violently, and his frame trembled.

As for Eveline, she acted the same to both—with a provoking kind of exactitude—showing not a shadow of preference to either.

"Yes, we had better go in," said Harold, and he turned to lead the way, more nervous now than his pale-faced friend.

The manner in which Launcelot Duke received his apprentices, coupled with the behaviour of Eveline, plainly showed upon what footing they stood in the house.

They had been so long in the household, and had been such faithful servants while they had been there, that they were looked upon by the worthy merchant almost as his sons.

"Well, my boys," said Master Duke, as they sat down to the breakfast, "we shall have a few hours' work this morning to get ready those diamonds for my Lady Richworth, and then we'll give up to jollity. Our most gracious queen passes at three, as you may have heard, on her way to the house of my Lord Talbot de Hargreaves, and a fine sight it will be, I fancy; better than all the fairs in the world."

"Yet I would not miss the fair for a fortune," cried Eveline.

"Nor I, nor I," echoed both the apprentices.

Launcelot Duke laughed gaily.

"I dare say not," he cried. "You young folks admire such scenes of senseless jugglery, and tumbling, and noise, and discordant music. So fear not; I will not spoil you of your treat. As soon as the clock strikes four, we will start. Everything is in readiness."

The morning passed laggingly enough, as can be imagined, for those who waited so impatiently; but at length work was over, and dinner eaten, and, in their holiday attire, the inmates of "Duke's Palace" came out on the front balcony.

The bridge presented the appearance of a scene in fairyland.

All business was, of course, suspended.

The people were thronging hither and thither in the gayest of gay attire; bands of music were playing; banners floated in the gentle breeze, gay devices sparkled in the light of the pleasant summer sun.

Everything was life, and fun, and jollity, and happiness, save for one.

And this one Edwin Archer.

Deep in the recesses of his heart, in spite of the sunlight, in spite of the gay music, in spite of the bright being who sat near him, there was the one thought —a thought of dread, a presentiment of coming evil—THE ECHO OF THE WARNING VOICE!

Yet he could not draw back.

It seemed, in his case, in truth, as if the order of the world was changed, and he was ruled by destiny.

At length there was a commotion visible in the crowd below.

The people hurried about more anxiously, more confusedly, and apparently more purposelessly than before; loud shouts rent the air, and the braying of trumpets, and the booming of drums were heard in the distance.

"They are coming!" murmured the crowd below, and the eyes of sweet Eveline Duke sparkled with anticipatory excitement.

The worthy merchant and his apprentices were scarcely less eager, for the sound of approaching music roused even Edwin from his thoughtfulness.

Puritanism had not as yet begun to spread among the people; and almost without inquiry, the nation accepted and reverenced the reign of the "Good Queen Bess."

In a few minutes their eyes were gratified with the wished-for sight.

First came a double row of trumpeters on horseback; then a number of Thames watermen; then a company of mounted soldiers, and then some of the lumbering vehicles of the nobility.

Then more music, more soldiers, more banners, more crashing noise, more show, more tinsel, and then the Virgin Queen, with my Lord of Essex by her side.

Behind her carriage came a number of gay lords, attired in the most splendid costumes that could well be imagined.

"What think you of them, Mistress Eveline?" asked Edwin Archer, turning suddenly to her as this portion of the cavalcade came in sight.

He started as he looked at her, as well indeed he might.

Her face was as pale as death, her bright eyes sunken in her head, her lips ashen and tremulous, her whole body convulsed with emotion, while her gaze was fixed with a kind of stony horror upon someone or something in the street below.

"What ails you?" exclaimed Edwin, gazing at her in surprise and fear, and speaking loudly.

Eveline seized his hand.

"Hush! as you love me, hush!" said she; "let not my father or Harold hear you. It was nothing but a sudden faintness. I would not, you know," she added, with a smile, "be the means of spoiling to-day's sport through my foolish weakness. Say no more of it."

The roses leaped back to her cheeks as she said this, for she caught the eyes of Harold Forrester fixed upon her.

But they were soon chased away again, for hardly had the tail of the cavalcade passed, ere the servant came out upon the balcony.

She was a very young, pretty, but cunning-looking girl, and as she neared her mistress, she watched well to see whether she was observed.

Then, quickly, she thrust into Eveline's hand a note.

"My Lord Housden's valet left it," she whispered, and sped away.

Eveline tore it open, read its few words, and then sprang up, her eyes gleaming, her face ashen, her bosom heaving.

"Oh, this is too much! too much!" she cried, as she left the balcony in haste, and disappeared from view.

Launcelot Duke himself had been too deeply engaged in the study of the scene before him to observe the movements of his daughter.

But Edwin and Harold had watched her well.

"What ails her?" cried the former, as he turned in wonder and fear towards his friend. "Some mysterious hand is at work to mar her happiness also. By heaven! would that I knew the villain, that I might wring from him a confession of his meaning!"

"Your watch is but a slack one, Edwin," returned Harold. "Did you not see the face and form of him who so discomposed her at first? It is some noble of the queen's court—a foreign-looking gallant, with dark eyes full of hateful meaning. Were he not beardless and a knight, I would swear that he was that villain Alsdon that came some weeks since to see our master. He has the same look and the same gait."

"And Eveline," said Edwin, musingly, "seemed moved and agitated by his behaviour. Alas! fine tinselled birds these to catch poor maidens by their glare!"

Harold scarcely heard these words.

He was intent upon the same subject in a different way, and was relieved fortunately from any further discussion by the merchant saying—

"Now then, lads; a little refreshment, and we start for the fair."

Harold, as we have seen, had beheld all that passed.

He had seen the mounted nobleman kiss his hand to Eveline; he had seen her blanching cheek and his hateful smile at her discomposure.

"There is a secret enemy here," thought he, "against whom my poor Edwin is as powerless as a child. I must be the one to watch, to guard, and to punish."

CHAPTER III.

ST. CHRISTOPHER'S FIELDS.

ALL the world that day was off to St. Christopher's Fields.

So, at least, it seemed to those who glanced at the roads thronged with pedestrians of both sexes, dressed in their holiday attire.

Nearly all had rushed to see the procession of the queen and her nobles; but all had now flocked back to the spot where throughout the day they had been enjoying the discordant music of the bands, the wondrous shows of itinerant humbugs, the dancing bears, dead and living monstrosities, fortune-tellers, dancers, and the hundred and one impostures that then, as now, made up the fair.

It was a fine open space, this spot named St. Christopher's Fields, and the shows being spread knowingly over its surface, afforded a chance to everyone to earn a living.

A crowd there was—scarcely what we should call a crowd nowadays—but still, when the diamond merchant and his daughter and apprentices arrived there, they looked upon the scene with a kind of wonder which we should laugh at.

To Edwin and Harold the place and its surroundings had a peculiar and terrible significance.

To Harold, of course, there could be but little enjoyment in such a scene.

What his feelings were in regard to Eveline Duke, I cannot here say.

I must leave that to my story to prove as it progresses.

However, it was evident that the intense pallor which had overspread her face when the queen's retinue had passed, and the mysterious letter she had received afterwards had taken a great and unaccountable effect upon him.

With Edwin Archer it was different.

His lighter nature was not to be permanently disturbed by anything; and, forgetting the danger which threatened himself, as he forgot the mystery that surrounded Eveline, he threw himself, with all his joyousness of heart, into the enjoyment of the moment.

The shades of evening at length began to fall, and as they did, other shadows seemed also to spring into existence.

Wherever they went, Harold felt, rather than saw, that they were followed.

In the crowd immediately around them there was to be seen suddenly a greater admixture than before of great swaggering bullies — regular swash-bucklers, with fiery faces and huge moustaches, elbowing their way through the people, and driving back those who opposed their progress.

Harold saw it, and his heart leaped within him.

He had no cause to fear for Eveline, for the plot against her was, of course, unknown to him.

His alarm was, of course, for his friend Edwin Archer.

But somehow or other he could not help connecting his peril with the mysterious letter to his master's daughter.

Apprentices, of course, were not permitted to wear swords; but Harold and Edwin had on this occasion concealed short weapons beneath their clothes.

Edwin was near Eveline, speaking rapidly to her of the gay scene around, when Harold, looking suddenly back, saw four or five villainous-looking ruffians whispering together and eagerly eyeing the group.

He hurried towards his friend, and clapped him on the shoulder.

"A word with you, Ned," he said.

Then he added, as they drew a few paces back from the others—

"The warning was not without its meaning. We are being surrounded. Keep good watch, for some deadly evil threatens us."

Hardly had the words escaped his lips when a shout arose near, and the crowd began to sway to and fro.

"It is beginning," said Harold. "This commotion is but to cover their design."

It was as he said.

One of the bullies had purposely insulted a bystander, and a fight had begun between two of the confederates.

Then the others who were employed to aid in the cowardly attack of the merchant's daughter, began to press back towards the group.

"Master Duke," cried Harold, "be on your guard. There is some villainy afloat here."

Launcelot Duke had just time to draw his sword, when the four ruffians who had met Alsdon in the "Red Cross" tavern on the bridge dashed forward, headed by Sharpley, and rushed towards Eveline.

In an instant, ere the diamond merchant or his apprentices could prevent it, the amazed and horror-stricken girl was seized and forced from the spot, while the ruffians closed round the abductors, and kept the way with drawn swords.

Both Harold and Edwin were so astounded by the unexpected turn of events that, for an instant, they knew not what to do; but, after a moment's thought, their weapons flew from their scabbards, and, side by side with Launcelot Duke, they rushed at the authors of the outrage.

A free fight began at once.

Those who had seen the outrage drew and took part with the merchant and his apprentices.

Those who had not seen it either shouted "Shame," or took part with the bullies.

The latter, however, purposely gave ground, either to make good their escape to the point where Alsdon awaited them, or to draw the victim they sought into more open ground.

For a long time it was impossible for these hired assassins to perform their deadly office.

In fair fight Edwin Archer, slim and pale, and womanlike as he was, was no insignificant match; and now that his blood was roused to fever heat by the sight of his beloved in the hands of desperados, he fought with the rage and courage of a lion.

"Down with the villains, down with them!" he shouted. "Ah, there is one for Eveline."

As he said this his bright weapon went plunging through the heart of Redlock.

This diversion, and the fall of the villain's body, caused an opening in the crowd which the friends took advantage of to make their way nearer towards the tall, cloaked figure, a glimpse of which they could see struggling through the crowd with Eveline in his arms.

But, just as they were advancing, a creeping, crawling figure emerged from the hustling throng—a man with a pale, cadaverous face, holding in his right hand a long knife.

No one saw him—no one could prevent his hideous deed.

The glittering blade was raised, and, quick as thought, was buried in the back of Edwin Archer.

"Murdered! murdered!" cried the unfortunate youth. "Avenge me, Harold!"

And with these words, he fell headlong to the earth.

CHAPTER IV.

MAT O' THE MIST.

DEAD!

There was no doubting it.

One glance at the pale face, the lustreless eyes, was enough to show that the spirit of the unfortunate youth had fled to a happier land.

It was a maddening moment for Harold Forrester and Launcelot Duke.

But eager as they were to follow and secure the abductor of Eveline, they were restrained by the sight of the bleeding body of Edwin Archer, whose murderer had slunk away, or been hustled out of sight by the throng.

Yet only for a moment.

"Bear him away," cried the diamond merchant; "time will show us his assassin. Let us follow the wretch who has stolen my child. Come, Harold, follow me!"

It was a comparatively easy matter now to force through the crowd.

Now that a murder, cold-blooded and deliberate had shown on which side right stood, the crowd unanimously took part with the merchant and his apprentice, and a lane was at once opened for them to pass.

But all efforts to discover the abductors were vain.

The tall man who had seized Eveline in his arms had not waited to see how matters had progressed, but had forced his way as swiftly as possible towards the dark lane that had been mentioned to Sharpley at the "Red Cross."

The carriage was here in waiting, the young girl was at once placed within it, and Alsdon—for he it was who had carried her off—having entered with her, the horses were driven off at a rapid pace.

When, therefore, the diamond merchant arrived there with Harold—pale, breathless, and in terrible sorrow—not a sign even of the carriage was to be seen, while all inquiries seemed useless.

The merchant's agony was fearful to witness.

All the more fearful because he did not give way to loud lamentations.

"Harold, my lad," he said, leaning for a moment on his shoulder, "I fear me we shall have two now to avenge. Poor Eveline! Poor Edwin! And they loved one another. Great God! who can have planned this injustice?"

"Heaven will guide us to this discovery," said Harold; "but come, let us return; let us carry Edwin home, and then, between us, we will concert measures for the recovery of Eveline—safe and sound, I trust—or the punishment of her base betrayer."

Poor Edwin!

When they returned to the spot, they found that the bystanders had formed a kind of bier, and were only waiting for their coming to carry him to his home.

Slowly and mournfully they bore him away to the house on Old London Bridge.

From out the frolicsome scene in St. Christopher's Fields to a darkened room!

Up to this moment there had been a severe struggle in Harold's heart.

Loving Eveline sincerely as he did, he had resolved to keep her secret, because his noble heart had imagined it would tend to her happiness to do so.

Now all was changed.

He saw plainly that whatever evil estimate she had formed of the gallant who had kissed his hand to her on the bridge, she had not been deceived.

He felt certain that this man had been the one to plan the outrage; and the diamond merchant had a right to know all.

When, therefore, Edwin had been laid out in his quiet room, with two high candles burning by his head, looking very calm, but scarcely more pale than of old, Harold took Launcelot Duke aside, and told him all.

The merchant listened eagerly.

"Heaven is against me!" he cried, when he had heard all. "Do you know who it was who thus addressed her?"

"Lord Housden."

Launcelot Duke uttered an exclamation of terror.

"A villain and rake of the deepest dye!" he exclaimed, and one who holds so firm a position with the queen that to breathe a word against him would be death! Oh! heaven protect her! *what* can be done?"

"You believe, as I do, that it was he who carried her off?"

"I do."

"Yes; and that Alsdon aided him. I will tell you, master, how we can approach him. I will lay my life down for Eveline, Master Duke, and if, when I meet him he tells me not of her, at least my sword shall hinder him from further mischief. My Lord Housden, they say, holds a grand jaunt and tourney to-morrow. Is that true?"

"Aye, true enough, at his house at Springfield. The queen, they say, is going."

"There, then, will I go to-morrow," said Harold, "and, no matter *what* happens, I will have speech with him. If he deny me," he added, his face red-dening and his eyes flashing, "the devil grant him aid. He will have need of it."

"Nay, we will go together," returned the merchant. "I shall have more authority than you. Heaven grant my poor girl its help and protection till then!"

The night set in dark and gloomy.

The horrid murder which had happened at the fair had damped the spirits of the people; and now the heaviness of the air, and the occasional flashes of lightning, caused them to disperse, nor wait for the heavy drops that were every moment promised by the black clouds in the east.

The household of the diamond merchant retired early.

But not to sleep.

Launcelot Duke saw only the vision of his beloved daughter in the hands of a libertine villain; while Harold, whose love for her, concealed so long, burned now with a flame more fierce than ever, was half mad with anguish.

If he could have met the ruffian and have thrown his life away upon his sword's point he would not have cared.

It was inaction which drove him to desperation; his helplessness to aid her which sent his blood boiling through his veins.

For some time he leaned out of his window and gazed upon the dark river, which more than once seemed to invite him to oblivion.

Presently, however, he was startled by a slight sound in the adjoining room.

He started up and listened.

At first he thought he was mistaken, for the adjoining chamber was occupied only by the silent dead.

But again he heard the noise repeated.

It was not the sound of feet, nor of voices in conversation.

It was like a wailing, sobbing cry.

"What can this mean?" thought he. "Surely we have not been mistaken? Surely our poor Edwin lives not?"

With these words he hurried to the door, and, passing a few steps along the dark corridor, entered the room of death, where lay the silent form, over which the tall candles shed a dim religious light.

For an instant all was silent.

Presently the sound was repeated.

And yet, as Harold Forrester glanced, no one was to be seen!

Bold as he was he must be forgiven if, in such an age, and in the presence of the dead, he felt an awe and alarm creeping over him.

But this feeling lasted but a moment, though the moist air blowing in from the window gave a chill, sepulchral atmosphere to the place, and caused the candles to send flickering, ghost-like shadows on the walls.

Advancing nearer to the bier on which lay the body of the murdered man, he said, boldly—

"Who is here?"

In an instant there rose from a kneeling posture beside the corpse a figure which caused him to spring back with alarm, which subsided, however, as its strange features became more familiar to him.

It was a figure about four feet high; the figure of a lad, but so distorted as to appear scarcely human.

His large head was stuck sideways on his broad shoulders, his back was humped, his arms and hands were unnaturally long, and his legs crooked.

His face was flat, with a long nose, and a wide, ghastly mouth; yet, from among the ragged mass of tangled hair that floated over him, gleamed forth two eyes, bright with intelligence and sorrow.

He laughed chucklingly as Harold started back.

"Did I frighten you, Master Harold?" he said.

"For a moment, I confess you did, Mat," answered the apprentice, kindly, as he saw that the eyes of the deformed dwarf were red with weeping. "But tell me, why are you here?"

The cripple pointed his long, skinny hand towards the bier.

"There," he said, "is the first cause. Edwin Archer was a good friend to poor Mat o' the Mist. Mat has come here to weep by him, and," he added, in a hissing whisper, as he struck his broad chest, "to swear to avenge him. The second reason is to tell you that this night, at twelve, my master wishes to see you."

The youth shuddered.

"The Headsman!" he said. "What wants he with me?"

"My master does not tell me all," replied the cripple; "but this I know, that my visit *here*, as well as your visit to him, must be secret from Launcelot Duke. If you divulge it to him he will *not* assist you, and without *his* aid you will never recover your Eveline. Nay, crimson not. Mat o' the Mist knows which way a loving heart beats in unison with another, though, alas! for him there will be no love on earth!"

He said these words in a mourning, wailing tone, as he approached the window.

"How do you quit this place?" asked Harold.

"By the way I entered. I will show you."

"And was it you who left the warning here for poor Edwin?"

"I know of no warning," returned Mat o' the Mist; "but farewell, time presses. Remember, at midnight precisely."

Then he swung himself out; and as Harold leaned out, he saw him running down like a monkey along the waterspouts, along projections, flying from one block of masonry to another, and at last dropping out of sight among the mists of the dark river.

"A strange being, truly," said Harold, as he covered up the face of the dead youth, which the cripple had unveiled; "worthy of so strange a master."

CHAPTER V.

THE FIGHT ON THE BRIDGE — THE HEADSMAN.

THE message of the Headsman, as may well be conceived, roused the curiosity of Harold Forrester to the utmost pitch.

That it had reference in some way to the recovery of Eveline, he sincerely hoped and believed; but, like all the other inhabitants of the bridge, he held the executioner in wholesome dread.

He was, in fact, a being well calculated to inspire awe.

From early youth he had been engaged in his terrible office, and yet, during all this time, few men had seen his face.

Masked when carrying out the dread sentence of the law, immured in his old house on the bridge at all other times, he had remained a man of mystery.

Not even his name was known.

That he had one could not be doubted, but no man seemed to have heard it.

There he lived in the house next the Middlesex gate of the bridge, with no other companion than the cripple, Mat o' the Mist, another being as mysterious as himself, and equally an object of awe and abhorrence.

In fact, he was known by most people, especially those who frequented the "Red Cross," the lowest hostelry in the neighbourhood, as the "Headsman's Imp."

Harrold Forrester, however, though his heart might be invaded by nervous tremors, had no such thing as cowardice about him, and, as soon as the clock warned for twelve, he made his way into the street, and hurried along the bridge towards the Headsman's house.

The night, as I have said, was dark and gloomy, and a storm had long threatened to burst.

But, though a few heavy drops had fallen, the tempest had apparently blown over, and the moon ever and anon burst through the drifted clouds.

All was very still as Harold quitted the door of the merchant's dwelling, and passed along the old bridge; but, as he approached his destination, he was convinced that some one was lurking in the shadow and watching his every movement.

He stopped and once looked round, loosening his sword in its scabbard ready for action.

But when he stopped the steps stopped too ; and, fancying that perhaps an echo had deceived him, he pressed onwards more quickly than before.

At a point, however, not far from the Headsman's dwelling there was a part of the bridge where the roadway was very narrow, and where there was, moreover, no place which would afford concealment to anyone.

Just as he had passed this, he turned sharply and saw by the light of the fitful moon the figure of a man gliding after him.

He turned so swiftly that the stranger could not avoid him.

"What want you with me ? " Harold exclaimed.

The stranger laughed.

"Is this bridge your own," cried he, "that you fancy I am following you because I am here ? "

"Men who do not desire to be taken for spies and traitors should walk openly and bravely through the streets," replied Harold ; "but since you desire no converse with me, pass on, and I will follow anon."

The stranger, whose features in the darkness of the archway he could not make out at all, but whose form appeared familiar to him, made no reply, but passed out into the moonlight.

In an instant, as the light fell on his face, an exclamation of anger escaped the lips of Harold, and, springing forward, he seized the man by the wrist.

"Villain ! " he cried ; " I know you. Where is Eveline ? "

"Are you mad ? " shouted the other, wrenching his arm from Harold's grasp, and drawing his sword. "What know I of you or your Eveline ? Let me pass."

Harold's sword at once leaped from its sheath.

"No, no, Master Alsdon ! " he cried ; "I know you well. Tell me where you and your villainous master have carried Eveline Duke, or by Heaven ! my sword shall drink your heart's blood ? Nay, look not around you. None of your hired assassins are here to aid you tonight. Speak or die ! "

"I tell you I know nothing of you or your Eveline," exclaimed Alsdon, as Harold rushed upon him.

"Then you or I shall die for the error," returned the latter.

And in an instant they were engaged in furious conflict.

Had he but known that before him stood the one who had ordered the murder of Edwin Archer, the diamond merchant's apprentice would, of course, have been still further infuriated.

As it was, he only thought of Eveline, being utterly unable to conceive a reason for the assassination of his friend by Alsdon.

The idea of his beloved's position, however, was quite enough to nerve his arm, and his treacherous opponent soon found that he had to contend with no mean swordsman.

"They teach apprentices to fight like gentlemen, I perceive," cried Alsdon, sneering, during one brief pause, or rather lull in the combat.

"Not sufficiently to prevent their being murdered," cried Harold, scarcely knowing what he said.

The effect on Alsdon was great, however.

A terrible curse escaped his lips, and he rushed at his opponent savagely.

"Ha!" exclaimed Harold. "What know you of the murder? Have I, then, before me the assassin of Edwin Archer?"

The manner of his assailant was quite enough to show him that he was correct to a certain extent in his surmise, and he seemed suddenly endowed with superhuman strength.

With a cry like a beast of prey, wrung from him by those last words of Edwin, "Harold, avenge me!" he dashed madly forward, and an exclamation of pain told, in another moment, that he had wounded his foe.

But there occurred an unexpected interruption.

The gate of the Headsman's house was thrown open, and the tall form of the mysterious man issued forth.

With his immense sword he dashed between them.

"Put up your sword, madman!" he cried, addressing Harold. "Would you fling away your life upon such as he? Quit the bridge quickly," he added, turning to Alsdon, "if you value your wretched existence."

For a moment Alsdon seemed disposed to resent these words.

Then he turned away.

"I care not," cried Harold, making a dash forward that caused Alsdon to start back. "He is the murderer of my friend, and I have sworn on Edwin Archer's dead body to avenge him. Let me pass!"

"You must pass over my dead body, then," cried the Headsman. "Come, put up your sword and follow me."

It would have been sheer madness on Harold's part to have attempted to resist.

The gigantic headsman could have disarmed him in a moment in the position in which they now stood, and so, reluctantly, he returned his sword to the scabbard.

Alsdon, on the other hand, took advantage of the Headsman's interference, and, abandoning whatever design he had upon Harold, hurried away towards the gateway of the bridge.

The executioner meanwhile, led the way to his house, and, the door being opened by Mat o' the Mist, they passed up into a room on the second floor.

It was a strange place this.

It overlooked the river, and was just beneath the place where the fleshless heads of the law's victims grinned, white and ghastly from their poles upon the old city.

Round it were rough portraits of people of both sexes, and strange knives and swords, and weapons of various kinds were hung on the walls.

At one end was a skeleton hand beneath a glass case.

About this hand there was a mystery.

To no one would the Headsman reveal it, not even to Mat o' the Mist; and, finding that he only frowned and was angry when questioned about it, people desisted, though their curiosity was none the less eagerly whetted.

"Young man," said the mysterious man, when they were seated, I have saved you to-night from an act of great folly. I would have saved Edwin Archer, but I could not. It was I who entered your house and placed upon his table by night the letter warning him not to attend the fair. Do you wish to share his fate?"

"I live to avenge him," said Harold.

The Headsman smiled grimly.

"Ah," he said, "you have much yet to do ere you can succeed in that; a long, intricate, and perilous course of travel. But of that anon. You desire first to rescue Eveline?"

"I do."

"Then take my advice. To-morrow, as you know, are the jousts at Springfield."

" I know it."

" The queen will be there, and my Lord Housden, to do her honour, will make a grand display—a display which the public will be permitted to see, that they may really have the opportunity of shouting : ' Long live the Queen ! Long live Lord Housden ! ' Demand to see him, to speak with him, and accuse him of the abduction.   If there is any scene, tell the queen your story. You know her jealous nature. She will at once ask an explanation, and my Lord Housden will be compelled to deliver her up to her father."

Harold listened to these words in amazement.

How did this man of mystery know that Lord Housden was the abductor of Eveline ?

Was he in his secrets ?

Was he an aider and abettor of this villain nobleman ?

But no.

The warning he had conveyed to Edwin Archer sufficiently proved this.

" And was it for this only you asked me here ? " he asked. " Why did you not send for me openly, or speak to my master ? "

The Headsman eyed him sternly.

" I suffer no man to pry into my actions," he said. " I do them as it pleases me to do them. With your master I have nothing to do ; my business is with you, and is not concluded yet. It was not only to advise you I sent for you hither, I have a sacred trust to repose in you."

" In me ! "

" Aye, in you. You must ask me no questions, however, for I can answer none."

He undid a drawer as he spoke, and took from it a small ebony casket bound with silver.

" This is the trust I have to deliver to you," he said. " Guard it with your life ; and on your life open it not until mortal peril threatens you, or until I am dead ; when the breath is out of my body, at that instant you are absolved from your oath. Will you take it, and swear to keep it and guard it well ? "

The eyes of the Headsman were turned upon him in earnest entreaty as he took the casket in his hand.

Yet he shuddered as he did so.

What terrible relic did it contain ?

What horrible secret would its opening disclose ?

" You hesitate ? " said the Headsman, sternly.

" No," returned Harold, boldly ; " no. I accept the trust, and swear to keep it with my life."

" As you hope for salvation ? "

" As I hope for salvation," repeated Harold, solemnly.

The eyes of the strange man kindled as the youth said this.

" Bravely spoken, my lad," he cried ; " and, mark me, if ever you are in danger —danger from which no earthly power seems able to save you—send for that casket, open it, and you will be saved—that is, remember, if your peril comes from enemies, and not through your own wrong doings. But now it waxeth late, and we must part. As to this interview, be silent as the grave."

The Headsman rose as he spoke, and, unfastening the door, called Mat o' the Mist.

In a few moments Harold was again in the street—the still, dark, shadowy street over the river—clutching his strange prize with a kind of shuddering resolve to keep it in spite of the world, yet full of dissatisfaction and wonder at the result of the midnight visit to the Headsman's lonely home.

"HOUSDEN FOLDED HIS ARMS, AND EYED ESSEX DEFIANTLY."

No. 2

CHAPTER VI.

THE JOUSTS AT SPRINGFIELD—THE ATTACK IN THE ARENA.

IT was a fine, sunny morning that followed the murder of Edwin Archer, and nowhere more brightly did it shine than in the lists at Springfield.

The mansion of Lord Housden was a splendid ancestral building, surrounded by a park and grounds of immense extent.

In the centre of the great park had been cleared a large space for the tourney which was to form part of the day's amusement.

Here a high stand had been erected for the queen and her favourites, while on both sides, and forming a semicircle, were the seats for the lesser stars of the nobility.

The other space was for those of the public whom the keepers of the gates thought fit to permit to enter, none being excluded, be it said, save those whom they knew to be bad characters.

In other parts of the park were glee-maidens, and dancers, and bands of music, and tumblers, and clowns, and what not.

For was not this my Lord Housden's birthday, and was not the queen there to show her gracious favour to him on that eventful day?

From an early hour a stream of people made their way through the grand gates of Springfield Park, and soon a merry, laughing throng was dispersed over the wooded pleasaunce.

Among these there seemed none who did not partake of the general jollity.

But to this seeming there were two exceptions, and those two were Launcelot Duke and Harold Forrester.

Without betraying his visit to the Headsman on the preceding night, he had prevailed upon his master to be guided by him, and both now, with hearts bounding with excitement, awaited the arrival of those who were, they felt, to decide their fate that day.

Strange to say, neither knew their exact course of action.

They felt that that was the place for discovery, but how they were to act was a matter they left to chance.

"By Heaven!" cried Harold, just as they reached a crowded part of the grounds, "there is one of the bullies who attacked us in St. Christopher's Fields. Let us attack him at once."

The merchant was about to reply.

But he was allowed no time.

"Be not mad," said a voice near them. "Wait and watch!"

They turned hastily, and there, standing beside them, was Mat o' the Mist.

"What know you of our business?" asked the merchant somewhat sternly, for the Headsman's Imp was no favourite with him. "Get you gone, and trouble not with what does not concern you."

The hunchback laughed chucklingly.

"The way of the world, the way of the world," he said; "but if you want to secure your daughter's safety, listen to reason."

"Let him speak, sir," said Harold; "he is a good friend to us."

"He will indeed be if he aids me to find her," replied Launcelot Duke. "Speak, boy, if you indeed know aught."

Mat o' the Mist grinned in his peculiar way.

"What I know, or think I know," he said, "I keep to myself, lest I should be wrong. But I say again, yonder villain is truly one of the bullies who attacked you in St. Christopher's Fields; yet it would be madness to attack him."

"And why?"

"He is but the instrument of others. His presence here may prove nothing; but it may prove that he is near his employer. Wait and watch; be not rash, and you will see anon that I am right. We may even see Eveline."

"Do you know this?" cried Harold, seizing his arm somewhat roughly.

"I know nothing," replied the hunchback, with a look of anger, "and if you are uncivil I will retire."

"I meant it not—indeed I meant it not," said Harold; "but hark to the sound of drums! They approach at last. Oh! that I was but noble that I might enter those lists and defy that villain to the death."

The lips of the hunchback moved, as if about to say something as Harold said this.

But he suddenly checked himself, and prepared, with the others, to enjoy the sights which would soon be before them.

In a few moments the cavalcade was seen winding its way through the park—trumpets braying, drums beating, banners flying.

First a number of knights, in resplendent armour; then the queen, having by her side my Lord of Essex, only lately restored to favour, yet even now once more tottering to his fall!

A bevy of lovely ladies followed, and in a short time, amid loud huzzas from the populace, "Good Queen Bess" took her seat in the stand prepared for her.

Then the knights entered the arena, those who were not to take part in the jousts forming a kind of semicircular bodyguard round the queen's stand, and the others retiring to their respective corners.

But very little delay now took place.

The trumpets sounded, the names of two knights were proclaimed, and two mail-clad horsemen took their places.

Another trumpet sounded, and they dashed forward, tilting with their headless lances, until even in the mimic fray one fell half senseless and bleeding to the earth.

Then loud huzzas and clapping of hands arose from the populace; and another knight came forward to combat the conqueror.

And so went it on, amid music and applause, until at length Lord Housden himself galloped into the arena with his visor up, and, after bowing lowly to the queen, took his place to meet the last victor.

His antagonist was a tall, broad-shouldered man, who appeared quite to outmatch the gay young courtier; and the anxiety of the excited people rose now to fever heat.

No hearts there, however, bounded so wildly as did those of Launcelot Duke and Harold Forrester, as their eyes fell upon the man whom they had come to seek, and whom they looked upon with such intense hatred as the abductor of sweet Eveline.

Harold, in fact, made a spring forward, but was restrained by Mat o' the Mist.

"Wait," he cried; "you will see more presently."

At this instant the trumpets brayed again, and Lord Housden and his tall antagonist met in full career.

Both were severely shaken, but both retained their seats, and, amid loud plaudits, they galloped back to their corners.

A lull for an instant, and then another rush, which sent the dust flying in clouds over the arena and the spectators around it; clouds which, on clearing away, showed the tall knight upon the ground, and Lord Housden sitting firmly and gracefully in the saddle, though blood from a recent wound was trickling from his arm.

Loud were the roars of applause.

Hundreds of handkerchiefs waved from fair hands.

Lowly bowed the victor before the queen.

But as he did so, and as Harold watched him, he saw that his eye sought another part of the stand.

A part where a bevy of young girls were watching the scene intently.

Harold gave but one glance at them.

Then a loud cry of astonishment and fury escaped his lips.

"See, see!" he cried, clutching the merchant by the arm, and pointing towards the spot where the pretty damsels, excited and pleased at the scene, were talking eagerly to one another. "Do you not see her?"

"Her! her! What mean you?" exclaimed the diamond merchant.

"There—there among the ladies of the court!—Eveline—your daughter."

The merchant looked.

"Great Heavens!" he cried, turning deadly faint; "it is she or her spirit! What can it mean?"

"It is for *me* to discover!" shouted Harold.

And then, in spite of the throng—in spite of the strong grasp of the hunchback—he forced himself to the edge of the arena, leaped over the barrier, and dashing across to where Lord Housden sat on his proud charger, seized the bridle, exclaiming—"A word with you, my lord; here, in this arena, as you value your life!"

CHAPTER VII.

THE QUEEN'S JUDGMENT.

THE populace who stood at the ropes, and the courtiers and ladies, were so astounded by the bold action of Harold Forrester that for a moment a profound silence reigned.

Lord Housden himself turned deadly pale, and for an instant was unable to speak; while even Harold was rendered voiceless by one glance into his deep black eyes.

It was not fear, however, that thus influenced him.

It was a wonder, a bewilderment, an inward question —

"Where had he met those eyes before?"

One other mutual glance, and Lord Housden drew his sword.

"What means this outrage, madman?" he cried. "What seek you?"

"Eveline, Eveline Duke, she it is whom I seek," exclaimed Harold, hoarse with excitement; "the girl you have stolen from her father. Give her to me, or by heaven——"

Lord Housden laughed derisively.

Then he beckoned to some of the retainers round him.

"Here, my men," he cried, "remove this fellow. He is some poor silly wight, whose senses some fair girl has stolen. See that no injury comes to him, for evidently he means no harm."

"Harm!" exclaimed Harold, as he drew his sword. "I mean harm to you if to no other on God's earth! Villain! Give back to her father the daughter you have stolen, or by heaven you shall live to lie no more!"

The glance of contempt that greeted these words so exasperated Harold that his brain reeled, his eyes flashed red with blood, and in another instant Lord Housden's fate would have been sealed, had not a bevy of retainers rushed forward and seized the impetuous youth.

"Take him away," cried Lord Housden, with pale lips, as he sheathed his sword; "place him in one of the vaults of my house. We will see to him anon,"

But this was not to be,

Queen Elizabeth had been no idle spectator of the scene.

She was the woman above all others who admired manly beauty and bravery.

"God's life, Essex!" she said, turning to the restored favourite, "that youth has blood in him that would not disgrace one of nobler rank. What can it all mean?"

Lord Housden was a thorn in the side of the favourite—a thorn of no ordinary magnitude; and it was only by compulsion that the Earl of Essex was present on his rival's grounds.

"He is, in truth, a noble-looking lad, your grace," returned Essex, catching at this opportunity of injuring his rival; "and see, my Lord Housden seems strangely confused. There is more in this than your grace can see from this place. If your grace will be advised by me, you will send for them, and know the meaning of this riot."

"By heaven! and I *will*, too, Essex," replied Elizabeth.

Then, turning to a page who stood beside her, she said—

"Quick, Lionel Ashley. Fetch my Lord Housden hither, and let that stripling, too, be brought to me. But, stay. See, my lord, another has joined them — an old man, too, and one, seemingly of good position. Quick, Lionel, and see they are all brought before me in my state-room yonder at once."

The queen had spoken truly.

Seeing the position of Harold, Launcelot Duke had sprang forward and endeavoured to follow his apprentice.

For awhile Mat o' the Mist prevented him, and, amid the throng, the merchant found it impossible to force his way to the barrier; but when at length he did reach it, he sprang over it with the agility of a youth, and rushed to the aid of his apprentice.

He had scarcely reached the spot where Harold stood, when the queen's page sprang to the side of Lord Housden.

"My lord," he said, "the queen desires your presence, and also the presence of these people here."

Lord Housden glanced at him an instant vacantly; then, with a muttered curse, he turned to his retainers, and bade them follow him — with the merchant and Harold.

Within a few minutes they stood in the presence of the wondering and angry queen, who, with some of her lords and ladies, had entered one of the grand rooms, where a raised, throne-like chair had been prepared for the queen's use after the jousts should be over.

Here Elizabeth waited in angry impatience the solution of the mystery.

It was a mystery of a nature which most thoroughly displeased her.

History explains why.

Of all crimes a favourite could commit, the most unpardonable was the fact of showing a preference for any fair demoiselle, no matter of what high degree.

The mere fact of being a favourite of hers made it an unpardonable offence to show love for another.

In an instant the idea had sprung into her jealous heart—

"There is some secret in this, maybe, that it will be well for me to know. My Lord Housden has some design upon me, mayhap."

And this simply from having heard a woman's name pronounced!

"Well, my Lord Housden, what means all this?" said the queen, who was striving with all her energy to keep down her anger. "Did I come here to see the jousts, or to see you well-nigh dragged from your horse by the populace? Quick! speak, or, maybe, I may give an order to quit Springfield at once, and——"

She hesitated.

She knew, in fact, how Lord Housden would interpret the words, and she felt that it was injustice to give judgment ere she knew rightly the circumstances of the case.

Lord Housden bowed respectfully before the queen.

"Your grace," he said, "I can readily explain. Yonder stripling, whom my men have brought before you, has conceived some mad notion that I have carried off a young girl—the daughter of the old man who stands by his side. Further, I know not."

The queen frowned.

"Bring them before me," she said.

The diamond merchant and Harold Forrester were in another moment in the presence of the queen.

Elizabeth's features, after the first glance at the handsome face and form of Harold Forrester, relaxed their sternness.

"Tell me sirrah," she said, "what means the outrage you committed upon Lord Housden in my presence? Know you not that you have committed what well-nigh amounts to treason?"

"Indeed," said Launcelot Duke, "I meant no treason towards your grace. I saw only the face of the man who had taken from me my daughter; and all thought of those near him was swallowed up in my desire to wrest her from him. My apprentice here is guiltless; he did but act upon my bidding."

"He is mad, your grace," began Lord Housden.

Elizabeth stayed him by an imperious gesture.

Then she turned again to the diamond merchant.

"Tell me, good master," she said, "what reason have you for deeming my Lord Housden guilty?"

Briefly Launcelot Duke told his story.

"I saw my child but now," he added, "and so did my lad here, sitting among the ladies of your court. I know it is she: she left me but yesterday. Can I so readily forget my own daughter?"

The queen turned towards Lord Housden.

"This is strange, my lord," she said. "Who is this lady?"

Lord Housden seemed astonished.

"Indeed, I know not what they mean," he said; "the only lady here of whom I know anything is my cousin, Lady Grace Harcourt, of whom your grace has heard me speak. But since this old man persists in his story, I would ask, for my own justification, that all the ladies here should pass through the room, that he may be well satisfied of his folly."

"Be it so," said the queen, whose curiosity was now fully roused, "be it so. Lionel Ashley, see that the ladies are summoned hither and passed in review before this gentleman and his apprentice."

"The villain will see now that she is hurried away by some secret door," whispered Launcelot Duke. " Oh ! Harold, I almost feel as if some terrible blow—some blow more dread than we can expect, is about to fall upon us."

After about ten minutes, during which the Earl of Essex talked in a rapid undertone to the queen, the ladies were brought in.

Among the very first was the one whom Launcelot Duke had seen among the bevy of pretty damsels at the jousts.

He sprang forward with extended arms.

" Oh ! Eveline, my child ! " he cried. " Thank God, I have found you."

The young girl drew back hurriedly, and waved him off.

" Sir, I do not know you," she said, in a low voice.

The Earl of Essex—perhaps more than the queen—observed the tone in which the words were uttered, and the trembling of the form which accompanied them.

" There is a strange mystery here, your grace," he said, boldly. " The girl speaks as if by compulsion."

Lord Housden, who stood in front of the royal chair, folded his arms, and eyed Essex defiantly.

" Am I arraigned before the queen, or before my Lord of Essex ? " he said, sneeringly. " Does not her majesty see that Lady Grace Harcourt knows nothing of these men ? Has her majesty need of the assistance of eyes which have not always seen too clearly for their own interest ? "

Essex's hand flew to his sword.

" God's death, gentlemen ! " cried Elizabeth, stamping her foot, " do you forget in whose presence you stand ? Come hither, Lady Grace, and you, Sir Merchant, and let me hear your explanation."

The merchant and Harold, both of whom appeared overwhelmed with surprise and horror, eagerly obeyed the summons, while the young girl tremblingly approached the queen.

" Do you know these gentlemen ? " asked Elizabeth, in her kindest tones, yet at the same time directing a piercing glance upon the shrinking figure before her, " tell me the truth now, and fear nothing."

" I know them not—indeed, it is some mistake — some fancied resemblance," replied the young girl, faintly

" Oh, Eveline ! Eveline ! " cried the merchant, who was trembling with terrible emotion, while the tears rolled down his pallid cheeks, " why, why do you deny me thus ? one who has been so good, so kind a father to you ? Oh, Eveline, look at me ! think of your sainted mother, and deny me not ! "

The earnestness of his words as he held forth his trembling hands towards her, touched the hearts of all present, save Lord Housden, who stood gazing in triumph upon the scene.

She whom he addressed also let fall a glistening tear, which dropped upon the fair bosom that heaved so violently and restlessly.

" Indeed, sir," she said in a tone of melting tenderness, " indeed, sir, I pity you ; indeed, my heart bleeds for you ! But you are mistaken. I am like one you loved, maybe—but cast *me* from your mind. I am not *she*."

There was an earnest pathos in all this which roused, more than ever the suspicion of the Earl of Essex, and in a lesser degree, that of Queen Elizabeth.

But the favourite prudently resolved to say nothing.

He would wait and watch.

" Well," said the queen, " since the young girl adheres to her word, there is no more to be said. Lady Grace, you may retire."

The girl bowed lowly, and slowly she turned to go ; her head leaning on her bosom, her tears falling fast, her whole form evidently convulsed with emotion.

All there were struck with her beauty —with her emotion—with the strange mystery that encircled her.

But what could they do ?

Only wait and wonder.

The queen, as soon as the door had closed on the young girl, turned to Launcelot Duke, saying—

" You, sir, pray may I ask your name ? "

" His name, your grace," said Harold Forrester, seeing that his master could not speak from the violence of his emotion, " his name is Launcelot Duke, the diamond merchant of London Bridge. I am his apprentice, and yonder stands, as my life is at stake, his daughter, Eveline, charmed by some terrible sorcery into forgetfulness. We will away now, your grace, if you will allow us, though—if——"

He hesitated, and looked from Lord Housden to the queen.

In the face of the former he saw furious rage struggling with forced calmness.

In that of the latter an encouragement to proceed.

"Speak on," said Elizabeth. "You seem a brave and loyal subject, and any reasonable request I will grant."

"It is for Mistress Eveline I speak," said Harold, "for you see her father is too broken down with sorrow to do so for her. What I would ask is that you would, in your great kindness, take her under your own protection. Evil is meant to her, your majesty, which your royal care could prevent."

"That is well spoken, and fairly, your grace," said Essex. "The youth but seeks justice."

"And he shall have it, too," cried Elizabeth. From this moment, Lord Housden, Lady Grace is attached to our person. If she belong to the merchant he need fear for her no longer. And now, since this matter is settled, let the jousts be continued. Let not my loving subjects deem that aught of evil has occurred. They will imagine that some war is threatened by the Spaniards, or some new civil commotion has broken out in our fair dominions. To the jousts, gentlemen—to the jousts!"

Then, turning to her page, she added—

"Lionel, see that the merchant and his apprentice have good refreshment ere they start. Now, my Lord Housden, lead the way."

Lord Housden bowed lowly, with a smile.

A smile that belied his heart.

"Curse her for a jealous old meddler!" he thought. "She has spoiled my game for a while, but she cannot always be upon the watch."

Had Launcelot Duke been more able to sustain the weight of his sorrow, Harold would have endeavoured to induce him to wend his way homewards at once.

As it was, however, the merchant appeared so thoroughly exhausted that a little refreshment seemed absolutely necessary, and Harold gladly followed the page into a room on a lower floor.

They had not been here long—indeed, the merchant had scarcely, as it were, recovered his speech, when the door was opened slightly, and a fair curly head appeared.

It was evidently the head of a boy of some sixteen years.

Having satisfied himself, apparently, that the coast was clear, he entered the room, and, in all the blaze of blue velvet and gold—the resplendent livery of the Earl of Essex—advanced towards Harold.

"A note for you," he said; "on your life keep its contents a secret."

Having delivered himself of which oracular speech, he went trippingly away.

Harold eagerly opened the missive.

It was very short but significant—

"I address you," it began, "because you are young, bold, and active, and, if I mistake not, love the lost Eveline. Words on paper are dangerous, so I will say no more now. I shall be at my private mansion at Horley Wood, on the second day from this. Come there at night and ask to see me. You will be admitted at once if you give the password, 'A friend to the good; a thorn to the evil!' Destroy this as soon as your master has read it.   "ESSEX."

"What a strange and mysterious network of villainy is coiling round us," said Harold to himself; "those words are the same that were on the dagger which the Headsman left in poor Edwin Archer's chamber. See here, Master Duke," he said, aloud, turning to his master and giving him the letter. "We have powerful friends to aid us."

The perusal of the missive roused the merchant from his lethargy."

He seized Harold by the hand.

"My lad," he said, "the earl is right; you are the one who will recover to me my lost child, and if you recover her and love her still, why——"

Harold's face flushed.

"Nay, speak not of that," he said; "the earl sees too much. But I will recover her, or perish in the attempt. And now, let me ask you, master, what your heart tells you. Is yonder lady that we saw just now, Mistress Eveline or not?"

"As God is in heaven, she is my child," replied the merchant.

"And so say I," returned Harold. "Now I shall know how to act. Let us away."

And within a few moments they had quitted the house, and avoiding the throng of busy pleasure-seekers made their way across the park towards home.

CHAPTER VIII.

MORE VILLAINY.

On the night following the jousts at Springfield, a terrific storm burst over London.

For years before the inhabitants did not remember to have seen such vivid lightning or heard such crashing thunder.

Yet in spite of this, and the rain which poured in an uninterrupted deluge, three of the ruffians, whom I introduced to my reader in the first chapter, presented themselves and were admitted to the "Red Cross" on Old London Bridge.

"A cursed night this to be out," said Sharpley, as he shook his drenched cloak, and approached the fire which the landlord kept ready for the use of his half-drowned guests. "But Alsdon is not one to be kept waiting. Wet or shine, storm or no storm, he is certain to be here."

"Then we may be sure," said Wormer, "that some dark work is to be done, and that some good money will be paid for it. However, while you are drying yourself, I'll just set light to a fire in the upper room."

"What for?"

"Because Alsdon knew that the Headsman was here when he paid his last visit, and he wants no listeners this time."

"All right; do as you please," growled Sharpley, "only let us have some strong ale to go on with."

In the space of about a quarter of an hour they were ensconced in the upper room, on one side of which was a wide latticed window, opening out over the river, while on the other side was a wide and black-yawning chimney, up which crackled a bright blaze, that, in spite of its being summer, gave, on this stormy night, a cheery and comfortable look to the place.

"Master Alsdon's plans have not turned out so well as he expected, I fancy," said Sharpley, to one of his two companions. "What think you, Skalton? Were not his looks most wondrous sour when you saw him to-day?"

"For my part, I think that neither I nor Hurlbut here have any of his good wishes, for he scowled at us as if we were his deadly foes," replied Skalton.

Sharpley laughed.

"Oh, that is nothing," he cried, "he never can look sweet. Even when he had that pretty wench, Eveline Duke, in his arms, carrying her to the carriage, he scowled at her as if he hated her. Perhaps he was envying my Lord of Housden. But, hush! I hear his voice."

In a moment afterwards the door was opened, and Alsdon appeared.

"Well, my brave fellows," he cried, in a voice, the cheeriness of which surprised them all, "you seem to be jolly enough, in spite of the absence of Redlock, eh?"

"Ah, well," said Hurlbut, in a sanctimonious voice, "it is the fate of all to die; some in bed, some in battle, some on the block. Better die bravely fighting as he died, than by the axe of the headsman."

"A truce to your croakings, you Puritanical raven," said Alsdon, with a visible shudder. "I come to bring you more work and more money. But first I must pay you for the last job."

A plentiful supply of gold was then meted out equally between the men, who clutched it with eager hands.

"You pay like a nobleman," said Sharpley.

As he spoke a chuckling, jibbering laugh sounded near them.

All started and listened, but all they saw was a flash of lurid lightning dashing across the angry heavens—all they heard was the crashing boom of the thunder, which shook the old bridge to its very foundation.

"I thought I heard a sound near us," said Alsdon, when the thunder had ceased rolling; "but maybe it was but the shrieking of the wind. I must confess, my lads, that last time I was here I committed a blunder."

Again the mocking laugh.

"Confusion!" shouted Alsdon, springing up and drawing his sword; "this is no fancy."

And dashing to the door he opened it and sprang out.

But all was quiet there.

A lamp shed a bright light over the landing, and there was no place where anyone could be concealed.

He returned and closed the door—breaking into a profuse and cold sweat as the lightning once more flashed across the horizon, and the thunder rolled forth its fierce and solemn warning.

"Search the room!" he cried, "there is some treachery or devilment here!"

But search as they might, they could discover nothing.

The walls were all solid; not a closet of any kind was there.

"We must be the victims of some strange illusion," he said, as he sat down again with his back to the great chimney. "I must hasten and finish our work and then away. I told you," he added, "that I had made a blunder when I was last here."

"Yes."

"That blunder was in getting you to spare Harold Forrester. Curse him! he is more in the way than I, or, rather, Lord Housden, ever dreamed. My lord had visions of a great future for the lad; but now he has gone mad for love of this Eveline, and is playing a desperate game, which will end in my lord's discomfiture if he look not to it. Well, our plan is easy. To-morrow night he visits the Earl of Essex, at Horley Wood."

Treachery already!

In these few hours Lord Housden had discovered the favourite's plans.

"Well?" said Sharpley, eagerly.

"He will pass along the great road towards East Point, and drive near Calthorp's Farm about nine. You know well the farm where you and I met, Sharpley, some months back?"

"Yes, I know it well," said the head assassin, "and well, too, I know the dark pool beside it."

"Good!" replied Alsdon. "You know, then, what I desire. This Harold Forrester, had he been discreet, might have been the friend, the confidant, the right-hand man of Lord Housden; and now, through his own folly, he has become a thorn in his side, which someone must draw forth. Not to mince matters, in fact, he must be got rid of, and no better opportunity presents itself for doing so than upon his journey to-morrow night."

"I see exactly what is to be done," said Sharpley, "and since you are so good a paymaster, you may depend upon your orders being obeyed."

"Verily," said the sanctimonious Hurlbut, "Master Alsdon can have nothing to complain in the way I did the business of Edwin Archer."

There was something inexpressibly loathsome in the crawling, serpent-like manner of this man; and Alsdon, bloodthirsty villain as he was, turned from him in disgust.

"I leave the matter in your hands, Sharpley," he said. "I consider you the leader, and when you tell me that he is dead, expect a good reward."

A bright flame rushed up the broad chimney as he spoke, and in an instant a dark mass fell into the midst of the fire, scattering the embers in all directions.

Alsdon and the others sprang up with a yell of terror, which was naturally increased by the sounds they had previously heard.

But none of them was able to tell what it meant.

In an instant it dashed towards the table, extinguishing the lamps, and making at once for the window.

Just as it reached the casement, and the men drew their swords to rush after it, the lightning flashed with terrible violence, illuminating every niche of the old window, and shining with ghastly brightness upon the face of the disturber of their deadly council.

"The Headsman's Imp, curse him! The Headsman's Imp!" shouted Sharpley.

And he darted forward.

But in vain.

The window was thrown open ere they

could reach it, and the lithe form of Mat o' the Mist dashed out, just as the terrific thunder boomed over the old city, rolling its horrid music fiercely over the bridge, and crashing as if in special anger over the house of crime.

In wild anger they leaned far out of the window.

But they could see nothing.

The rain, and the darkness, and the mists of the river, had swallowed him up, and all that they could hear in the lull of the storm was his mocking laugh as he sprang from buttress to buttress towards his home.

"Curse him, he will betray all," cried Alsdon. "What can be done now?"

"Fear not," said Sharpley, who cared not for risk, and was only fearful of losing the opportunity of a good haul;

"he could have heard nothing perched in the chimney yonder. He must be the devil's imp indeed if he was there long amid the smoke and flame."

Alsdon, however, was not so confident.

He feared lest his plan should be marred; and more than that, the cripple must have heard his words if he did not see his face, and thus he was committed to the crime.

However, regrets were useless.

"Well, Sharpley," he said, "I leave it to you. Kill him, and I care not then for all. They may seek for Alsdon, but they will not find him."

These words passed for nothing at the time, and when the hired assassins parted from their employer they were forgotten.

But they recurred with wondrous force to their memories in after days.

CHAPTER IX.

THE JOURNEY TO HORLEY WOOD—THE ATTACK BY THE DARK POOL.

WHETHER acquainted or not with the machinations against him, Harold Forrester made no difference in his preparations.

The merchant, of course, knew of his proposed journey, and was eager to accompany him.

But this Harold would not hear of.

He felt confidence in himself, more confidence, in fact, when he was alone; and besides, he was certain that the Earl of Essex, having demanded his presence, would resent as an affront the companionship of the merchant.

"God speed ye and bless ye," said Launcelot Duke, as, in the dusk of the evening, Harold leaped upon his horse at the door of "Duke's Palace." "Look well to your pistols, and be watchful as you go, for you know not what enemies may know of your journey, and be upon the watch to destroy you."

"Fear not," said Harold. "Heaven will guard me, for I have right on my side. I shall keep good watch, however, and give them no chance of surprises. Good-night—I will not say farewell."

With a light heart Harold Forrester put spurs to his horse and started on his road towards East Point.

Secure—for Eveline—in the guardian-

ship accepted by the queen, he felt now that he had time to work.

Lord Housden would have no time now wherein to work his fell machinations against her; and he had therefore no occasion to precipitate matters, but proceed calmly and deliberately to work.

The enmity of Lord Housden and the Earl of Essex was, of course, most favourable to him.

The latter he knew to be a brave and noble soldier—a favourite under compulsion—loyal only because his head was in danger.

To him, therefore, he could trust in all things, and he determined unreservedly to yield himself to his alliance and guidance.

Eveline Duke being safe (for that the young girl he had seen at the tourney *was* Eveline Duke he was quite certain), Harold must not be blamed if a certain amount of ambition mingled with his dreams of the future.

He saw himself the friend of Essex; his trusted messenger, his confidant; rising step by step to the top of the ladder, and becoming ultimately the husband of sweet Eveline.

These dreams occupied him while he was riding along the streets of London.

But as soon as the green lanes of Hertfordshire came in view, the darkness warned him of the necessity for caution.

He remembered the treacherous murder of Edwin Archer; he knew that Lord Housden was the instigator of the murder and abduction, and he was well aware, also, how desperately he had roused the anger of Alsdon's patron.

With such a desperate and powerful man it would have been madness to play; and as, therefore, his swift horse plunged into the darkness, he took a rapid survey around to see if he were followed.

To his mind fear was an utter stranger, or perhaps the gloomy nature of the road might have had no unnatural influence, and he might have felt induced to wait for a companion.

As it was, however, he plunged along gallantly, rushing by the hedgerows, until at length, in the distance, glittered the waters of the dark pool.

Knowing nothing, except by mere suspicion, of any plot against him, he dashed on quickly as before.

But he had no sooner reached the edge of the water (which, to some extent, encroached upon the high road), than three figures rose up—springing up, as it were, out of the pool itself, and confronted him.

No words were used, no challenge given; the men attacked him furiously and in silence.

CHAPTER X.

ON THE BRINK OF THE DARK POOL.

In an instant Harold Forrester knew that some crime of a deadly nature was threatened.

If the men had spoken—demanded his money, or ordered him to return the way he had come, he would not have thought this.

But not a word was spoken.

Evidently they were there for murder and nothing else.

Any argument was useless, therefore, but the argument of the sword, and he prepared consequently to defend himself against them for dear life's sake.

All had been well chosen for the murderous deed.

The pool, lying there, dark and dismal, with trees dipping hushingly into its black waters; the lonely road far away from all human habitations, made up a gloomy picture, which suited well the hideous act which Sharpley and his companions had been commissioned to accomplish.

Harold Forrester, however, felt no fear in his breast.

He knew himself to be at a disadvantage: to be in a position, of course, of great peril.

But he had faith in the justice of his cause and his strong right arm, and after a moment, backing his horse, he sprang lightly from the saddle.

He would have put spurs to his steed and fled.

But he had not the chance.

Two strong hands clutched the bridle; and he felt that on the ground he would have more play for his sword than on the saddle of an unmanageable horse.

Planting his back against a wide-spreading tree, therefore, he awaited the attack.

"Come on, ye villains," he cried, as he pinked his first assailant in the shoulder; "come on—to your death. Are ye mad, that you thus attack a peaceable traveller without telling him in what he has offended?"

"We must have your life, Harold Forrester," replied a hoarse voice, which was completely strange to him, "and there is, therefore, no need of words!"

The cold-blooded manner, and the voice in which this was said, would have been enough to have chilled the blood of many.

It only rendered Harold more determined, and he began to assail his enemies more recklessly than before.

It soon was evident, however, that unless some aid came, and that quickly, the uneven conflict would end in the death of the brave young apprentice.

Three men—armed well—used to the sword, and utterly reckless of life or death, were more than a match for one, however full of energy or daring; and, wounded slightly in more than one part, Harold was just beginning to yield, when a loud, shrill cry close at hand caused all to start round.

Then a dark form sprang into the scene of conflict, and with a shout of defiance ranged himself on the side of Harold.

It was Mat o' the Mist.

Even in the darkness the three hired assassins recognised his distorted form.

"The Headsman's Imp, curse him," exclaimed Sharpley; "now, then, is our time——"

Our time to rid ourselves of him, he meant, and would have said.

But Mat o' the Mist gave him no time to frame the words, much less to put the threat into execution.

Strong and active we have already seen him to be; but he proved now that he was no mean swordsman.

Poor lonely creature!

What had he to amuse himself with during his solitary vigils in the house of the Headsman on the bridge?

He could not always be watching the rushing waters of the dark river; or the swaying to and fro of the poles with the traitors' heads; or listening to the moaning of the restless wind among the tall houses.

So, to amuse himself, he had oftentimes taken the Headsman's huge sword and practised in his solitary chamber, until he could wield his weapon with the strength and the grace of a cavalier.

He put his knowledge to good use now.

Springing, as I have said, to the side of Harold Forrester, he soon turned the tide of battle.

Wounded as he was, Harold felt himself roused to more vigorous exertion, and Sharpley and his companions soon found themselves hard pressed.

Mat o' the Mist style of fighting was most extraordinary.

He seemed like two men.

Here, there, everywhere at once, as it seemed, he so distracted his opponents that they knew not on which side to expect the assault.

Though three to two, therefore, the villainous murderers found themselves soon placed on the defensive; and, seeing that they were yielding ground, Harold shouted to his strange assistant to assume the direct attack and destroy them.

Mat o' the Mist responded with a will.

Suddenly dashing forward, he overthrew Hurlbut, and, flinging him on his back on the brink of the pool, held his head beneath water.

Harold Forrester, meanwhile, sprang forward, and, seizing Sharpley by the throat with his right hand, sent his sword clean through the chest of his companion Skelton.

"Victory! victory!" he shouted.

And hurling the quivering body of the man far from him, he released his hold on Sharpley's throat, and attacked him furiously.

Sharpley, however, brutally courageous as he was, was thoroughly thrown out by the unexpected turn of events, and with a feeling that some strange influence was protecting Harold, and that Mat o' the Mist was really in league with the devil, he made a feint to strike and then fled into the darkness.

Harold did not pursue him.

It was not, in the deep darkness that overspread all things, worth while to do.

So he hurried to aid Mat o' the Mist.

The hunchback, however, had no need of help.

As Harold Forrester turned, he sprang up from the body of Hurlbut.

"He's dead!" he cried. "Ha! ha!"

Harold knelt down and looked into the puritanical ruffian's face.

The cripple's words were true.

He was indeed dead.

Two of Alsdon's hired villains had gone to their account.

He and Sharpley only, of all Edwin Archer's assassins, lived to be destroyed.

"Mat!" cried Harold, pressing his hand, "how can I ever reward you? You have this night saved my life, though how you came so opportunely to my aid I cannot fathom."

The lad chuckled.

"Ah! ah!" laughed he; "Mat has his secret ways of finding out things which you know not of. But come, my Lord of Essex will be waiting for you. There is your horse grazing yonder. Mount then, and away!"

"My Lord of Essex!" repeated Harold, in astonishment; "what know you of my visit to him?"

"Ha, ha!" cried Mat, "that is another of my secrets. Seek not to discover how I knew it. I shall never divulge my means of obtaining knowledge. Go, Harold; and go with a stout heart!"

"Well, well," said Harold, as he again wrung his hand; "I will not attempt to fathom your secret. Farewell, and Heaven preserve you. If ought comes of this visit to the earl, it may not be beyond my power to reward you in some way that will please you. Again farewell."

In a few moments after this he had leaped upon his saddle, and was once more dashing away towards East Point.

CHAPTER XI.

TREACHERY AGAIN.

BEING somewhat beyond the time when the Earl of Essex expected him to arrive, Harold found that nobleman greatly excited and disturbed.

His handsome face was flushed, and he was pacing to and fro in his room when the page (whom we mentioned as being at the jousts at Springfield) announced the diamond merchant's apprentice.

The earl had no feeling of anger, however, towards Harold.

He was only in fear of treachery.

"Ha!" he cried, advancing with undisguised pleasure, as our hero entered, "methought some evil had befallen you. One knows not in these days what one has to dread. Every man, I fear, may at any moment have the queen's anger turned upon him. She grows old and cankered now, and her mind is become as crooked as her carcase."

"Fine words these to use towards the queen," muttered Luke Haverley, the earl's page, who was present, and heard all. "What will my Lord Housden say when he hears that?"

Neither the earl nor Harold, however, dreamed for one moment that the lad with the immovable countenance was noticing what was passing between them.

"You were correct in your surmise, my lord," replied Harold; "by some means or other, which I cannot fathom, my visit here this night was known to my enemies. I was attacked by three ruffians near the Pool by Calthorp's Farm, and had it not been for the opportune arrival of a friend, I should never have reached your lordship's house."

A dark cloud settled on the earl's brow as he listened.

"This is some of Housden's work," he murmured, "and yet, such is my position that I can do nothing against him."

"I thought, my lord," said Forrester, bowing low, "that you were just now in great favour at court?"

"Alas! no," returned Essex, throwing himself wearily into a chair; "the queen is capricious; she feels the weight now of her seventy years, and is spiteful to us young courtiers because her mirror tells her that her wrinkles are getting deeper and more numerous. Luke, go, get some refreshment. Master Forrester here must be fatigued after his long ride."

The refreshment being brought, and the door being closed, Essex began to open his heart, little knowing that concealed behind the tapestry was one who heard and greedily devoured every word that was uttered.

"You are a brave lad," said Essex, smiling pleasantly upon Harold: "few men, however great their wrongs, would have dared to act as you acted at the tourney."

"Ah! but, my lord, love will do much," added Harold. "Although Eveline Duke knows it not, I love her more than my life, and would willingly sacrifice it to save her!"

"And you are sure that the young lady whom you saw at the jousts was she?"

"Sure? aye, as sure as that I now listen to your question."

"Then why—why does she deny not only you, but her father?"

"Indeed, I know not," said Harold; "she must be under some strange and evil influence."

"And is Lord Housden the only one whom you suspect?"

"No! there is Alsdon, his creature; the one who is first in all the villainy which this new royal favourite plans. He is the prime mover in this affair; he is the one, I believe, who pointed out to Lord Housden first the beauty of my master's daughter. Would that I could have the villain at my sword's point!"

Lord Essex smiled.

"I fear me," he said, "that you would find it difficult to do. In my mind there is no doubt that Alsdon and Lord Housden are one."

"Impossible!"

"Not so. They are never seen together—they have *never* been seen together. No, Lord Housden is too cunning a villain to trust anyone with the commission of his infamous projects. He does them in disguise himself, and is sure, consequently of not being betrayed.

"But come, let me tell you my object in bringing you hither. I much fear that this same villain has obtained so great a mastery over the queen's mind that my very life is in danger. Now tell me, are you bound for a long time to Master Launcelot Duke?"

"For another year."

"And would he keep you to this were he to know that advancement, fame, honour, awaited you in the service of another?"

"I know not," said Harold, whose heart swelled with strange ambition as the royal favourite spoke. "Master Duke has ever been kind and good to me, and I believe would do anything to further my well-being; but I should not care to act in anything without his permission."

"Certainly not," replied the earl; "but put this to him when you return. Say that Lord Essex fears to have need of you, and ask him boldly to permit you to enter my service. Believe me, you are born to be a soldier; you have it in your eye, in your bearing, and I will swear, in your heart. And remember, if I strike, I strike for you, too. Eveline's safety shall be assured you— Eveline's hand shall be yours."

Harold flushed and paled alternately as the earl spoke these mysterious words.

"You certainly rouse me with your speeches, my lord," he said. "I will ask my master; but I fear me what poor aid I could afford your lordship is overrated by you."

The earl smiled genially and leaned over towards him.

"Walls have ears they say," he said, in a low tone, "so I will whisper to you the most important part of my wishes. Take this letter; it is sealed, you see, and unaddressed. Keep it until you hear from me. When a person comes to you, be it man or woman, and says to you, 'The time has come,' open it, and follow the instructions contained therein. Until that time keep silent on this point; and mark me, you shall not lose your reward."

Harold took the letter and placed it in the breast pocket of his doublet.

"I will defend it with my life," he said, and when the time comes for action, depend upon me for acting promptly."

"Good," said the earl, "I put full faith in you. And now, since you must be very weary, take some more refreshment and let me offer you a bed till morning."

"I will take the refreshment gladly," said Harold; "but I must return home to-night. I will not leave my master too long alone without first preparing him for it. After the attack upon me this night, there is no knowing what evil may threaten him."

Soon after this Harold took leave of the earl, and, mounting a fresh horse, started off at full speed towards London.

His mind was full of wonder.

What could it all mean?

The Headsman of the old bridge had not long delivered to him a casket almost with the same injunction.

Was there any real connection between these two mysteries?

Not long after Harold came another horseman, who carefully avoided him, and even went a different route, as far as possible.

This was Luke Haverley, the treacherous page of the Earl of Essex.

His heart was replete with evil excitement.

He had heard enough to cause his master's head to fall.

The question was, to whom was he bearing the news?

CHAPTER XII.

DON FERNANDO.

I⊤ will be remembered by my readers that, in the first chapter of my story, I mentioned the fact that Harold Forrester and Edwin Archer were foster-brothers.

I must say a little more of this, at this point of my story, in order that my readers may understand more clearly the events which now followed each other in rapid succession.

On Gladwell Heath, near the banks of the Surrey side of the river, stood a semi-ruinous building.

For years it had stood uninhabited, until at length an old woman of dark and gloomy aspect, and her daughter, a pleasant young creature of some two-and-twenty years of age, came to tenant it.

They did very little to it.

Two of the rooms they rendered somewhat habitable; the remainder was left as it had been for so long before, free to the fury of the storm.

The younger of these women had a child at her breast.

The husband—so she said—had been a mariner, but had been drowned at sea almost on the day when her babe was born, and she had come hither with her mother to be alone and away from the world.

Such people as Mistress Lewarden and her mother would, in the present time, have excited not the slightest notice.

They would have been regarded as curiosities, and that is all.

In those days, however, anything out of the way caused a commotion at once; and it was not long before the mother—Mistress Halcott—began to be called Mother Halcott in the neighbourhood, and be deemed nothing better than a witch.

The good people round about, and they were but few, had no further reasons for this absurdity than that Mistress Halcott was old, decrepid, had a black cat, and was often to be seen alone on the dark heath, apparently communing with the stars.

One evening, about six months after their arrival, a loud knock came at the door; and on opening it, they started with astonishment at seing the tall form of a man standing in the doorway.

It was a dark evening; in fact it had been dark and stormy all day; and at first they did not observe that by his side were two little children.

"Let me enter," said the stranger, "and fear nothing. I am alone, with the exception of these two little ones, who can hurt no one."

His voice was singularly sweet and pleasant; and instinctively the two women experienced a sensation of confidence in him.

"Enter, sir, and welcome," said Mistress Halcott, and in a few moments he had seated himself by their cosy fireside, with a child on each knee.

He was a dark-visaged man, swarthy, like a foreigner who had travelled in tropical countries.

His hair was black as the raven's wing, and his dark eyes, too, and piercing.

"Mistress Halcott," he said—"you see I know your name, and yours too, Mistress Lewarden—I have come here to place a trust in your hands. I leave England to-morrow, to return—when, I know not. I wish to leave in kind hands these two children. Will you take them from me?"

The two women looked at him in surprise.

In the first place, how knew he their names—in the second place, did he expect them to take the children for nothing?

"HAROLD AND THE YOUNG EARL BORE DOWN ALL BEFORE THEM."

No. 3

"Well, you see, we are poor people," began Mistress Halcott.

The stranger smiled.

"Yes, yes, I know," he said, "you are poor. I will leave ample provision for their keep for a year, and at the end of each year I will forward more. Now, you must understand that these lads, though nurtured by the same mother, are not brothers. You will find their names clearly marked upon their clothes. Explain to no one how they came hither. Let them pass as your nephews, and as to their future, wait till you receive instructions signed with my name."

"And what is that?"

"Don Fernando."

"Only that?"

"That is all you need know."

"But one thing, sir. Tell me how is it that you knew my daughter's name? She is spoken of here by the same name as myself."

"I knew her husband," replied the Spaniard, with some emotion. "A brave and worthy man he was. But enough of reminiscences. I must away."

And with these words he strained the two boys to his breast convulsively, and kissed them repeatedly, while tears of anguish rolled down his bronzed cheeks.

The two little things, who were only about three years old, seemed to understand his sorrow, and kissed him again and again.

Then suddenly he tore himself away.

"Here," he said, placing a heavy purse in the hands of Mistress Halcott, "here you will find abundance for the first year of their sojourn here. Farewell, and forget not the name of Don Fernando."

A few minutes more and he was gone, and the wondering women were left alone.

What he had promised he faithfully fulfilled, and they as faithfully fulfilled their trust.

The names of the lads they had found on the clothes, as stated; the one Harold Forrester, and the other Edwin Archer.

The latter seemed to be the favourite of Don Fernando, however.

Whenever a letter came he always sent some special present for him; and as years sped on, his best blessing accompanied it.

So time passed, and the lads were fifteen, educated as well as lads could be at such an age, and loving each other like brothers.

There came a letter from Don Fernando, saying that they were to be apprenticed to Launcelot Duke, the diamond merchant of the Bridge. It said also that the writer was going far away West, and that his return was uncertain.

Hardly had the boys quitted Mistress Halcott's cottage, than a man, evidently in disguise, came to the place and demanded to see them.

But Mistress Halcott had been too well schooled to tell secrets.

Letters from the Spaniard had warned her against giving information to any one unless he gave the name.

And failing this the stranger went away with an oath on his lips, and they saw him no more.

Since then, the two had been educated and brought up by Master Launcelot Duke; both had fallen in love with the lovely Eveline; and Edwin Archer, to all appearance, had gained her heart.

Yet such was the love which Harold bore his foster-brother that he was content with this, rather than that Edwin should suffer one heart-pang for him.

Seventeen years had now passed by.

Poor Edwin Archer was dead, by the hands of a murderer, and Harold was his declared avenger, and the friend of the Earl of Essex.

And on the evening after the apprentice's visit to the latter, we once more pay a visit to the house, or rather the cottage of Mistress Halcott.

The place had not improved in reputation with the lapse of time.

The reputation which, justly or unjustly, Mistress Halcott had obtained for witchcraft had strengthened instead of decreasing, and, as the weight of years fell upon her, the poor old creature seemed to take a delight in the idea, and at length went so far as to suffer herself to be consulted as an oracle, by the ignorant people round about.

As it often happens, the prophecies of the most ignorant persons have a semblance of truth, and having more than once "hit the right nail on the head," as the saying is, Mistress Halcott had attained quite a reputation as a prophetess.

On the evening after Harold's visit to the house of the Earl of Essex, Mistress Halcott and her daughter were sitting by the fire, with a third person—the child of the latter, now grown into a fine, handsome girl, when a knock came at the door.

Just such a knock, just such an hour, just such weather as it had been seventeen years ago.

Mistress Lewarden sprang up and opened the door, and there—standing in the semi-darkness, was a tall, cloaked figure—the figure of a giant with long hair, wildly fluttering in the breeze.

"Is this the house of Mistress Halcott?" he asked.

"It is sir."

"I will enter, then, if you will allow me," he said; "I have a wish to consult you."

He walked in, and then, for the first time, they observed that he wore a mask.

The women almost trembled in his presence.

There was something about him, in fact, which inspired awe.

They would have trembled more if they had but known that it was the Headsman of Old London Bridge who was with them.

"I have been sorely troubled of late, Mistress Halcott," he said, "by dreams and visions, and I have come——"

"Step this way then, good master," said the old woman in a shrill voice, and with a nervous look at her daughter. The latter always deprecated what she termed "her evil doings," and prophesied that evil would certainly come to her in the end.

The Headsman accordingly passed into the adjoining chamber, and the old woman, having trimmed her lamp, requested him to be seated.

"What do you desire to know, sir?" asked the old woman.

"They say you are in league with spirits," replied the Headsman, sternly; "if so, I desire to know the future; to see the faces of those who must fall by my fatal axe."

Mistress Halcott uttered a smothered cry of terror.

"Who, then, are you?" she asked in a gasping voice.

"The Headsman of London Bridge."

For a moment there was silence.

Then the old woman seemed to recover courage, and approaching the other end of the room, drew aside a curtain.

Poor, infatuated woman!

She had adopted now all the paraphernalia of the witch's craft.

"You are, I know, strong enough to bear all you see," said Mistress Halcott. "I can see you are a strong and a brave man."

"Yes. Do as you please. I shall not shrink from it," replied the Headsman, sinking into a chair.

For a time all was silence.

Then a kind of sleepy feeling overcame him.

He seemed wafted away from earth on zephyr wings, and then suddenly a vision came before him, clear as if it stood in the blaze of the noonday sun.

He saw himself standing at the gate of the old bridge, leaning on his axe and block.

At first all around was vacancy.

But in a moment, from out the mist came trooping figures whom he well knew—figures of lovely women—of old men whose hair had grown grey in the service of an ungrateful country—young men in the flush and pride of youth—all passed by him and eyed him with reproachful eyes.

He knew them well.

Each one of them had suffered beneath his fatal axe.

And as he stood there beneath the broad gateway, with its iron bars hovering, as it were, threateningly above his head, the tears of pity rolled from his eyes.

But what is this to him?

This is but the past.

What of the future?

He was not long to be kept in suspense.

From out the darkness, at length, came a solitary figure: a tall, commanding figure—that of a young man in all the gay dress of the court gallants.

The Headsman clasped his hands, and watched eagerly for the face.

It was turned towards him after a moment, and the executioner awoke with a shudder gasping, in tremulous accents—

"Great Heavens! My Lord of Essex."

When he recovered full possession of his senses, he found the old woman bathing his forehead with some perfumed water.

"What cursed charms have you been practising upon me?" he cried as he sprang up.

"Ungrateful man," she answered, "did you not ask me to conjure up for you a vision of the future, and now do you upbraid me for it?"

The Headsman pressed his hand to his brow, and glanced around him.

Confused as had been his ideas, he now well remembered what had been his object in coming to the cottage.

"Forgive me," he said; "I had forgotten myself. But the vision you conjured up before me was a terrible one—one that was beyond even my power of endurance. Yet fear not; I will reward you well. Give me some refreshment, if you have any, and we will have further converse."

The old woman at once obeyed, and in a few moments returned, bearing a tankard of wine.

The Headsman drank freely of this, and having emptied it at two draughts, set it down on the table.

"Tell me," he said, "what know you of the birth of Harold Forrester and Edwin Archer."

The question seemed to take the old woman aback.

She had not forgotten the injunctions of Don Fernando.

"I know nothing of them," she said, "and even if I did, would tell nothing."

The Headsman's eyes gleamed with pleasure.

"My good Mistress Halcott," he said, "I asked it but to try you. Then you have revealed nothing to anyone of their birth, or how they came into your hands?"

"Nothing, as Heaven is my judge."

"Know you that one is dead—murdered?"

"Dead—murdered!" repeated Mistress Halcott, raising her hands.

As she did so, there was a loud knocking at the door, and even before she could proceed into the front room, the door of the chamber in which they sat was thrown open, and a dark, swarthy stranger appeared.

"Don Fernando!" exclaimed Mistress Halcott in wonder.

And then to her greater surprise, the Spaniard and the Headsman exchanged a hasty glance; and their hands were grasped in a mutual grasp of friendship.

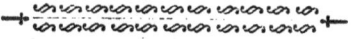

CHAPTER XIII.

A SECRET INTERVIEW.

No wonder was it that Mistress Halcott gazed with astonishment as she saw the Headsman and the mysterious Spaniard exchange a friendly greeting.

After so many years, how did they know one another?

Don Fernando, however, was not altered beyond recognition.

There was still the swarthy complexion, the coal-black hair, the bright eye, the upright form, and he smiled as she gazed in undisguised wonder at him.

"I am but little changed, Mistress Halcott," he said, "very little, and that surprises you. You see how I trusted you. Had I not known that my dear ones were in safe custody, my face would have shown many a deeper furrow!"

Mistress Halcott trembled.

What had she just heard? Was not one of these "charges" dead—murdered?

And would he not exact a strict account from her?

The Headsman saw at once her emotion, and guessed its cause.

By a quick glance he enjoined silence, and said, turning to Don Fernando—

"We have much, I doubt not, to say to one another. Come with me; I have a boat in waiting, and it will not take us long to row to London Bridge."

"But my dear ones, are they safe?" asked Don Fernando.

"*I* can best tell you about them," said the Headsman cheerily. "They have long, as you are aware, been beyond the care of Mistress Halcott. Take a glass of this good ale here, then come with me, and I will tell you all."

Don Fernando, having partaken of this simple refreshment, passed into the outer room, where, approaching Mistress Lewarden, he placed his hand upon her shoulder.

"In an hour or two you will see one," he said, "whom you have long believed lost. Nay—interrupt me not—he will return to you, never more to leave you until death; but I beg of you—as I have behaved well to you and yours—to ask him *no* questions in regard to me."

Then, stooping down and kissing her daughter, who sat near and gazed at him, half in wonder, half in fear, he placed a heavy purse in her hand and hurried with the Headsman out of the cottage.

During the row from the shore of Gladwell Heath to London Bridge, scarcely a word was exchanged between the two strange friends.

In fact, it was so dark and misty when they started, that they had enough to do to keep clear of obstructions, and as they drew nearer to their destination, a heavy fog had settled on the bosom of the stream.

They pulled on steadily and slowly, however, and presently they fancied that they could descry close at hand the "Red Cross," which showed to thirsty people at night that Wormer had accommodation for the wayfarer.

This had scarcely appeared, when a shrill whistle resounded on the night air, seeming, truly, as if it with difficulty penetrated the thickness of the fog.

"What is that?" asked Don Fernando.

"That is my double—my faithful companion," replied the Headsman. "We call him Mat o' the Mist, and, truly, a child of the mist he is. He saw us, as you observe, before we beheld anything, even the huge fabric itself."

The Headsman whistled in reply, and again Mat's guiding signal rang out.

Thus aided, the men soon reached the point they desired, and sprang ashore.

"You live in a strange place," said Don Fernando, as soon as they were fairly settled in the executioner's room. "I fancy that with all my experience, and after all the dangers I have undergone, I should go melancholy mad in such a place. But, tell me, where are the boys, and how has fortune used them?"

"Fernando," said the Headsman, "you are a brave man, and can endure sorrow."

"Sorrow!" almost shouted the other. "Have you then bad news to tell me of them?"

"Nay, nay, be not so hasty," replied the other. "It is not so bad as you imagine. Listen, and interrupt me not, and I will tell you all."

"Say on," said Don Fernando, calmly.

But this calmness was only assumed.

His heart, in reality, was profoundly agitated.

Briefly as possible the Headsman described the events which had taken place since the arrival of the two lads at the house of the diamond merchant, the fair in St. Christopher's Fields, the murder of Edwin Archer, and the abduction of Eveline Duke.

Don Fernando listened in silence, as the Headsman had asked him, but the burning of a mental volcano was observable beneath his placid demeanour.

Even though the sun of the tropics had tanned his brow, a pallor overspread his face, while his clenched hands, too, and rigid way of sitting, showed how strong was the effort required to repress his emotion.

"And so," he said, in a calm, cold voice, when the Headsman had finished his narration; "and so they have killed Edwin?"

The Headsman did not reply, but rising from his seat, approached a secretaire, and drew from it a paper.

This he placed before Don Fernando.

"Read this," he said, "and implicitly believe it. But, for a time, keep your knowledge a secret."

Don Fernando took the paper and read it eagerly.

As he did so, the colour returned to his cheeks, the brightness to his eyes.

Then he turned to his companion.

"You can vouch for this?" he said.

"Aye—on my life!"

"Then, by Heaven, we can concoct and execute a plan which will yet confound them!"

What this plan was we must leave the future to elucidate. We must turn now once more to Harold Forrester.

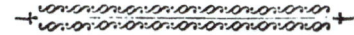

CHAPTER XIV.

FALLING SHADOWS.

DAYS sped rapidly by, and yet no tidings reached Launcelot Duke in regard to his lost child.

Convinced though he was that the lovely girl he had seen at the jousts was his own sweet Eveline, he yet knew himself to be human, and spared no trouble to inquire in quarters where the slightest chance existed of her being found.

But all to no effect.

The lady whom Lord Housden declared to be Lady Grace Harcourt, was at Court under the protection of Queen Elizabeth.

But *she* made no sign.

Business at "Duke's Palace" went on in a very dull routine.

Even if Harold Forrester had had no deeper interest in Eveline than as his master's daughter, the place would have seemed dull enough for him.

Master Duke, in fact, seemed in no spirit to address any one, and went about the place in silent sorrow.

Loving Eveline, therefore, as he did, it may well be imagined how full of excitement and anxiety was the heart of Harold Forrester.

Wherever he was engaged, or however he was occupied, her form would appear to him, sad, pale, full of eager grief.

At length, at the end of a week he had quitted his daily duties, and was passing along the old bridge towards the abode of one of his companions, when a hand was placed on his shoulder.

He started round, with his hand on his sword, expecting an enemy ready for attack.

Instead of which there was a short figure draped in black, evidently the figure of a woman in disguise.

"Your name is Harold Forrester?" said the Unknown.

"It is. What want you with me?"

"Nothing more than to give you a message. THE TIME HAS COME."

And with the words the figure turned, and passed rapidly away.

Harold's heart beat violently.

He recognised the words at once.

The message had come from the Earl of Essex. And so soon!

He at once turned back towards home.

On reaching his own room he hastily took from its secret hiding-place the sealed letter given him by the Earl of Essex, and, with trembling hands, opened it.

It ran simply as follows:—

"When you open this be assured that treachery has been at work, and that I am in danger. If you have a courageous heart, and are willing to fight your way to distinction, collect together about twenty daring spirits, and hurry with them to my house at Horley Wood. If more, so much the better, provided they can be trusted; but have a care that you are sure of your men. Tell your master that not only your good, but his daughter's is involved in this, for the great enemy and traitor I have to combat is Lord Housden, her abductor. Two days will probably be time enough for you to accomplish this enterprise. So, on the evening of the second day, I shall be anxiously awaiting you at Horley Wood. Until then, adieu. "ESSEX.

"The pass-word to my presence will be 'NOT YET TOO LATE.'"

Harold sat down, and passed his hand over his fevered brow, closing his eyes for a moment, as if to convince himself he was not dreaming.

"This is more than I could have pictured to myself in my wildest visions," said he. "A letter from Essex—a secret mission entrusted to me! But, there, the mission has to be performed, not talked about; and on its performance depends the future of Harold Forrester. Now, then, for my master."

And, despite the hour, he hurried towards Launcelot Duke's room.

In order to explain all this, and much more that followed, we must return for awhile to the Earl of Essex.

Naturally enough, the attack which had been made upon Harold on the occasion of his journey to Horley Wood had excited considerable suspicion in the mind of the earl.

In fact, he had long known his position to be most insecure.

Ever since the time of his last disgrace, the queen had been strange in her manner towards him, had listened to the whisperings of his enemies, and had acted even with such cruelty that she denied him the presence of his wife and his favourite physician in his illness.

He kept good watch, therefore, and when, at length, the hour came when he was to present himself at Court, he took leave of his beautiful wife with much emotion, and, accompanied only by his secretary, Cuffe, departed on horseback to London.

On arriving at the palace and entering the hall, he observed that the glances of all around were strange and unusual.

But, with the grand spirit which always unfitted him for the servile society of courts, he passed on towards the queen's chamber without announcement.

As he reached the end of the grand gallery leading to the royal room, Lord Housden advanced to meet him.

"One word with you, my lord," said he.

Essex turned upon him haughtily.

He knew him for the traitor that he was, the time-server, and the sycophant, though he only suspected him as yet as the hirer of bravoes and assassins.

"Speak quickly then," said the earl, "for I have business with the queen."

"Of that I desire to speak," replied Housden, in a tone of pretended concern. "I am posted here specially to inform you that her majesty does not desire to see you."

Essex reddened.

"Then if my life depends upon it, I *will* see her," he cried.

And thrusting aside Lord Housden, he strode on, along the corridor, into the queen's private chamber.

Lord Housden could have prevented this catastrophe.

He could forcibly have turned Essex from the palace, creating disturbance and scandal, no doubt, but nothing like the storm which he knew would inevitably result from such a breach of court etiquette as this.

But Housden had no desire to put a veto upon the earl's rashness.

He desired his downfall.

What then could he do better than let him rush headlong to his own ruin?

Essex found the queen alone.

She was pacing the chamber with violent strides; her face was pale, and her hands were clenched together in nervous excitement.

She started round as Essex entered; and even the brave earl was for an instant daunted, or rather awe-stricken, by the terrible tumult of passion visible on her countenance.

He bowed lowly.

But she took no notice of his reverence.

"By God's son!" she cried, standing before him and stamping her foot, "I am no queen! You are above me! Who gave you command to come hither?"

"Your grace sent for me," replied Essex, repressing with difficulty his haughty temper, "and I could do nothing else but obey."

"I must have done with this, my lord," returned the queen, seating herself in her chair, and speaking in a voice which chilled the blood of the handsome young courtier. "I had told you you might retire from court, and you returned to find those whom you fancied to be your enemies, but who were in reality but guarding me against your conspiracies."

"Conspiracies, madam!" repeated Essex, with a frown.

"Aye, conspiracies, my Lord of Essex," said Elizabeth, "against the one ' whose mind has grown as crooked as her carcase.' God's death, sir!" she added, fiercely, warming as she remembered the words which had been repeated to her and which had caused her heart to palpitate with intense fury, "God's death, sir! do you fancy that I do not hear of your doings? Ungrateful man, leave me while my passion is yet only rising, lest I call my guards, and have you sent where other traitors have gone before you!"

"Call your guards, madam," answered Essex, boldly, "I care not for them. But let me say this much. I am not a traitor, and I am not ungrateful; for what, pray, am I to be grateful? What, since I have been at court, have I been but a puppet for you to raise up and cast down; now in favour, now out of it, just as your jealous temper willed it. A soldier placed at the head of a rabble army to make room at court for a lying sycophant! I return from Ireland to you for justice, and find nothing but degradation and disgrace."

The queen here essayed to interrupt him.

But he would not stay the torrent of his anger.

"Nay, hear me out, madam for I *will* speak. For my own life's sake, and for the sake of that dear one whose sweet face was your first cause for jealousy and distrust, I *will* take your advice. I will leave this palace ere you call your guards; but when I knock at its doors again it shall be with such a host at my back, that even Elizabeth of England shall not dare refuse me admittance without honour!"

The old queen, whose health, and, therefore, whose courage was now somewhat on the wane, seemed paralysed by this audacious speech.

She sank back in her chair of state aghast, gazing at her old favourite with an expression in which furious anger was mingled with astonishment, sorrow, and regret.

Essex took immediate advantage of this.

He knew well that all depended now upon his making his escape from the palace ere she summoned her guard.

So, with a bow, in which there was a slight suspicion of mockery, he passed from her presence, and made with all speed towards the entrance hall.

At the gate his horse was being held by his secretary, who, knowing the dangerous aspect of the political horizon, had not deemed it right to deliver over to a stranger the care of the steeds.

"Quick, Cuffe; mount and away!" cried Essex as he vaulted into the saddle.

"Whither?"

"Follow me, and ask nothing," said Essex; "my head will feel loose upon my shoulders until I am at home, and with an army at my back."

These words caused a tinge of colour to invade the generally pale face of the secretary.

This was exactly what he had long been hoping for.

Cuffe, in fact, had the most untiring and boundless faith in his master.

A soldier himself, he regarded Essex as the impersonation of address, courage, and astuteness, and he had the same faith too in his popularity.

He feared nothing for his safety, even now, therefore.

Although, indeed, his enemy was the Queen of England.

"Now is the time for our advancement," thought he.

And keeping a good look-out behind him, he pressed eagerly after his master.

Unpursued, as far as they were aware, they reached Essex House in the Strand, the town residence of the earl, whose beautiful grounds reached the borders of the Thames, where so many days of happiness had been spent in times gone by, where the queen herself had appeared—where, in fact, the young earl had held his head above all in in England.

At the gate Essex drew rein, and leaped off his horse, but as Cuffe was about to knock, he stayed his hand.

"Enter you not, my lord?" asked the secretary in great surprise.

Essex smiled bitterly.

"Enter *here*, my good Cuffe?" he said. "Of little use would that be to me without an army at my back. The flames of the queen's anger are lit against me. Know you not that?"

The secretary had heard nothing.

He had only surmised.

"You have as yet told me nothing, my lord," he answered.

"True, true," replied Essex. "These constant turmoils turn my brain. I have fled from the presence of yonder crazy queen, threatening her with riot and insurrection. I have thrown down the gage, and be well assured she will take it up."

"What do you intend, then, my lord?" said Cuffe, calmly, though his heart was throbbing with emotion.

"Go you at once to the Earls of Rutland and Southampton—to Lord Sandys and Lord Mounteagle, and bid them meet me here to-morrow night, without fail. Go then to Colonel Mortimer and Captain Haslyn, and tell them the time has come. Say no more. Give them no satisfaction if they desire to know further; I would have none with me who will not come at my first call, without knowing why I call them."

"And you, my lord, are you safe — alone?" said Cuffe, anxiously.

"Aye—safe enough. Here, take my horse, and be swift with your work, for I shall return ere midnight."

Cuffe at once obeyed, and the Earl of Essex, hurrying away passed down a narrow lane leading to the water-side.

On his way he put on a small mask, which entirely prevented his features from being recognised.

Arrived at the stairs at the water's edge, he called a boatman, and directed him to row him with all possible speed to London Bridge.

This was the safest plan.

No one could have expected to find the rebellious earl on the river at such a time.

It was the nearest route, moreover, and, more than this, he would be certain to meet no friends who might delay him on the route.

Very silent and still he sat in the boat as they neared the clumsy old edifice which spanned the broad bosom of the river.

No shudder passed through his frame as he viewed the traitors' heads.

Why should he have viewed them with anything but indifference, though even then he was on the point of stirring up an insurrection against a powerful monarch?

Was he not thirty-three years of age, in the prime of youth and vigour?

Was not all the world bright and beautiful to him, in spite of the malignity of a jealous old woman?

It was absurd to talk of danger.

He would raise a rebellion; thousands would flock to his standard.

The people loved him; they would everywhere hail him as a deliverer, and when he was in a position to impose terms, he would be the leading man in England, and the queen—in spite of Housden, in spite of Sir Walter Raleigh, and his other enemies—would admire him all the more for his daring.

Such were his golden dreams, as he floated quickly along.

But the reality came when his boat bumped against the stairs on the Surrey side of London Bridge, and he leaped out.

"Await me here," he said to the waterman, as he gave him a gold piece, "and on no account take another fare."

Then he hurried up the steps and made for the bridge gate.

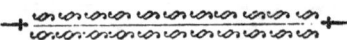

CHAPTER XV.

THE FIRST CONFLICT.

ON entering the narrow roadway, he looked hastily this way and that, to see if he were watched. and then hastened on with rapid strides towards "Duke's Palace."

Arrived there, he knocked lightly at the door, removing his mask as he did so.

The maid-servant—the same that I mentioned in my third chapter—started, on seeing the finely-dressed gentleman.

Her guilty thoughts suggested that it was none other than Lord Housden, whose letters to Eveline she had so often been the means of carrying.

But she was soon disabused of this notion.

"Is Master Harold Forrester at home?" asked Essex; "if so, I wish to speak with him."

"He is at home," replied the maid, "and has a friend with him. Whose name shall I give him?"

"Tell him I come from Horley Wood, that will be sufficient."

Harold well understood the summons, and, with a heart which leaped in his breast, he hastened to the door.

He had expected to see Cuffe, or even a messenger of less importance.

He was astounded when he saw the earl.

"My lord," he cried, "what brings you here? No evil, I trust?"

"I know not if it be good or evil," replied the earl; "but it is business of great importance. Lead me to some room where we can converse in private, for I must not be seen here. By the way, is your master at home?"

"He has this moment gone out," said Harold, as he closed the door.

"That is well," replied Essex. "I have every faith, be it said, in Launcelot Duke, but when matters are secret, it is as well to have as few confidants as possible."

As soon as the earl had reached Harold's room, Essex began—

"You received, of course, my summons?"

"I did," replied Harold; "and have acted upon it."

"How many friends of yours do you expect will rally round you?"

"About thirty."

"That will not now be enough," said Essex; "matters have assumed grander dimensions. I had thought that I should have but to defend myself—whereas, it seems, I have to take the offensive. But I will talk no longer in riddles—I will explain all."

Briefly he told the interview between him and the queen.

"And who, think you, has betrayed you?" asked Harold.

He had thought that he alone was present when the earl had expressed himself so disrespectfully of Elizabeth, and he consequently, and naturally enough, imagined that Essex might suspect him.

"I have good reason for knowing," said the young earl, "that accursed page of mine was present during our interview. He disappeared that night, and I am certain, though I will not swear to it, that I saw him whispering with my Lord Housden's page at the Queen's Palace. But enough of that— there has been a traitor, at present it matters not who it was—we will leave him for destruction hereafter. We must now consult for the present. In the first place I will explain to you my plans. I am about to collect together all those whom I know to be my friends —my staunch friends and partisans— and on a certain day I shall ride through London at their head, calling on the citizens to rise."

"And think you they will, my lord?"

"Aye, all loyal subjects will gladly follow my standard," replied Essex. "Remember, I do not make war against the queen, but against her advisers— not against a woman who is but the shadow of her former self, but against those enemies of mine who are now foremost in her counsels."

"And when will you make this attempt, my lord?" asked Harold, who, during this conversation, was impressed most notably with the madness of the whole design.

"Next Sunday," said Essex. "There will be a meeting on that day at Paul's Cross, where a sermon will be delivered. I will then address the people—call upon them to arm themselves—and with their aid force my way to the presence of the queen. Vengeful as she is, she will be glad to make terms with me, when she sees that the people are at my back."

As he spoke these words, the door was opened, and Mat o' the Mist entered unceremoniously.

"Fly, fly, my lord!" he cried. "Your life is in danger."

Essex turned in surprise, almost in anger.

How was it that his presence was known there?

"What mean you?" he said, gazing in surprise at the distorted figure before him. "Why, Master Forrester, what imp of darkness have we here?"

"As honest, true, and brave a lad as ever lived," said Harold, quickly, "though Nature has been so unkind to him. Tell me, Mat, what is it?"

The cripple was used to have such words as these addressed to him. So he took no heed of the earl's jeering remark.

"The bridgeway opposite our door is swarming with armed men," he said. "I heard one of them, pointing to this house, say, 'He is there. I will swear it.' Hark! hear you not their summons?"

Surely enough, as he spoke there came a thundering knock at the front gate.

The earl frowned angrily.

But no fear was visible on his brow.

"And what was this man who pointed out the door?" he asked, as Harold rushed down to forbid the opening of the gate.

"He was dressed as a waterman," replied Mat o' the Mist.

"Curse him! it is the treacherous vagabond that rowed me hither," said the earl. "My escape then is cut off?"

Harold, who at the first knock had rushed from the room, at this moment re-entered.

"The door, my lord," he cried, "is doubly barred and bolted, and for a time, therefore, we are safe from them. Hark! how the vagabonds are battering at the gate. They are my Lord Housden's men, if livery tells anything. I saw them from the front window."

"How is escape possible?" said Essex. "My boatman has turned traitor, and—"

"Excuse my interruption, my lord, as time is precious," cried Mat o' the Mist; "but where did your lordship leave your boat?"

"At the stairs on the Surrey side."

The "Headsman's Imp" chuckled.

"Good, good!" he cried. "You shall have your boat. Harold, see that my lord descends upon the stonework below the window. In ten minutes I will be there, skiff and all."

And with these words he sprang to the window, and leaped out into the dark night.

"This way, my lord," said Harold; "we must make good our escape as best we may; for hark!—the door sounds as if yielding to their efforts."

As he spoke there arose a loud shout—

"Open here—in the name of the Queen!"

Essex smiled bitterly.

"It shall soon be open in the 'Queen's name' at your house, my Lord Housden, if my friends are but brave and true. Now then, Master Forrester, which is the way?"

Harold at once led him to a passage outside his chamber, at the end of which he opened a kind of door, used only to lower goods to the boats below at low tide.

Fortunately for Essex it was low tide now, and the broad buttresses uncovered, or all chance of escape would have been cut off.

"Here, my lord, is a ladder," said Harold. "Mind how you step, though, for, by heavens! they have burst the door, and you must hasten."

Essex laughed.

"You would teach a soldier who has stormed and taken towns, the use of a ladder, would you?" said he, and darted downwards as quick as thought.

Harold would have followed him at once, but as he was about to do so, there was a rush of men into the narrow passage, and he stopped to close the wooden door, hoping that, frail as it was, it would prove a momentary check.

"Burst it open! Quick—quick, this way!" he heard them cry as he descended.

"Your friend is a long time," said Essex, calmly, though he heard the shouts, and knew how imminent was the peril.

"He will be here in a moment," answered Harold; "I see the flash of his oars."

As he spoke, the doorway was burst open, and down the armed band swarmed along the ladder.

"Yield, on your life!" cried the leading party, trying to reach Essex.

But at this moment Mat o' the Mist reached the spot, and leaped on shore.

Then he and Harold formed a barrier between the earl and his enemies.

"Fly, my lord, fly," cried Forrester; "your life is of more consequence than ours."

"If your lives are in danger, I remain," cried the brave nobleman, facing about again.

"No, no," shouted Harold as he dashed aside the eager swords of the armed retainers of Lord Housden; "escape at once and fear not for us. We know well the river, and can escape where you would be lost."

"Farewell, then, for awhile," cried Essex, and leaping into the light skiff, he was soon whirling away along the rapid river.

A howl of rage and disappointment arose from the men.

"Cut them down! destroy them!" shouted the leader; they are both traitors and villainous hirelings of a rebel; at them, and fling their vile carcases into the water."

And with these words he dashed forward once more, with the whole pack of yelling and excited retainers, and attacked Harold and Mat with redoubled fury.

CHAPTER XVI.

THE ESCAPE AND THE CALL TO ARMS.

THE position of Harold Forrester and Mat o' the Mist was one naturally of great peril.

That they could escape they had told Lord Essex simply to induce the brave young nobleman to depart; and he, imagining that they knew all the ins and outs of the bridge so well that they could easily make good their retreat from the retainers of Lord Housden, had consented to depart.

At the moment, however, that they bade him go, they knew well that they were playing a desperate game.

For a time they would be enabled to keep back the enraged retainers of Lord Housden.

But only for a time.

Had their foe, in fact, chosen to give over the use of the sword, and rushed forward in a body, they could have driven the two friends into the river.

Fortunately, however, this idea did not occur to them, and they contented themselves, therefore, with simply adopting the ordinary rules of fighting.

Mat o' the Mist saw plainly, and more plainly than Harold, that the conflict could not last long.

Knowing the river well as he did, he was aware that the tide was rising rapidly, and that in a very short space of time the piece of rough stonework on which they stood would be submerged; and that whereas their enemies would escape by the ladder, he and his friend would be left to the mercy of the river.

Swimming at this point was next to impossible, except to one who, like Mat o' the Mist, was, as it were, amphibious.

What was to be done?

"Harold," Mat cried, just as he withdrew his sword from a too eager foe, who toppled over into the river, "can you keep them at bay yourself for a few moments?"

"Aye; and if I cannot, I can fling myself into the water."

"Good; then I will save you."

So saying, Mat plunged into the now eddying and seething water, and disappeared.

For full five minutes Harold, panting and nearly tired out—wounded, too, in more than one place—stood up before his eager enemies.

Just when he was yielding ground—when, in fact, he felt certain that he could hold out no longer against such odds—a dripping figure sprang to his side, and Mat o' the Mist cried—

"Seize this rope—jump with me, and fear nothing."

Harold did not hesitate a moment.

To remain was to court death.

In leaping there was at any rate a chance of safety.

Grasping the rope, therefore, he sprang forward with Mat, knowing not whither he went.

There was a blinding dash of spray, a bump against some hard substance, and he felt his feet touch dry land.

He was on the next buttress.

"Now climb for your life," cried Mat.

Harold had not the slightest conception where he was climbing to; for, long as had been his acquaintance with the bridge, he had not been accustomed, as Mat had been, to wander about its dangerous places as a pastime.

However, in a few minutes he found himself standing on a broad projection, along which Mat easily guided his steps, until they reached the wooden gate through which the Earl of Essex had so lately escaped.

"But where is the ladder?" asked Harold in surprise, as he saw the armed men below huddling together, with the water rapidly rising above their feet.

The hunchback chuckled.

"I took the ladder away first," he said; "else what would have been the use of reaching this point? See! they are about to climb on each other's shoulders to reach this doorway. We will hurl them down as they ascend."

A yell of execration rose from the crowd of armed men below as they caught sight of the two friends in the doorway, and the idea was at once suggested that they should ascend by climbing on one another's shoulders.

In fact it behoved them to do something.

The tide was now rising rapidly, and to remain where they were was to court a slow but certain death in the darkness.

If they had the least idea, however, that they would be able to enter the house by these means, they were most wofully mistaken.

The first man that showed himself at the narrow opening was hurled instantly into the foaming river, where he was at once carried away by the current.

The second shared the same fate; and no third appeared.

A consultation was held, and they had just decided upon consigning themselves to the mercy of the river, and endeavour to reach the shore by swimming, when a voice from above them said—

"You below there, listen a moment."

"We listen," replied their leader.

"If you will deliver up your arms, then," said the voice, which was that of Launcelot Duke himself, "we will permit you to ascend. No attempt at treachery, remember, will be of any avail, for we can see what you are doing, and you must ascend one by one. Deliver your arms up first, and then we will let down the ladder to you."

There required but little consultation as to this.

The rising of the water was a conclusive adviser, and accordingly, without further words, they began their disarming.

After all the weapons had been handed up, the ladder was let down, and they began slowly to ascend.

There was an idea in the hearts of of more than one of them that, when once they entered the house of the diamond merchant, they might make a rush for revenge.

In this they were most disagreeably disappointed.

The last man had scarcely set his foot upon the floor of the passage when the clash of arms was heard, and about a dozen soldiers, headed by an officer, appeared.

"We arrest you all in the queen's name," said he, advancing. "It will be best to submit quietly, as we are well prepared in case of resistance."

The leader of Lord Housden's men was utterly astounded.

"What means this?" he cried. "We are here by the express orders of Lord——"

"A still tongue shows a wise head," interrupted the officer, with a frown. "I wish to hear no names. It is sufficient that I am here by the order of no lord, but by command of the queen."

Resistance, of course, would have been useless; there was nothing for it, therefore, but to yield with a good grace; although, in very truth, the leader of Lord Housden's men was utterly confused and bewildered by the extraordinary turn of events.

They knew well that Lord Housden was at present in favour with the queen—that she had ordered the arrest of the Earl of Essex; and they supposed naturally enough, therefore, that he was but carrying out her orders.

However, in the face of an armed force, they yielded, attributing the change to the well-known caprice of the queen.

Within half-an-hour, therefore, the men had departed, and the old bridge had re-assumed its usual air of solemn tranquility.

On the evening following, Harold Forrester had made his way at an early hour towards a tavern in London, not far from the precincts of Tower Hill, where he knew he should meet the principal of those upon whom he could reckon for assistance.

As a rule Harold's life was of that quiet order that he abstained from association with the City apprentices, who in this reign were in the hey-day of their riotous insolence.

They were rarely seen on the side of wrong, but their achievements had been so praised that they began to conceive themselves by far too important a portion of the State.

From this, of course, resulted a reck lessness which ended in open riot and debauchery.

Although, therefore, there were many brave and honourable spirits among them, neither Harold Forrester nor Edwin Archer had for years associated with them.

In spite of this fact, however, Harold knew that he had secured to himself sufficient respect among them to obtain the aid of some of the best members.

He was quite right in his supposition.

When he entered the large room at the tavern where that evening the apprentices were holding their meeting, he was received with acclamation, and his proposition for a conference with closed doors was hailed with cheers.

His plan was quickly explained.

Among the apprentices of London, as in fact among all the citizens, the Earl of Essex was most popular, and his name consequently was received with loud cheers.

"Long live the earl!"

"Down with traitors!"

"Clubs and staves for ever!"

The greatest enthusiasm prevailed.

With difficulty, indeed, was it that Harold Forrester could give them any details.

Every one of them was eager to be off at once home to secure arms and prepare.

Harold, consequently, found an easier task than he had imagined.

Instead of the thirty volunteers of whom Harold had spoken to the Earl of Essex, he had obtained, before he had left the place, the aid of one hundred and fifty with the promise of fifty more.

CHAPTER XVII.

THE INSURRECTION.

ABOUT eleven o'clock at night the whole company started for Horley Wood.

In order to avoid exciting suspicion, they went in companies of six or a dozen, taking different routes, and arranging to meet at a spot near Calthorpe Farm, and close by the dark pool where the attack had been made upon Harold upon his last journey.

Only those who could ride had been allowed to join, as it was well known that the movement which Essex intended would be made so quickly and suddenly that foot companies would be of no service.

Horses, of course, it was beyond the power of the apprentices to supply.

These it was known would be ready for them at Horley Wood.

There is no necessity to describe the journey in detail.

Being unsuspected, the whole of the hundred and fifty volunteers arrived in safety at the rendezvous, and proceeded, under Harold's guidance, to the earl's house.

They found the place in a state of great excitement.

Everything was ready, and the young nobleman had resolved to trust his fortune and his life to this last cast of the die.

Lords Mounteagle, Sandys, and Southampton, with Colonel Mortimer and the rest, were already there; and, in fact, the whole of the preparations for the rising were complete.

The Earl of Essex greeted Harold with enthusiasm.

Tears started to his eyes when our hero drew him to the window, and showed him the band of volunteers which he had so quickly collected.

He grasped him by the hand.

"Harold Forrester," he said, "you shall be my captain-general; with those brave fellows of yours, and the retainers of my friends here, we can enter London with the certainty of success."

"When do we start, my lord?" asked Harold.

"We must be at Paul's Cross by ten in the morning; among the hundreds assembled there we shall be sure to find many friends, and we can make a dash upon the palace and secure the queen's person before even our intentions are known; for 'Essex and Freedom' will be the cry, and wherever that is heard, thousands will flock to our standard."

History tells us how vain his hope was.

By eight on the following morning the young earl was on the road.

He kissed his wife affectionately at parting, and bade her be of good cheer, and spoke of victory as certain.

But when with tearful eyes she saw him depart, though he had three hundred and fifty men at his back, including his most staunch and most resolute friends, something like a terrible dread of the future stole over her heart.

Throughout the Earl of Essex's unfortunate career, it had always been his peculiar bad luck to have to do with traitors.

While, therefore, the earl and his companions were galloping along towards London through the sunny morning, treachery had already been at work.

His movements and his intentions were well known at the palace.

By order of the queen the religious meeting which was to have been held at Paul's Cross was prohibited by the mayor, and although no military force had been as yet ordered into the streets, meetings of all kinds were ordered to be dispersed.

When, therefore, the earl and his friends galloped in hot haste to the Cross, they found only a few loiterers.

At the sight of the brilliant cavalcade, headed as it was by the most popular nobleman of the age, the people began to shout—

"Long live your honour!"

"God bless the Earl of Essex!"

This was the only result, however.

Not a single hand was raised to help him. In vain he shouted—

"The queen is in danger, arm! arm!"

The people only shook their heads, talked together in knots, and let him and his companions pass.

"The people are mad," cried Essex; "or else treachery is abroad. Follow me; this way, gentlemen."

At a gallop the excited earl led them through the most crowded streets of the city, shouting as before—

"Arm! arm! the queen is in danger!"

Either the people did not understand him, or they saw no cause for the rising, or they knew that an insurrection would be followed by terrible slaughter.

At any rate, though they still cried "God save your honour," not a single man in the whole of London armed himself to aid him.

No matter how much enthusiasm was in the heart of the young earl, it was impossible for him to deny that for the present, at any rate, he had made a mistake.

"We must retire to Essex House for awhile," said he, as they halted near Temple Bar.

He would have said more, but at this moment an extraordinary apparition came leaping out of Strand Lane.

It was Mat o' the Mist.

Without any ceremony he sprang upon the Earl of Essex's horse, saying in a hurried whisper—

"The troops are assembling. The queen herself has addressed them, and ordered them to seize your lordship's person. Fly, my lord; fly for your life's sake."

Then he said, as if to himself—

"Harold, too, in danger, at the very moment when Eveline could be saved!"

"She shall be saved," cried Harold, who at this moment had come to the side of the earl. "Tell me quickly, where is she?"

"When the queen heard of the insurrection she at once ordered away all the ladies of the palace," replied Mat o' the Mist in a hurried and eager voice. "My Lord Housden, of course for the sake of securing the person of Eveline Duke, has offered the use of his mansion, which the queen naturally accepted at once. The house is guarded only by a few retainers, who expect no attack, and her rescue would be easy."

Harold listened eagerly.

"I will rescue her or die," he said, when Mat o' the Mist had finished.

"Aye, and by heavens!" cried Essex, "while I have the power I will assist you in saving her. Forrester, we will start at once, before the troops can intercept us. Eveline once saved, your heart would be free to serve me; and to-morrow we must start for the north."

"Follow me to my Lord Housden's," he added, in a loud voice; and in a moment the cavalcade had turned about and were galloping rapidly back again towards old London Bridge.

They found no interruption on their passage; and the earl and his companions never drew rein until they reached the door of Housden Hall.*

---

* History supplies us with the materials for describing the insurrection which Essex raised against Queen Elizabeth when he found himself so rapidly declining in favour, and beset, moreover, by jealous enemies. There seems no doubt that, influenced by some secret motive, she purposely goaded him on to this act, which ultimately proved his destruction; but it is altogether incomprehensible how—with her feelings towards him personally—she should have permitted him to suffer on the scaffold. In describing this strange episode in a strange reign, we have of course taken some liberties with history —in regard to dates and names—but the general facts are correct.—[Author of "THE HEADSMAN."]

"EVELINE, WITH A QUICK LUNGE, WOUNDED HIM IN THE SHOULDER."

CHAPTER XVIII.

THE RESCUE.

IT was just as the hunchback had said.

The strong-minded queen, fearing that real disturbances would arise from the angered feelings of her deposed favourite, had really dismissed all her female attendants to a place of safety, while she remained behind with her courtiers, and one or two of the older ladies. In fact, far-seeing as she was, she had guessed the earl's plan.

Her own person would be what he would endeavour first to secure.

Eveline Duke—for that it was Eveline Duke seemed evident enough, strange as might be the influence which had been exercised over her to make her deny her own father and her lover—could, of course, make no objection to the proposal.

Lord Housden was, by her own word, her guardian.

How, then, could she, by any process of reasoning, object to go to his house?

So, then, when Harold Forrester, with the Earl of Essex and his followers, arrived at the gates, she had been at the mansion some hours, and with one or two of her newly-made friends was at a window overlooking the road.

She started in surprise when she beheld the body of armed men approaching.

Her heart beat violently in her breast, she knew not why.

Something, however, seemed to tell her that the approach of the cavalcade had something to do with her.

More highly did it beat when she saw approaching the doorway Harold Forrester and the Earl of Essex.

She started up.

"Oh! can it be possible that my lord of Essex has succeeded?" she cried. Can it be that he, too, Harold——"

She stopped and glanced round in a frightened way, as if she had let slip a great secret, but fortunately for her, the other girls were too much occupied in wondering at the approach of the brilliant cavalcade to notice her words.

The earl advanced to the door, and knocked violently.

An armed retainer appeared at a window above.

"What want you, my lord?" he said.

"I come to demand the instant delivery of Mistress Eveline Duke," cried Harold Forrester. "I am here for her father; and if she is not delivered to us at once, we shall secure her by force of arms."

Why, if she was not Eveline Duke, did these bold words cause such a flutter in that maiden's bosom, as she listened at the window?

The man made no answer, but hastily withdrew his head, and in another instant the rattling of bolts and chains was heard.

"They are going to defend the place," said Essex. "We must surround it so that none can escape."

"But why," said Harold, his love even becoming for the moment secondary in face of the noble conduct of the unfortunate earl—"why, my lord, expose yourself to such danger, when flight would not only save you, but aid your cause?"

"Enough—enough!" he said. "Did you not, two nights since, risk your life to save mine? Have I not sworn to aid you?—and, moreover," he added, gaily, "do I not wish to see your mistress in safety, that I may have you with me with a whole heart?"

He turned then hastily away to give the necessary orders to his followers.

He forgot to impress upon them the necessity of rapidity of action, for the approach of troops in any numbers might at any time render flight necessary.

The attack was commenced without any further ceremony; the apprentices and others dismounting from the horses with which the earl had supplied them, and attacking the door with stones and other weapons, while the others answered the desultory firing which came from the windows.

It was evident that the house had but few defenders, but the anxious looks they cast towards London showed that they hoped every moment to see a large body of troops approaching to their rescue.

But this hope appeared entirely fallacious.

The assault, conducted regularly, despite the loss of two or three men, was at length successful, and with ringing cheers the followers of Essex burst into the great hall of the building, headed by Harold and the earl himself.

Housden's retainers fought well and bravely, and would even now have disputed every inch of ground, but Essex advancing, cried—

"One moment! Stop this fight— this useless shedding of blood. I have enough at my back to render it easy for me to slay every one of you, and pull the place down over your dead bodies. But there is no need of this. We come simply for Eveline Duke; when she is surrendered we leave you all in peace."

A hurried consultation accordingly took place among the men, and it was at once decided to yield.

It would have been madness to have done anything else, for there were not a dozen of the defenders altogether.

The word having been given, Harold, followed by Essex, sped upwards to the room which was indicated by one of men, and in a moment he stood in the presence of Eveline, who stood before him, pale—statue-like—terror-stricken.

"Oh! Eveline," he cried; "come quickly. I am here to save you—to carry you away to a father whose heart is breaking for you. Come, lose not a moment."

She gazed at him with eyes full of tears.

"I thank you for your interest, sir," she answered with emotion; "but indeed —indeed you are mistaken. I pity you for the noble love you seem to show; I pity him that he has lost a daughter; but I am not she, and cannot leave this place."

Her look, her words, her agitation, her whole presence told Harold's heart that he had not erred.

"Mistress Eveline Duke," he said, "I assume the responsibility of claiming you; and with the Earl of Essex and three hundred men to back me, you cannot resist. Come, for you shall accompany us!"

He seized her wrist with gentle force,

and led her away just as a loud shout below was heard of—

"The troops—the royal troops are coming."

The retainers, had they been in greater numbers, could, no doubt have made another attempt at resistance.

As it was, Essex and his friends swept by them like a whirlwind, and in a few moments they were once more on horseback, and galloping away towards London.

Eveline Duke sat before our hero on his horse, but she had not gone many yards before, with an exclamation, which sounded like "Oh! Harold," she fainted on his breast.

London Bridge was of course the only means by which the royal troops could make their way towards Lord Housden's house.

Essex, therefore led his men by a circuitous route in order to avoid them.

But the news of their doings had spread rapidly, and a regular plan had been adopted to intercept them.

Of course, the attack on Housden Hall was not known, or the rescue of Eveline Duke; but it was known on London Bridge that the earl and his men had gone at a gallop along the Dover Road, and it was surmised that should he return, it would be by the same route.

When therefore they imagined that they had successfully eluded all chances of attack they came face to face with a large body of heavily-armed troopers.

What was now to be done?

Had Harold been alone he would not have cared; he would have fought bravely with the rest, and taken his chance of life.

But, encumbered as he was by the clinging form of Eveline, who had even now but half regained consciousness, he was helpless to do anything.

He looked inquiringly at Essex.

"I know your thoughts," said the earl; "you must keep in the centre, and we must fight. There is no help for it. Forward, gentlemen, let us cut our way through."

The commander of the royal troops had expected, of course, to see the cavalcade draw rein, and was prepared to demand in a loud and blustering voice, their surrender.

He was somewhat disconcerted, therefore, when he beheld the whole glittering array of swordsmen coming upon him at a galloping charge.

The troops, who were infantry, armed principally with long spears and pikes, immediately prepared to receive them, but such was the impetuosity of Essex and his men, and the ferocity with which they cut and slashed with their long swords, that the young earl and Harold bore down all before him.

They had dashed forward some distance in their wild rush before they perceived that they had been entirely cut off from the main body of their friends.

The young earl looked round him somewhat wildly.

Other troopers were hurrying up the narrow street to the aid of their companions.

"To return would be madness," he cried; "let us gallop onwards."

Putting their horses to increased speed, therefore, they dashed on once more.

The troopers knew them to be fugitives by their gestures—by their wild and pale features, and at once formed in line across the street.

But Providence seemed to watch over Essex and his friend.

Dashing among the bristling pikes they forced a passage like lightning, and with a wild cheer rushed away towards the bridge.

Arrived here they drew rein opposite the house of the diamond merchant, who sprang to the door himself.

"Here is Eveline, Master Duke," cried Harold, as he delivered her into the arms of the old man; "we have saved her—let it be your duty to keep her from harm. Enemies will be here to take her from you, but I cannot remain to aid you. It is through the earl here that she is safe and sound — to him, therefore, my right arm belongs, in this, his emergency."

"God bless you, Harold," murmured Launcelot Duke as he pressed the hand of his apprentice; "go whither you list; keep out of danger for my sake, and be assured that when you return Eveline shall be safe."

He said this, though in very truth, at the moment that he spoke, he knew not how he was to secure her safety.

"Good!" said the earl, "we must now away. Come, Harold, let us return to the scene of conflict, by a circuitous route. We must join our friends, if possible, and I can show them how and where to cross the river without nearing this bridge which seems so fatal to me."

With these words he waved his hand to the merchant, and, with Harold, galloped back towards the scene of conflict.

The merchant, meanwhile hurried with Eveline into the house and up into her own chamber, where, with the assistance of the maid-servant, he soon succeeded in restoring her from her state of semi-consciousness.

"Where am I?" she asked, in a dreamy way, as she opened her eyes.

Then as she saw her father bending over her, and recognised the chamber in which they were, she started up with a look of horror.

Before she spoke, however, she glanced round her with eager eyes, to see if any-one was near.

Then she threw herself upon the merchant's breast.

"Oh! father, dearest father," she cried, "why did Harold bring me hither? You know not the danger—the terrible danger in which my presence here places you. Your life—your honour, both are at stake—else would I not have denied you as I have done?"

The merchant pressed his hand to his brow.

"This seems some dreadful dream," he said. "What can its meaning be? Explain to me, my child, or I believe in very truth that my senses will give way."

The young girl shook her head, still clinging to him fondly.

"No, no," she cried; "I can explain nothing now. There is no time—let me rather hasten from this place. Your enemies may be here even while we speak. Once beyond their reach, and I will tell all."

As she said this, there was a loud knock at the outer door.

All started and turned pale.

"Stay!" cried the merchant, as the servant was about to hurry away; "let me go down. I will see first who it is before I allow the door to be opened."

So saying, he hastened down to the door, and gazing out of the window above it as he went, he saw the Headsman of the Bridge.

The mysterious executioner, as well as the being whom, in common with so many, Master Duke had been in the habit of calling the Headsman's Imp, had always been regarded by the merchant as a being of ill-omen.

For a moment, therefore, he hesitated ere descending to the door.

But only for a moment.

He remembered how he had striven to save Edwin Archer—he remembered that he was the friend, too, of Harold Forrester.

"And, besides," murmured the stout-hearted old fellow, "if he means mischief—why then, after all, it is but man to man."

Hastening down accordingly, he opened the door.

"Let me enter at once," said the Headsman; "you have already delayed too long. I wished no one to see me here. Bolt the door, and let no one else in."

In a moment the merchant had complied, and had turned towards the executioner inquiringly.

"You would ask," said the Headsman, "why I am here. I will explain. I am aware that Harold Forrester and the Earl of Essex have rescued your child from that villain Housden, and that she is here. This is no place for her. You will only bring utter ruin upon yourself, and all connected with you, if you keep her here an hour."

"But what can I do?" asked the merchant distractedly; "I have no friends who could secrete her for me: few, indeed, who could assume the responsibility."

The Headsman smiled grimly.

"In times of need friends are seldom found," he said, "more especially when the frown of the great overshadows them. You need go nowhere for a friend, however; I am here to save her. Where I will take her no one will think of searching."

"But how are we to go? Not by the front of the house," said Duke; "the neighbours would——"

"Fear not," replied the Headsman. "She must be disguised. You have, of course, some of Edwin Archer's clothes? She must hasten to put them on as a disguise, and we will go together. I have a disguise for myself in my pocket. Mat o' the Mist has by this time a boat ready at the stairs, and within an hour, with this tide, your child shall be safe!"

The merchant's heart was too full for words, and he silently pressed the hand of the Headsman in token of his gratitude.

Very little time was expended in preparation.

In a quarter of an hour there issued from the merchant's door Launcelot Duke, and what appeared to be a lad of sixteen, and a broad-built, tall man, with shaggy moustache and beard, nearly concealing his features.

They were only just in time.

In five minutes after, a troop of horse, headed by Lord Housden, galloped up to the door and knocked loudly.

CHAPTER XIX.

EVELINE'S STORY.

In order that our readers may understand the extraordinary condition of mind to which Eveline had been brought, we must narrate, in our own words, the story which her father heard with astonishment and anger.

When she had been carried away, as we have seen, by Alsdon, at the fair in St. Christopher's Fields, she had lost all consciousness.

Her terror, in fact, caused her to go off into a swoon, from which she only recovered to find herself in Lord Housden's house.

Where she was, she, of course, was unable to tell.

She was in a room overlooking the beautiful park.

But where?

She was soon told.

She had not recovered consciousness long when a young girl entered the room.

She said nothing, only glanced in and then went out.

Then, in a few moments, the door was once more opened, and Lord Housden himself came in.

He bowed in the extreme of gallantry, as was natural to one bred in a Court like that of Elizabeth, and then approached her.

"Mistress Duke," he said, "you see before you one who has risked his life for you—who has worshipped you so long, and been scorned by you so long, that he has become desperate, and has brought you hither, even though he thereby runs the jeopardy of the queen's hate."

During this speech, which was given with all the smiles which in those days were thought a necessary part of courtship—studied pieces of gallantry to cover evil designs—Eveline Duke stood gazing at him proudly, angrily, and, moreover, wonderingly.

"I know not what you mean, sir," she cried. "You have either made a great mistake, or you are mad. I know you not, and understand not your words. All I ask is that you will allow me to return to my father."

He threw himself on his knees before her.

She gazed at him still proudly and angrily.

Yet he refused to move.

He was so utterly conceited of his own appearance and his power of fascination, that he could not imagine it to be a matter of any difficulty to cajole a woman into loving him.

"This is an insult, sir," she said.

"No, no, my sweet one," he cried, "no insult. What insult is it for a man to tell truly how his heart is fixed upon the possession of one fair being—one only out of the thousand beauties that throng in London? I love you, Eveline, more than all the world besides; I have watched you, when you least knew it, for a long time, and I have sworn that you shall be mine and mine only. I am wealthy; I am in the queen's favour; no nobleman at Court has more influence than I have, and as Lady Housden you will be the gem of the palace."

A curl of inexpressible contempt wreathed itself over the lips of Eveline Duke at these words.

His wife!

The idea was simply detestable.

She had heard far too much of his character to be deceived by his idle talk.

And, besides, was not her heart elsewhere?

"You have named yourself now, my lord," she said, "and I know you. I can well understand now the desperate manner in which you brought me here. I am aware of your career at Court. I am aware of your position, bought by bribery and deceit. But I will not waste time in discussing that. Enough that, though meeting you now face to face for the first time, I hate and despise you. I demand to go, and if the queen is in this house, as I have reason to suppose, I will demand her aid in releasing me."

Lord Housden rose.

A cruel smile was on his lips.

He saw at once that all persuasion was useless.

The manner and the tone in which she spoke was enough to prove that she thoroughly meant all she said.

He took a seat near her, and looked her steadily in the face.

"Mistress Duke," he said, in a cold, hard voice, "I have endeavoured to prove to you my love."

"Love!"

"Aye; despise it if you please, but I *do* love you; you are the only being I ever could bring myself to love, and I intend, since you contemn me, to show you to what a length of wickedness such passion as mine will drive a man."

"I can believe anything of you."

"Aye; but," said Lord Housden, savagely, "you do not suspect *how* my anger will affect you. In the first place, now you have reached this house you lose your identity. You are Eveline Duke no longer."

She gazed at him in amazement.

Well she might.

What could he mean?

"I do not understand you," she said, "pray explain yourself. If *you* are mad, *I* am not, and I am certain that I *am* Eveline Duke and none other."

He smiled.

"I will prove," he said, "that your name is Lady Grace Harcourt."

Now, indeed, she thought him insane.

What was to be done, however?

She was there in his power.

So she would humour him.

Gain time, in fact, until some other person came, when she could make appeal against his frenzy.

"Explain yourself, then," she said, gently, "and I will listen patiently."

He smiled.

Perhaps he penetrated her thoughts.

At any rate, he quickly took advantage of her calmer mood.

"I am going to tell you a little story," he said; "but I will make it as short as possible. It will not, perhaps, seem interesting at first, but it *will* be as it progresses."

She made no reply, and consequently he proceeded—

"Some years ago there was a certain Lord Elliot, who was in high favour with the queen. He was in such favour that, as time went on and she heard rumours that he was doing strange things unbecoming to a soldier and a gentleman, and detrimental also to the royal interests, she refused to believe it.

"So it is always with the queen.

"She is too vain to believe that any-one has ceased to study her.

"So it went for a time—he deceiving her, betraying her in everything, and she refusing to give credit to the insinu-ations of his enemies.

"At length, however, she awoke from her dream of security.

"She found he was not only acting the traitor, but deceiving her in the meanest and most despicable way.

"He was, in fact robbing the ex-chequer.

"How did he do this?

"By a very simple method.

"He went in league with some who were considered to be the leading mer-chants in England, and pretended to give them orders for large supplies of goods to the palace.

"These goods, of course, were never seen.

"They never, perhaps, were in ex-istence.

"So it went on for some time.

"Then my Lord Elliot flew at higher game.

"He grew sick of simple merchandise.

"So he resolved to try the diamond merchants. He did so.

"For a long time, however, he could find no one to suit his purpose.

"Then at last he did, and the one he found was *your* father."

"It is false!" cried Eveline, stamping her foot indignantly. "It is false! My father never committed a dishonest action."

Lord Housden smiled.

"You anticipate," he said. "No one yet has spoken of dishonesty."

"I know well what you mean," re-turned Eveline. "My father is——"

"The same as other men, only mortal," replied Lord Housden, "and so, being mortal, and being promised a great reward, he agreed to Lord Elliot's terms

"These terms were by no means bad.

"In fact, your father worked his cards so well that he had arranged to have half before the slightest commencement was made.

"Things went on swimmingly for some time.

"But at length the defalcations be-came so great that they could no longer be ignored, and being traced to Lord Elliot, he was arrested, thrown into prison, and suffered death.

"He was so far honourable, however, that he did not desire to implicate anyone.

"Willingly, therefore, he never men-tioned names.

"As bad luck would have it, however, one or two names *did* ooze out, and among those who were thus unfortunate was Launcelot Duke."

"Again I say you lie," cried Eveline, "else he would not be alive."

"Oh, yes; he was fortunate," said Lord Housden. "The papers which would have been his condemnation could not be found; consequently he escaped, and the queen has forgotten that he was one of the delinquents; but now it is different. The papers implicating him have been found; they are in my possession, and at any moment I can be his death!"

These last words were said in a loud and resolute voice.

It was easy to see what they meant, or, rather, what *he* meant.

He would have no pity.

If she roused his anger her father would most certainly suffer.

"And how, pray, my lord, am I to know whether this is true, or some dis-torted story which you have told me to make me subject to your desires? You must give me proof ere I give credence to you."

"That I cannot give you, except in one way," replied Lord Housden, with a cold, glittering look in his eye, which told how fierce was his determination. "I tell you that I love you—that I have sworn you shall be mine—that, in fact, you shall be my wife; and yet I do not intend to use any violent means. I tell you that I hold your father's life in my hands—that, if you consent to be mine, I will destroy the evidences of what has been the scandal of the Court for years. If, however, you do not consent to remain where you are, I shall set you free, but, within four hours after your departure, your father will be prison. It is for you, therefore, to choose for yourself and for him."

The young girl knew not what to do.

What could she answer?

Seeing her hesitation, he proceeded—

"All I require of you at present is that you will remain in this house as my ward. Your name for awhile will be Lady Grace Harcourt. It may be a trial for you, no doubt, but it will be the saving of your father's life. I will leave you for awhile; but I swear, by Heaven! that if you refuse me, your father shall die an ignominious death upon the scaffold."

Then once more the cold, glittering glance, and he quitted the room.

Need I say more at this point?

What could the helpless, imprisoned girl do but comply?

And so she consented to half his proposition.

That is to say, she agreed for a time to go by the name of Lady Grace Harcourt, and to deny all knowledge of her father and lover.

How she escaped and reached her father's house on the bridge, we already know.

We must return now to the time when, in company with the Headsman of Old London Bridge and her father, she quitted the house to take her way up the river.

CHAPTER XX.

ALSDON RECEIVES AN UNEXPECTED CHECK.

LORD HOUSDEN, as we have seen, was just too late.

When he and his armed men reached the diamond merchant's house, Eveline and her protector had already proceeded some way on the river.

"Whither are we going?" asked Launcelot Duke, when they were out of harm's way.

"To Gladwell Heath—to the woman who so well took care of Edwin Archer and Harold Forrester. With no one will your daughter be safer than with her."

A gleam of pleasure overspread the face of the diamond merchant.

"Indeed, yes," he said; "she will be safe there."

But it was not only for this reason he was gladdened at heart.

His life had been clouded of late.

Why had it been so?

He partook greatly of the superstitious condition of the age, and he knew that Mistress Halcott had the reputation of being a witch.

Might she not be able to reveal to him something of his future?

He would try, at any rate.

Very little was said until they reached Gladwell Heath.

There, without apparently having been watched by anyone, they arrived in safety, and leaping on shore, Mat o' the Mist hurried away to apprise Mistress Halcott of the arrival of her new *protégée*.

The circumstances were soon explained, and very readily the old woman accepted the charge.

Well she might.

Other mysterious charges had paid too well to permit her to think of refusing.

It was arranged that she should remain at the cottage still dressed in male clothes, and that no inquiries in regard to her should be answered.

The Headsman and Mat o' the Mist had no hand in this.

Having told Mistress Halcott who they were, the Headsman stood aloof, and allowed the diamond merchant to make his own arrangements.

This being done, and a sum of money having been given to Mistress Halcott, the Headsman suggested a return to London Bridge.

But to this Master Duke demurred.

He had resolved to tempt the fates, and see what was looming in the future for him.

"I have business here near at hand," he said to the Headsman; "so if you would not mind returning with Mat o' the Mist, I will follow you in an hour or two."

"Yes," replied the Headsman; "I will go on in advance, and see how matters stand ere you return."

The merchant watched him from the door, and then hurried to his daughter.

"A truly worthy man that, Eveline," he said. "And now that he is gone, let me hear from your lips the story you were about to tell me in regard to Lord Housden. Mistress Halcott here will, I know, excuse us a moment. On yonder mound we can sit awhile, and I can hear all."

The mound to which he alluded was not far from the cottage, and overlooked the river.

Sitting down here, Eveline narrated to him the whole of her miserable adventures.

The merchant listened sadly.

"Then you believed me guilty?" he said, when she had ceased speaking.

She threw her arms round his neck and eyed him reproachfully.

"No, no," she cried; "I *never* believed it."

"Then why have you yielded so far?"

"Because I knew him for the villain that he is—because, in fact, he might have forged papers that would be your ruin. I acted for the best, dear father, I am sure I did, and the end will prove it."

The merchant mused a moment.

"We are in great danger, my child," he said, "I can see that. The Bridge is no longer a safe place for us. And Harold, too."

"Ah! what of him?" asked Eveline, eagerly.

So eagerly, that the blushes rose to her cheeks at her own temerity.

The merchant laughed, though sadly.

"Ah!" he said; "I would that Harold, brave lad, had seen that blush. I fancy his heart has run away with him, and if yours is of the same mind——"

"Nay, father," said the still blushing girl, "you know he saved my life, and I owe him a debt of gratitude. But tell me, whither can we go?"

"Well, that remains to be decided," said the merchant; "*you* must remain here for awhile, while I must return to the Bridge and see that our home is taken care of."

"Surely Harold is there and will see to the old house," said Eveline. "There is danger in London for you."

"Harold is not there to care for it," returned the diamond merchant. "He has gone off with my Lord of Essex. Once he had saved you, he cared apparently very little for anything else. But hark! who comes here? I should know his face. Here, quickly, place——"

He was about to hand to Eveline a small crape mask.

But he had no time.

The stranger advanced rapidly, and stood before them.

It was Alsdon.

Eveline knew him well.

But though she trembled with dread she did not permit her emotion to be seen.

The dusk of evening had now come on, and it was impossible, even for one who knew her well, to tell who she was.

In fact, her disguise was so good that she looked like a young man, in spite of the roundness of her limbs, which could be seen so plainly in her tight hose.

"Well met, Master Duke," said Alsdon. "I would have a word with you."

Launcelot Duke drew himself up haughtily.

"Methinks, sir," said he, "that were I to seek speech with *you*, it might be considered no matter of surprise. But how you can dare face me, knowing all I have suffered from your master and yourself, is fair matter of wonder for me. Tell me, sir, where is my daughter?"

He saw plainly that Alsdon had not recognised Eveline, and he resolved to keep up the illusion.

Alsdon laughed.

"You still adhere then to that mad idea," he cried. "Why, your Eveline, though like Grace Harcourt, would never queen it as she did at the palace of Elizabeth. You are mad to fancy it was she. She had pity for you, and even shed a tear at your expense; but afterwards, when she saw your conduct in all its folly, why she laughed and jeered at it. A vendor of stones and his apprentice coming to claim a lady whose blood runs as purely as that of royalty! It was laughable indeed; and yet, so I hear, it was likely to have gone hard with you for it."

"How so?"

"Why, someone whispered in the queen's ear that you had some underhanded purpose in your eagerness to rescue the girl. People have not forgotten the past, and how sham dealings in diamonds were known to have been made——"

"Hold there!" returned the diamond merchant, restraining his furious anger awhile for the sake of Eveline; "enough of such mad talk as that. It is not of that you came to speak, but of something more important and to the purpose. Say what is it?"

"It is readily explained," returned Alsdon; "I wish to speak of Harold."

"Of Harold Forrester?"

"Yes; of him. The queen has need of him," said Alsdon.

Launcelot Duke smiled sneeringly.

"The queen has need of *him*, and yet knows he has been rebellious?"

Alsdon smiled.

"You know very little of the world," he said, or you would have scarcely made that remark."

"Why so?"

"Simply because his rebellion has been the means of bringing him under notice. If mad-cap Essex had not dreamed of a crown or a martyrdom, then Harold Forrester would never had the chance of an earldom, as he has now."

"Then the queen will ennoble him because he has defied her authority?" said the unconvinced merchant.

"No; but simply because she believes that he has been seduced from his allegiance by the wicked folly of the Earl of Essex. At any rate," added

Alsdon, "I am the bearer of a royal message. It matters not to me whether you act up to it or not."

As he spoke he gave a piercing glance at Eveline Duke.

In spite of the disguise, he began to fancy that something was wrong.

Why, he knew not.

But he felt himself being deceived.

"Who is our friend here?" he asked, suddenly.

"A friend of Harold Forrester," replied the merchant, quickly. "But now let me give you my answer."

He advanced close to Alsdon as he spoke.

His eyes were ablaze with anger, his whole manner agitated, his attitude threatening.

Alsdon guessed there would be an explosion and prepared for it.

"Give it quickly," he said, freezingly, "as, though I willingly do my lord's pleasure, I do not wish to take insults also."

"Those who dabble in dirty work must expect to be defiled," returned Launcelot Duke. "You are the slave—the serf of an infamous libertine—a villain and a coward, whom I spit at and defy. Go, cur—go, miserable ruffian, hired kidnapper and assassin, and tell him I laugh at him, and defy his threats; and that Harold Forrester, sooner than take service under the queen, at his bidding and yours, would fling himself headlong from the topmost turret of the bridge, and find rest and release from tyranny in the wild waters."

During this conversation Eveline, as may be imagined, was no idle spectator.

Her heart beat wildly in her breast, as she heard her father's bold and angry words, and when at last she saw the livid face of Alsdon in his passion, she, woman-like, pressed her hand anxiously over her bosom.

This action was not lost on Alsdon.

"This must be a woman—what if it is Eveline," he thought. "And yet, how could it be?"

At any rate, he could soon ascertain by wilfully widening the quarrel, and seeing what part the suspected stranger took in the contest.

He drew his sword.

"Have a care, old man," he said, "how you insult me and my master. I might be inclined to chastise you for your insolence."

The merchant drew his sword at once, while his eyes darted fire.

"Have a care, hired ruffian as you are, how you attack one who can well defend himself," he cried. "Youth has left me, that I allow, but I have not forgotten how to thrust and parry. So begone, and tell your master how I reject and scorn his offer on behalf of Harold."

Alsdon had now drawn his sword, and, irritated beyond measure by the haughty and bold bearing of the diamond merchant, he lost all control, and sprang forward.

It was with great difficulty that Eveline could prevent the escape of a cry of terror at seeing her father assailed by one so much younger, and so much his superior in size and strength.

But she knew well the danger of discovery, and, though her heart beat wildly in her bosom, she restrained herself.

One thing, however, she resolved.

If her father were in any way getting the worst of it she would interfere.

The opportunity was not long wanting.

The merchant, in spite of his knowledge of the art of fence allowed himself to be drawn into wild and somewhat reckless fighting, and, by degrees, in consequence of this, he soon found himself yielding ground.

Alsdon took immediate advantage of this, and with his eyes sparkling with hate and malice, he pressed still more eagerly forward.

The diamond merchant saw the error he had made, and endeavoured, by steady fighting, to retrieve it.

But time was not allowed him.

As he stepped back, his foot caught in a rugged projection in the ground, and he fell.

Alsdon sprang at him to deal the death blow at once.

But there was one there to save.

In an instant Eveline rushed forward, seized the weapon which had dropped from the hands of her stunned and helpless father, and stood over him to defend him at the peril of her own life.

This action, and the manner in which it was done, seemed to dispel the suspicion which had arisen in the mind of Alsdon.

Had he known his opponent he would rather have yielded or fled, than that his sword should end her life.

But as it was, all suspicion being dispelled, he fought all the more desperately because he had not expected the interruption.

But though Eveline had never before wielded a sword, she seemed now inspired by a kind of natural instinct.

She fought coolly and well.

Yet, of course, such a contest could only be ended in her favour by chance.

Suddenly, a long, shrill whistle rang out upon the evening air.

Alsdon started and slightly turned his head.

In an instant he found how fatal was his error, for Eveline, with a quick lunge wounded him sharply in the shoulder.

He sprang back with a slight cry of pain, just as a second and more shrill whistle resounded from the riverside.

"We will have this out another time, young sir," he said, "remember that you have made a deadly enemy of Henry Alsdon, and that he never forgets or forgives."

So saying he dashed away, while Eveline, with a thankful heart threw down her sword and knelt by her father's side.

CHAPTER XXI.

THE EARL PLAYS HIS LAST CARD.

WE must leave Eveline and Launcelot Duke now for a time, while we follow the fortunes of Harold Forrester and the Earl of Essex.

They received no further molestation on their route; and in due time arrived in safety at the spot where they had left the earl's retainers still fighting.

No fighting, however, was now going on.

In fact, both soldiers and rebels were gone,

When they found that neither Harold nor the Earl of Essex were with them, the rioters at once deemed it prudent to give way.

Several of their number were wounded, and they knew not, of course, where they would be likely to find their leader.

Before starting, however, on their wild and hazardous expedition, arrangements had been made in case of defeat, and a rendezvous made, and, consequently, as the adventurers were on horseback and their foes on foot, they resolved to take advantage of the circumstance to make good their escape from the battle-field where no honour could possibly accrue to them.

So with a loud shout to one another, they turned about and dashed away at full speed along a wide and easy road, which led them towards Richmond.

A few shots were fired after them.

But in vain.

The soldiers had been taken by surprise, and except a trifling wound here and there, they had been unable to effect any evil against Lord Essex's men.

The rendezvous had been made by Essex near a part of the river which it was easy to ford, and on reaching it they leaped from their horses, tied them to the trees, and formed an impromptu encampment, towards which numbers soon flocked from the neighbouring villages with provisions.

Here they remained some time without seeing anything of Essex or Harold.

In fact the latter could, with difficulty, make their way towards the place of meeting.

They had horses, truly, but they had not the advantage possessed by those who rode together in large numbers.

However, by dint of hard riding, they contrived to elude their pursuers, and, dashing merrily along the road, at length reached the pleasant sylvan retreat where their friends awaited them.

Very little was said on the journey.

The Earl of Essex, in fact, seemed to have upon him some slight anticipatory dread of the gloomy fate awaiting him.

Harold, on the other hand, felt his mind in a turmoil of anger and disappointment, and bewilderment at the conduct of Eveline.

Consumed as he was by an irrepressible love for her, he saw no chance now before him of succeeding in his suit.

Unable, of course, to fathom the extraordinary conduct of Eveline, he attributed it, as was natural with a jealous lover, to some secret affection for another.

Agitated thus, therefore, as they were, by varied and conflicting emotions, no wonder was it that they scarcely spoke on their journey.

When they arrived, however, at the rendezvous, their spirits quickly revived.

The sight of the three hundred and fifty soldiers lying scattered about on the greensward, smoking their newly-discovered treat, tobacco, and drinking copiously from huge tankards of ale—laughing, joking, singing—inspired the young earl with some degree of renewed courage.

It looked certainly like the nucleus of a victorious army; yet how could such an army be organised?

CHAPTER XXII.

THE ATTACK ON HORLEY WOOD—THE SURRENDER.

THE Earl of Essex had seen already that the citizens of London were not disposed to join him.

Where, then, should he look for men?

As he had said, in the north.

There were many there discontented.

Many Catholics, who had fled from London to avoid the persecutions to which they were subjected by Elizabeth, would join him.

Then, again, he would have to oppose Queen Bess, the adherents of Mary Queen of Scots, who were burning to avenge her imprisonment and death; and, if all else failed, he could throw himself into Scotland and declare on the side of King James, who he dreamed, rashly enough, might even now be becoming anxious to seize the sceptre which he could see was destined for him in the future.

All these ideas passed through his mind as he threw himself from his horse and sat down upon the greensward amid the cheers of his retainers.

"Oh, if I had ten thousand such men as these," thought he, "how the old she-wolf would gnash her teeth and tremble."

But, alas!

His prophetic thoughts, as we know, were never destined to be realised.

After half-an-hour's rest, the cavalcade once more leaped on horseback, and, under the personal guidance of the young earl, crossed the river.

Then, at full speed, they made for Essex's house at Horley Wood.

Lady Essex, when she saw her young and handsome husband enter the room where she sat, cared not for conventionality or appearances, but threw herself into his arms and fairly sobbed for joy.

She had never expected to see him again.

He had not much time, however, to indulge in this dalliance.

The apprentices and men-at-arms having been disposed as best they could about the place, a council of war was held, at which Lady Essex was present.

Divers opinions were given on all sides; but at length on every hand it was decided that the campaign—if there was a chance of being one—should take place in the north.

It was a wild and headlong plan.

But the enthusiasm of Essex carried all before it.

Where doubts and fears had before existed, only halcyon dreams were in vogue.

The counsel thus went far into the night, and all arrangements had been proposed and agreed to, when Harold Forrester, sword in hand, and followed by some armed retainers, burst into the council chamber.

"To arms, gentlemen! to arms, my lord!" he cried. "The queen's troops are at the gate, and are surrounding the house!"

Lady Essex sprang up, and clung around her husband, as if to protect him, while the assembled gentlemen rose quickly and drew their swords.

Instant action was necessary.

Yet all seemed paralyzed.

Lord Essex was the first to recover himself.

"Where are my men-at-arms?" he cried; "have they pressed into the courtyard?"

"Yes," replied Harold, "they have all entered, though in doing so they have had to give up their horses, for there was no room for them. It was by my desire they did this. I know not if I acted rightly or wrongly."

"Right well," cried Colonel Murray; "but now we must hasten down and dispose of our forces as best we can."

In less time than it takes to narrate it, the members of the council had passed down into the courtyard and given instructions to the three hundred and fifty men who formed the garrison.

Among this number were mingled, as I have said, gentlemen and apprentices, military men and armed retainers.

But there was no distinction of persons.

Everyone fraternised.

Everyone was eager to do his best to aid the nobleman whom they loved.

In a very short space of time the house had been placed in a proper state of defence; and then, passing along the ramparts, a man blew a trumpet, and demanded to know the meaning of the assembling of a hostile force.

"We come here to demand the body of the Earl of Essex, who is now in open war and rebellion against our most sovereign lady, Queen Elizabeth," returned the leader of the troops, in the pompous manner peculiar to the times. "If, therefore, you wish for pardon for your late insurrection, deliver him up, open your doors, and let us enter."

The man had his answer ready, and no delay, therefore, was experienced.

"We know nothing of the insurrection you name, or the pardon you offer, when we are in no need of one," he replied; "but this we do now, that we are all here faithful adherents of the Earl of Essex, and, rather than deliver him up to anyone, we will die true at our posts."

"Your blood, then, be upon your own heads," cried the leader of the soldiers, and the trumpeter at once saw that they were preparing for the attack.

It was not long before the thunder of

cannon was heard, mingled with the sharp rattle of small arms.

In those days walls could stand against artillery, for the strong stone work was only assaulted by means of small, unwieldy guns, with but little comparative force in them, and which, if fully charged, would as often burst and injure besiegers as besieged.

The defenders lying down behind the stone ramparts, and only popping up as occasion required, contrived to fire upon the enemy without standing in any peril themselves, and consequently, finding that they were suffering injury without being able to knock over any of the defenders, gave over all active attack till morning.

They contented themselves with keeping strict watch to prevent anyone's escape.

During the hours of semi-darkness, they resolved to throw up some works, which would bring them more on a level with the ramparts, and thus enable them to fire at them point blank.

The Earl of Essex recognised the danger of the position, and knew, therefore, that escape might be their only alternative.

He, above anyone in that house, knew the means of flight.

But he resolved not to speak of it till the last moment.

To speak of the possibility of flight, would, of course, be to suggest the chance of defeat, and would discourage the men.

As soon, therefore, as the sound of artillery had ceased, he quitted his friends with Harold under some pretence, and made his way towards one of the highest turrets of the building.

Anyone who had seen him ascending the spiral staircase, lamp in hand, would have imagined that he was about to take a survey of the surrounding country, and the forces of his enemy.

So, indeed, thought Harold; though how it was to be done at night he knew not.

The earl, however, soon explained his object.

"Harold," he said, in a firm though sad voice, "I have led you all into danger, and it is my duty, therefore, to provide as well as possible for your safety in case of defeat. And now I am going to show you how I have done so."

So saying he opened a door, and showed to our hero a small chamber at the very summit of the tower, containing a couple of chairs and a small round table, besides a case full of books, queer, ancient-looking volumes.

"Here is my favourite resort," he said, "in summer whenever I have a chance of escape from the turmoil and trickeries of court. And here, too, when I am absent does my sweet wife sit and read, and cast anxious, loving glances towards the palace far away, where my fate was being decided and changed each hour. But she knew not what a strange place she was sitting in. She little knew what secret lay concealed within it. Observe this."

As he spoke, he advanced towards the bookcase and stooped down.

In an instant it slid back, and revealed an aperture.

A dark, yawning gulf, wherein could faintly be distinguished a staircase.

"Follow me," said the earl. "I spoke not of this to the others, lest I should discourage them by talking of flight; but to you I can say that this is a sure and easy method of escape in case we should be driven to it."

He led the way into the gulf, which, under the influence of the light soon assumed the dimensions of a circular shaft, in the centre of which was a spiral staircase.

Down this they went—down, down, down, until the air became chill and sepulchral.

Then, at length, they halted.

"We are now in the bowels of the earth," said Essex, far below the foundations even of Horley House, so that even if the place were burning above us, the fire would not reach us."

"But there is no place where three hundred men could conceal themselves," said Harold.

"Not here," replied the earl. I spoke of the stragglers. Follow me, and I will show you a spot where a thousand men could hide in complete security."

He led the way now along an ascending passage, until they reached a doorway, or, rather, an opening, which was entirely choked up with shrubs and weeds, but which the fresh air that fanned their foreheads told them was the point of egress into the open country.

"Here," said Essex is a door which has not been used since Roger Bardoleer fled with his wife into the woods to avoid his murderers, a hundred years ago. But come, with our well-sharpened swords we can make a way through."

In a few moments they had quietly cut away sufficient of the branches to enable them to pass into the wood.

All here was still.

Save only the melancholy sighing of the trees.

"Was I not right?" whispered Essex. "This place will afford concealment to the whole troop if it so turn that I am to be driven from my home. But come, let us return, and think no more of flight. The knowledge that we can assure safety to my dear wife and my friends, will be enough to nerve me in the battle."

Harold caught his arm as he was about to re-enter the subway.

"Stay, my lord," he said, "if it be so easy to enter and depart, I have a plan to suggest to aid you."

"State it, then, quickly," said Essex, "but let it be no suggestion of flight for me. That will be the last resource of all."

"My plan is by no means one of flight," cried Harold. "It is to enable you the better to defend this place against your enemies. Have you no friend somewhere in the vicinity of this place who can send some armed men to your assistance, and thus create a diversion by making an attack upon your enemies outside the wall?"

"Good," cried Essex. "My head has been so distracted with recent events that I had not thought of this. If you are willing, and have courage to undertake the mission, hie to Sir John Armstrong, at Castle Armstrong, not five miles distance from this: explain to him all that has happened, and bid him, as an old friend and comrade, to arm and come to my aid."

"But," said Harold, "there are troops even now between me and the high road. How am I to make my way through them?"

Essex smiled.

"The troops are between us and Horley House. The secret passage by which we came hither extends so far into the

wood, that we have passed completely under our besiegers. You can go straight on through this wood, therefore, and in returning, yon avenue of lofty beech trees will guide you to this spot—hasten now, good Harold, and God speed you."

Without further delay, Harold Forrester darted away through the beech trees, and soon disappeared from the sight of the young earl.

Essex had scarcely reached the door of the subterranean passage, when from out the shadow of the trees, issued a figure, which, brave man though he was, made him fall back in alarm.

It was a figure, tall, masked, and heavily cloaked.

One well known to my readers, but not as yet to Essex.

It was the Headsman of Old London Bridge.

"My Lord of Essex, a word with you," he said.

"Who are you?" asked the earl.

"It matters not," replied the other; "I am a friend, and come to warn you ere it be too late. You have begun a mad insurrection, counting upon the assistance of men who have not the courage to join you. Throw not away your life for cowards and traitors, but fly at once."

"And leave my wife and my friends to perish?" cried Essex. "Never!"

"I said not so," replied the Headsman. "I have heard all you have told Harold Forrester, and I know that you can fly in safety at any moment. Therefore I entreat you, as you value your noble life, to delay not another moment."

"And yield myself to the kindness and mercy of her most gracious majesty, the Virgin Queen?" cried Essex, scornfully. "No, no, let me die, rather!"

"I said not so," replied the Headsman. "Fly to France, or to any other distant land, until her anger is appeased, or until her days are numbered. Then return to take the position you deserve, and punish your enemies."

Well would it have been for Essex had he followed this advice.

He could not resist the feeling that the one who spoke to him was really a friend.

But he was far too ambitious to yield.

"THE SURPRISE AT THE OLD RUINS."

He could not endure, in fact, the thought of submission, which would accord to Elizabeth the triumph of knowing that he was beaten.

"My friend," he said, "I thank you, for I believe you truly sincere; but I cannot accept your counsel. However, tell me, I beg, how you came here unnoticed to my enemies, and why you speak to me with such a solemn air?"

Clearly and unreservedly the Headsman told the story of the vision which he had seen at the cottage of Mistress Halcott. The earl listened calmly.

Then he said—

"With such a she-wolf as Elizabeth on the throne, such visions, good friend, have every chance of being fulfilled. Give me your hand, for I forgive you already. We shall meet again, maybe, when you will ask me to forgive you once more, and then and now I will do so freely."

"For whom, then, do you take me?" asked the other, in surprise.

"For the one you are, I feel assured," replied Essex; "the Headsman of the Bridge beneath whose axe, maybe, my ancestors have fallen, for people give to you a long and mysterious life. I thank you again for your counsels, but I cannot take them. Farewell."

"Once more, once more, my lord," cried the Headsman, still grasping the earl's hand, "let me entreat you. There are more than a thousand soldiers surrounding this house, and all chance of combatting them is folly. Beyond there in the high-road are two fleet steeds. Go; bring my Lady Essex, and fly to happiness and freedom."

In spite of the sigh that involuntarily escaped his bosom, the infatuated earl tore himself away, and, after a wave of the hand, disappeared amid the undergrowth.

The Headsman stood and looked after him with folded arms.

"You are right, mad earl," he murmured; "we shall meet again."

Then he turned, and rapidly left the woodland.

The Earl of Essex meanwhile hurried up into the turret, and descending among his friends, found them in great anxiety with regard to him.

But, in spite of the warning of the Headsman, he rallied them.

"I have been reconnoitring the enemy," he said, "and I find we shall have tough work of it. In an hour or two, however, I expect a goodly reinforcement from one of my oldest and staunchest friends."

"Pray heaven, then, that they come quickly," said Colonel Murray. "From what I have seen of the enemy they mean business, and they are in such numbers that we could never resist them if they tried to storm the battlements."

"Horley Wood has stood a siege before now," said the earl, proudly; "and if they can pass the moat without losing half their number, then my men are not such shooters as they should be. Come, Murray, and you, Lord Sandys, you have fought under me in Ireland, and know well the science of war Let us go the round of the house, and see to the defences."

The three accordingly started on their errand, and visited the sentinels, cheering up the watchers with kindly words, and taking observations, as far as they could, of all that was passing without.

But in the middle of all this the thoughts of Essex were elsewhere.

They were with Harold Forrester and Sir John Armstrong, his staunch friend.

At length, after seeing to everything as far as they could, they re-entered the house.

Essex then once more excused himself to his friends, and re-ascended to the top of the turrets, and fearing least Harold Forrester might await him below, descended to the very end of the subterranean passage.

He had not very long to wait.

Harold Forrester had found an inn where he could obtain a horse, and the five miles there and the five miles back were soon traversed.

Presently his form could be distinguished hurrying along on foot up the beech avenue.

The heart of Essex beat high.

Five hundred men will follow him soon.

Such were his thoughts.

But at last he was fated to disappointment.

"What news, good Harold?" he cried, as he sprang forward to meet him.

"My lord," replied Harold, "all I need say is that you have good men and true in your house yonder, and with them you must fight the fight. Sir John Armstrong——"

"Is from home, and his coward retainers will not arm without his word of command. Say, is it so?"

"Alas, my lord," said Harold, "I will delay you no longer, but tell the truth. Sir John refuses to come."

"Refuses! Heaven's furies! Why, I saved the coward's life three times in Ireland! I have stood by his side when his right arm was broken and the savage troopers were dashing upon him. What reason does the knave give for declining?"

"I explained all to him," replied Harold, and the answer he gave to me was this—'You have told me enough to prove that all attempts at rebellion are in vain. If the people in London had responded to his call, then there might have been some reason in proceeding; but now I cannot think of helping him in his madness. Anything I can do for him by way of intercession with the queen, I will do, but nothing more.'"

"Then, by Heavens!" cried Essex, fiercely, "we must ourselves drive these knaves from our doors, and when we return triumphant from the North, we will burn his house about his ears."

And without further preface, the earl turned upon his heel, and led the way back into the house.

The earl said very little to his friends about the disappointment he had received.

He told them that the reinforcements he had expected were, for some reason or other, unable to join him, and that they must do their best to fight out the battle alone.

"We must drive these knaves back to London, and then make all haste to the north."

The dawn of day was now rapidly approaching, and soon the garrison was able to see the extreme peril of their position.

The earthworks of the enemy were quite as high as the battlements, and were heavily mounted and manned.

Yet Essex did not despair.

Nor did he claim their assistance selfishly.

Before the first gun had thundered forth its challenge to the fight, he told all who desired to do so to quit him.

To the honour of all there, be it said, that whatever others might do, they at least were faithful to him.

Not one man budged from his post, nor did one, indeed, show the slightest disposition to quit his position of danger.

Here, at least, the once mighty earl was respected and believed in.

At length the first cannon-ball came with a whiz from the enemy's works and went crashing against the inner wall.

This was the signal for action.

The sharpshooters on the walls at once began to fire at the besiegers, and from both sides the firing for a long time was fast and furious.

There was no doubt that Essex had the best of it.

His men were by far the better protected, and their hearts, too, were in their work.

The young earl, as may be imagined, was filled with exultation as he beheld the earthworks of the enemy crumbling away, and the queen's troops drop one after another.

The pleasing vision came before his mind of the exasperated queen cursing her courtiers, dismissing her attendants, and giving mad orders for the death of the beaten commanders, while he and his victorious men were galloping away towards the north to spread the news of the royal defeat.

All day the fight continued with varying success, but towards nightfall the fire of the queen's troops slackened.

They were either short of ammunition or they had resolved to wait for next day.

The truth, had Essex but known it, would have astounded him.

The fact was that, finding themselves overmatched by the little garrison, they had sent to London for reinforcements.

All through the night everything was quiet.

The dawn of day showed that Essex had too soon indulged in hopes of triumph.

Double the quantity of men that had originally advanced to the attack now surrounded Horley House, while battering rams and scaling ladders were to be seen in plenty.

An immense number of men were employed filling up the moat, and it was easy to be seen that a vigorous attack could only for a few hours be repulsed.

Under these circumstances it would have been utter madness to have thought of a lengthened defence.

All that could be done, consequently, was to hold their own as best they could until nightfall, and then, under the cover of the darkness, to make their escape.

To do this was a work of no ordinary difficulty.

Upon those who were filling up the moat the defenders on the ramparts fired unremittingly, despite the incessant fire from the earthworks.

Every now and then, too, large stones and melted lead were poured down upon the heads of the assailants.

Again and again scaling-ladders were raised against the wall, but were hurled back by the intrepid defenders.

Thus it went on during the whole day, with much loss on both sides, until at length night closed over the scene.

When all was once more quiet, Essex called his leaders into the council chamber.

As eager and as brave as he, they had no conception of his wishes in doing so.

They had recognised with joy the results of the day's fighting.

Naturally they expected that the news would spread, and that hundreds would flock to his standard.

But Essex knew otherwise.

He had around him truly a band of brave and faithful adherents.

But there was evidently no chance of the arrival of others.

Why, then, sacrifice the few noble souls who still adhered to his waning fortunes?

"Gentlemen," he said, "my cause is hopeless, and I am resolved to fly."

A murmur of dissent passed through the assemblage.

They imagined themselves on the road to victory and glory.

"Nay, gentlemen," he said, "hear me out. The numbers opposed to us are such that it is impossible to defeat them ultimately.

"No one comes to swell our ranks, and from the answer I received from Sir John Armstrong, when I sent to him, I have no hope of succour from any."

He then told them the story as he had heard it from Harold Forrester.

"My plan," he said, "is this. I have a secret mode of escape for all. Let us, then, fly, and leave this house empty for them in the morning. I shall fly to Essex House, and then, if they will promise to accord me a fair trial, I will yield myself not to the queen, but to my country."

Various arguments were used to dissuade him from this.

But in the end he prevailed.

In fact, his arguments were feasible ones.

There was evidently no chance whatever of a successful insurrection, and as for flight to a foreign country, Essex refused even to hear of it.

So everyone having heard the plan, Essex led the first detachment up into the tower, whence they descended to the subterranean way.

Then the second detachment, among whom were the sentinels, were quietly withdrawn from the walls, and the old house was left in total quiet.

When all were ranged in the wood, and so near the enemy that they could see the men clustered round their watch-fires, they passed quietly away in parties of fifty.

Essex insisted upon being last, and he, accompanied only by his wife and Harold Forrester, took his way towards Essex House.

Even the company of Harold he did not desire, for in the present state of affairs he desired no one to share his perils; but our hero refused to leave him, and at full speed, therefore, they dashed along the dark high-road.

On arriving at Essex House, the unfortunate earl was surprised to find every window ablaze with light.

"Go to the door and demand to see Cuffe," said the earl. "There may be treason here."

Harold had no need to ring, for the little group had been seen by a watcher at the window, and Cuffe, the earl's faithful friend, rushed forth.

"Fear not, my lord, but enter," he cried; "they are all friends here."

The earl at once entered, and there, to his astonishment, he found Lord Sandys, Colonel Murray, and all those whom he imagined he had left behind him in the vicinity of Horley House.

They had hurried to London by a less

circuitous route, and were there before him.

"Be not angry, my lord," said the brave colonel; "we knew not what treachery might be lurking here, and until we know you to be in safety, we cannot leave you."

Early morning found the earl and his friends once more in council, in the midst of which there came a loud knocking at the gate.

There, in all the pomposity of conscious power, were the emissaries of the queen, and first and foremost among them was my Lord Housden.

Essex turned pale as he saw him.

Not with fear, but anger

"There will be no justice where that villain is," cried Harold. "It is a shame and an insult that he should be sent hither."

Presently, and by Essex's order, the Commissioners were ushered in.

Among them were several true noblemen—friends to Essex as to the queen—who wore on their faces the impress of real sorrow.

"My Lord of Essex—," began Lord Housden.

Essex interrupted him fiercely.

"'Sdeath, gentlemen," he cried, turning to his friends, "am I fallen so low that I must submit to this?. You, my Lord Lorton, you speak to me your wishes. I refuse to hear what this traitor has to say."

Lord Housden's hand was on his sword in a instant, and a collision would most certainly have taken place had not the friends of Essex closed round.

"No fighting can be allowed here," cried Colonel Murray. "If ye come to murder my Lord of Essex, say so, and we will string you up to the trees in yonder garden, be ye Queen's Commissioners or not."

A word from Lord Lorton at once appeased Lord Housden.

A smile of malignant triumph crossed his lips, and he drew back while Lord Lorton advanced.

"Stay, my lord," said Essex, "I will spare you the trouble of explaining to me your visit here. You come to arrest me, and, on one condition, I will offer no resistance to your wishes."

"Name it, then, my lord."

"It is that, on your words of honour as gentlemen, you will here undertake that I shall have a fair and public trial?"

"That, my lord, we will swear," said Lord Lorton, "for there are many here who believe you in their hearts to be the victim of some foul treachery. Gentlemen, have I spoken rightly? Will you undertake this?"

The Commissioners, even including Lord Housden, drew their swords, and having kissed the blades, replied—

"We undertake it, solemnly."

"Then here," said Essex, "is my sword. It is an honourable one, and has done, on many a field, good service to my native land."

Then, with a sigh, he resigned it into the hands of Lord Lorton.

"And now," said Lord Housden, "as my words now have no reference to my Lord of Essex, I conclude I may be allowed free speech?"

"Speak on, my lord," said Essex.

CHAPTER XXIII.

THE TOWER.

HOUSDEN glanced round him imperiously.

"I hold here in my hand," said he, "a warrant for the arrest of one Harold Forrester, who is a follower of my Lord of Essex."

"I am here," cried Harold, advancing boldly.

Housden turned to one of his attendants.

"Here, Horsley, is your prisoner," he said. "See that he escapes not."

"My Lord Housden should remember better than that," cried Harold, as he yielded up his sword. "It is my Lord Housden who believes more in his heels than in his sword."

A fierce frown was the only answer which Lord Housden gave to the taunt, and in a few moments the Earl of Essex and Harold Forrester, having taken leave of their friends, were conducted by their captors into the Strand.

Very few persons noticed them as they passed by.

In fact there was nothing in their appearance to distinguish them from a company of gentlemen on a ride of pleasure.

There were no men-at-arms—no mail-clad attendants.

The Earl of Essex had trusted to the word of honour of the queen's commissioners, and we shall see how well they fulfilled their trust.

Meeting, consequently, with no obstructions on the road, they soon arrived in the neighbourhood of the grim old Tower of London.

There were very few people about, but as they crossed Tower Hill, a tall, cloaked figure passed them.

Strange coincidence, truly.

It was the Headsman of the Bridge.

Seeing at once who the prisoner was that was being carried to the gloomy fortress, the Headsman tried to pass by unnoticed; but as Essex, with a gay smile, waved his hand to him as a token of recognition, the mysterious man uncovered his head, and bowed in respectful sympathy.

He turned and watched the little cavalcade until the gates of the gloomy Tower had closed behind it.

Then he turned mournfully away.

"The doom of the earl is sealed," he said, "but as for Harold Forrester, he must and shall be saved."

Had Harold been in a position to overhear these words, they no doubt would have afforded him some comfort.

But in very truth, in peril as he was, he thought more of the condition of the Earl of Essex than himself.

He had confidence in his own fate, but for the young earl it seemed truly as if the sun had set.

Essex himself, notwithstanding the dark aspect of affairs, could not persuade himself that any danger threatened his life.

He knew well—he felt, indeed, that his favour at Court was gone—he saw in his mind's eye the triumph of his enemies, these and his own retirement from the public gaze.

But would not that, after all, be as well?

What could be better, he tried to persuade himself, than the solitude and quiet of Horley Wood with the company of his sweet wife?

However, he was not long occupied with such thoughts.

He had other and more important matters to claim his attention.

He had demanded a fair trial, and he had been promised one.

I shall not describe the trial here.

It is no part of my story, which must soon diverge from the unfortunate earl, and follow yet more closely the fortunes of the hero and his friends.

It will suffice to say that, after a protracted scene of lying and recrimination, the Earl of Essex was found guilty of high treason, and sentenced to death.

The Queen had watched this trial anxiously.

She had hoped against hope that he would be acquitted, and yet (strange anomaly in human kind!) she could not so much as raise a finger to aid him.

She had stamped and raved when she had heard of his insurrection.

She stamped and raved now that she heard of his condemnation.

And yet, from her subsequent conduct, she seemed to blame *him* because he was not found guiltless.

The truth in all this is easily explained.

She wanted to see him at her feet; to hear him supplicate her for pardon; to feel and know her power over the noblest and handsomest, and bravest man in all England.

And this, even in the hour of his extremity, he refused to do.

All expected a scene when she was called on to sign the death-warrant.

They were disappointed.

She signed it without delay, and with a firm, bold hand, as the existing manuscript proves.

"This will awe him into subjection," she thought.

See how wrongly she judged him!

Time went by. The morning appointed for the execution came.

Yet Elizabeth received no token that he desired to appeal to her for mercy.

Whether or not the story of the ring

and the Countess of Nottingham is a true one, we will not pretend to say here.

It has been made a part of history—where fables are often made good use of.

At any rate, one cold, grey morning saw the scaffold erected in the inner court of the Tower, whence the earl and Harold Forrester could see it from their barred window.

Why this precaution was taken we cannot say, unless because the well-known popularity of the earl gave reasonable fear of a rising in his favour at the last moment.

The earl had long since given himself up for lost.

He had taken leave of his dearest friends, even of that one dearest of all—his young and beautiful wife.

"I am to die through the caprice and folly of a mad old woman," he said, as he pressed his loved one to his breast, " who will regret my death when my head cannot be fixed again upon my shoulders. Have a care of her, Lucy, and let not the she-wolf seize my lambs. When you leave me, think of me as dead. Let no thought of to-morrow break your rest, for that is the least of all to be considered— a swift and painless death! When you leave this place, hurry to Horley Wood, and take our children away to some safe hiding-place until she dies, which, mark me, at her age, and with the indulgence of her evil passions, will not be long ; and then Heaven grant England a king who will rule her well."

"A king like you, my Essex," murmured his fond wife.

And presently they parted with such a burst of agony and sorrow, that even the stern gaolers turned away their heads to hide the tears that forced themselves down their rugged cheeks.

And so, as I have said, after a peaceful night, the earl rose and dressed himself, and looking out, saw the drizzling rain falling on the grim apparatus of death.

His heart did not fail him.

If any one feeling was uppermost in his heart it was anger.

Anger against the infirm old tyrant who, through caprice and spite, desired to snatch from him his life at the very moment when he had begun to find its beauties and its uses—in the very commencement of his prime.

At length the hour came, and he was led forth.

Of his execution I have little to say.

He met his fate as a good man and a Christian should meet it, and that is all.

But one thing deserves recording, wherever, even in the slightest degree, the shame of a bad action may be perpetuated.

His rival, Sir Walter Raleigh, was present purposely to see it, and witnessed the extinction of a good and noble life from one of the windows of the Tower.

Harold Forrester, doomed to be near, knelt and prayed in his cell !

CHAPTER XXIV.

A COUNCIL OF WAR.

THE Headsman of the Bridge had, in accordance with his duty, and what he also considered his fate, performed the office of executioner on Lord Essex.

At such a moment it would, indeed, have been strange if the words which the young earl had said to him in the wood near Horley House had not recurred to him.

But, as he stood there, leaning on his axe, and almost feeling a culprit, by the side of the handsome young earl, whose life he was to take at the bidding of a tyrant, he resolved that no words of his should make that hour more bitter for the victim.

Essex, however, had not forgotten, and turned towards him with a gay and genial smile as he held out his hand.

"I told you not long since," he said, "that there would come a time when I should again have to give you my forgiveness. The time has come ; and freely and from my heart, I give it you."

The warm shake which he gave to his masked and mysterious companion fully attested the truth of his words.

"My lord," said the Headsman, in a

voice full of emotion, " why did you not accept my warning? Why did you not fly when I——"

"Enough," said the young earl, interrupting him almost sternly, " men, I fancy, will never understand me or my motives. I have played a game and lost it. I should have been a fool had I not been aware in the first instance that there was a losing side to it as well as a winning. Farewell, and may God bless you."

When this tragedy was over, the thoughts of the man of death naturally reverted to Harold Forrester.

That he could ever bring himself to act the part of executioner to one in whom he felt such an interest—one, in fact, whom he may be said to have loved as he did Harold—seemed impossible.

In fact, if such an event as the execution of this other young life *was* destined to take place it was doubtful whether the honour of the axe would be accorded to the apprentice.

Hanging, even despite the fact that he had been guilty of the respectable crime of high treason, would probably be his fate.

Of two things, however, the Headsman was determined.

In the first place, he would not be his executioner.

In the second place, if he could, at the risk of his own life, effect his escape from the Tower, it *should* be effected.

The Headsman at the Tower was known by the name of Reuben.

Why, was a mystery.

A hundred times he had been heard to declare that it was *not* his name.

But as all persevered in so denominating him, he made no objection to it.

"As they do not know my real name," he said, " they have a right to christen me something. So let them call me what they will."

He was a great favourite among the warders of the Tower.

Taciturn to a degree, never mixing much with any, he had yet a reputation for kindliness of heart.

A reputation, be it said, well earned by constant acts of goodness and charity to those whom he felt to be in need of aid.

It was upon this reputation, this good name, which he had so justly obtained, that he intended to depend now for the escape of Harold.

"Well, Reuben," said a tall, raw-boned Scotch archer, who stood at the gate of the queen's courtyard of the Tower, " he died nobly."

"Aye, right nobly. But of him no more, Maxwell," replied the Headsman. " Never before did my axe tremble as I raised it to strike. But I nerved myself, and struck well and surely, for his sake."

"Art going to see thy friend Forrester?" asked the Scot. " The governor is not near at hand, and no one will see thee."

"Not now; with my hands even now red with the blood of his dear friend and patron, I should make but a sorry visitor. To-night, however, I would visit him; for now that the queen and her new counsellors have tasted blood, heaven only knows when the heads will cease from dropping."

His words were prophetic.

History tells us how many victims, including Cuffe, the faithful secretary, fell to appease the wrath of the infuriated queen.

"Good," replied Maxwell. " Present yourself this night, then, at nine at this gate. *I* shall be on duty, and you can pass in unnoticed."

The Headsman then dropped a piece of silver into the Scot's hand and departed.

That evening a council of strange import was held in the upper room of the executioner; up there in his turret chamber, where only the swaying heads of traitors could hear their whispers of treason.

It was a strangely composed assembly.

There were present the Headsman, Launcelot Duke, Don Fernando, and Mat o' the Mist.

The shades of evening had fallen over the river as the Headsman finished narrating his plan for the rescue of him who was so dear to all of them.

With this plan I need not now occupy myself.

It will be developed in full as I proceed with my next chapter.

"Well," said Mat o' the Mist, " if Harold once gets on those outer walls that you talk of, I must be much changed if in ten minutes he doesn't hold in his hand a stout rope to clamber down by."

"Yes," returned the Headsman; "I have full confidence in you; but we must not all follow you. Too many would be worse than none. A thousand could not save him by force, whereas one or two could save him by stratagem."

"Granted then that he is saved," said Don Fernando, who, strange to say, was the most anxious and eager of all present, "what provision is made for his safety after? There can be no doubt that the queen will be as inveterate against him as she has shown herself against all the friends of the poor murdered Essex."

The executioner smiled sadly.

"Don Fernando, I can well appreciate your eagerness," he said; "but let us save him first."

"You must excuse me for my impatience," cried Don Fernando, "but when I think of his future—of the hopes just ripening for him, I may be forgiven if I see, in the course of events, nothing but a maddening labyrinth of sorrow and disappointment."

The Headsman pressed his hand.

"Yes, yes," he said; "I well understand your feelings. But, to tell the truth, I am at a loss myself as to where we can safely stow him until all danger is passed. There is no doubt that when his flight is known, Master Duke here will be in as bad odour as a man can be, and that a temporary absence from the bridge would be advisable. So I propose if he once gets clear of the Tower, to row hastily up the river to Mistress Halcott's and fetch Eveline away. She is no longer safe, now that Alsdon knows that even a friend of Master Duke's is there. Once there we will consult as to our future proceedings. But come, time presses, we must be up and away."

It was just approaching the time when it was necessary to enter the boat, and make for the gloomy fortress.

As far as the outer walls of the Tower the Headsman could accompany them.

But no farther.

He had then to land, and to begin his perilous task, within the old State prison itself.

Everything had been arranged for secrecy.

Certainly the Headsman had no reason to suppose that he should be suspected of any design for the escape of Harold.

Nevertheless he had resolved that no unusual commotion should be noticed within his house.

He left a light burning, therefore, in his own study—that quaint old room, with its ancient panelling, and its armour and the skeleton hand beneath the glass case—and then led the way down a staircase which, even in the memory of Mat o' the Mist had never before been used.

"Time was," he said, as he conducted his friends down the cold and damp-smelling steps, "when this house belonged to famous conspirators; and many a party, no doubt, of plotting nobles have made their way to fresh air again by this secret road. We are conspirators in our own small way, and you will see that it will require a clever spy indeed, to observe our movements."

On reaching the bottom of the staircase, the damp that was oozing through the walls plainly proved that they had reached a point below high-water mark.

The Headsman paused for no explanation, however, but pushing open a little wooden door, to which he ascended by a flight of steps, bade the others follow him.

Mat o' the Mist was the first to obey.

He sprang up and rushed through the Headsman's legs more like a monkey than a human being, and when the rest of the party reached the top they could just see in the gloom of the dark night that a large boat had been brought up close to the opening.

Brought up right under the shadow, where no one could observe their movements.

In a few moments they were afloat on the river.

They had very little need of precaution.

Not a soul seemed to be afloat on the bosom of Old Father Thames.

Very few people, too, were on the bridge, and those few who leaned over the railings of its unfrequent openings, saw, of course, nothing peculiar in the fact of a boat suddenly darting from one of its dark arches.

And so, unnoticed, they arrived at the Tower stairs.

Not the stairs leading in to Traitor's Gate, but those by which they could ascend to Tower Hill.

"Now," said the Headsman, "I must leave you."

"And which point are we to remain at?" asked Don Fernando.

"Mat o' the Mist will see to that," replied the man of mystery. "I must not pause now, but enter upon my task while my nerves are strong and my head clear."

In a few moments more he had landed, and was stalking along the rising ground which led to the western gate.

CHAPTER XXV.

AN INNER MYSTERY OF THE TOWER.

THE clock on the old Tower tolled forth the hour of nine as the Headsman presented himself at the gate.

"You are punctual, as usual," said Maxwell, laughing at his own grim joke.

"Yes," replied the other; "but tell me who is at the inner gate?"

"Harford."

"That is well," said the executioner. "The time has gone now when I could enter with the order of my Lord Essex. But I suppose Harford will not refuse me a word with my friend?"

"Not he," replied Maxwell; "he has not forgotten the good you have done him and his."

It was as the worthy Scot had predicted.

It required but a few words to open Harford's heart to his friend.

"Don't remain long with Forrester," said the gaoler, as he led the Headsman up the echoing staircase. "The constable is absent now, but who knows when he may return?"

Within a few minutes the executioner, who, in spite of his strong nerves, was trembling with excitement, found himself in the presence of his young friend.

"How long do you wish to be?" said Harford, who was evidently in a nervous state of mind.

"A quarter of an hour will do well. Come up again in that time. All I wish with this youth is to warn him against the mad and reckless folly that hurried Essex to his doom."

In another moment they were alone.

Harold, of course, had not the slightest conception that any attempt was to be made to release him.

He had heard the conversation, therefore, between his friend and the gaoler with much disquietude.

Had the Headsman come there to lecture him in his misery?

His mind was soon disabused upon this point.

"Harold," said his strange friend, in a quick undertone, "I am here to save you. But, until I discover one thing, it is useless to talk of my plans. Have you ever heard whose cell this is?"

"Yes," replied Harold; "the gaoler has told me that it was from this cell that Sir Roger Blakeleigh escaped, and that none knew how he did so."

"Thank heaven!" cried the Headsman; "the story is true, my lad. Sir Roger did escape, and yet not a bar in yonder window has been touched these hundred years. This fortress was built for other purposes than those of a State prison. See this."

So saying he crossed the room, and made his way to an angle of the wall.

Then he paced to and fro three times, and counted the stones each way.

Then, with a start of satisfaction, he turned to the wall, and inserted his knife in a crevice between the stones.

One wrench, then another.

Wonder of wonders!

The great stone glided away, and revealed a dark opening.

"There," said the Headsman—"there is your way of escape. Come hither, and observe it well, for we have little time to talk."

He pressed the lower stone, and the upper one at once rolled into its place.

Then, with his knife, he showed Harold the way to loosen the secret door, and, returning to the table, sat down.

"How can I ever thank you for your interest in me?" cried Harold.

The Headsman interrupted him.

"We will talk of that another time when you are free," he said. "Now listen to me. As soon as I am gone and the gaoler has locked you in once more, do not wait for anything, but make your way through that opening. You will have no light, but you can safely descend in the darkness, and you will find no interruption. At the bottom of the staircase you will come to a passage, which will lead you out through a kind of porthole on the battlements. There you will hear repeated again and again the peculiar signal of Mat o' the Mi.t. Answer immediately you arrive on the ramparts, and Mat will throw you a rope. Hold this fast, and he will in a moment be by your side. You can then fix the rope, and descend to the boat that is waiting for you. Hush! we can say no more, the gaoler is approaching."

In a few moments the door was opened by Harford.

"The constable has returned," he said, "else I would not hurry you. But he seems in vast ill-temper about something."

"We have said our say," returned the executioner.

Then he pressed Harold Forrester's hand evasively.

"Farewell, my friend," he said; "do as I have bidden you, and you will run no risk of failure when the moment of trial comes."

Then Harold was once more alone.

He waited to hear the keys turn and the echoes of footsteps die away.

But no longer.

Then he darted eagerly forward.

The knife was quickly inserted; the stone obeyed its mysterious impulse, and rolled away from the opening.

He gave one wistful look at the lamp.

Then he sprang into the gloom, and applying no strength, for none was required, rolled it back into its place.

He was in utter darkness.

What if alterations had been made, and there was no outlet below?

How then could he re-enter his cell?

But these thoughts did not check his advance.

He held by the iron balustrade, and slowly and cautiously advanced.

Presently, as his eyes became more accustomed to the darkness, he saw below him a faint glimmering of light.

This was evidently the commencement of the passage which was to take him out upon the battlements of the Tower.

On he went now with renewed courage.

It was a long descent.

But he did not lose courage.

Down he went again more quickly, in spite of the utter gloom, and presently arrived at the commencement of a long stone corridor.

It was not exactly here, however, as the Headsman had told him.

Probably he had concealed some of the perils of the way, in order not to allow any feeling of discouragement to rise in in his breast.

As he advanced, he could hear plainly the sound of voices not far off, and presently he passed in full view of a number of armed men in a distant chamber.

They were not near enough to him, however, to observe him, and, indeed, had they seen his dark figure moving stealthily along that disused corridor, they would have been more likely to have fled from him as some ghost than have pursued him as an enemy.

Harold did not wait to make any inquiry in this respect.

He knew that, discovered or not discovered, his way led forward.

And so, hurrying on he at length came to a part of the corridor which suddenly narrowed.

Through this he could plainly feel the fresh air, and without thinking of what might be on the other side, he at once plunged through.

In another instant he stood in the dark night out on the second range of battlements.

How was he to descend to the next tier?

For a moment his heart failed him; but after an instant he saw directly in front of him the stone steps by which the sentinels descended, and rapidly rushing down this, he found himself on the broad river terrace just as the shrill signal of Mat o' the Mist rang out upon the night.

He answered at once.

Then there was a second call, and he rushed to the parapet.

He had not long to wait, for after a moment a coil of rope came whizzing up into the air.

He caught this ere it fell, and held it

firmly, twisting it about his body, and fastening its end to one of the balustrades.

In an instant, as it seemed, Mat o' the Mist was beside him.

One grasp of the hand, and then the cripple was busy fixing the rope's end.

"Now, then, Harold, go first," he cried; "the rope is safe enough now, and you know I can clamber down anywhere."

There was no time for hesitation or mock sentimentality.

Harold at once leaped upon the parapet, and swinging himself over, was soon gliding rapidly down the rope towards the boat.

Another moment and he was in the grasp of his friends.

Then, tumbling, clambering like an ape, came Mat o' the Mist.

"Fire away," he said; "here is the rope, and it will puzzle the devil himself to find out how you escaped."

There was no time to discover, though all wondered, how he had contrived to make his way to them without the rope being fastened at the top, but so in some way he had.

They were soon spinning away along the river with the tide as swiftly as all their strong arms could urge the light boat along.

Their destination was, as we are aware, the cottage, or rather the ruined habitation of Mistress Halcott, and with the quick tide, it was not long before they reached the margin of the lovely heath.

Somehow or another the Headsman had contrived to inform Mistress Halcott of the intended visit, as late as was the hour; therefore both she and her daughter and Eveline Duke were ready to receive them.

Firmly convinced that no one had observed their movements, they were gathered round the fire in the large room, planning the means of concealment for a time, when a slight noise without attracted the notice of Eveline.

Without communicating her fears to the others—not wishing, in fact, to alarm them, when, after all, the sound might be only the sighing of the wind amongst the trees—she rose, and opening the door, softly passed out.

No one observed her departure.

In fact, they were far too busy at their own thoughts and words.

However, it was not many minutes before they were startled by a loud and prolonged cry for help.

They all started up.

More than one had recognised the voice; and Harold, springing first to the door, shouted—

"It is Eveline! Quick! to the rescue!"

When they reached the outside of the house, they discovered the young girl lying apparently insensible on the ruined steps, and a crowd of armed men pressing around her.

"Stand back, ye villains!" shouted Harold, as he and his companions cleaved a space with their flashing swords, "back, as ye value your lives."

But the odds were terribly against them.

In the darkness it seemed as if a hundred men had risen up from the lone heath for their destruction.

CHAPTER XXVI.

THE TRAITORS ON THE RIVER.

IN order to explain how it was that the Headsman and his friends were followed so quickly to the old ruin on the heath, we must return for a moment to the time when the Headsman quitted the Tower and hurried to rejoin his friends.

He was so absorbed in his own thoughts that he did not observe anything unusual in the aspect of the stairs where he had landed.

Had he, however, been less preoccupied he would certainly not have failed to observe that a boat was moored close up to them, and that a man was half lying at the bottom of it.

As it was he passed on unheedingly, and, as he entered the boat of his friends, he said—

"It is all right; he will be here soon."

There was nothing in this, truly.

But events that shortly followed proved that these words meant a great deal.

This man would not have taken any notice of the circumstance again had it not been for his companion.

This companion was one our readers are well acquainted with.

None other than Sharpley.

Sharpley, the hired bravo and assassin.

He had always been a thief and a ruffian, but when he took service as it were with Alsdon, he left off for a time his minor villainies.

In spite of the good pay, however, which he received from his patron, he had not saved a groat, and when, on the afternoon of the day when Essex was beheaded, he entered the little room at the sign of "The Red Cross," he threw himself with an oath into a chair by the fire, saying—

"Curse my luck! Dame Fortune seems to have set her face dead against me."

"Why, what's the matter now?" cried an old, red-faced, bottle-nosed villain of the name of Casker, who had succeeded Wormer in the business. "You seem down in the mouth to-day, and yet last week you were boasting of your gold."

"Gold?" cried Sharpley. "Yes, I *had* a few golden coins then, but now a silver shilling is all I can show. Bring me ale and some bread and cheese to that amount. Then I shall be cleaned out—in fact, ruined, and must to business."

The landlord at once obeyed his guest's bidding, and without compunction took his last shilling.

"I say Casker," cried Sharpley, as he drank a huge draught from the foaming tankard, "I say, Casker, I shall want that boat of yours to-night."

The landlord smiled grimly.

"All right," he said. "Anything good in the wind?"

"I don't know yet," returned Sharpley. "I haven't even made up my mind where I'm going. I only know that I must make some money—somehow."

"Very well; I don't want you to tell me any of your secrets," returned the landlord. "You can have the boat."

So, when it was dark—in fact, when it was nearly dark—Sharpley quitted the room in the tavern, where he had sat since the afternoon, and going down by the way by which Alsdon had often descended, passed into the light skiff that was moored ready for him.

Then he shot rapidly away, and in a few minutes he pulled up at an old house, whose crumbling walls were washed by the river, even at low water.

He soon returned, in company with a thin, scarecrow of a man.

A scarecrow, truly, but possessing immense strength.

They seated themselves in the boat again silently, and rowed back towards the Bridge.

Before they reached the stairs at Tower Hill, they again stopped.

This time the scarecrow of a man got out and hurried off.

In a few moments he returned with another man, and then they rowed down the river once more, and stopped under the shadow of the Tower Hill stairs.

Then Sharpley and his scarecrow friend hastened off, leaving the third man to take care of the boat, and keep a sharp look-out.

What I am about to describe may appear digressive.

But it is not so.

It is necessary to explain the circumstances in order that the reader may understand what occurred presently to the worst of Alsdon's hired villains—Sharpley.

Near Tower Hill lived a man of the name of Abraham Moss—a man who, in those days, had a thousand facilities for making money.

Hated as was his race, he was yet sought after; for he bought and sold anything, from a rag to a diamond; and though always dirty and greasy, he was in reality in possession of abundance of money, although, as usual with his race, he invariably declared himself on the verge of ruin.

This man was assisted in his business by a daughter—a lovely girl of eighteen —and a Christian youth, who, indeed, had been induced to live with the Hebrew through the charms of the dark-eyed Esther.

Sharpley's object in paying a visit to the Jew may readily be guessed.

His object was purely robbery.

Robbery and murder, if circumstances rendered that necessary.

However, he did not intend to attempt anything openly.

He was going to the Jew's as a friend, that he might the better betray him.

He had known Abraham Moss for a long time, and had done business with him.

Moss, in fact, was not particular in his bargains.

He, like all others of his race, was ambitious to obtain the largest possible quantity of anything for the smallest possible price, and this being so, he was not very nice in the questions he put to anyone who desired to sell.

But recently Sharpley had not brought him anything.

He had dealt only in plausible stories, spoken of his connection with Lord Housden, leaving Alsdon, the "go between," entirely out of the question, and borrowed, absolutely borrowed, of the Jew.

It was not often that Abraham Moss was betrayed into such a weakness as this.

But Sharpley had put his request well, and having obtained the money and spent it in grovelling dissipation, he was as far off having the means or the inclination to pay as the man in the moon.

This, however, was to form his excuse for the visit which was to begin by a demand for money, and end—he cared not how.

CHAPTER XXVII.

THE MURDER.

ABRAHAM MOSS smiled, and rubbed his oily hands together with evident satisfaction as Sharpley and his friend entered.

"Goot evening, Mashter Sharpley," he said; "good evening, sir (to the villain's friend.) I am very glat to shee you. Walk in, walk in."

They were ushered in through the shop, if such a store of nondescript articles can be termed a shop, and found themselves presently in a room where there were some attempts at elegance.

Abraham Moss was no miser at home.

He had, as we have said, a handsome daughter, and on such days as the shop was closed, they had little feasts together, and sat there dressed in their best.

For Abraham Moss loved his child.

Well he might.

She was devoted to him, had smoothed his way of life since her mother had died, and moreover was very beautiful.

Beautiful and attractive in her semi-oriental costume, which showed off to advantage her exquisitely moulded figure.

Unprincipled receiver of stolen goods and usurer as he was, Abraham Moss had a heart for her—a heart open and generous, even to smiling on the suit of the Christian youth who, so strangely in such an age, had linked his fortunes to his.

"Well," said he, as they entered the room and closed the door, "well, what can I do for you, Master Sharpley?"

"A great deal," replied he; "in fact I have a great project on foot—a project which promises abundant reward; but —yet, I had better explain first."

"Just so," said Abraham Moss, morally buttoning up his pockets.

"Well, the truth is, I'm in love. Fancy *me* in love," said Sharpley, with a forced laugh, all the more unnatural because he was attracted at the moment by his scarecrow friend, whose eyes were taking in everything in the room.

"I can't very well," said the Jew.

"Well, I *am*, but it is not with a woman but a fortune. I have hit upon a widow, a fine, handsome woman, who has a snug business. All I have to do to obtain her hand is to deck myself out in gorgeous array, and propose. But to do this requires money. I can't go on such an errand in such guise as this, and so I've come to you to ask you to advance me thirty pounds."

The Jew raised his hands deprecatingly.

"Thirty pounds, my friend," he cried; "why, I don't possess it. Pisness is very pad; and then, you know, Mashter

Sharpley, if I had it, you owe me now feefty pounds."

A cloud darkened Sharpley's brow.

"I know that very well," he said; "but when I marry this widow I can pay you all. If you don't lend me this thirty, I don't see very well how I can pay you the other. Come, Moss, I'll give you a promise to pay in a month. Long before that I shall be married and settled, and——"

"Mashter Sharpley," interrupted the Jew, in a voice almost angry, "I have not got the money."

A significant glance passed between Sharpley and his fellow-ruffian.

This was easy to be understood.

It meant plainly—

"I see all quiet measures are in vain; we must resort at once to ruder plans."

"Well, I'll tell you what," said Sharpley, "I've come for the money, and the money I must have. I can't go without it." The Jew was alarmed.

There seemed a murderous look in the eyes of his visitor.

So he rose from his seat abruptly.

"Vell, vell, Mashter Sharpley," he said, "since you are so very importunate, I must go and see what I have by me. I must go and ask Esther; she keeps my sthrong box."

And he was shambling towards the door.

But Sharpley stopped him.

His crafty mind soon told him that the Jew had no intention of fetching the money, but of obtaining aid to resist any attempt at robbery.

"No, no," he said; "we can transact any little business ourselves, without the assistance of other people. *I* can take any message you wish to your daughter; but until we have finished our business you don't budge."

The Jew turned pale.

His heart, too, fluttered with fear, but he thought it best to dissemble, and assume a coolness and courage he was far from feeling.

"Very well, shentlemen," he said, quietly, reseating himself; "if you don't want me to fetch the money, so much the better."

"I don't want you to quit the room," replied Sharpley, "simply because I know that you don't intend bringing back with you any money, but simply assistance to get rid of us. This does

not exactly suit my plans. If you want us to go quietly, the way is easy before you. Simply write on a slip of paper, 'Give the bearer thirty pounds.' Sign this, address it to your daughter, and my friend here can bring it to me."

The Jew was now fairly trapped.

He could no longer dissimulate.

"Mashter Sharpley," he said, "you *must* take no for an answer. My pisness has been ferry pad of late, and I haven't got it, 'pon my soul, I haven't got it."

Sharpley's bad passions were now thoroughly roused.

"Very well," he said, quietly, but with a deadly resolve in his voice which made the old Jew shudder, "since you won't lend thirty, you shall a hundred. Orke, see to the door."

His scarecrow companion at once prevented any attempt of the Jew to depart, for Sharpley had for some minutes had his eye upon a box, from which he had seen the Jew often take money.

In an instant it was in his grasp, and in another it would have been wrenched open, had not the Jew, with some of the energy of youth, sprang across the room and seized his arm, at the same time shouting—

"Help, there, Esther! help, there, Arthur! Thieves! murder!"

Sharpley was compelled to drop the box to defend himself against the Jew, who had already drawn a knife from his girdle, and wounded his enemy in several places.

Meanwhile, as Orker was about to rush to his assistance, a heavy thump against the old door warned him that he had better stick to his post.

Arthur, in fact, had heard the cry, and, urged by the young Jewess, had armed himself, and flown at once to Abraham's assistance.

He had now an opportunity of showing his valour, and saving as he hoped, the life of his beloved's father.

Again and again his strong shoulder was applied to the rickety door, and after a few efforts it burst open.

The violent entry of Arthur nearly upset the scarecrow, and the young man at once rushed to the aid of the Jew, whom Sharpley had now forced on his knees, and was about to cut down with his sword.

"'COME ON,' CRIED ORKER, 'LEAVE THE GIRL ALONE!'"

This diversion enabled Abraham Moss to rise, but it was only a temporary diversion.

Orker soon rushed upon Arthur, and a desperate conflict was the result.

Had Esther been able to raise an alarm, Sharpley and his villainous comrade would soon have found the perilous nature of their enterprise.

But there seemed a spell upon her, and, overcome by a horror she could scarcely herself comprehend, she sank, helpless, voiceless into a chair.

Meanwhile, terrible things were going on in the room.

Arthur's attention was divided between the Jew and himself.

He had no mean adversary, but he saw that without help, the Jew would inevitably fall a victim to his strange foe.

So, whenever he saw Sharpley gaining any advantage, he turned quickly round to his master, and put Sharpley off his point.

This, however, could not last long.

Just as the Jew fell gasping again on his knees, and Arthur turned once more to aid him, Orker sent his sword flashing through his chest close to the shoulder.

It was all over with him now as regarded the combat.

He felt himself fainting from loss of blood, the shadow of death already hovered over him, yet he staggered away out of the room, and reaching the outer room, cried—

"Esther—your father—they are murdering him!"

Then he fell prone upon his face.

The spell seemed suddenly to be lifted from the pretty Jewess, and she tottered away towards the room where the terrible conflict had taken place.

She was not in time to afford any aid, if, indeed, any aid could have come from her feeble hand.

Her father already lay on the ground, stabbed to the heart, and Sharpley and Orker, having seized their booty, passed her as they made off.

A villainous light illumined Sharpley's eyes as he went by.

But Orker drew him away.

"Come on," he cried, "leave the girl alone!"

"But she may ruin us."

"Bah, they won't believe the word of a Jewess against us; and the Christian youth is as dead as a maggot. See where he lies yonder. Come on."

And he dragged his more murderous companion away, leaving poor Esther still kneeling by her father's murdered body, and Arthur lying on his face in the room beyond.

CHAPTER XXVIII.

DISCOVERY.

IN spite of the cries of the old Jew, not the slightest suspicion of the dreadful deed had been aroused in the minds of any of the neighbours.

In fact, the store of Abraham Moss stood somewhat apart from the rest of the houses, and nothing but a loud outcry from an open window would have reached the ears of any of them.

No one, therefore, opposed them on their way.

Hurrying, therefore, along the street, they made their way towards the river side, and having, before their arrival, given a peculiar whistle, found the boat waiting for them at the bottom of the wooden steps.

They were soon afloat on the bosom of the dark river.

"There has been a rare to-do down here," said the man whom they had left in charge of the boat. "A tall fellow in a cloak and a mask came down the stairs soon after you went away, and shouted out to some friends of his on the river; then a large boat shot from the centre of the stream under the Tower walls, and I distinctly saw a prisoner escape. It was no use my giving the alarm, for they were off and away with the tide up the river, and besides, I thought I might spoil your game."

"I wish we had only been a few minutes sooner," cried Sharpley; "we would have stopped their game. But, come, it is not even now too late to make something of this."

"How?" cried Orker.

"We will seek Lord Housden and tell him all. He will be glad enough to learn of this escape in time to prevent other mischief. Pull away, my friends, with a will. I know well where to find him."

He carried this infamous project, born of spite and the meanest malevolence, at once into execution.

Lord Housden he found at his usual haunt, and as soon as he heard what had occurred, a bright idea shot through his brain.

"They are gone to Mistress Halcott's on the heath, I'll be sworn," he cried. "That is where the Headsman would most certainly have thought of taking them at first. I will send Alsdon and some twenty of my men after them at once; and we will see whether these fellows will thus dare authority."

We have seen how, through the quick hearing of Eveline Duke, the party of fugitives were saved from a fatal sacrifice within the cottage, and from this point we resume our story.

The numbers of the attackers were so great as compared with the defenders, that it seemed truly a hopeless task to attempt a conflict.

And yet surrender was worse than defeat.

The first meant a return to imprisonment, and the implication, too, of all Harold's friends; the second might mean an honourable death.

"What want you with us?" cried Harold, in a loud voice, as he and his friends cleared a wide space to enable Mistress Halcott and her daughter to carry the still insensible Eveline into the cottage.

"In the first place," cried Alsdon, whom they now saw plainly was in command of the attacking party, "wedemand the surrender of your person. You have escaped from the Tower, where you were placed by command of the queen, and you must return thither with me."

"And is that all?" asked Harold, with a tone of irony.

"No; we demand also the surrender of the man yonder, who is known by the name of the Headsman of the Bridge.

He is suspected of aiding your escape, as is also Launcelot Duke, the merchant, who stands by your side, and whom I am also empowered to arrest."

"And is this the sum and total of your modest requests?" asked Harold.

"It is."

"And by what authority do you enforce them? Have you scrip or writing from the queen?"

A savage frown lowered on Alsdon's brow.

"Little time was given to her majesty to write orders," he answered. "I come hither at my Lord Housden's bidding, who was himself commissioned by the queen, and without writing of any kind, I intend to arrest you. You see how many men are at my back; therefore, if you value your lives, surrender."

In any other circumstances the diamond merchant would have counselled prudence.

But prudence had no charm now.

The re-arrest of Harold would most certainly end in his death; and there was not one there who would not rather have seen him die there on the open heath, with a sword in his hand, than on a scaffold at the bidding of the queen.

"We reject your offer, and will fight to the death!" cried Harold.

And the devoted band prepared resolutely for defence.

"On, my men!" shouted Alsdon, "cut down the madmen!"

The men thus incited, made a dash at our friends, and the desperate and unequal fight proceeded.

There was little hope of sustaining it long.

Had they had more notice of the assault, they could have sent the women off by a backway, and clambering up the ruins, have kept the assailants for some time at bay, by firing on them with their pistols from the walls.

But this, of course, was not possible now.

So, though a feeling akin to despair was in their breasts, they planted their backs against the walls, and again and again hurled back the tide of assailants.

The men, who were, of course, hired partizans, and had no heart in their work, were not equal to such work as this, and when volley after volley from the pistols of the brave little band were poured in upon them, they again and again drew back, and huddled together in disorder.

"Curses on the cowards!" shouted Alsdon. "Come on; follow me. Are you afraid of a handful of men?"

The men thus roused, made a fierce rush.

They knew well that in such an assault numbers must prevail.

The little band of friends knew it too, but prepared, nevertheless, vigorously for the defence.

The battle, however, was fast being lost.

Don Fernando was already down, and Harold himself was wounded, when a great shout of triumph was raised in the rear of the assailants.

"Hurrah! Apprentices for ever!"

"Aye, aye; come on! We'e in time."

The voice of the last speaker brought joy to the hearts of that valiant band.

They knew it well.

The shrill, cracked voice of Mat o' the Mist, who in another minute came clambering down a tree, and dropped, as if by magic, in the midst of the affray.

"The Headsman's Imp! Curses on him!" cried Alsdon.

But he had more to do now than to shout and curse, and to threaten destruction to others.

He had to save himself and his friends.

They were literally now between two fires, for the apprentices whom Mat o' the Mist had brought to the rescue, attacked them without delay from behind, and the little band was roused to fresh exertions by the knowledge now that rescue had arrived.

The suspicion which had so long haunted Harold's mind he now resolved to solve.

Without regarding what was going on around him, therefore, he made a rush at Alsdon, and in a few moments they were engaged in a desperate single combat close by the door of the cot.

No one noticed them.

In fact, everyone had his own duty to perform.

Alsdon knew more than any of his followers the danger of capture, and, in spite of the arrival of the new force, whose numbers they could not be aware of, he shouted to his men to resist to the last, and cut their way through to freedom.

In spite of the quick change in the state of affairs, he had time to change his thoughts also.

A moment ago, and he saw everything in his hands, even the gratification of a deadly and undying revenge.

Now he would have preferred death to capture.

Why, we shall presently see.

Harold, meanwhile, had the best of it.

He, of course, had now all the exhilaration of a man who finds himself on the winning side, after being plunged in despair, while Alsdon's attention was divided between defending himself and giving directions to his men.

Very soon it was shown how perilous his game was.

Harold, making a sudden rush, struck his sword from his hand, and at the same time wounded Alsdon so severely that he fell on one knee.

He at once dashed forward to give the *coup de grace*, and had seized Alsdon by the throat when the heavy beard always worn by the man of guilt fell off.

Fell just as a gleam shot on his face from a lamp within the cottage.

Harold had had suspicions before, as I have already said.

But they were suspicions and surmises only, and he was so unprepared for this sudden realization of them that he loosed his hold upon his enemy's throat, and staggered back.

The secret of years was thus in a moment discovered.

Alsdon and Lord Housden were one and the same.

Harold's astonishment saved the life of the villainous noble, for, as he let go his hold, Housden sprang to his feet.

"Perjured villain! traitor!" shouted Harold, springing forward again.

But he had missed his victim now.

With a sudden rush, Housden burst into the ranks of his men.

"Fly, fly!" he said; "in good order if you can, but fly. We are overpowered, and to attempt to gain victory would be madness."

In a few words, swiftly spoken, Harold made known to his friends the discovery he had made, and urged the necessity of endeavouring to effect his capture.

But the attempt was useless.

The apprentices were, of course, without any information in regard to the discovery which Harold had made, and hearing only the continued clashing of arms, they considered it their duty simply to aid their friends in escape.

When, therefore, Alsdon and his friends attempted to cut their way through they were met with little if any opposition; and in the space of a very few minutes, the treacherous lord had reached the wooded margin of the river, where his men had left their horses.

The apprentices did not pursue; and when Harold had succeeded in making them understand who it was who was thus escaping, the galloping of a horse told that all attempts were now useless.

"So far so good," said Harold, as he wiped his heated brow, and gazed upon the field of battle, where bodies of men were lying in death's grim majesty; "and yet nothing is gained save a brief spell of liberty. Lord Housden, villain as he is, is still the queen's favourite, and I——"

A hand was placed on his shoulder as he thus soliloquised aloud.

Turning round quickly, he saw Don Fernando standing by him, his right arm in a sling.

"Fear not," he said, in a voice whose tone betrayed weakness from loss of blood. "Lord Housden's favour with the queen will be but of short duration. Had he killed me he might indeed have gained a longer triumph. But I am saved, thank heaven, to bear witness against his treachery, his villainy, his imposture!"

"Aye, he is an impostor," cried Harold, for this very night I have discovered that Lord Housden and Alsdon are one."

"I saw his face as you tore his disguise from him," returned Don Fernando; "but that is not the reason I call him an impostor. I cannot explain now, for we must hasten to leave this place while we have time. But this very night I will tell you all, and lift the veil of mystery which has so long enveloped you."

While the apprentices threw the dead bodies of their enemies into the river, and attended to their own wounds, our small band of friends hurried into the cottage to consult upon their movements.

Various suggestions were made, but for some time the conversation was not observed by Harold, who was too busy listening to Eveline's explanation of the cause of her faintness—the sudden view which Lord Housden gave her of his face, and his fiendish words of triumph to his men.

But he had another reason why he so eagerly noted her words and actions.

He saw plainly from them that she loved him, and that discovery was more than enough to compensate him for all the troubles he had, or was to suffer.

With a pressure of the hand he left her at length, and going to his friends, said—

"Gentlemen, I heard while I was in the Tower that the house of my Lord of Essex at Horley Wood was entirely deserted, that the queen had taken possession of it, and had sealed the doors, but no living soul is within it. I know a secret way into the building, and there in the basement we can conceal ourselves until all has blown over."

This daring proposition was at once discussed, and finally agreed to; and, in the course of half-an-hour, the party, well armed, set out for Horley Wood.

CHAPTER XXIX.

THE MYSTERY OF HAROLD'S LIFE.

THE fugitives reached Horley Wood before morning broke, and, without exciting any notice, made their way into the forest.

Here Harold soon found the spot which the murdered Earl of Essex had pointed out to him, and through this he led his companions up to the old tower and down again to the basement storey.

Not a living thing did they encounter, and it was evident from the smell of all around that the beautiful mansion which had once been the abode of the happy nobleman and his beautiful wife, had long been deserted.

That morning, after a meal which had been provided by Mat o' the Mist in the neighbouring town, Don Fernando began the story—the mystery of Harold Forrester's life.

"You must understand, my friends," said Don Fernando, "that my story has to do with the Housdens—the real Housden family—and so you must hear me patiently to the end, and reserve your surprise.

"My last words will sufficiently explain all.

"You must understand that thirty years ago there were not two more inseparable friends than Lord Edward Housden and Athol Forrester.

"Their fathers' estates down in Devonshire adjoined.

"These fathers were staunch and old friends, and, naturally enough, the sons came to be incessant companions, and were at length unhappy out of each other's society.

"Their thoughts—their habits—all were the same.

"Their fortunes seemed for a long time to be guided by Fate in the same grooves.

"Both fell in love at the same time, and married on the same day; both lost their wives and fathers within the year; and both having engaged in the same political intrigues, incurred the displeasure of their sovereign, and had to fly the country.

"At this point, however, the strange similitude of their fortunes ceased.

"On the evening of their departure they had agreed to go together to a certain place, the hut on the heath occupied by Mistress Halcott and her daughter, and in her care deposit their infant sons.

"They knew her well as the wife of a worthy sailor, who had sailed often with Lord Housden's father, and who, now they were compelled to abandon their native land, was willing to pretend to be dead for a time, and follow the fortunes of his masters.

"He little knew, poor fellow, how long his devotion would keep him from his dear ones.

"If Lord Housden and his friend had started but a few hours before, they would have avoided a terrible catastrophe.

"As it was, they had been hiding in the house of a friend, and had no conception that their hiding-place was known.

"The night on which they started for the heath was a wild and stormy one, with a heavy wind roaring and raving like a weird spirit through the trees.

"Otherwise they would certainly have seen the forms of the men who were waiting for them near the gate of their friend's park, and have heard the scrambling of their feet as they hurried to their horses to begin the pursuit.

"They had been too cowardly to make any open attempt while in the vicinity of their friend's house, but Lord Housden and his companion soon heard the clattering of their horses' hoofs close behind them.

"They soon reached an open part of the road where there was no chance of interference, and the pursuers, dashing on more madly than before, called loudly upon them to stop.

"'Stop! on your lives, stop!'

"But they only rushed on the faster.

"Then several shots were fired, but without effect, and the chase was continued more madly than ever.

"Soon Lord Housden and Athol Forrester found that their horses were no match for those of their enemies.

"They were heavy chargers, splendid steeds in battle, but not fitted for a race for life.

"On, however, they urged them.

"Life and death were in the scale, and they hoped that some lucky chance might enable them to elude their pursuers.

"Perhaps, even, some persons might be met on the road, who might be pressed into their service.

"But no such aid was forthcoming.

"Fate seemed to have declared against them, and when not very far from the heath, the pursuers, four in number, were upon them.

"Lord Edward and Athol were about to turn and defend themselves, when a shot from one of their cowardly foes struck the latter in the chest.

"He had just time to gasp forth, 'Save my child!' just in time to aid his friend in securing the boy, when he fell from the saddle— dead!

"Another shot, which was intended

for Lord Edward, was buried in Forrester's horse's chest, and the animal, rearing upon its hind legs, flung himself, mad with pain, in among the pursuers.

"Of this momentary check, Lord Housden took immediate advantage.

"Driving his spurs into the flanks of his frightened steed, he dashed away like one demented, until reaching a turn in the road, he suddenly drew rein and leaped off.

"Then, with the two children, he hid quickly behind a hedge, having first struck the horse a violent blow with the whip, which sent him scampering off at full speed towards London.

"It happened, fortunately, as he had hoped.

"The pursuers imagined, naturally enough, that he was still fleeing from them at full speed, and consequently, dashed off after the riderless horse, passing quite close to the dark spot where the fugitive cowered beneath the hedge.

"As soon as they had passed away in the gloomy distance, Lord Housden rose from his place of concealment, and, with all the speed he could, made his way to the cottage of Mistress Halcott on the heath.

"The two children, whom, of course, he was compelled to carry all the distance, naturally impeded his movements, but he reached the place at length, and, as you know, safely deposited his precious charges in the hands of that worthy woman."

As Don Fernando said these words, Harold Forrester interrupted him.

He had several times been about to speak, but had been checked.

Now, however, he burst forth impetuously.

"Why," he cried, "I understood it was you who left me and Edwin at the cottage of Mistress Halcott?"

Don Fernando smiled.

"Have patience," he said, "and you will understand all. Well," he continued, "I need not tell you anything concerning that interview. You know it already.

"As soon as he had made arrangements for their future safety, he quitted the cottage, and with all haste made for London, where he succeeded in reaching, not without some difficulty, the house of Halcott, the brave and faithful servant.

"It had been his intention to sail as quickly as possible for foreign lands, but fortune had not so willed it.

"Those who had pursued him were indignant, as may well be supposed, at being deceived by a simple trick, and were savage in their determination to discover the one who had so cleverly eluded them.

"By some means or another they discovered that he was hiding in London.

"Where, they knew not; but the mere fact that he was known to be in the City was quite enough; for, as you know, London is not so large a place that it is safe for one to be hid from the sovereign's wrath.

"John Halcott, the trusty seaman, soon discovered that enemies were on the watch, and at his house, therefore, the son of his patron had to remain for a long time.

"At length the time came when the vessel in which he desired to sail was positively to start, and all preparations had been made, when, on the very evening fixed for starting, Halcott came home with the news that their retreat had been discovered.

"What was now to be done?

"To go out was as dangerous as to remain in.

"However, John Halcott rose superior to the occasion.

"He engaged the services of two trusty comrades, gave out that a friend had died suddenly, and, at a given hour, the body was brought, enveloped in a sheet, and carried down towards the river's edge to be carried to the other side.

"No one interfered with them.

"Rumour had been busy in the neighbourhood, and report said that he had died of a terribly infectious disorder; and those who sought for Lord Edward thought it prudent at present to abstain from anything but watching from afar.

"So the dead body was permitted to go out without any interference; and, indeed, until it reached the water's side, there was no thought of anything like pursuit.

"The boat was ready at the landing-stairs; John Halcott in the skiff stood up ready to receive the supposed dead

"THE MYSTERIOUS BURDEN."

body, while the two men handed it to him.

"At this moment six men, headed by a tall man in military costume, rushed towards them.

"'Stop there, in the name of the law,' shouted he.

"As you may imagine, no one attempted to obey him.

"On the contrary, the boat pushed off, the two men leaped in, and the six men were left standing in furious rage upon the stone steps.

"'A boat here; five gold pieces for a boat!' shouted their leader.

"But in vain.

"There was not a boat within hail, and the skiff containing Lord Edward went dashing away with the tide towards the Pool. All pursuit was useless now.

"The pursued had so great a start that, in the darkness of the night, their light skiff could never have been caught up, and within a few hours, Lord Edward and his trusty friend were sailing down the river towards the sea."

CHAPTER XXX.

TRAITORS AT HOME.

"I SHOULD occupy days were I to tell you," continued Don Fernando, "the adventures which Lord Edward went through in the wild and lonely countries he passed through. I have now to do with those who remained at home.

"Finding that there seemed no chance of Lord Edward returning to England, the steward he had left in charge of the estate took a diabolical idea in his head.

"He would repay the trust reposed in him by betraying his master and substituting his own son for his.

"To do this with greater effect he sent his son away for a time to some place abroad, where he not only contracted foreign ways, but also a bronzed complexion, which made him seem as if he had been travelling.

"The villain—Thomas Ryder by name —knew well that able and real friends were at work at court to reinstate Lord Edward in the good opinion of the sovereign.

"He kept up a regular system of espionage, and at length discovered to his intense satisfaction, that Lord Edward had been pardoned; that all bar to his returning to England had been removed, and that if he chose to return he could even proceed to court.

"Now was the time.

"His son—Henry Ryder—was produced, recognised by *his own father* as the heir of Housden, and a story well trumped up was brought forward to prove that Lord Edward Housden was dead.

"Since then this impostor has been received at court as Lord Housden.

"And now comes the most important part of all.

"Lord Housden discovered that the real heir to the Housden estates had been brought up by Mistress Halcott, and had been placed as an apprentice to Launcelot Duke.

"He at once concocted a scheme of murder, and the horrid scene at St. Christopher's Fair was the result.

"But here again an error was committed.

"In the hurry of departure on that fatal night, when Lord Edward and Athol Forrester fled for their lives, the clothes of the children were changed.

"The one who was called by Mistress Halcott Edwin Archer was, in reality, Harold Forrester, and the one who was called Harold Forrester was, in reality, Edwin Archer, heir to Lord Edward Housden.

"I, then," cried Harold, seizing the hand of Don Fernando, "I am Edwin Archer, and you—oh, I feel it, I know it — you are my father, Lord Edward Housden?"

"Yes, my boy," exclaimed Don Fernando, as he embraced his son, with a voice broken by emotion, "I *am* Lord Edward, and you, who were saved from murder by the mistake committed at the fair by the impostor's ruffians, are my son, and heir to my wealth."

"Then why," asked the Headsman, who had listened with emotion to every word that had fallen from Lord Edward's lips, " why do you not at once claim your rights, and oust the villain from his false position? *I* know well that your story is a true one, though *why* I know it to be so, even *you* are unaware."

" I cannot yet prove my rights," replied Don Fernando, "and it may yet be a long and weary time ere I *can* do so. I have nothing by which I can show my identity; and until I obtain that it would be madness to attempt anything. I have learned, however, that the father of this pretended Lord Housden repents bitterly of his former crime, and would, had he the power, be eager to repair the bitter injustice he has done."

" And why can he not do so?" asked Harold, impetuously.

" His son has concealed him somewhere; absolutely imprisoned him in a cell, I believe, where he can hold no communication with his fellow creatures. Until I can discover him, nothing can be done."

" And would he acknowledge you and betray his own son were you to find him?"

" I know it. He is an old man now, and in bad health; and, in fear of the grave, would tell all. But tell me, Harold (I will call you so until we are reinstated in our rights), where you have put the box with the valuable papers?"

" I have it not with me," replied Harold; " it is in my secret drawer at the house of Master Duke."

" That is unfortunate," said Don Fernando (it will be more convenient to continue that name for the present). " No doubt by this time the house has been invaded by the partisans of that villain, and it will be a matter of great difficulty to get the casket, even if it has not been already seized and destroyed."

Mat o' the Mist, on hearing this, came forward.

" Be not uneasy on that score," he cried. " *I* will undertake to obtain that. I will go to-night."

" Aye, and he *will* get it, too," said the Headsman, " if it be there to get.

But tell me, Lord Edward; you have known me long, you have trusted me, and always found me a true friend. Have you no conception who I am?"

Lord Edward thought a moment.

" No," he said; " your mystery has been always unfathomable to me."

" Then for you," replied the Headsman, " I will do what I have not done for many years. I will unmask."

And so saying, he withdrew from his features the mask, without which no one had seen him before.

Don Fernando gazed at him in wonder and dismay almost for an instant.

Then he said, in a voice low with suppressed emotion—

" Athol Forrester! Can it be possible?"

" Aye, my old friend," exclaimed the Headsman, with a voice which trembled with feeling, " it is true that I am that most wretched of men—deprived now of even the child of my love.

" When I fell from my horse, I was, as *you* thought, dead. But in reality I was only stunned. The ruffians who pursued us looked well at me, but pronounced me lifeless; and when I woke to sense again, I crawled away into a field, where I was found by some farm labourers in the morning.

" As I lay there through that night, which seemed never ending, I made in my maddened state of pain and anguish a vow to heaven which I have faithfully kept.

" I vowed to yield up my identity, to become a terrible instrument of vengeance in the hands of the law, and to see my enemies, one after another, swept away by my hands ere I took my own name and position once more.

" Events have prevented me accomplishing all I desired to do.

" But with the exception of this pretended Lord Housden, all my foes have fell under my terrible axe.

" I hope I shall have the last satisfaction of beheading that treacherous villain, then I shall be happy, and shall relinquish my task for ever."

CHAPTER XXXI.

HOW MAT O' THE MIST WENT IN SEARCH OF THE CASKET.

THERE was abundance of things to talk of and wile away the day, for friends re-united after so long an absence have many old reminiscences to think of and adventures to wonder over.

Evening at length came, and Mat o' the Mist prepared for his solitary journey.

Harold was eager to accompany him.

But to this proposal Mat turned a deaf ear.

He could do better by himself.

"You see," he said, "if force were required two of us would be of no more use than one. No, no. I'll go alone. Don't be alarmed if I am absent some time. This will have to be done entirely by stratagem, and I have crafty people to deal with."

So, unaccompanied by anything but the good wishes of all, Mat, in the dark night, crept away, well armed, but dis-guised in all the rags he could collect, so as to resemble a beggar.

He had a difficult and a dangerous task to perform.

Of this he was well aware.

But he did not for a moment shrink from it.

Well he knew his own deformities.

Well he knew that his blear eyes, his great, mis-shapen head, his distorted body, were bye-words among his neigh-bours of the bridge, and more especially Lord Housden's men.

But he trusted to his disguise, which he resolved to make more complete when he entered London.

On entering the wood he found that he was within the circle of a large military camp.

The soldiers who had been left scat-tered about to watch over Horley House had now been joined by a large body of troopers, who were part of an expedition going north, in consequence of some rumoured restlessness among the people.

Here they were, then, forming a perfect cordon round the wood, their watch-fires blazing merrily, and crowds sitting round the genial glow, joking and singing, and watching with eager-ness the preparations for supper.

There was no possibility of Mat passing through them unobserved.

The only way, therefore, was to pretend that he had been lying asleep in the wood, and to advance boldly in among them, trusting to the chance that no one would recognise him.

He began, therefore, suddenly to sing out the first verse of a song well known and popular at the time—

"The beggar gets plenty of money,
    Yet greed put not down to his score;
A dry crust eats better than honey,
    When ill-luck comes oft to his door.
Happy and blythe 'neath the greenwood shade,
The beggar's a merry and artful blade."

And singing thus he advanced boldly to one of the watch-fires.

The soldiers had heard his voice.

But thinking that it was one of their own comrades that was singing, they had taken no notice of it.

The appearance, therefore, of Mat in his fantastic rags, created a hearty burst of laughter.

"Hullo, Master Scarecrow," cried one of them, "where do you hail from?"

"From the moon," replied Mat, "where there are no knaves, and where there are no soldiers required to catch them."

A roar of laughter followed this sally.

"Well done," cried one of the troopers, "the rogue has wit; and if he will give us another verse of his song he shall sup with us."

"To the devil with your supper," thought Mat.

But he knew well that if he showed any signs of impatience he would be suspected.

"A supper is good, but a penny lasts longer," he said. "However," he added, flinging himself down before the fire in an easy attitude, which provoked another laugh, "as you want another verse of my song I will give you one.

"The heart of the beggar is open—
    Always free to give aid to his friends;
He takes what he gets without grumbling,
    And the smallest piece never offends.
And the beggar and soldier good mates should be,
For the soldier does nothing—and so does he."

In spite of his anxiety to be off, he sang the stave with right good-will; and, despite his rags and his hideous face, he produced a most favourable impression.

"What were you doing in the yard?" asked one of the soldiers, as he finished his song, and prepared to do justice to some excellent beef that was put before him.

"Well," replied Mat, "I have had a very bad day's work. All the people I have met seem to have left their money at home, so I took a long snooze in the woods, after eating some roots, and here I am—

"Quite ready to dance, quite ready to sing,
   If I hear but the sound of the good metal ring."

"And where are you off to when you leave this?" asked one of the troopers.

"To fair London city," said Mat. "I'll have no more of the woods. Roots are food for rabbits or beaten soldiers, but for a jolly beggar who loves his ale and his beef, and the smile of a pretty lass, why, the town is the best place after all."

Poor Mat!

He knew that by saying such things as these he turned the laughter of the soldiers against himself.

But he cared not for that.

His heart was hardened against jibes and jeers.

All he wished for was at *any* hazard to bring his mission to a successful issue.

A roar of laughter followed this sally, and the soldiers feeling merry over their cups—for ale was brought plentifully from a neighbouring tavern—suggested that he should travel with them to the North and be their jester.

Mat put on a comical look at this.

"No, no," he said; "if you like to fight for glory, have the kicks with it, by all means. But while *I* can pick up halfpence by merely putting on a wry face, and pleading starvation with a full belly, why, I'd rather keep to my trade and be out of the way of the fighting."

And after quaffing a large draught of ale he rose to go.

There was no opposition.

The troopers were sorry to lose the company of such a jolly good fellow, but as far as suspecting him, there was nothing of the kind.

So they bade him good luck, subscribed a few pence for him, which Mat pocketed with a great show of pleasure, and, though full of eagerness to be off, walked away slowly, singing to himself as he went.

As soon, however, as he had got fairly beyond the light of the watch-fires, he dashed off at a rapid pace to make up for lost time.

There was no fear now of further interruption.

He met no one on the road but a few stray travellers, of whom, as it was not necessary to avoid suspicion, he asked no alms.

In fact, he was resolved not to assume his character of a beggar again until he reached the neighbourhood of Old London Bridge.

It was morning ere he came in view of the Tower, however, and as people were now flocking along the roads, and a number of troopers, too, could be seen hanging about, he dropped into a halting walk, and made his way to the nearest inn.

That he was footsore and weary was no untruth, and if he halted it was nothing more than might be expected after such a journey as he had made.

When he entered the inn he begged a crust of bread and cheese and some ale, which was readily accorded by the good-natured landlord, and going outside, he sat at a little table beneath the shade of a wide-spreading tree to eat it and listen to the talk.

There were several soldiers and some country-people grouped round the table, having a kind of early meal—breakfast in fact, of bread and cheese and ale; and the name of Horley House pronounced again and again attracted his attention.

So he lengthened his meal, and listened eagerly.

"The colonel's a long time coming up," said one of the troopers; "I should fancy that he wants to arrive when all the fun is over."

"Where is the rendezvous?" asked a comrade.

"At Horley House," replied the other. "I should think the men were in the old house by this time."

"What do they want at Horley House?" asked his companion.

"There is a great quantity of gunpowder and military stores there, which will be of immense use to the expedition," said the other; "it was only lately that they discovered that they were here, and, as the property of the executed Earl of Essex, they are now the property of the crown. So the queen will save her stores; and, between you and me, our colonel will find another excuse for delay."

Mat fairly trembled as he listened.

Horley House to be filled with troops?

In what fearful danger then were his friends?

For a moment his mind seemed to lose its balance.

What was he to do?

Should he return and warn them, or should he hurry on?

He determined on the latter.

To return might be to arrive when all was over, when his friends had either escaped, or had been taken prisoners, whereas, if any mishap had befallen them, he could do them no better service than to save the papers which would prove their identity.

Their unparalleled misfortunes, and the proved treachery and imposture of the so-called Lord Housden might be the means of restoring them to royal favour.

Having nothing more, therefore, to learn, Mat o' the Mist hastened on with his meal, and started at a rapid pace from the tavern.

He had meant to remain there during the whole of the day.

But he had good reason for not doing so.

He had, in fact, recognised in one of the men who had spoken a man who knew him well, a partizan of Lord Housden.

However, it was still far from his intention to enter that populous part of London during the day, for even the disguise he had adopted would not save him from recognition in the neighbourhood of his old haunts.

So, having put a safe distance between him and the inn where he had breakfasted, he went to a little spot where he procured the necessaries for a day's consumption, and then made his way to a wooded part of the country, not far from the high road.

In those days pleasant forest land almost joined the bustling city; and here, then, amid a dense mass of verdure he was able to lie concealed and watch those who passed on the highway.

Had any prisoners as yet been taken to London from Horley House, he would have seen them pass, and he saw none.

But still this proved nothing.

They might be kept behind until the arrival of the colonel, of whom the troopers spoke in such unceremonious and disrespectful terms; or, perhaps, the danger was still coming, and Horley House was yet to be invaded.

Having nothing else to occupy his mind, a thousand thoughts of this kind naturally rushed through his brain.

But still his path of duty was clear before him. He must pass on to London and do as he was required there.

At length, after a day which seemed truly as if it would never end, the darkness came on, and Mat once more pressed onwards with all speed.

His natural friend in all cases was the river, and towards this accordingly he made; and coming upon its banks beyond Whitehall, he took possession of a small skiff he there found moored, and with the strong tide hurried down the river towards the old bridge.

As he approached the old building, something at once struck him.

The only two houses where lights were to be seen were the inn, which we know already by having been kept by old Wormer, "The Red Cross," and "Duke's Palace."

From the latter a broad sheet of light glowed over the river.

It was evidently occupied.

The question was, by whom?

Certainly it was not by friends, for no one could enter it without forcing their way in; and none of Launcelot Duke's friends would have done such a deed.

It must, then, have been forcibly entered by enemies; and to find out who they were and in what numbers, must be Mat's first duty.

CHAPTER XXXII.

MAT'S SECRET.

THE question to be decided now was, which was the best way to effect an entrance?

If Harold had been with Mat o' the Mist he would have suggested at once bursting into the house, and demanding by what right the place was invaded, feeling doubtless all the more incensed now that he knew who he was and what treachery had been used against him by a villainous impostor.

But Mat o' the Mist, distorted as he might be in body, was in no way distorted in mind.

He had, in fact, a cool and collected brain, which carried him through life better than many a man of superior appearance and pretentions.

Eager, therefore, though he was to secure for Harold the papers which were to give to him his birthright, he repressed his impatience.

He resolved, however, to make use of his peculiar aptitude for climbing, and his knowledge of the bridge to have a peep at the interior of the house.

Having glanced round him, therefore, to see that no one was on the watch, he secured his boat to the wooden posts near the stairs, and clambered along the parapet of the bridge, only a few inches in width, as he had done on the night of the escape of the unfortunate Earl of Essex.

On reaching the wooden door in the wall, of which we have spoken, he found it securely fastened within; but, clambering upon the sill of the window, he was able to see into the large room, which had always been used as a dining chamber by the merchant.

Here, collected round the centre table, were about twenty men, military-looking idlers, who seemed as if they had doffed their armour for the sake of comfort.

"It would be of little use my entering here at present," thought Mat, as he clambered down again. "I must go round to the bridge, and see what information I can pick up."

He had scarcely reached the bridge gate when he was hustled by a number of men, who seemed bent upon some important errand.

He at once joined the crowd, which stopped before the house of the diamond merchant.

One of them at once advanced, and knocked loudly at the door.

It was opened in a moment by one of the troopers.

"What do you want here?" he said, gruffly.

Mat o' the Mist creeped up closer.

He was just in time to hear the answer.

"Have you one Sharpley among your number here?"

"Yes," replied the soldier. "He is upstairs with my comrades."

"Tell him he is wanted," said the other, "and I will await him here."

Sharpley, though irritated by being disturbed in a game of chance that he was winning, hurried down nevertheless to the door, thinking that it was some messenger from Lord Housden.

"What want you with me?" he said, gruffly, as the stranger and four or five men stepped into the entry.

"Is your name Sharpley?" asked the other.

"It is."

"Then I arrest you in the queen's name," replied the new-comer. "Men, see that he does not escape."

Had Sharpley had any desire to resist it would have been useless.

He had left his weapons upstairs, and the men who seized him were well armed.

"For what am I arrested?" he cried, furiously.

"For the murder of Abraham Moss," replied the stranger. "Quick, my men; hurry him out, or we shall have those half-drunken companions of his attempting a rescue.

They had only entered the street and closed the door just in time, for the heavy tread of the soldiers was heard descending the stairs.

Once out of the house, however, they soon hurried him away, leaving Mat o' the Mist standing there in wonder.

"MAT'S STRATAGEM."

He knew nothing of Abraham Moss and his terrible death.

Neither did he imagine what a direct and important effect the capture of Sharpley on that charge would have upon the fortunes of Harold and his friends.

When the bustle of Sharpley's arrest was over, and the streets had settled down into the usual quiet of the night, it must be confessed that Mat o' the Mist felt a chill, a dreary sense of loneliness creep over him.

On the bridge it was certain he had nowhere to go to.

The Headsman's house was closed; "Duke's Palace" was closed; and nowhere else could he at any time have found a welcome.

For that night, however, his task was done.

In the present state of excitement in which those at "Duke's Palace" were in at the arrest of their leader, it would be useless to attempt any secret entry, and he therefore quitted the precincts of his old haunts, and went in search of a resting-place for the night.

For this purpose he hastily made his way along the road which led to St. Christopher's Fields, of blood-stained memory.

In a little lane, which struck away in a zigzag, hesitating kind of direction, from this plot of waste ground, he stopped at a little house, or, rather, cottage, and though there was no sign of any living thing within, knocked loudly.

After he had repeated this operation three times, the door was opened by a diminutive old man, who, upon seeing Mat, uttered a grunt of satisfaction, and bade him enter.

Mat soon found himself in a little room, lighted by a dismal lamp—a room so curious in all its surroundings, that, had we time and space, it would have merited a more detailed description.

Suffice it to say that its contents were a collection of all the old rubbish that it seemed possible to bring together in so small a space.

"What brings you here at this untimely hour?" asked the old man. "Had I not known your knock, I should not have opened the door."

In reply, Mat o' the Mist explained to old Solomon Ambrose the errand upon which he was engaged, telling him that he could give him more information in the morning.

The old man then led the way to an an upper room, where he left Mat to make himself comfortable for the night.

There were more attractions for Mat in the old cottage than the presence of old Solomon.

Solomon, in fact, had a daughter, and distorted and hideous as the Headsman's Imp was, he had found in her a congenial spirit.

Lucy Ambrose was also a cripple, but with a face which her worst enemies could not call anything but beautiful.

A slight defect in her walk, in consequence of an accident in her infancy, had caused her to be the butt of the neighbourhood; for, in those days, as in these, people were always too ready to hold up to scorn the unfortunate and the wretched.

Mat o' the Mist was, of course, far more deformed and unhuman than poor Lucy; but, in spite of his misshapen form, she had recognised his goodness of heart, and an affection of a strong and unselfish nature had sprung up between them.

Mat never thought of her lameness, but of her beautiful face, and would wonder, when the young girl talked to him and gazed at him in kindness, that she had anything to say to or think of such a miserable creature as himself.

It was to see Lucy that he anxiously longed for to-morrow, and, in spite of the late hour at which he had presented himself, he was up with the dawn.

There was a little strip of monotonous garden at the back of Ambrose's cottage, and into this Mat descended.

The garden could have been increased to an unlimited extent by carrying it into the immense waste ground beyond, had any energetic spirit presided over the cottage.

As it was, however, what the little piece of ground wanted in extent it made up in the tasteful way in which it was laid out and tended.

This was all due to Lucy Ambrose; and Mat, as he wandered along the neatly-kept paths, saw a reflection of the one he loved in every plant and flower.

During the whole of that day, Mat o' the Mist remained at the cottage of

Solomon Ambrose, and, when the strange pair of lovers parted, it was once more evening.

Mat had succeeded in keeping his presence in London a secret, and he had ascertained also that Lucy Ambrose would consent to become his wife as soon as Harold and his friends were out of danger.

With this assurance, Mat, as he supposed, went happily away towards the old bridge to fulfil the mission which had been entrusted to his care.

CHAPTER XXXIII.

MAT'S STRATAGEM.

IT was now mid-winter, and although it was scarcely eight o'clock, the bridge, when Mat approached it, was enveloped in a shroud of darkness.

In fact, when he passed by Duke's Palace, there was an air of loneliness about it that made him shudder.

Not a single light was to be seen in any of the windows, and long disuse already began to show itself in the dusty and rusty appearance of the whole exterior.

There was no possibility, of course, of entering the house by the front way; and Mat, therefore, after taking a hurried observation of it, proceeded to the rear of the premises, and made his way along the parapet to the casement where he had made his observations before.

All was dark within.

Everything was as quiet as the grave.

Now or never, then, was the time.

To make his way through that window was the difficulty.

But there was no time for hesitation.

He must break the glass, and if the sound betrayed him, he must conceal himself until the alarm had passed over.

Without waiting, therefore, for any further consultation, Mat dashed the hilt of his sword through the pane of glass which was nearest the catch of the window.

Fortunately the wind was very high, and part of the glass fell out into the river, so that very little noise could be heard inside the house.

After a lapse of a few minutes, therefore, Mat passed his hand through the opening, undid the catch, threw open the window, and entered the room.

Having closed the casement again to prevent any suspicions, he advanced on tiptoe towards the inner apartment.

The door of this was closed, or, rather stood ajar, and it was no difficult matter for Mat to discover the reason why his entry had not been observed.

He could hear plainly the voices of men and the clinking of glasses.

Here, in the very room where Harold had explained to him that the casket was kept.

However, he must wait.

And while waiting, he could lie concealed and listen.

The men within were evidently under the influence of drink, although as yet they could scarcely be accused of intoxication.

After listening, therefore, a little while, Mat hit upon a bold plan, and, throwing open the door, walked into the room.

The two troopers who sat there were at first so astounded at the apparition that they could not speak.

In fact, as Mat saw at once to his satisfaction, they were strangers, and had never seen him before.

"Why, what devil's imp have we here?" said one of the troopers, with a loud laugh.

Mat merely grinned at this insult, and threw himself carelessly into a chair.

"Well, I am an imp, so people tell me," he said; "but my master is not the devil, but the Headsman, his agent."

"And whence came you now?" cried the man.

"Why, since you have taken my master's occupation from him, and shut him up in prison, I have been hiding away in this house, and living upon what few scraps I could pick up; but now my companions, the rats, have become so ravenous that I have been compelled to quarrel with them; so if you have any human kindness left in you, you will give me something to eat and drink."

Both of them during this speech had eyed him narrowly. But without suspicion.

They were already pretty well pleased with themselves and the world, and so were not in the humour to be suspicious.

Their scrutiny only showed them a wretched, misshapen, beggarly fellow, whom it would be inhuman to wreak revenge upon, even if he were a servant of those who were their master's enemies.

So they resolved to receive him well.

"Well, you are not over good looking, but I suppose you are a human being," said one of them, "so help yourself to what you can find to eat, and here is some of the merchant's best wine to wash it down with."

Mat o' the Mist, although he had not been allowed to leave Solomon's house with an empty stomach, was obliged to feign hunger, and set to with right good will.

Having found that he had so easily become popular with the troops at Horley Wood by indulging in a few songs and jokes, he adopted now the same plan, and in course of a very short time, he found himself on excellent terms with his companions.

"The wine is getting very low," said he, after a bit. "I know where Master Duke keeps his best: his special bottles, for his own drinking; I will go and fetch some."

He returned in a few moments with the merchant's choicest wine, which he knew well that Launcelot Duke would not begrudge under the circumstances.

The strong liquid soon had its effect upon the already half-drunken men, and they gradually began to nod in their chairs.

"We shall have to make a night of it here," cried one of the men. "I feel too heavy to move."

His companion only answered by a nod of the head, and fell back in his chair, in a deep sleep, while Mat o' the Mist, who knew the advantage of caution, pretended to do likewise.

It was not long before the second trooper relapsed into the same state of insensibility.

Then, gradually, Mat opened his eyes and glanced round him.

The room was evidently the one which Harold had pointed out to him as that which contained the casket.

There, in fact, was the bureau invitingly before him.

But he hesitated even now.

If he attempted to open it the troopers might awaken, and, of course, they would at once suspect that he was on some secret errand.

He resolved, therefore, to adopt a plan which would effectually prevent their interfering with his actions.

Going stealthily to a cupboard at the corner of the room, he took from it a long coil of stout rope, which was used for fastening up the merchant's heavy chests.

At the end of this he made a large loop, which he very cautiously dropped over the head of the trooper.

Then slowly he drew it tight, and proceeded to bind each limb slowly and methodically.

He had ever and anon to stop and watch the movements of the man's companion, who slept a most uneasy sleep, and every now and then started under the influence of some frightful dream.

Neither of them, however, woke; and presently Mat o' the Mist commenced the same operations upon the second man that he had performed upon the first.

He had scarcely succeeded in thus securing his two captives, when the first one woke and gazed about him with a stupid stare.

After a moment he became conscious that Mat o' the Mist was engaged upon something extraordinary, and he endeavoured to jump.

Mat, in fact, had discovered, in attempting to open the bureau, that it had been relocked, and the key that Harold had given him was of no use.

He had, therefore, procured a crowbar, and it was when attempting to force a door open with it that he aroused the trooper.

"What in the devil's name are you doing?" cried the soldier; "eh—eh, what's this?"

The last exclamation was drawn from him on finding himself not able to move and, fancying that he must be dreaming he tried to raise his hand to rub his eyes.

In this, however, he was foiled, for his wrists were firmly bound to the heavy chair.

He saw now at once that he was the victim of a trap, and loud and long were the curses which he invoked upon Mat's devoted head.

The second trooper was, of course, awakened by a noise, and joined his misfortunes to those of his friend.

But, with the exception of their power to swear, they were both helpless.

They glared at Mat with a ferocious malice, but that worthy only answered them with a grin, and proceeded all the more hurriedly with his work.

"I don't mean to harm you," he said; and if you behave yourselves, I will let you go directly I have got what I want."

"And then, when you set us free," thought they, "we will pay you well for your trouble."

"The fool! He will undo his own work."

This was the mistake they made.

They had not to do with a fool, but with one cleverer than themselves, as they found out ere long, to their cost.

By dint of hard work, Mat succeeded, after a few minutes, in forcing open the bureau, and the casket, which had been thoroughly described to him by Harold, was soon in his hands.

As soon as he had stowed it away in his pocket, he drew forth a pistol and approached the two troopers, who, of course, had slept off some of their drunkenness, and were fully aware of the absurd position in which they were placed.

But absurdity was not the worst of it.

There was also danger.

For, if Mat o' the Mist left them in their present position, they knew well they would have to remain in that house fully a week without seeing a human being.

There was a good chance, therefore, of their starving, and they were inclined to be as civil as possible to their captor.

One of the troopers accordingly burst into a hoarse laugh.

"You are a clever young imp, to say the least of it," he cried; "but since you have obtained what you want, it is to be hoped that you will now restore us to liberty."

"In order that you may take it from me, and fling me out of window," cried Mat. "No, no, I have a little more sense left than that; but as you have been friendly, I will see that you have a chance of freedom as soon as I am safe myself."

As he spoke he raised his pistol.

"You see this," he added. "This is loaded, and I am a good shot. I shall cut the end of your bonds, and then I shall retreat backwards to the door. If either of you attempt to move before I have quitted the room, I shall fire."

Taking up one of the knives from the table, Mat then so cut the cords that a little exertion on the part of the prisoners could release them.

Then, sternly and slowly, he made his way backwards towards the door.

It was quite evident that Mat o' the Mist was serious.

That, in fact, he meant what he said, and that the slightest movement on the part of the captives to take undue advantage of his leniency, would be followed by a bullet which would end the earthly career of one of them at least.

So neither of them moved.

In fact, if they had done so it would have been more for the sake of easing themselves after their close bondage than with any idea of escape.

They wisely concluded that Mat knew every inch of the house, and that before they could free themselves he would be off by some mysterious mode of exit, of which they, of course, would know nothing.

So they waited a reasonable time until he had time to go, and then, freeing themselves of their bonds, proceeded to search the house—not, indeed, for the purpose of interfering with Mat's flight, even if they discovered him, but only out of pure curiosity to see if he had really been able to make good his escape in so short a time.

But they might have spared themselves the trouble.

The house was still and solemn, and with the exception of themselves, tenantless.

Mat o' the Mist had been away long since, and was hurrying back with the turning tide towards Whitehall.

CHAPTER XXXIV.

SHARPLEY'S VIEW OF THE FUTURE.

WHEN Sharpley was arrested, as we have seen, and hurried off to prison, his mind was in a turmoil of excitement.

Yet it was not in respect to the crime with which he was charged that he was so anxious.

What he thought of—what he longed to know was—who had betrayed him?

Even in his helpless, imprisoned state, he hoped to be able to make his sting felt; for he was now full of money, and could reward anyone who would be the instrument of his venomous hate.

But how was he to find out?

If he mentioned Orker, or the other man, he was at once connecting himself with the crime.

Perhaps these men had been arrested too—perhaps they had "peached upon him;" if so, the very fact of his seeming to know them would convict him.

So, though his mind was full of eagerness, he restrained his impatience, and decided upon biding his time.

One person, however, he resolved to see—one person he was determined should be fully aware of his position, and should extricate him from it if earthly power could do so.

This was Lord Housden.

To him, therefore, he at once sent, and having done so, he seemed to grow quite contented; and during the day after his arrest, joked and played games with his warders as if nothing particular were the matter.

Evening brought Lord Housden.

Sharpley had sent to him quietly and as secretly as he could, and he came, disguised so well, be it said, that when he entered the cell the man who had so often been employed to do his villainous work knew him not.

He had sent for an advocate to make the best of his sorry case; and when the cloaked figure, with slouching hat, entered the cell, he thought at once it was this man.

But Lord Housden soon undeceived him.

He threw aside his cloak, took off his hat, and before Sharpley could address a word to him, turned to one of the warders.

"You can leave us together," he said; "I am the prisoner's lawyer, and have permission to see him alone."

The man bowed and withdrew.

"Now," said Lord Housden, frowning savagely as the man departed, "what does this mean? Were you not satisfied with what work I gave you—what pay I gave you, that you must needs go about a sneaking, cold-blooded murderer, when I would have given you money?"

"Well, my lord," replied Sharpley, "you see my habits have been very extravagant of late, and, though your lordship supplied me well with money, still, you see, that wouldn't stand against gambling."

"Gambling! curse you! What do fellows like you want with gambling?" almost shouted Lord Housden. "Leave that to your betters. Besides, if you had asked me, I would have supplied you."

"Not as the Jew's cash-box did," thought Sharpley.

However, he said aloud—

"I did not care to do so. Besides, this was no murder. The old fool was killed in self defence in a violent struggle. Your lordship *can* know none of the particulars."

"I do—*all*," replied Housden. "Both your accomplices are in custody, and I have seen them. They declare that they will turn Queen's evidence against you. The one, it seems, is innocent of all but the knowledge of the theft; the other aided you, but he did not kill his man. He attacked a Christian youth, who lives to give evidence against you; and the man's daughter can also swear to you."

"Curse that Orker!" murmured Sharpley. "I knew it would have been best to have killed that girl and made sure of the youth. Well," he added, aloud, "since you know all, my lord, the question now is how are you going to get me out of it?"

These words were uttered with such

insolence and quiet resolution, that Lord Housden was amazed.

"How am *I* to get you out of it?" he repeated. "I have nothing to do with it. You have got into the mess yourself, and you must get out of it the best way you can. It is no matter of mine."

Sharpley shrugged his shoulders.

"I see I must explain more fully," he said.

"Precisely," replied Lord Housden, with suppressed anger, "for at present I am utterly in the dark."

"Well, then, I will do so," said Sharpley, "as simply and as plainly as I can. You will admit, of course, that I have served you well?"

"Yes."

"That you have even thought sufficiently well of me," added Sharpley, "to entrust me with many of your secrets?"

This was said pointedly, and Lord Housden knew it.

It was a covert threat.

"Well, and what can this come to?"

"It comes simply to this," said Sharpley, "that I have not a single soul in the world to help me but you, and that I must—in fact, I *will* depend on you for my release."

"Then let me tell you once for all, Sharpley," replied Lord Housden, "that you depend upon a broken reed. Had you been in difficulties through me, I might have strained a nerve to aid you. As it is, your own bloodthirtiness and greed have brought you into this strait, and you must get out of it the best way you can. I absolutely refuse to assist you except as regards money, and when *I* refuse, you know that I mean it."

"Then I tell you what," said Sharpley, "when I swing, so shall you beside me."

Lord Housden grinned defiantly.

"All *you* can say against me," he said, "you are quite at liberty to say. Say it, and swing also. I will be there to see you. But set aside all foolish ideas of *that* sort. I have brought you some-thing here which is better than all lawyers. I have seen these men—your confederates. They will confess everything; your case is hopelessly desperate; there is the only remedy that *I* can see."

And as he spoke he placed on the table a small bottle.

It was marked "Poison."

A sarcastic smile wreathed itself over Sharpley's coarse lips.

"Why are you so solicitous to prevent me the trouble of dancing in the air?" he asked.

"You told me once that you had one person who cared for you, and who would, doubtless, grieve to see such an unseemly exhibition," cried Lord Housden. "But you can take it or leave it. Your case is desperate. You will most certainly be condemned; most distinctly the judge will refuse to listen to any talk of pardon, in fact, you are as good as dead; and if I were to use my voice in your behalf, I should simply be ruining myself and not aiding you. So fully understand that no entreaties, no threats will move me except in so far as money will aid you in your defence. Come what may, I swear I will do no more."

Sharpley saw the truth of this.

He knew that Lord Housden could do him little good, except, indeed, *after* condemnation; but this conviction did not prevent his resenting the cold-blooded and murderous style in which Lord Housden gave out his feelings.

"So, so, my lord," he said, as Lord Housden bade him good-night, "so, so, then, if you cannot help me out of a halter, I'll help you into one. Towers," he added, to one of the warders, as they re-entered the cell, "let me have pen and ink. A letter to Fanny will bring her herself, I know, and a few directions will find Harold Forrester. If he knew what I know, how small would my Lord Housden feel! But, then, his lordship if not even now aware that I hold him in the palm of my hand, and that when I choose I can close my fingers and crush him."

CHAPTER XXXV.

SHARPLEY'S STRATAGEM.

THERE were three days yet to come before the trial.

There was time, therefore, to let Harold Forrester know, and to obtain his advice and assistance before then.

In answer to his letter, there appeared on the next day at the prison a young woman—pretty, meek, unassuming.

This was Fanny.

How such a being as this ever came to love such an unmitigated villain as Sharpley, it would be difficult, by any process of logic, to discover.

But that she did so was quite evident; for, on entering the cell, she flung herself on his neck, heedless of the presence of the warders, and burst into a torrent of tears.

"Oh, Sharpley!" she cried, "this is very awful. Only tell me you are innocent; say so, and I'll believe you—indeed I will—and do anything for you."

Fanny being the one person in the world whom Sharpley had never deceived the one person he loved and respected—had a right to receive a truthful reply.

But she did *not* get one.

I need scarcely say this.

To tell her the truth would be to blight her life; to cast her from him; to throw away wilfully all chance of her doing anything for him.

So he merely pressed her to him, saying—

"Of course, Fanny, I am innocent. Why should you think it possible that I could be guilty?"

Fanny looked up, beaming.

"I never thought you guilty," she said. "But tell me, now, what it all means. I am so bewildered and terrified with the whole matter that I feel all in a whirl."

Poor thing!

She had never received any education, except what she could drag for herself out of wretched circumstances, and her whole aim and hope lately had been to see Sharpley settle down a little, and marry her.

So she listened wildly, though with implicit faith, to the lie which Sharpley concocted for her deceit; and, though she confessed herself somewhat confused by the description he gave of the scene at the old Jew's, she fully believed that he was the injured party, and that the usurer had attacked him, and attempted his life.

So far so good.

"But," pleaded Fanny, "I hear it said that the man who went with you to old Moss's swears you killed him deliberately for his money."

"It's a lie; all a wicked lie," cried Sharpley, stamping his foot on the stone floor; "it is all concocted by that wretch, Housden, to destroy me. He has a reason, I suppose, for wishing me out of the way, and this is the method by which he seeks its accomplishment. But I'll prove my innocence. I can. And if anyone suffers for all this it will be himself. Now, Fanny, if anyone can save me it is you."

Need I say how eagerly Fanny responded to this appeal?

So eagerly, in fact, that the ruffian, for the first time in his life, felt compunction.

"However," he whispered to his dark heart, "he would reform after this. He would never again launch out into the villainies which had come to be a portion of his life, but would settle down, as Fanny called it, and be a new man."

Wretched creature!

How could he fly from the pursuing demon of Remorse?

How wash out the stains of blood?

He sat down and wrote a brief letter.

It ran thus:—

"MASTER HAROLD FORRESTER,—I am in prison for murder, and have very little chance of getting free again. In fact, I feel that I am a lost man, and what comes of me out of prison won't have a voice to speak to you with; so, before I go, I want to relieve my mind of a burden. It's a great secret for you, and something that will repay you for all the evil I've done you in the past, and enable you to triumph, too, over that villain, your arch-enemy, Housden. Do not be afraid to come; do not think I'll betray you;

the one who brings this will tell you better than that. Disguise yourself well, so that not even that traitor will know you if he met you, and I will tell you a story that will make your hair stand on end, and will give you the means of proving it too. "JOHN SHARPLEY."

This was all very well.

The writing of it relieved his mind, and made him feel as if he really was at last on the way to vengeance.

But then came two questions.

Harold Forrester was proscribed, and flying from the law.

How was he to reach him? and, if he *did* succeed in reaching, would he trust himself to such a man as he was?

This last question, however, he only asked himself.

To tell Fanny would be to confess his own guilt.

"It will be a difficult matter to find him," said he; "but I think you'll have time. They've left 'Duke's Palace,' on the Bridge, and they've left Mistress Halcott's on the heath; but perhaps Mat o' the Mist (you've seen him, and he's got nothing to fear) may be found wandering about the bridge, or somewhere in the neighbourhood, and *he* would be the one to take your message. At any rate, Fanny, I'll leave it all to

you, and if you don't succeed in three days, come back to me."

And so the poor, confiding being left him, and he was alone once more.

Alone, for he considered the presence of the turnkeys as nothing.

Fanny, now cast upon a cold and uncharitable world, listened with a strange bewilderment to the icy and unfeeling clang of those prison gates.

What was she to do? where was she to go?

These were the questions she kept constantly asking herself.

Where was she to go first?

These were the questions she kept constantly asking herself.

Where was she to go first?

This to the unfortunate victim of a deluded love was a perfect mystery.

Yet she did not falter.

She loved Sharpley, and, like the fair Saracen, she started out upon her errand with little better than a name to guide her.

She knew that the life of her lover—so, at least, *he* said—depended upon her exertions.

She little knew how much of other people's fortunes also were confided unwillingly to her care.

CHAPTER XXXVI.

A STRANGE FRIEND.

ON quitting the presence of the troopers, Mat o' the Mist hastened into the adjoining room, and let himself out through the window by which he had entered, ran along the parapet as before, and was soon in his little skiff hurrying away up the river towards Whitehall.

He had divested himself of his beggar's garments at the house of Lucy's father, and made up his mind on this occasion to proceed to Horley House by the coach.

What he had heard from the soldiers at the inn convinced him that things could not be right at Horley House; but, nevertheless, there could be no other destination for him.

Whatever clue there was to the whereabouts of his friends he would there find it.

It was night-time when he reached the end of his coach journey, and hurried towards the house where the unfortunate Earl of Essex and his wife had spent so many days of happiness.

Had he not heard of the rumoured occupation by the soldiers he would, of course, have hurried on by the secret door, and have surprised them with his good news.

As it was, however, he was aware that caution was necessary.

He, therefore, made a tour round the building, and was scarcely surprised, though alarmed, to behold that every window in it was lighted up brilliantly, showing how fully the place was occupied.

His heart sank within him.

What was he to do now?

How ascertain the strength of the garrison and the fate of the fugitives?

It was indeed impossible for him to tell whether the secret way had been discovered or not; but this was no time to give way to idle fears.

He must risk all, or he could discover nothing; and so, making his way to the entrance of the secret way, he began gliding along the subterraneous passage which led to the turret top.

He had not proceeded far when he heard the sound of voices, which, of course, told him the necessity of caution, and caused him to advance more slowly, expecting to come upon some of his enemies.

But in this he was agreeably mistaken.

He had not gone very far when he heard the voice of a woman, and, suddenly turning a corner, he came upon a sight which cheered his heart.

In a cellar which adjoined the passage were seated Don Fernando, the Headsman, Launcelot Duke, Eveline, and Harold, who welcomed him with a suppressed shout of applause.

In a moment a meal was provided for him, and while he was engaged in it he told the story of his adventures.

He had saved the casket.

That was *one* great step in advance.

But there was yet another thing in regard to which they were still as far behind as ever.

Proofs of all kinds were of no use until they had discovered the whereabouts of the old steward.

As long as this was a secret, all of them would be compelled to remain either where they were or in some place of concealment.

Once the imposture of the pretended Lord Housden was proved, all would be well, but not till then.

Many conferences were held during that night.

It seemed that the fugitives had seen the approach of the troops, and had made their way from the turret-top as soon as the first trooper had entered the building.

Since then they had had no alarms, and Harold had procured all the necessary provisions.

The result of the conference was that Harold and Mat should, in disguise, make their way to London, and then pick up what information they could.

The arrest of Sharpley, however, was for the first time a stumbling-block in their path.

Little did any of them imagine that Sharpley at that very moment was burning to see some of them; not to injure them, as was his wont, but to aid them in their secrets.

Little also did they think that Fanny, as an emissary of his, was even now in search of them.

In the morning, early, Harold and Mat set out.

They had very little data to go upon; but some presentiment was in their hearts that they would not return empty handed.

They reached London the same evening, performing their journey in the same way that Mat had done before, and at once began their inquiries.

Little, however, did they learn in the neighbourhood of the old house, to which they naturally took their way.

People knew that Sharpley was in prison; they were aware that he had been arrested for murder, and that was all.

However, they were just leaving the place in despair when a woman accosted them.

It was Fanny; but, of course, neither of them knew her.

"Oh, sir," she cried, addressing Harold, "can you tell me what I am to do? I have been watching this house *so* long to see if I could find some intelligence of Harold Forrester or Mat o' the Mist, or Master Duke, and I can hear nothing of them. I was told to tell no one my business, but to-morrow is his trial day, and I'm well-nigh distracted."

"This is strange, indeed," murmured our hero.

Then, turning to Fanny, he said—

"My good woman, I know well all the persons you name, but——"

"Oh! then do take me to them," she cried, impetuously; "do——"

"Stay," said Harold, interrupting her; "in the first place I cannot remain here to talk. I must proceed to some more secluded spot and hear all you have to say."

Without further explanation Harold and Mat led the way quickly in the direction of the house of old Ambrose, where the latter said they could talk in confidence; and, arriving there, they were soon in possession of a private room.

Then Fanny, who saw no use in keeping back her information any longer, and, in fact, chose rather to risk a little peril than lose a chance for Sharpley on the morrow, told the whole of her story.

"And, oh!" she added, as she concluded her narration, "if you *do* know Harold Forrester, pray ask him to come. There is *no* danger, Sharpley would never betray him. See, here is the letter for him."

"Well," replied Harold Forrester, "I am the one you seek."

"You!"

"Yes; but this Sharpley is one of my deadliest enemies; he has ever been the first to do me injury. Listen, and I will tell you."

Fanny listened in amazement to the catalogue of her lover's sins, as detailed by Harold.

But, truth to say, she was less interested in their number and consequence than in the question, "Would Harold come after all?"

As to Sharpley's crimes, Harold might be mistaken; at any rate, as to his desire to do harm.

All her mind was set on the one idea— "Would Harold come?"

In reply to our hero's words, therefore, she could only reiterate her words, and beg him to follow her.

Harold and Mat had at once a serious conference.

There was evidently no time to be lost.

There was no knowing how much would come out at the trial, and if Sharpley should be condemned, a sharp watch would be kept over him, and the danger of detection would be greater.

At length he resolved to go.

Upon Sharpley he really thought he might rely, though how he could aid him, accused as he was of murder, he was unable to see.

"I will go," exclaimed he, at length; "but what I can do to assist Sharpley I cannot say."

It is needless to describe the ecstacies in which these words put Fanny.

She was profuse in her thanks, and

insisted on kissing Harold's hand; but he soon put a stop to an unpleasant show of gratitude by reminding her that time pressed, and they must think about disguise.

In this he was assisted by Solomon Ambrose.

He was dressed up as a lawyer, and Mat as his clerk, and in this character looked by no means the frightful object he seemed in his other and ragged clothes.

On presenting themselves at the door of the prison, they were readily admitted; and Harold, having said that he had come by direction of Master Alger (whom Fanny had named as Sharpley's lawyer), he was soon admitted into the cell of his old enemy.

Fanny remained in the hall of the gaol.

Sharpley's features became of a leaden hue, and they turned red when he saw Harold and Mat enter; but he contrived to address the warders in a tolerably firm voice when he asked them to withdraw.

"So you have come? you *have* trusted me?" he said in surprise.

"I have," Harold answered. "My life is in your hands. It remains to see if you will betray me."

"Forrester," replied Sharpley, "I have called you hither, not to betray you, but to tell you a great secret. My Lord Housden is an impostor, and you——"

"I know now that you mean no more than what is good to me," interrupted Harold, seating himself. "I know all my story. I know that my father is the real Lord Edward Housden. What I require is the proof, the living proof, in the person of the old steward, the father of the impostor."

Sharpley was astonished, as may well be supposed, at hearing Harold's words.

"Well," he cried, "you surprise me. And is your father living?"

"He is."

Sharpley smiled in triumph.

"Good, good," he said; the reign of the impostor will soon be at an end. But now for our compact. *I* know where this old steward lives—I can give you such information as will take you to him; but in return for this you must do me a service."

" And what is that ? "

" You must aid me to escape."

" How ? "

" Ah! that must be left to time," returned Sharpley. "I have, however, sufficient faith in your word that if you will pledge yourself to assist me at the proper moment, I shall be perfectly satisfied."

" But this murder ? "

" It was none," returned Sharpley, " I swear it. The old man attacked me like a demon, and the lad attacked my companion. I did but kill him in self-defence. It will be proved to-morrow, though that will be of little use towards saving my neck from a halter."

" It will do this much, however," said Harold, " it will satisfy my mind. Well, I give the promise."

As he said these words, the door was opened, and one of the turnkeys entered.

He glanced round him with a suspicious air, and then went out again.

" Can't you send someone else to hear the story ? " said Sharpley, nervously. " I don't like the look of that man; he seems suspicious."

" Certainly he appeared to eye us very closely," said Harold; " but my interest is too far excited to go away now. However, it is not worth while for both of us to run this risk. Mat, leave the prison and wait for me at your friend Ambrose's house. If I am not there before morning you will know that something has happened, and you can then hurry and inform my friends. If they ask where you are going, say you are going to fetch Mr. Alger."

" That will be best," said Sharpley, nervously; " but if we are not allowed time for explanations, see that someone is in court to-morrow, and he shall receive, through Fanny, the whole of the information required."

Mat o' the Mist at once acted upon this suggestion, and quitted the cell.

When he reached the prison gate, the turnkey said to him—

" You are leaving then before your friend."

" Yes; I am going to fetch Mr. Alger."

The man grinned.

" Ah! that is well," he said; " for, until Mr. Alger comes, your friend cannot quit this place."

A chill ran through Mat's body at these words.

But he did not betray by any motion, or by any convulsion of feature, that he had heard the utterance of words so fatal to the safety of Harold.

He only said " very well," and went out, grieved and alarmed at leaving his friend in such a position of peril, yet confident that it was his duty to save himself that he might aid in saving him.

CHAPTER XXXVII.

THE TRIAL.

MEANWHILE we must return to Harold and Sharpley.

" These men," said the latter, " do not seem as if they were going to disturb us again, so I will proceed.

" You have heard all, you say, and you know, consequently, that the real name of Lord Housden is Ryder.

" It is now nearly two years since his father began to show signs that all was not well with him.

" His health was really giving way, and as he saw death hovering near him, he began to think of the evil he had done, and to wish to make some atonement for it.

" He knew through his son who you and Edwin Archer were, but, of course, he was not aware that you had been changed, and that Edwin was not the heir.

" Indeed, I only learned the fact from overhearing a few words let fall accidentally by Lord Housden.

" You have the means, of course, of proving to him that you are the heir, and what I advise you to do is at once to seek him.

" Of course, there will be some difficulty in the way."

" He is well watched, I suppose ? " said Harold.

"As to that, I know nothing," returned Sharpley. "From all I am aware of, I should fancy that Lord Housden looked upon it as a matter of impossibility for you to make such a discovery."

"He does not know, then, that my father is alive and with me?" returned Harold.

Sharpley glanced at him in amazement.

"Your father alive?" said he. "Impossible."

"Nevertheless, it is true," replied Harold, smiling. "It was from his lips that I learned the wonderful news which has so changed my position in life. But proceed; there is no knowing how soon we may be interrupted. Tell me at once the name of the place where Master Ryder is stowed away; and as to the difficulties, I must surmount them as best I may."

"Well," said Sharpley, "he is in a place situated some thirty miles from London to the north; a place which no one would believe to be inhabited. In fact, it is neither more nor less than a shepherd's hut on the mountains. There is a village near it called Orton; when you enter it you can inquire at the 'Orton Arms,' for Margrave. He's the man that keeps the hut and watches over the poor old steward. How you're to disguise yourself, and how you're to manage with him, I leave, of course, to you."

He had scarcely uttered these words when the door was flung open somewhat unceremoniously, and a number of armed men entered.

Their footsteps had not been heard along the corridor, and it seemed, therefore, as if they had been eavesdropping.

At any rate, one of them advanced towards Harold.

"Master Forrester," he said, "your presence here has been discovered, and in the queen's name, therefore, we arrest you for high treason."

Harold and Sharpley exchanged a look of alarm and bewilderment.

They knew denial was useless.

"I surrender at once," cried Harold; "though for the traitor who did this no mercy must be expected if I escape my threatened fate."

As he spoke he glanced at Sharpley, whom at the moment he must be forgiven for suspecting.

Sharpley saw the glance, and at once interpreted it aright.

"Before heaven," he cried, "I have had no hand in this. All I have told you is solemn truth, and all my hope is for your escape."

"It is right," replied the leader of the troopers; "this man is innocent of all participation in your betrayal. How we learned your presence here you will never know; but it was from no one in the prison. If you are ready now, we will depart, as time presses."

Harold at once walked in among his guards.

"Farewell, Sharpley," he said, as he did so. "Even from my dungeon, maybe, I shall be able to make use of what information you have given me. Endeavour, however, if you can, to let others know what you have told me, that they may work while my hands are tied."

In another moment he had quitted the cell, and Sharpley was once more alone with his turnkeys.

"Give me paper, and pen and ink," he said, excitedly. "To-morrow is the day of trial, and I have something to prepare. Now you have taken my friend away, I must trust to myself."

"But you have Alger, your advocate," said one of the turnkeys.

"Bah! he cannot do what I wish," replied Sharpley. "He knows the law, and can quibble, no doubt, with the best of them; but as for anything else, he is of no use to me."

The materials were accordingly brought, and, for a time, Sharpley, was engaged in writing down the whole of the particulars which he had given to Harold Forrester.

This occupied some considerable while, for, in those days, as my readers are aware, writing, at any rate fluently was an art known to few.

When he had finished, however, he retired to bed, fastening the document in the breast of his doublet.

On the next morning early he was led away to the court-house.

Murder was in those days, unfortunately, a matter of so ordinary an occurrence that the trial of such a man did not attract a crowd of any magnitude.

But there were a large quantity of the Hebrew tribe among those who were there, and these, as may be imagined, eyed Sharpley with eyes expressive of demoniacal hate.

Sharpley, however, though he saw his two companions there — the very men who had betrayed him—seemed to care nothing for himself.

All he was anxious for, in very truth, was to discover some one among the audience who could assist him in helping Harold Forrester.

The conviction, in fact, was strong within his mind that he must suffer; and, as the one who had brought him to this pass was Lord Housden, it had become in his mind an overwhelming belief that the one object now of his life must be to destroy him.

In giving him the poison the impostor had imagined that he had acted in his own interest.

He was wrong.

He was making Sharpley a more desperate man than before, and giving him a deadly weapon to use *in extremis*.

Presently the judge entered and took his seat on the bench.

Still no one.

Not even Fanny!

Yet Sharpley did not despair.

He was certain, from the very fact of Mat o' the Mist not returning to the prison, that he had suspected something, and that, even at the last moment, something might turn up for the best.

However, he was soon fully occupied.

The trial began.

The advocate for the prosecution was full of bustle, show-off, and excitement (counsel were in Queen Bess's days the same stuff as now), and he found himself, villain and murderer as he was, put in possession of facts, and accused of crimes of which he had never dreamed.

Ever and again he was on the point of bursting out indignantly, and denying the allegations against him.

But his counsel restrained him.

"This is all folly," he said, with a wave of the hand, and loud enough for the judge to hear—"this is all folly, and we can easily dispose of it. Leave it entirely to me."

So, though trembling with anxiety to speak his mind, Sharpley subsided into quietude once more, and the trial proceeded.

Very anxious were the Jews in the court, and very eager seemed one or two persons also, who were in a private part of the room, to hear the evidence, and evidently delighted they seemed at everything which seemed to tell against him.

Sharpley watched these narrowly.

That is to say, when his attention was not distracted to other objects by an anxiety to see those who would carry his letter to Harold's friends.

And a discovery he soon made rendered him the more resolved to risk all to punish Lord Housden for his cold-blooded refusal to aid him.

Two of these persons were Esther Moss and her Christian lover.

The third, disguised as he was, he recognised by an accident as Lord Housden, himself.

There was evidently in the mind of the impostor a dread of something coming.

Perhaps he had heard tidings of what Sharpley's desperation had driven him to.

Be this as it might, he listened to every word with marked, and even intense eagerness, and was undoubtedly pleased whenever anything was said which criminated the prisoner.

Evidently Lord Housden desired to get rid of him.

For this, Sharpley did not care.

Except for one thing.

If he suspected him, he could, in all probability, remove the old steward from his place of concealment.

Soon, however, though feeling half crazed at the non appearance of Fanny, or anyone to whom he could communicate what he desired, he found himself called upon to give his version of the story.

As we have seen before, Sharpley was no coward, and now that he knew that his life depended upon his address and courage, his bravery did not desert him.

CHAPTER XXXVIII.

SHARPLEY gave a clear and distinct account of the fatal evening, concealing, of course, his own villainy, and making it seem as if the old Jew had attacked him without cause.

He accused those who had been with him in the transaction of having made false statements for the purpose of saving themselves from punishment, and threw himself on the mercy of the Court.

"I have lived," he added, as honestly as I could; but in these times honesty is a difficult trade, and, in fact I found it almost impossible to stick to it. If, however, I have done things at times worse than another, it has been at the bidding of other people. These people I shall not name now, but I may do so, eventually. In the meantime I declare myself wholly innocent of this crime, and throw myself entirely on your merciful consideration."

He gloried in the uneasiness which he saw plainly visible in the manner of the impostor as he hinted at the possibility of his betraying the names of his employers.

But what he saw with most pleasure was that his clear, succinct account of the scene at the house of the Jew had made an evident impression on the minds of all in court.

Time went on.

Half-an-hour passed, and—while yet no sign of Fanny or Mat had appeared—the court delivered judgment.

Glorious uncertainty of the law!

The verdict was—

"NOT GUILTY!"

A spasm of emotion was observable on Sharpley's face when he heard it.

Then the blood rushed up into his face, and he glanced in triumph round him.

But the best thing that occurred to him was the change within him.

"I am saved," cried the new spirit in his heart. "Providence has given me a chance of redeeming the past, and I will do it!"

There was a strange commotion and gathering among the members of the Hebrew fraternity, when the verdict was given; but they had heard it, knew it was impossible to reverse it, and accordingly, shuffled off quickly, lest they might waste a moment's more time in their business.

Sharpley was at once set free, and, as may be imagined, made his way in all haste for the door of the court.

Only once did his evil passions get the better of him.

This was when he caught sight of the two approvers glancing at him with looks of evident fear.

For an instant the thought crossed him—

"I will wait and give those fellows their due."

Then his better genius whispered—

"No, no; you are permitted to live for something better."

And accordingly he cast upon them a look of ineffable contempt, and passed away.

Lord Housden hurried from the court before him; and as Sharpley, the observed of all observers, made his way along the road, he pointed him out to some armed ruffians who were concealed in a dark archway.

"You see him," he said; "before morning bring me proof of his death, and a hundred gold pieces shall be yours."

" ONLY TELL ME YOU ARE INNOCENT, AND I'LL BELIEVE YOU,' SHE CRIED."

CHAPTER XXXIX.

SHARPLEY ACTS ON HIS OWN ACCOUNT.

WITH Harold Forrester in prison again, and, of course, guarded with more jealous care than ever; with Mat o' the Mist and the others hidden, he knew not where, the task to which Sharpley had devoted himself was truly a difficult one.

Nevertheless, he did not experience the slightest approach to faltering, and he resolved at once to hurry home, and fashion a feasible plan for his future guidance.

He had not observed the by-play on the part of Lord Housden and his men, of which he was the object; but, nevertheless, he was certain that he would be the subject of his old patron's revenge, and, knowing the style and the means which he had always adopted to further his detestable ends, he was very careful as to the company that followed him home.

The men to whom Lord Housden had given the mission of murder were, however, in no hurry to perform his bidding.

The reward he had offered for their villainous task was a good one.

One readily seized upon, and one readily and willingly earned.

Yet not to be lost by hurry.

So they watched him home, saw that he could remain there for the night, and planned the murder for the following night. They were boastful and reliant.

There were six of them, strong, active villains, up to any kind of ruffianism and cold-blooded crime; and what could *one* man do against so many?

Sharpley, meanwhile, on arriving home, saw a sight which astounded him.

Well it might.

Fanny and Mat o' the Mist, sitting by a comfortable fire, with a mess ready on the table near them.

He started back in surprise.

"Why, what on earth——," he began.

But he had no time to say more.

In an instant Fanny was upon his breast, weeping, laughing, and then weeping again, and it was some time before they subsided into anything like sober senses again.

When they did, however, Sharpley's face beamed with satisfaction.

"I'd hardly have believed it possible that things should have turned out so exactly as I could have wished them," he said; "but, there, I've given over my old ways, and resolved to begin a new course, and so, I suppose, things are going to take a new turn with me also."

He thought too greatly of this.

Almost as if he ought to be rewarded for doing right, after a long life of misdoing.

However, there was one thing certain.

He had really made up his mind to commence a life of right doing, and failure would not daunt him.

He explained at once to Mat o' the Mist the same that he had told Harold.

"No delay must be allowed to take place now," he said, in conclusion. "The queen is nearing the hour of her death, I am certain, and she becomes more vicious and more angry every day. There is no knowing how soon Harold may fall beneath the axe of the executioner, and the disclosures in regard to his parentage must be made at once, that it may fall like a thunder-bolt upon her and her impostor favourite."

"I will start, then, at once," said Mat o' the Mist. "And you?"

"I shall only be in your way," said Sharpley. "I shall be watched by the emissaries of Lord Housden, and, no matter where I may be, I shall not be safe. No, I will remain here in London; here in this place and scarcely stir from it. You will know where to find me, and I will appear, depend upon it, the instant my voice can be raised for good. But tell me, how did you know that Harold was taken, and how did you come hither."

Mat at once explained how his suspicions had been aroused.

"When I left the prison," he added, "I knew not what to do or whither to go, and was about to give up in despair and wait till to-day, and then enter the Court and chance being recognised, when I met this lady."

"She heard my wishes with alarm.

"What!" she said; "go to the Court and be recognised? You will be known at once. No, no; rather let *me* go thither in disguise and you remain at Sharpley's.'

"Were you then in Court, Fanny?" asked Sharpley in surprise.

"I was—in male attire. No one knew me; no one observed me, in fact at all; and though I nearly fainted with joy to hear of your acquittal, I restrained myself, and hurried away alone to this place to be here to greet you. I knew not what might be construed from a meeting in the street. So you see, love has made me heroic."

Mat took his leave.

He had learned all.

Good news and bad alike; he had found out as much as he could, and the next thing was to act.

He said adieu, therefore, at once.

He even shook Sharpley by the hand.

To him that hand was only that of an old enemy.

The owner of it had been acquitted of a murder, and he naturally, therefore, regarded him as innocent.

Fanny had done so all along; and when, therefore, Mat had gone, she gave full vent to her joy.

She sprang upon his knee, clasped her arm round his neck, and kissed him again and again.

"Dear—dear!" she said. "Oh! how glad I am that you are here safe once more. Oh! I forgive you all the past! I know you have been sinful and foolish; but you'll never be so again. Tell me—tell me you never will. For my sake say so!"

"My girl," said Sharpley, "I can promise it with my whole heart. When I stood in the dock a strange change came over me as the words were pronounced that told me of my safety; and depend upon it, if I starve for it, I will never go into evil ways again."

You may imagine how he was rewarded for those sentences of contrition.

And you may imagine, too, how sweet were the kisses that rained upon him from her clinging lips; how exquisite the pleasure, as those warm arms encircled him.

Yet presently the thought occurred to him—

"Am I worthy of all this?"

And he put her away from him gently.

"Fanny," he said, "it is getting late, and your friends will wonder where you are. Come and see me again to-morrow evening."

She was grieved at the sadness which had so suddenly taken the place of his joy; but she was overburthened with joy herself to take such a thing to her heart.

"Poor fellow! I've no doubt he has enough to worry his brain," she thought; and so she pressed him once more to her pretty, fluttering bosom, promised to come again next night, and was gone.

Sharpley heaved a sigh as she departed.

A change so wonderful had come over his spirit, that he could scarcely sometimes believe in his own identity.

He congratulated himself upon this, as being a kind of foreshadowing of a new life.

He never dreamed that it might be the warning of a more awful change still!

"Well, well," he said, rising after a moment from the seat he had occupied by the fire, and drinking off a large glassful of spirits, "well, well, I mustn't delay here. I know what is my duty, and I'll do it. It was no good my hampering their movements by the presence of a proscribed devil like me; but if I can do it by myself, I'm bound to try."

CHAPTER XL.

THE SHEPHERD.

No one who had taken the trouble to observe the man who, about ten o'clock on that night issued from Sharpley's house, would have imagined that it was that worthy himself.

He was good at disguises.

When in the employment of the impostor Housden, he had been compelled always, at the slightest notice, to launch out into some desperate adventure which required the use of sagacity as well as courage, and he had adopted, consequently, nearly every possible disguise save that of a female.

In other instances he had not considered it necessary for him to adopt any secrecy with his landlord.

But in this case it was different.

He desired to have it imagined that he was still within.

So, having assumed the garb of an old man—not only old, but decrepid—he lit his lamp, placed it conspicuously near his window, and crept down the stairs towards a gate which led to a backyard.

From this there was a mode of egress into the street.

On arriving here, a bold thought struck him.

He desired to see the efficacy of his disguise.

How then could he do this better than by knocking at his own door and asking for himself?

He accordingly proceeded at once to put this plan into execution.

Hastening to the front door with a hobbling gait, he knocked.

The landlord came grumbling to the door.

Sharpley knew well there was no fear of this man's ascending to the room.

He had left strict orders that he was, on no account, to be disturbed.

"What is it you want?" asked the landlord, gruffly.

"Is Master Sharpley at home?" inquired the supposed visitor.

"Yes; and he won't see any one."

"Are you sure?"

"Quite sure. Come again in the morning."

Sharpley was standing during this in the full glare of a lamp.

It was evident his disguise was impenetrable.

"Very good," he said, as he turned to go, "I will return in the morning."

The door was then closed, and he was just making his way somewhat hurriedly from the house, when two men came out upon him from a shadowy corner, where they had been lying in wait, and where they must, consequently, have heard all that had been said.

"One moment, master," said one of them. "Didn't I hear you ask for Sharpley?"

Sharpley looked intently at them.

"Yes, I did," he answered, at the same time grasping a pistol in his pocket; "What then?"

"Oh, no offence, old fellow," replied the man. "Only we wanted to see him, and if he's out, why one might as well sheer off."

"He is not out," replied Sharpley; "he is in his room, so the landlord says, and refuses to see anyone. You'd better knock and see."

And then, with a slight inclination of the head he turned to go.

The men made no attempt to stay him on his way.

They had entirely failed to recognise him, and yet, when Sharpley had placed some distance between himself and them, he gave a sigh of relief.

"I need fear no more," he said, "those fellows little think that their imprudence has saved my life, and spoiled their plans of villainy."

He had, in fact, recognised in those who addressed him, two of Lord Housden's men: former companions; now they longed for his blood!

This meeting proved to him more than ever the necessity of haste.

He knew now that Lord Housden was on the watch to destroy him, and he must, consequently, be more eager and rapid in his movements.

Arriving presently at a waste piece of ground, he dived into the darkness, and threw off his disguise entirely.

At the place where he was going recognition was necessary to effect his end, and for a short time at any rate, he had his time before him.

As soon as he had disposed of his disguise, he hurried towards a tavern where he was well-known, and where he knew he could borrow a horse, and was soon dashing away at full speed towards a dark and unfrequented road.

He did not spare his horse.

Away he went in spite of the desperate gloom of the night.

Away, away, with the will and energy of one who knows that life and death depend upon his haste.

It was not at such a very late hour, therefore, that he arrived at the sign of the Orton Arms, which he had spoken of to Harold.

A sign had long ago been agreed

upon between Sharpley and the landlord when anything had to be done in private.

So, when he entered the bar and ordered his glass, he made the sign, and as soon as he had drank, he walked carelessly towards the rear of the premises, and was there joined by Boniface after a few minutes.

"Well, what brings you hither?" cried the latter. "Your master, Lord Housden, was only here yesterday."

Sharpley could scarcely repress a start of surprise and alarm.

But he did, nevertheless.

"I am aware of it," he said, "but a few circumstances may entirely alter everything. He has commissioned me with a most difficult task; but, tell me, has he seen *him?*"

The last word was spoken with a peculiar pronunciation, as if to express something secret.

In fact, Sharpley had a reason for being vague.

This being really the first he had heard of a visit of Lord Housden to his father, he might compromise himself greatly by pretending to what he knew nothing of.

Lord Housden, in fact, might have removed his father from the old place of concealment, and in that case his present visit was utterly useless.

"Yes, he saw him," returned the landlord, "but nothing of any consequence occurred. I know that he was there, and that was all."

"Well, that's what I understood, myself," said Sharpley, "from what instructions he gave me, it seems that the old fellow is getting very unmanageable. However, where's the shepherd?—I'm going over."

The landlord grinned.

"Well, if you're going over there," he said, "it strikes me you'll have to go alone."

"Why?"

"Look in here."

He pushed open a door as he spoke, and Sharpley looked in.

There, seated by a fire asleep, evidently no natural slumber, but the effect of heavy drink—was the shepherd.

"He's been drinking then," said Sharpley, secretly delighted, but speaking in an angry tone; "what am I to do? If I were to return to London and tell Lord Housden that I had not seen *him* to-night, my very life would not be safe. How am I to get across the moor without his guidance? It is as dark as pitch everywhere."

"Well, I don't know what you'll do," replied the landlord; "but you can see at once that he's no good, and you can't go alone."

"No, no!" said Sharpley, "I must chance it. But I have not the key! Here, Margrave—here, wake up!"

A drunken grunt was the only answer.

Another shake, and he opened his eyes.

"What do you want—what are you disturbing me for, eh? What! Sharpley."

"Aye, Sharpley," cried that worthy; "what's the meaning of this? I have a message from Lord Housden to his father, and here you are too drunk to guide me. Out with the key and let me go."

The shepherd put on a look of intoxicated cleverness.

"No—no!" he spluttered. "Lord Housden has warned me against you. You are an artful card. He was here last night and bade me beware."

Sharpley purposely, as he spoke, upset the glass which stood on the table near.

He had no desire that the landlord should hear these words.

Fortunately, however, Boniface had made for the door in consequence of some disturbance without, and now approaching, said—

"Well, I'll leave you to settle this affair between you. I'm wanted."

And so he went.

Just in time.

Another moment, and the shepherd, drunk as he was, would have told all.

"Come Margrave," cried Sharpley, "be quick and let me have the keys. I'm in haste."

The shepherd stood up, staggering terribly.

"Keys," he said; "no. I give up no keys. You are a traitor. Lord Housden has told me all. Help, help, there——"

He had no time to say more.

His voice had no sooner been raised than Sharpley, who saw him fumbling about for a weapon, dealt him a tremendous blow in the face with his fist, which sent him headlong to the ground.

Then he struck his head violently, and lay senseless.

Sharpley waited a moment before attempting to act in any way.

The shepherd was a heavy man, and the sound of his fall was great.

But, somehow, fortune seemed to smile on Sharpley's efforts.

The noise outside in the tavern bar was so incessant that no one observed it, and in a few moments the adventurer, therefore, had searched the pockets of the recumbent man, and obtained what he required.

Then he quietly issued from the room,

took another glass at the bar, and left the inn.

"I don't envy you your journey," said the landlord, as he went out.

He laughed.

Things were at present going on so well with him that he felt in good spirits.

"Oh, it's nothing," he said. "I know the way pretty well. Good-night."

"Good-night."

And so he went out into the darkness, making his way quickly from the high road into rough lands, and up rugged paths and steep hills.

CHAPTER XLI.

THE SCENE IN THE MOUNTAIN HUT.

THE hut where the father of the impostor had so long been immured was situated on the slope of a wild succession of hills, open unto the chilly blasts of the east wind.

It had at one time been inhabited by a man and his family, but for a long time only one chamber in it had been used, and that by one who was powerless to leave it—the wretched steward of the Housden estates.

The place was built in the most wretched and primitive manner.

It was, in fact, little better than a hut formed of mud and rough stones.

Any man in possession of all his strength and freedom could, of course, have easily forced his way out of it.

But he had the will and strength, without the means of using them.

The room, if such a term could be applied to such a miserable hovel, was about ten feet square.

The floor was the bare ground, and to a thick post in the centre of this was chained a man.

A man reduced to a living skeleton, yet whose eyes burned with a fire that seemed to tell that he lived in the hope of one day achieving a purpose.

What was that purpose but one?

The punishment of the son for whom he had sinned, and who requited him with chains and dungeon.

A fire burned in a little grate on one side, where a very small modicum of heat could reach him, while a bed of some coarse material was so placed that he could throw himself upon it whenever he designed.

For food he depended upon the shepherd.

And a bad dependence that was.

The man brought him food often, but then he often forgot it, so that sometimes, for days together, he was without sustenance.

To give Lord Housden his due, that was not part of his orders.

He did not desire his father's death.

Or rather a superstitious dislike of being himself instrumental in bringing it about.

He, therefore, gave Margrave strict instructions that, in spite of all other things, his father should always be supplied with the best of everything.

On the evening on which Sharpley was hurrying towards him through the darkness, he was sitting moodily before his fast-dying fire, looking into the flames and fashioning, maybe, among their fantastic leapings and twirlings, visions of old days—now gone for ever.

Suddenly a rush of feet was heard above the moaning of the wind.

CHAPTER XLII.

SHARPLEY'S END.

THERE was a loud clattering in the adjoining room, and then the door was quickly opened, and Sharpley entered, breathless.

"I am—pursued—curse them!" he cried, gaspingly, as he reclosed the door, and proceeded to barricade it.

The prisoner, for a moment, glanced at the intruder in amazement.

To one in his position, anyone entering his place of concealment in such a manner would have been an object of suspicion.

But a cloud settled on his brow as he recognised Sharpley.

The latter, in fact, had always been to him a bitter enemy.

He knew him in the first instance as the easily bought tool of his son, and willing, and even apparently eager, to carry out any of his evil wishes.

Now, of course, he naturally looked upon his arrival as a token of some fresh evil and disaster for him.

"Bird of ill-omen," he said, "why are you here? What fresh ill-luck have you brought me?"

"No ill-luck," returned Sharpley, speaking rapidly. "I am no longer in your son's service—I come to save you—to set you free—now—this night."

"You jest—you jest at my misery," cried the wretched man.

He had been so long in misery that he could not believe so sudden a revolution of events.

"No, no! As heaven is above us, no!" almost shouted Sharpley; "but there is one condition."

"Name it, name it," said the other, feverishly.

"That you will swear before the Eternal Being who has to judge you—you know not how soon—that you will reinstate the rightful Lord Housden in his property, and expose the imposture of your son."

"Yes, yes, I swear it—I swear it! But how can this be done?—I know not."

"I will tell you all; but interrupt me not, for your son's bloodhounds are on my track. Even now as I hurried over the hills I heard the sounds of pursuers, and I know not how many they may be. While, therefore, I release you from your bonds, I will tell you all."

But the bonds which held the impostor's father were strongly forged, and the file was still rasping—rasping, when he had told the whole of his story.

The legs of the prisoner were free, but not his hands.

"You have sworn to do all this?" said Sharpley, eagerly.

"Aye—so help me, heaven! Let me do this right, and I shall die happy."

Had Sharpley been an even worse man than he was, it would have required a most incredulous mind to disbelieve him.

There was no mistaking his earnestness, and Sharpley laboured away with a will.

Just as one of the hand-fetters was off, the sound of men's voices were plainly to be heard close to the hut.

They were shouting to each other, as if in encouragement.

Sharpley's hands trembled for an instant, but then, with a savage kind of resolution, he worked away again.

"Stand up," he said, "or your legs may be cramped, and you will not be able to escape. There—so—lean forward, so that I can work the file more readily."

"But tell me," whispered the old man, "what is your plan? If these men are here in search of me, how can we defend ourselves against a whole crew of them, when I am, in fact, without arms?"

Sharpley smiled.

It was not a smile of derision; nor a genial one either.

It was the smile of one who sees that a supreme moment has arrived, and is resolved, in spite of all, to do what is right.

"Fear not," he said; "your safety will not have to be battled for. They will knock loudly at the door and demand admittance, which you will refuse. They will then commence to batter down the door, and if you are not then free, the sound of the file will be drowned in the noise. As soon as you are free, you can rush up yonder ladder, and drop from the roof outside. As soon as you reach the ground, fly for your life."

"But you ?"

"Oh, I!" laughed Sharpley, bitterly, "leave me to myself."

It was the laugh of one who had made up his mind for the worst that could happen.

He had no wish, truly, for death.

But he feared it not now if he had to die while engaged in doing good.

As he uttered these words the sound of voices came near, and a loud knock came at the door.

In an instant Sharpley put out the lamp.

"I can work just as well in the dark," said Sharpley, in an excited whisper.

And away he worked eagerly in the dark.

"Open here," shouted a loud voice. "Open, or we shall batter the door down."

"Courage, friend," whispered Sharpley, "and when I have done fly and think no more of me."

"Open here," again was shouted, and then heavy blows were heard on the door.

But still steadily rasp, rasp, rasp went the file, while the hard breathing of the two excited men, and the very beating of their hearts could be heard in the little room.

One more link was worn through.

There was only one now remaining.

What if this last link should bind them to misery, after all!

"Curse them! Break down the door," shouted a voice which both knew, but the sound of which sent a terrible chill to the mind of one of them.

It was that of Lord Housden.

Sharpley's heart beat quicker at this; but he delayed not.

On he went, rasp—rasp—rasp, working away till the sweat stood out like large beads on his forehead.

Now a loud crash came at the door, and the timbers shivered again.

"It is of no use," said the old man, whose limbs were now trembling with fear and excitement. "They will soon break in, and death then awaits us both."

"No, no," said Sharpley, eagerly.

"No; courage, courage! In a few moments I shall have finished. Remember all I have told you. As for me, I fear me the end of all is come. But—"

As he spoke, another tremendous blow on the door sent some splinters flying about in the darkness.

There was evidently not a second to lose.

"Quick," said Sharpley, "take the file and finish this yourself. I must defend the door."

So saying, he placed the file in the hands of the steward, and rushing to the door, placed his shoulder against it in such a manner as to form a kind of prop.

Every blow now dug into his flesh, and sent a quiver of agony through his frame.

But he yielded not an inch.

He had resolved to risk all, even life, in this effort, and the agony only made him the more determined that his enemies should not triumph over him at the last moment.

Finding that they were now resisted still more than before, the assailants, lighting flambeaux to enable them better to see their work, directed a perfect shower of blows against the door, driving it further into Sharpley's flesh, and turning him sick and faint, in spite of all his resolution.

A few minutes more, and he saw plainly he must yield.

"Quicker, quicker," he whispered; "my strength fails."

Another minute passed.

One of intense excitement and agony.

Then he heard the file drop.

"It is done," said the steward.

"Fly! fly then!" cried Sharpley, "by the ladder yonder, and may heaven protect you!"

"And you—you, my deliverer ? "

"Go; wait not for me. I will follow presently. Go quickly, for I can hold out no longer."

The steward delayed no more, but, rushing up the narrow ladder, disappeared.

The silence remained unbroken without.

Evidently no suspicion was excited.

Another minute passed, and then a combined and vigorous dash was made upon the door.

Further resistance was in vain.

In fact, to have remained in his present position would have been simply to court insensibility and death.

Suddenly springing back, therefore, he drew his sword, just as the door was flung in almost upon him, and a crowd of armed men, some bearing torches, rushed in upon him.

Lord Housden turned ghastly pale when he saw that the prisoner was no longer there.

"Villain!" he shouted, dashing at Sharpley; "where is the captive?"

Sharpley kept him at sword's length.

"Your father," he cried, in a voice which all could hear, "whom you have villainously immured in this lonely dungeon so long, has long since escaped, and is now beyond your power. Tremble, wretch, for your downfall is at hand; and in the hour of your ruin, remember that I, whom you sought to murder, have been the instrument of it."

Lord Housden, almost foaming at the mouth with rage, said no more, but attacked him furiously, while some of the men spread themselves about in search of the fugitive.

Housden, however, had no idea of conquering Sharpley in a fair fight.

Finding that the latter was becoming far too strong for him, he shouted to his men to aid him, and in another instant Sharpley found himself attacked by four at once. He saw plainly now that his last hour was come.

No help was near—no possibility existed of its arriving.

All he could do was to sell his life as dearly as possible, and most of his thrusts consequently were aimed at Housden.

But such a conflict could be but of short duration.

The odds were too great; and wounded as he was by the sharp woodwork of the door, he soon began to feel the deadly faintness caused by loss of blood.

He made one more desperate lunge at his special enemy, and wounded him severely in the shoulder; then the place seemed to turn with him, and pierced by three swords at once, Sharpley fell with a groan, and rolled over upon the ground—dead!

A smile of happiness was, in spite of his fearful end, visible upon his lips.

He believed himself to have redeemed the past—and let us hope he did.

"Leave that carrion here," cried Lord Housden, "and search high and low for the fugitive. The blow that accursed fellow's sword has inflicted on me has made me feel sick and faint. Seek high and low; the old fellow cannot have fled far, and if you find him, kill him, without a word!"

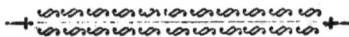

CHAPTER XLIII.

WHAT PASSED BETWEEN HOUSDEN AND REDCLIFFE AT WAPPING.

SEEK the men did, urged on by Housden's repeated promises of reward.

The men now with him did not thoroughly know the man who led them, or it is certain they would have taken no notice of his promises.

The hut and the surrounding acres were carefully searched, but no trace of the escaped steward could be found.

One of the men suggested that the hut may contain some secret exit.

"If I thought so," said Housden, with a bitter imprecation, "I would raze it to the ground. But I am certain that it does not. Nay; he got away with the help of yonder ladder. But no matter. I shall yet have him."

"At any rate," he thought, "I feel far safer than I did a short time ago. Sharpley can tell no tales now. At one time I thought I could find no better man; but I was mistaken. Fool that I was not to have taken Redcliffe into my service. As soon as I return to London I will seek him."

Aloud he said—

"Come—let us leave this place. But wait," he added, as he took a link from the hand of one of the men. "Collect the smaller articles of furniture and break them up."

Speedily the men did this, and placed the pile in the centre of the hut.

Immediately Housden thrust the link

at the bottom of the pile, and, with a grim, sardonic smile, watched it until the flames shot upward.

When the flames had taken a firm hold he beckoned to the men to depart, and the party at once made their way towards where they had left their horses, that was, fastened to the trees beside one of the many deep, dark, and dismal pools which abounded in this part of the country.

They had just reached it, gliding like shadows in and out of the trees, when they observed a man rushing towards them.

At first they could not understand what he was shouting as he ran, but in a few moments they made out that it was "Fire!"

He was, of course, attracted by the fire at the hut, and which was now burning furiously, and lighting up the dark country in every direction.

Housden motioned to his men to stand aside, for he did not wish them to be seen.

The next moment the man was close beside Housden, still running and shouting with all his might.

As he came on a level, the light from the distant fire fell full upon his features.

Instantaneously, with a wild cry, Housden, sword in hand, dashed upon him, seized him by the throat with one hand, and bore him backwards.

"Wretch!" he said, "I am not mistaken—it is Margrave."

Aye, he was not mistaken; it was the shepherd whom he had selected to watch over his father, and who continually neglected his charge to get drunk.

But he was not drunk on this occasion.

Nay, he appeared to be perfectly sober.

At any rate he immediately recognised Housden.

Clasping his hands frantically together, he implored for mercy.

"Ay, I'll mercy you, curse you!" thundered Housden. "Villain, this is what you call minding the man I placed in your charge."

"I did mind him," gasped Margrave, his wide-open, terrified eyes seeming ready to start from his head, "but Sharpley——"

"Did I not warn you against him?"

"Yes, yes; but he nearly murdered me, and——"

"He did not kill you. Nay, that was left for me to do. A man that betrays me dies!"

As he spoke he deliberately passed his blade through Margrave's heart.

With a low moaning cry the man fell to the ground, his last words being an appeal to heaven for vengeance.

The men with Housden were certainly astonished at what had been done.

But they knew better than utter a word, and when Housden told them to raise the murdered man they did not offer to disobey.

Margrave was taken to the edge of the pool, and placed down for a moment.

Housden then directed the men to pick up a large and very heavy stone, and, with a piece of rope fasten it to his body.

This was speedily done, and then the unfortunate shepherd was lifted, swung backwards and forwards for a few moments, and then thrown into the pool.

The body sank like a piece of iron.

"Good!" muttered Housden, with a low, demoniacal chuckle. "Another removed. Ha! nothing is better than removing a man when you no longer require him. The old saying that dead men tell no tales, I always have, and always will, treat with the most profound respect."

The horses were mounted, and the party made their way towards the Orton Arms, Housden taking particular care to be the last, so that, in case it might be required, he would have a better chance to run. However, not a soul was met with on the road.

At the tavern door stood the host, watching the flames in the distance.

He also at once recognised Housden, and hastened to bow respectfully.

Then he ran to the horse's head and held it while his lordship dismounted.

The host did not have to look twice at him to see that he was in a furious temper.

The men were about to dismount—for of course they thought themselves entitled to some refreshment—when Housden stopped them.

"Wait," he said; "at present I have no further need of your services."

The men started in astonishment.

But they did not think it worth while to make any remark.

Had they questioned him they considered it quite possible that they would forfeit their reward.

They were correct, too.

"In a minute or two," continued Housden, "the host will bring you out each the sum agreed upon, and having partaken of what you desire without dismounting, you can make your way to London."

So saying, he entered the hostelry, beckoning to the host to follow him.

"Have you seen Sharpley lately?" he asked as soon as he had seated himself.

The host at once knew that something extraordinary had happened.

His reply was immediate.

"Not lately," he said.

"Sure?"

His lordship's fierce eyes were fixed full upon the host's face.

The latter, fortunately, did not quail.

"Certain," he said, "unless he has been here disguised."

"When did you last see Margrave?"

"Not very long ago. In fact, it was a short time ago, only. He suddenly caught sight of the fire over yonder, and, thinking it was the hut on fire, he rushed off like the wind. *Is* it the hut?"

"It is. The prisoner managed to release himself and escape. But before he went, he set fire to the hut. You have not seen him?"

"No. He would not come here, because he must know I should detain him."

"Five hundred gold pieces for you if you can succeed in tracing him. Without money, without friends, he cannot travel far."

"You may depend upon it that I will keep my eyes open. In fact, I will cause inquiries to be made in every direction."

"And your reward will be certain. In the meantime, you heard what I said to those men?"

"That you would hand them a certain amount each? Yes."

"The amount is twenty crowns each."

The host bowed.

He had not the faintest suspicion of what was about to follow.

"Well, continued Housden with all the coolness in the world, "it so happens that I have no money with me."

The host stared.

"Then, I ask your pardon," he said, "of course, they cannot be paid."

"Yes, they can, easily. *You* will produce what money you have."

The startled host might have been knocked down with a feather.

But, forcing a smile, he said—

"Your lordship is perfectly aware that, were it in my power, I would willingly advance any sum I might——"

"Silence!" was the stern interruption. "You are about to say that you have no money."

"True. And, had I said so, I should have spoken the truth."

"Not so. You would have told a lie."

"How can your lordship expect me to have money when I do no trade worth speaking of?"

"If you have no money of your own, you have money in your possession."

"The devil!" muttered the discomfited host, "how did he know?"

Housden continued, but not too quick, for he gloried in the man's uneasiness.

"Yesterday, at a certain hostelry about ten miles from here, I saw a man whom I know to be a travelling goldsmith.

"I heard him tell a person that he was coming on here to deliver a certain sum of money to you, which money you were to hand to a certain person as soon as he claimed it."

"I cannot deny what you say. The money *was* left with me, but I cannot touch what is another's."

Housden burst into a loud, ironical laugh.

"Since when," he sneered, "have you turned over such a new leaf? Time was when you took a delight in thrusting your infernal fingers into another man's pockets. You know what I mean?"

"I do. But you forgave me for that."

"Yes, and placed you here, for the simple reason that it struck me you might one day be of service. The day and the hour has come. Produce the money, or you remain here but little longer."

There was no getting out of it.

The host, like plenty more, was in the power of this fiend.

He must obey, or abide the consequences.

With a deep sigh he withdrew.

Reappearing after a few moments, he placed a small oaken, brass-bound box before Housden.

Housden opened it and found that it contained quite enough money for his purpose.

Counting out the various lots, he handed the coin to the host, telling him to pay the men.

This the host at once did, and Housden heard them ride away.

"They have gone," said the host, returning; "they took the money, but without thanks. They do not appear to be at all satisfied, for when I asked them what they would drink, they made no reply."

Housden laughed.

"Here," he said, "is the box. All that you have to do is to guarantee to the owner that the person who borrowed the money from you will faithfully repay it. And I will give you a handsome bonus for yourself. Now, a bottle of wine, and I must set out."

"You are wounded, I fancy."

"Slightly only. I shall be attended to as soon as I reach London."

"The roads are sometimes dangerous."

"Aye; and so am I."

The host said no more.

He procured the wine, and his lordship, having partaken of what he required, mounted his horse and set out for London.

At first he went at a walking pace, for he was thinking of what next he would do.

But at last he put spurs to his horse, and rode on at a gallop.

"Yes," he muttered, "I must employ Redcliffe. He is the man. I certainly was a fool not to accept his services when he offered them long ago. Had I done so, Harold Forrester, and all my enemies, might have been slain; while the girl I covet—but she shall yet be mine! I will possess her if I have to spend every shilling I possess in the attempt."

* * * *

At the period of this story, Wapping was not the busy place it now is; nor did it contain a fiftieth part of its present population.

Also where there is now a hundred houses, there was then but one or two.

The greater number—all of wood, with one exception, and constructed in the most extraordinary manner — were situated near the river.

Originally the houses were built for, and inhabited by, watermen, who got their living in a more or less honest fashion; but, gradually, they shifted their quarters, and the houses were speedily taken possession of by a lot of ruffians, who acknowledged as their "chief," a man of the name of Redcliffe —or, as his men pronounced it, "Red-Cliffe."

The exception in the long row of dirty wooden houses was the one in the occupation of this man.

It was called the "Parson's Retreat;" the reason being that at one period, it was in the occupation of the Vicar of Wapping.

It was a very large house, built of stone and brick, though the quaintly-constructed balconies were of British oak.

The front looked out upon a narrow—and always filthy—lane, leading to the high-road, though both ends were guarded against the intrusion of strangers by badly-constructed wooden gates.

The back faced the river, the steps leading from the yard always touching the black water.

It was freely said that in this house many terrible crimes had been committed, but the authorities could never bring anything home to the occupants.

The night following Lord Housden's visit to the "Orton Arms," Redcliffe, for a wonder, was "at home."

He was seated in one of the rooms on the ground floor.

A fine chamber it was, though somewhat small, with a very high-vaulted ceiling and stained glass windows, though numbers of them, being broken in many a fierce fight, had been mended with rags and paper.

Of what could be called furniture there was none.

A large, cranky deal table in the centre of the carpetless apartment was the most prominent article the room contained.

A huge fire of logs burned brightly on the broad hearth, and before it, smoking a pipe of tobacco—then but just introduced into this country—stood Redcliffe, or, as he preferred to be called, "Captain" Redcliffe.

He was somewhat tall and stout, but decidedly awkward, for he had a habit of standing more on his left leg than his right.

A more coarse, bloated, and brutal-looking wretch it would have been difficult to discover in London, or, perhaps, anywhere else.

He was attired in what, at one time, no doubt, had been a very handsome doublet. Very likely he had stolen it from one of his victims.

Now, however, it was faded and wine-stained, while in many places unskilful fingers had tried to mend it.

He wore black hose and somewhat high boots, armed with long spurs.

A long, basket-hilted sword was the only weapon he carried, but there were several weapons upon the rickety table, mixed with wine bottles and food.

Beside a bracket—Redcliffe called it a "candelabra"—into which was stuck a dozen tapers, lay a letter.

It was from Housden, and intimated that Redcliffe might expect him at the hour of ten.

But the note was not signed "Housden," or even "H."

Nay, the initial was "A," which, of course, signified Alsdon.

"Ten," muttered Redcliffe, as the chimes of Old St. Paul's were wafted across the waters to his ears. "Well, I suppose I must wait another hour. Ten, of course, means eleven or twelve.

"No matter, I will wait. Rather! Important business should not call me out.

"So he is about to knuckle under at last, eh? No doubt of it, else why this letter?

"But I wonder what has become of Sharpley? We shall—— Hillo!" he roared, as a loud knock came upon the door, "who the devil, is it?"

The door opened, and a small, red-headed, ragged little boy popped his head in.

"Gentleman to see you. Think it's the one you expects."

"Show him in," said Redcliffe.

He remained at the fireplace, and still continued to puff the smoke from his pipe.

Another moment, and a cloaked figure entered.

"Glad to see you, Master Alsdon," said Redcliffe. "Take a seat."

"Put down that pipe, otherwise I cannot remain here."

"No? You don't like it? Ah! you'll alter your opinion some day."

"It is scarcely likely. But let us to business."

"To business it is."

"Listen. It is possible I may accept the offer you made me some time ago."

Redcliffe bowed.

"I am your man," he said. "And there's not a better man in London to transact secret business. By the way, have you seen anything of Sharpley?"

"Have you?"

"No—not since his trial. I saw him a month before his capture. That was at the "Red Cross" on the bridge, and there I succeeded in twisting a score of crowns out of him at the table. I cheated him as as easy as possible and, by the Virgin, he had not the faintest suspicion of it. That proves what a fool he is Ho, ho!"

"Was, you mean," said Housden.

"Was?"

"Ay, was."

"You have seen him then?"

"Yes, and have done what the law failed to do."

"What! killed him?"

"Ay, killed him!"

Redcliffe stared and seemed confused. But it was only for a moment.

Then he said—

"In fair fight, of course?"

"Yes; on this occasion it was in fair fight. But you must understand that, if I feel inclined to make away with a man who is an obstacle, I do not stand upon ceremony."

"Nay, nor do I," said Redcliffe, slowly, as he placed his pipe down, and seated himself very carefully on the edge of a chair; "but let us see now if we can come to some arrangement, my lord."

Housden started up.

"Why do you say that?" he asked.

"What?"

"My lord."

"Because I know that you are Lord

Housden; though I must admit you are cleverly, although simply, disguised as one Alsdon."

"Let me tell you that you make———"

"My lord, if we are to transact *business* together, let us be open and above board to each other. It will be all the better. I can keep your secret, of course, and my men would only know you as Alsdon."

Housden hesitated a moment.

Then he said—

"Be it so. I need not ask, however, who told you who I really am. It was Sharpley."

Redcliffe shook his head.

"You are wrong," he said; "I never *could* get anything from Sharpley. I don't suppose he preserved your secrets out of pure love for you. No; it was because he fancied I might take his place. But now, my—I mean, Master Alsdon—what is the first business you wish to place in my hands?"

"First, you are aware, I pay well?"

"Yes, I *have* heard that much."

"Proof of it," said Housden, as he threw a heavy purse on the table.

An eagle could not have darted upon a rabbit more quickly than Redcliffe pounced upon that purse.

"It contains?" he said.

"Money," was the brief reply.

"Aye, a hundred pieces, perhaps."

"More, I fancy. But you can count it anon. Now, carefully listen to what I say. One of my greatest enemies is one Harold Forrester."

"Forrester? I know him."

"How?"

"Well, I have seen him many times."

"I am glad to hear it. You will not have to establish his identity."

"But why trouble yourself about a person who is already a prisoner?"

"He was a prisoner before—placed in one of the strongest cells in the Tower. Yet he managed to escape, assisted by another of my enemies."

"His name?"

"The Headsman of Old London Bridge. As to his name, no one knows it."

That Redcliffe was considerably affected at the mention of the Headsman was evident at a glance.

He rose, and as he stuffed the purse into a specially constructed cavity in the breast of his doublet, he said—

"He is not only an enemy of yours, but he is of mine. He has foiled me over and over again. I must confess that he appears to be a man possessed of the most extraordinary powers. At any rate, he has been known to glide through———"

"Hish!" interrupted Housden, impatiently; "those wild stories may do for children. They will not do for me. The Headsman, whatever his name, is an ordinary mortal."

"No doubt. But at times he appears to be possessed of the devil's own powers. Upon my soul, I can give you a good instance, and may I lose this purse—which, by the Virgin! I want badly—if what I say is not the truth.

"By order of a certain gentleman, I, some little time ago, received a lady. This lady, you must understand, had designs upon the gentleman. Fact was, it would be greatly to her advantage if he was *removed*.

"Therefore she consulted me.

"But, in the meantime, her intention became known to the gentleman.

"He placed himself in communication with me, and so, when the lady came, I knew what to do.

"I need not tell you what passed, but, in less than an hour, that lady was dead.

"Not my fault, you know. She was thirsty, and drank some wine, which, *unknown* to me, was poisoned.

"She was placed in a sack, with four heavy stones—stones nearly twice her weight—and I and one of my men—my right hand, as I call him, Dick Ralston—took her out by the yard, our intention being to drop her into the middle of the river.

"We had reached the steps, when, on my soul, we were startled to see a tall, dark figure standing upon the steps.

"I should tell a lie if I said we were not alarmed.

"We were so startled that we dropped our burden.

"We looked at the river.

"There was only our own boat. Now, how the fiend, could this man, whom we quickly recognised as the Headsman, have got there without a boat?

"Without saying a word we returned to the house.

"When we came out again, there was

the sack and the stones, but the body of the lady and the Headsman had vanished as completely as if the earth had opened and swallowed them up."

"And your boat had also vanished?" said Housden, with a sneer.

"Nothing of the sort — it was still there."

"Well, was there a sequel to this very extraordinary story?"

"There was; this is it—the body of the lady was restored to her friends."

A light seemed to break in upon Lord Housden.

"Was not the gentleman's name Master Reginald Groome?" he asked.

"It was. And the lady was his wife. You see the reason for all that occurred.

"Master Groome was thirty-five years older than his wife. He was wealthy, and his wife had a lover with nothing."

"What you have told me shows how this accursed Headsman interferes with matters which do not concern him."

"You are correct. But is it not possible that you could do something towards getting him dismissed from the office he holds?"

"I might, but it is not worth while. The queen has a great belief in him. She considers him the very man for the office of executioner. If I attempted to weaken her opinion, she might suspect something."

"True. Well, Harold Forrester, you fancy, will escape with the connivance of the Headsman?"

"I do."

"Then?"

"Think—*think*, man!"

"It would be as well to put the Headsman out of the way?"

"Assuredly. He would not be the first Headsman who has suddenly disappeared."

"He would not," grinned Redcliffe. "Well, in a few hours I shall have formed a plan, and, before I attempt to execute it, I will consult you."

"Do so. Now comes another matter. You know Duke's Palace?"

"Well, and the proprietor, who, I am told, has much neglected his business of late. Then there is his daughter——"

"Eveline," interrupted Housden, "and it is of her I would speak. I may as well tell you plainly that I love her—

that I have sworn she shall be mine, and——"

"But," interrupted Redcliffe, "*what of your wife?*"

Had a thunderbolt fallen at Housden's feet he could not have been more astounded.

With flashing eyes he started up, and, in a voice hoarse with rage, said, as he laid his hand upon the hilt of his sword—

"From whom did you get your information? Answer me, or your life pays the forfeit!"

Redcliffe expressed no alarm—indeed, he smiled grimly as he reached his pipe.

"Do not be rash, my—Master Alsdon," he said; "nothing is gained by it. What does it matter that I know you have a wife? The secret you have so long kept will not be exposed by me.

"Besides, when you say that my life will pay the forfeit if I do not answer, you are only saying what is ridiculous. If I placed my hand on this piece of rope, this chamber would be instantly swarming with men who would do as I told them. But I will tell you who informed me. It was your late secretary."

"The hound!"

"He ran away from you?"

"He did, with a large sum of money."

"Ay, and he lost the whole of it at the 'Red Cross.' There it was I met him. He told me he was quite destitute, and so I took compassion on him and brought him here."

"Where is he now?"

"Dead and buried. He quarrelled with one of the men. There was a fight, and the secretary was killed."

"Well, I see you know more of my affairs than I dreamt of."

"Rely upon it, I will not take advantage of it. But what of Eveline Duke? Where is she now?"

"At Horley House."

"Is it possible?"

"Yes, she is there; but she does not know that I am aware of it. I did not hear of it until to-day."

"Who is she with?"

"I cannot say."

"Leave the matter to me, and you will find that I will place her safely in your arms."

"Do this, and one thousand crowns shall be yours."

"SHARPLEY AT ONCE SEARCHED THE POCKETS OF THE INSENSIBLE MAN."

"SUDDENLY SPRINGING BACK, SHARPLEY DREW HIS SWORD."

Redcliffe's blear eyes twinkled.

A thousand crowns! It was a handsome sum. And it would be paid, too, in the event of success.

Yes, he had just received proof of his lordship's liberality.

Housden rose, drew his heavy cloak about him, and pressed his hat over his eyes.

"You will join me to-morrow night at the 'Manor House' at Charing Cross," he said. "And I shall expect you to have your plans complete."

"I shall devote hours to them. But at what time shall I join you?"

"Ten."

"Good. For whom shall I ask?"

"Lord Housden. Had you not known who I really was, I should have appointed elsewhere."

"I shall be at the 'Manor House' without fail," said Redcliffe, as he brought his hand down upon a small bell.

Almost immediately a man, very much after his own stamp, but evidently more active and powerful, made his appearance.

"My right hand," said Redcliffe—"Dick Ralston."

Ralston bowed very low, but it is needless to say his bow was not returned.

Housden simply nodded.

"Dick," said Redcliffe, "conduct this gentleman to his horse. Assist him to mount, and then see him safely through the gate."

Housden turned and followed Ralston from the house.

Perhaps it was as well his lordship was accompanied to the gate by Ralston; for as they proceeded, he saw several horrible-looking ruffians creeping silently along beside the rotten houses.

They were always ready to levy blackmail, and they cared not who from.

CHAPTER XLIV.

OF THE EXTRAORDINARY FASHION IN WHICH HAROLD IS TAKEN OUT OF PRISON, AND OF HOW HE ESCAPES FROM LAWYER BELLWOOD.

To return to Harold.

Of course, when arrested he considered it certain that he should be kept in the same prison as Sharpley—at any rate, for the present.

He was soon to find out how mistaken he was, and to what extent some men would go for money.

The men, five of whom were attired as soldiers of the queen's guard, while the sixth, the leader, was dressed as a captain, conducted their prisoner down several long and dimly lighted corridors, and, at last, a sleepy warder who followed them, threw back the door of a heavy cell, and Harold was placed within it.

But, to his intense astonishment he was not left alone.

Nay, after a few hurried words, the captain and the warder withdrew, leaving the five men standing at the door.

The warder, hurried on by the surly captain, hastened to the governor's room; and into this the captain was ushered.

The governor was a man of at least seventy—very short, and so bloated, that he could walk only with the greatest difficulty.

Before him, on a small table, was a small slip of parchment, bearing a heavy official stamp.

"Well," said the governor, "are you correct?"

"Quite. It is Harold Forrester, and we have secured him."

"Good! Excellent," said the governor, as he rubbed his fat hands; "you are a sharp and clever man. This capture will be a feather in your cap, Captain —er—let me see——"

"Captain Roberts."

"Ay, Roberts—yes. Well, now I will go and attend to the prisoner. You have done your duty; I have got mine to do. A prisoner of such great importance cannot be too well looked after."

"Do not trouble yourself."

"Eh?"

"I say, don't trouble yourself. I will attend to the prisoner."

"You! How? You are not governor."

" True—nor am I Captain Roberts."

The podgy governor staggered back in astonishment.

" Are you mad ? " he asked.

" Nay, quite sane, I fancy."

" Well, if you are not Captain Roberts —the name is here on this warrant— who the devil are you ? "

" No matter. I repeat that I am not Captain Roberts, nor do I know there *is* such a person. As to the warrant, it is a forgery."

" A *what?* " gasped the almost petrified governor.

" A forgery."

" You tell me this to my face ? "

" Certainly I do."

" By heaven and earth ! you shall suffer for this rascally——"

He had placed his hand upon the bell-rope beside the fireplace.

But, at the same instant, the supposed captain presented a petronel, or pistol, at his head.

" Pull it," he said, calmly—" pull it, and I will scatter your brains upon the wall."

The instant the governor saw the pistol, he dropped into a chair, burying his fat face in his hands.

" Look up," growled the captain, " and don't make a fool of yourself. Listen to what I say."

" I am lost ! " groaned the governor. " My appointment will be taken away, and——"

" Nothing of the sort ! " interrupted the captain. " Listen, I tell you, to what I am about to say. Now—do you listen ? "

" Yes—yes—yes ! "

" For certain reasons I am desirous of taking Harold Forrester away from here. Let him go with us without interruption, and I will place in your hands—this very instant—the sum of one hundred crowns. Look up, curse you ! "

" I listen—I listen."

" Do you agree ? "

" What—what am I to do ? "

" Do ? Why, agree to my proposal, and at once."

" If I refuse ? "

" I will kill you as surely as you sit there ! "

" I agree then ; but I must have the money at once."

" 'Tis here," said the supposed captain, as he threw a purse upon the table. " Count it."

The governor did so, and pronounced it to be correct.

" Good," said the captain. " Now burn that warrant, and forget that you have seen me."

" But the warders ? "

" Give them a piece or two each, and they will keep their mouths shut. Now, remain where you are for half-an-hour."

" But your men—do they not belong to the Queen's Guard ? "

" No, but their clothes do. They were stolen from the Tower."

" Then you will not tell me who you really are ? "

" Oh, if you desire to know particularly you shall. But you know me well enough. I have been in your care enough times. My name is Robert Coe."

The governor leapt from his chair.

Only too well did he know the lawless ruffian who frequented the " Red Cross," and who had been in his care dozens of times.

But, on this occasion he was wonderfully well disguised.

A man of keener penetration than the wine-loving governor would have failed to recognise the man.

Coe did not wait for the governor to recover from his surprise.

He passed out of the door with the simple—

" Half-an-hour, mind."

As he retraced his steps to the cell in which Harold had been placed he took from his pocket two articles.

The first was a thick kerchief, the second a small coil of thin, but strong rope.

During his absence Harold had plied the men with all sorts of questions.

But without result.

They did not reply to one.

Our hero offered them money, but they would not accept it.

The reason was simple.

They knew it must come to them soon, for they would take it.

" Harold Forrester," said Coe, as he entered the cell, " you are to be removed from here to another prison. All prisoners from whom violence is to be expected are always secured, and you will be no exception to the rule."

"I promise that I will offer no resistance."

"I refuse to accept your promise. Here," he added, to the men, "is the rope, secure his hands behind his back."

Harold offered not the least resistance.

Of what use would it have been surrounded by six armed men?

He, however, had not the faintest idea as to what gross indignity was to be offered him.

His arms were no sooner tied than Coe came behind him, and, in an instant the kerchief was placed upon his eyes.

"Wretch!" cried Harold, "what is the meaning of this? Take off the bandage, instantly, or, by heaven! you shall repent it. No warrant authorises you to so insult a prisoner."

"Silence," growled Coe, "or we will stop your tongue."

"I will *not* be silent. I will appeal to the governor. Were my hands free——"

He was not allowed to say more.

Coe took a handkerchief from one of the men and tied it firmly over Harold's mouth, thus rendering him totally incapable of speech.

Another moment and he was being hurried along the several corridors.

Then there was a pause.

The loud clanking of chains, and the withdrawal of heavy bolts was heard, and our hero was again led on.

He could tell now that they were in the open air.

Not a word was uttered by either of the men as they went on.

Two linked their arms in Harold's, while the others brought up the rear.

Captain Coe led the way, nor did he hesitate for an instant.

"I am in the power of the impostor Housden," thought Harold; "this time my life will to a certainty be forfeited. Poor Eveline! These men are in Housden's pay—what will they do next?"

Captain Coe led the way through a number of narrow lanes and alleys, and at last the Thames was reached.

Coe whistled, and from out the darkness shot a boat.

Harold heard the plash of oars, and so knew where he was.

What was the meaning of this?

Were they about to take him in the middle of the river and slay him?

The whole party were quickly in the boat.

"Southwark steps," said Coe, shortly.

The waterman bent to the oars, and the boat glided towards the Surrey side.

It had not got a hundred paces from the shore when a little figure darted forward.

It was Mat o' the Mist.

"Ah!" he muttered, as he surveyed the fast disappearing boat, "you are quick and clever, Master Coe, but you are not quicker than Mat o' the Mist. Southwark steps, eh? Well, there is no boat, but I can do without one."

Thereupon he sprang into the river—which, fortunately, was calm—and struck out towards the boat.

He was an expert swimmer, it is true; but, nevertheless, it required a very great amount of courage to plunge into the river on a dark night.

He was running a very great risk; for if, by any chance, either of the men in the boat made out his figure, he would probably have been shot dead.

On the Surrey side near Southwark steps a huge barge was moored.

A solitary lantern burned in the bows, but not a soul was visible on board.

No doubt the crew were asleep.

Mat swam round the barge, and contrived to hold on to one of the life chains.

From this position he could both see and hear.

Harold and the men landed first.

Coe stopped to talk to the waterman.

But what he said was of little importance.

He paid him twice the ordinary fee for rowing them across the river, and a gold piece "to keep his mouth shut."

Then he landed, but, before ascending the steps, he gave the waterman a parting warning to the effect that, if he *did* open his lips, he could make up his mind to die a sudden and violent death.

As soon as Coe was at the top of the rotten old steps, Mat was at the bottom, but he took care to keep in the shadow of the wall.

It was fortunate he did so, for Coe, on arriving at the top, turned and looked towards the river, apparently watching the direction taken by the waterman.

Then he joined the men, who took their way down Swan Lane, so called on account of a large hostelry, which, however, at the period of this romance, had long been closed.

The lane was of great length, but it boasted only one house on the right; and it was here that the men stopped.

They did not have to wait long.

The door was quickly opened, and the party admitted.

Mat watched close by, and, when the party had entered, he went rapidly past the house on the opposite side.

"Yes," he muttered, "I am right. It *is* the house occupied by that rascally lawyer, Bellman! Soh! *he* is concerned in the plot. How many more is his lordship about to employ? But I will be even with them yet, or my name is not Mat o' the Mist. Thank heaven, I can climb like a cat. With the assistance of the water pipe, and the various projections, I can reach the roof of that house if I think proper.

"But, alas! I have no fire-arms. The only weapon I have about me is a dagger.

"Nevertheless, if poor Harold had that and his arms free, it would go hard with some of them.

"I must wait and watch. If I could— Ha!" he added, as he saw the curtains drawn at the windows of the first floor, "Bellwood is in that room, I'll warrant.

"If I could overhear what is said. Well, why cannot I do so? Surely I can easily reach the balcony.

"Well I know I should run a great risk, for if they discovered me my life would be forfeited in a few seconds.

"But I *must* run the risk. Yes, yes —to leave him alone would be cowardly. Ha! why did we visit that Sharpley at all?"

Up and down the lane he looked.

But there was not a soul in sight.

Creeping to the house he listened.

Satisfied that no one was near the door, he took hold of the water-pipe— then a square tube made of wood, and secured by monstrous staples.

An ordinary person would have found it utterly impossible to climb it.

Mat, however, could climb like a monkey.

Then, again he was so light.

With the assistance of the staples, and the various other projections invariably to be found in wooden houses, he was speedily upon the balcony; still, he found his movements considerably impeded by his wet garments.

The curtains, as we have seen, had been drawn.

But, through a small rent in one of them, Mat could distinctly see all in the room.

As to what was said—that he could overhear most distinctly.

But we will enter the house.

Harold, bound and blindfolded as he was, was taken into one of the rooms on the ground floor.

Here, in but a few seconds, they were joined by Lawyer Bellwood.

At the time we introduce him he was close upon seventy, and a more crafty looking man could not have been found.

This was the man who had taken a large share in putting Henry Ryder into the shoes of another; in other words, it was principally through him that "Lord Housden" was enjoying what was the property of our hero and his father, "Don Fernando."

The instant he saw Harold he chuckled with delight.

He whispered in the ear of the man who had admitted the party, and Harold was led away.

The men followed.

Four were to descend when Harold had been safely placed, while one man was to remain without the door.

"Take the bandages from his eyes and mouth," said Coe, "but do not untie his hands."

"Now," he said, when the men had gone, "what do you think of it, eh?"

"You have not told me how you effected this important capture. He was never released?"

"Nay. But I will tell you the story."

When he had finished the lawyer laughed heartily.

"By Satan!" he said, "you acted very cleverly."

"Well, now as to the amount."

"We did not agree to any, I think. But follow me upstairs."

"No," said Coe, when they were in an upstairs room, "no amount was agreed upon, it is true. But you will remember what you told me.

"It was this— 'You can, if you think proper, try your hand in the matter. If you can get Harold Forrester into your hands and bring him here, I will guarantee that Lord Housden will hand you five thousand crowns.'"

"And so he will, and I am prepared to advance a thousand now."

"You are?"

"I am."

"Over with it, then."

"But, look you, in order to make more certain of the amount, you must complete the task you set yourself."

"Complete it? Why, curse it, have I not already finished?"

"No — *he must be killed.* Lord Housden, when he arrives here, must see him dead."

"I thought he wanted the satisfaction of slaying him, himself?"

"I say that he must be killed. There is danger, not only to Lord Housden if that lad lives, but also to me."

"I see — I see. Well, as to his death, there need be no difficulty. I will kill him myself."

"How?"

Coe significantly touched the butt of his pistol.

"Anyway you like," said Bellwood, "so that he is killed. Now here is a bottle of wine. Help yourself, while I procure the money. Then I will write a letter to his lordship telling him to come on here at once."

"Ay, ay; and, look you, tell your man to take my men to the kitchen. Have you anything for them?"

"Plenty of ale."

"That will do."

"Five thousand!" chuckled Bellwood as he descended the stairs. "Why, *he* will pay me ten thousand—yes, and more than that."

Assisted by his man he attended to the wants of the men, the while he assured them that their leader would pay them well for their share in the "good work."

We now return to Mat.

Every word that had been uttered he had heard.

He nearly dropped when the words — "He must be killed" fell from the lawyer's lips.

"My God!" thought Mat; "unless something is done at once, his life will assuredly be lost. Ah! would that my good master were here!"

"In what part of the house has he been placed."

He was soon to learn.

In less than five minutes the lawyer re-entered the room.

"Look you," he said, "are these men your regular associates?"

"Nay. I employ them occasionally."

"As I thought. Then, if you take my advice, you will give them the amount agreed upon and let them go."

"All?"

"All but the man at the top. Thus, as they will not know what is done with Harold Forrester, they will not be able to talk."

"That is true. I will do as you say. And I know they will be glad to get their share and go."

"In this bag you will find one thousand crowns. Pay them out of that."

Coe counted the contents of the bag, and then, selecting for each man the sum agreed upon, he left the room with the lawyer.

The opportunity was not to be lost.

Mat now knew that Harold had been taken to the top.

He knew, too, that if he remained on the balcony, one of the men coming out might see him.

He at once tried the window.

By means of his dagger he pushed back the catch.

The next instant the lower part of the window was open.

Mat darted in, closed the window, shot out of the room, and stood upon the landing.

Distinctly he could hear many voices below, as well as the rattle of tankards and money.

Mat's best chance was now, when all this noise was going on below.

Feeling his way along the passage, he found the stairs, and noiselessly ascended them.

On the next landing, exactly across the top of the stairs, a tattered pair of curtains were drawn.

On the landing itself, stuck against the wall, burned a taper.

Against this, his face towards Mat, was the man who had been placed on duty outside the door of the room in which Harold had been placed.

Mat saw at once that he was a powerful man, and that he was well armed.

Nevertheless he did not hesitate.

The thing to do was to take him utterly unawares.

So, as the man slightly turned, he sprang forward, and, before the man could draw back, he seized him by the throat.

Nevertheless, the man contrived to draw his dagger; and he aimed a tremendous blow at Mat's head.

This he avoided, and the next instant, he had plunged his own blade into the man's throat.

Down like a log he fell, one cry only leaving his lips.

The key was in the lock, and Mat, after listening at the head of the stairs, opened the door.

"Master Harold!" he whispered.

Our hero, with a low cry of intense astonishment and joy, sprang forward.

"Mat!" he cried; "you?"

"Ay, ay! I am here—here to save you," replied Mat, severing with his dagger the cords which bound Harold's hands. "If we are—but hish!"

The noise of the tramp of many feet was heard.

It was the men departing.

Soon the street door closed, and then the lawyer and Coe entered the room below.

"We must lose no time," said Mat; "they may come here at any moment."

Stooping, he unfastened the belt of the fallen man, and handed it to Harold.

Attached to it was a sword and a dagger.

Our hero instantly fastened it about his waist.

"The five men have departed," said Mat; "Captain Coe alone remains. The only other persons in the house are, I believe, a lawyer and a man-servant. If we pass cautiously down the stairs we may escape without arousing those below.

"If we can, you will have plenty of opportunity of punishing both of them anon. But if we chance to arouse them you will have to fight for your life."

"Ay, and I am *prepared* to fight," replied Harold.

"Come, then, I will lead the way."

The dagger still grasped in his hand, Mat led the way.

They made not the least noise, and they would have reached the street door without arousing the precious pair of rascals had it not have been for the man-servant.

As they crept on to the first landing, the man, lantern in hand, was ascending.

No sooner did he see Mat than he yelled with terror, dropped the lantern, and fled down the stairs as if the foul fiend himself was at his heels.

The lawyer at once darted to the door, and, as quick as lightning, Mat dealt him such a tremendous blow in the face with his clenched fist that he fell backward, nearly knocking down Coe, who was close behind him.

The latter had drawn his sword, for he thought it possible someone he should not care to see was at the street door.

But when he saw Harold, free and armed, he gave a howl of astonishment.

"Wretch!" cried Harold, as he sprang into the room, "we are now on even terms, and, by the Virgin, here you fight! And mark it well—it is to be a fight to the death!"

For some few moments, however, Coe was unable to recover from his surprise.

But then surprise gave way to rage, and, like a tiger just about to be baulked of its prey, he rushed upon Harold, thinking to instantly cut him down.

Meantime Mat was guarding the lawyer. He told him that if he dared to attempt to rise, he would put him beyond the power of again driving a pen along a sheet of parchment.

Did the lawyer attempt to rise?

Nay, nor even to move.

As for the man-servant, he had quitted the house, for Mat heard the door closed.

Standing over the prostrate lawyer, Mat watched the fight.

It proved to be a desperate one indeed.

In less than two minutes Harold had wounded Coe twice.

The second, in the breast, was a severe one, but it did not cause Coe to pause.

On the contrary, the effect was to madden him beyond description.

Not the faintest idea had he that Harold was such a swordsman.

As to himself, he was decidedly not skilled in the handling of the sword, at any rate, not in fair fight.

Presently he succeeded in inflicting a slight wound on Harold's left wrist, but the very next instant his blade was torn from his grasp, and he fell, pierced to the heart.

"He is dead," said Mat. "Leave him where he is. Now," he added to the lawyer, who was in a fearful state of terror, "get up—quick!"

Bellwood, with difficulty, got upon his feet, and Mat dragged him into the room.

"Can you handle a sword?" demanded Mat.

"No, no," stammered Bellwood. "No —no—spare me—spare me."

"Ay, ay, we'll spare you. Sit in that chair."

And Mat dealt him a blow which sent him into the nearest chair.

"You see," said Mat, "this man was in league with this brutal wretch, who is called Captain Coe. His name is Bellwood, and he transacts the legal affairs of Lord Housden. He arranged with Coe to murder you."

"No, no," gasped Bellwood; "that was Coe's proposal. I did all I could to prevent——"

"Infernal liar!" thundered Mat; "I was on that balcony and overheard all you said."

"If he cannot use a sword," said Harold, "he can the pen. Listen to this."

He had picked up a letter.

It was to Lord Housden, and Bellwood had just written it.

It ran as follows—

"My Lord,—I have glorious news for you. Harold Forrester has been brought to this house by Captain Coe, of whom I think you have heard. At one time he used to 'work' with Redcliffe. Set off as quickly as possible, and you will see the youth lying dead in one of the rooms.
"C. B.

"To the Manor House at Charing Cross."

"Villain!" cried Mat, "you deserve instant death."

"We will spare his life," said Harold, "but we will take care he does not move from this room until his lordship, as he calls himself, arrives."

"Until he arrives?"

"Ay. Take this piece of rope, and tie him securely in that chair."

Mat, with a broad grin, at once set about this task.

The dastardly lawyer's howls for mercy, his offers of money for release, were something to hear.

The only reply Mat gave him was that, if he did not stop his tongue, he would give him the soundest thrashing he ever had in his life.

When Mat had bound him so that it was utterly impossible he could get away, Harold took a piece of cloth and fastened it firmly about his mouth.

Then he took a pen, and, on a piece of parchment, wrote in large letters—

"By order of Harold Forrester, who has slain the man in this room. Lord Housden, impostor and murderer, your time is approaching!
"Harold Forrester."

This he pinned on the lawyer's breast

Then he sealed the letter, and with Mat left the chamber.

But a sudden thought struck Mat, and he returned, fell upon his knees, and took from the body of Captain Coe the remains of the one thousand crowns, something like six hundred.

"I know two apprentices," he said, "who are down with a severe illness. Their parents are so poor that they are unable to procure the proper necessaries. This money will be a god-send to them. They shall have every penny."

The lawyer looked what he would have said.

Just as they reached the street door, it was opened suddenly, and a man entered.

It was the lawyer's man-servant.

No doubt he thought that Mat had gone

No sooner did he see him than, with a yell, he was about to rush away.

Mat, however, was a little too quick for him.

He seized him and swung him round.

"Fool!" he said, "do you want to be killed?"

"No, no; I am as innocent of anything as a child."

"Well, you *look* innocent, certainly. But had you entered that house you would have been killed. We have left two men in there, with orders to kill anyone who enters the house."

The man groaned dismally.

"Captain Coe is killed," continued Mat, "and so is the lawyer. Now, do you wish to enter?"

"No, no; but I have a lot of things in there."

"Leave them for a few days. But you can enter if you like."

"No, no, I don't want to be killed," whined the man.

Turning, he shuffled off.

Mat then locked the door and pocketed the key.

"Depend upon it he will not return," said Harold, "at any rate, not for a few days. Now we will at once cause this letter to be sent to Lord Housden at the Manor House."

"But how will he enter?"

"He will knock, no doubt, and if he gets no answer, he will break into the house."

"Come, now, Master Harold, with me."

"Whither?"

"To my master's quarters."

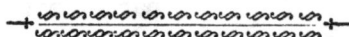

CHAPTER XLV.

OF WHAT TRANSPIRED AT THE MANOR HOUSE.

CAPTAIN REDCLIFFE, like others of his class, was in the habit of making any number of promises, but he broke almost as many as he made.

The appointment he made with Lord Housden, however, he certainly meant to keep.

He knew well enough that it might mean any amount of money in his pocket.

But he did *not* keep the appointment.

On this occasion it was not owing to his own fault.

He was visiting a person at some little distance from his own "home," when he was suddenly arrested on suspicion of being concerned in the assassination of a gentleman whose body had been found floating off Wapping Stairs.

Resistance was useless. He was alone, while the officers who arrested him numbered six.

He was promptly disarmed and conveyed to prison.

There he bribed a turnkey to convey a message to Lord Housden.

It stated the reasons why he would be compelled to absent himself.

Housden at once interested himself in the matter, but Redcliffe was not released for four days.

He then made his way to the Manor House.

The hour was late, but Lord Housden expected him, and was awaiting him in what was called the study.

Before we describe what passed between them in that room, we will pay a visit to another, or rather, to a vault in the basement of the building.

This was one of four wine vaults, but it had been roughly fitted as a living and sleeping apartment.

For over twelve months it had been occupied by a lady, and that lady was the wife of Lord Housden, or rather, Henry Ryder.

A short time before Redcliffe arrived, Lady Housden, as usual, was slowly pacing the vault, lost in thought.

But every now and then she paused to listen.

That she was anxiously expecting someone was certain.

Despite her fearful sufferings since her marriage with Lord Housden, and which had been carried out with the greatest secrecy, and in defiance of the fact that she had been for twelve long months a prisoner in the vault, her extraordinary beauty still remained.

Four years before we introduce her she had been a visitor to one of the queen's maids-in-waiting, and had attracted the attention of her majesty, whilst she had gained the respect and admiration of everyone with whom she came in contact.

Then, suddenly, she disappeared.

The queen caused inquiries to be made in every direction, and large rewards to be offered, but without result.

She was never again heard of, and it was supposed that she had met with foul play.

Housden took her into the country, where the marriage took place, and, owing, as he said, to certain family matters, prevailed upon her to preserve silence.

But at last her suspicions were aroused, and she declared she would proceed to London, and seek an audience of the queen.

Housden then said he would take her to Court, and publicly acknowledge her.

One night they set out, as the poor lady thought, to proceed to the house of a friend.

Housden, however, took her to the Manor House, and she was at once taken to the vault.

Housden, of course, had made all the necessary arrangements, and had engaged a woman—a perfect fiend—named Martha Habrond to be her gaoler.

This woman, though old, was as active as a girl.

She watched over her ladyship night and day.

By day she sat in a huge oaken chair before the door.

By night she lay across the threshold, on a mattress.

Three female servants were in the house, and of these, one had taken compassion upon her ladyship.

This was a young girl named Jane Robertson.

Time after time she had had brief interviews with the poor lady, and they had come to a perfect understanding.

Jane determined to assist her ladyship to escape.

But, alas! the opportunity never came —the old woman gaoler was ever on the alert.

There was no getting at her at all.

Housden paid her well for what she did, and he repeatedly swore that, if for one instant she ceased her watchfulness, he would kill her.

And the woman soon learned enough of Housden to know that his threat was not an idle one.

Jane was wise enough to keep on good terms with the old woman.

Frequently she brought her a bottle of wine or spirits, of course in the hope that she would make herself intoxicated.

No such luck.

Though the hideous old woman would, as the saying goes, have swam in liquor, she always remembered Housden's threats, and restrained herself.

Then Jane resolved to drug her.

She was acquainted with the apprentice to an apothecary, and from him she obtained a drug the effects of which would throw a person into a state of unconsciousness for hours—only a glassful being required for this purpose.

On the very night Redcliffe was expected she had placed the drug in a bottle of wine, and this she presented to the old woman.

Having in like manner received many a dozen bottles, it was not likely that the woman had the faintest suspicion that this one was drugged.

In ten minutes she drank half a tumbler of the wine, and in another five she lay upon the mattress, to all appearance, dead.

So like death did this unconsciousness seem, that Jane was at first alarmed.

But she remembered that the apprentice, whom she knew to be remarkably clever, had assured her that, unless taken in large quantities, the drug was harmless.

As Redcliffe was admitted, Jane descended the stairs, and pulling the woman and the mattress from the door of the vault, secured the key and unlocked the door.

Her ladyship at once started forward.

"Hish! my lady," said Jane, "or we may attract attention."

"You have succeeded?"

"Yes, there she is. All danger from her is over."

"She is not dead?"

"Nay, she is unconscious. But she is as good as dead, I fear; for his lordship, if you succeed in escaping—and, oh! I pray God you may—will have his revenge."

"Did you procure what I asked you?"

"Yes, yes; here they are."

And from the folds of her dress Jane took a pistol and a dagger, the latter a slight, but terrible weapon, in the hands of a determined person.

These her ladyship received, and, with the greatest coolness, secreted about her person.

"What of the man who is expected?" asked her ladyship.

"He has just arrived."

"You saw him?"

"I did," replied Jane, with a shudder. "And a more repulsive-looking blackguard I never beheld."

"I have heard him spoken of. He is the leader of a gang of desperate ruffians,

Depend upon it, he has been hired to murder me."

"Oh, no, no! Do not say so!"

"I am sure of it. Remember what his lordship said when he came here four days ago; 'Be careful to say your prayers, for you have now but a few days to live.'"

"Jane, you must do me yet another service. He is speaking to this man in the study?"

"Yes."

"Conduct me then to the little ante-room you spoke of."

Jane started.

"My lady," she said, "it would be madness. If discovered, you would be killed on the spot."

"As well die there as anywhere else," was her ladyship's reply. At any rate, if discovered, *you* will not suffer. Here is the case of jewels I promised you. Take them, and be ready to fly."

"No, no, my lady. No matter what may follow, I will not leave you."

"Think—think!"

"I *have* thought. I will *not* leave you."

"You are a brave girl, and, one day, you may be well rewarded for your devotion. Now take me to the room."

"Does your ladyship persist?"

"Yes, yes. What passes between the two I long to know."

Jane turned and left the vault, followed closely by Lady Housden.

A small staircase on the right of the kitchen was ascended, a passage, and another short flight of stairs.

Then Jane paused.

"His lordship keeps the key in his bedchamber," she said; "remain here, and I will fetch it. Is your ladyship nervous?"

"I am as calm and as collected as ever I was in my life," was the reply.

Ay, she was not only calm and collected, but determined also.

Never before had Jane seen such a look on that beautiful face.

She quickly procured the key, and noiselessly opened the door.

It was a very small room, which at one time was used by Housden's secretary.

On the opposite side was a narrow door.

It was locked, and, the key being out, her ladyship was able not only to hear, but to see.

The conversation between Housden and Redcliffe was, at first, as may be supposed, of the latter's unexpected arrest and imprisonment.

Then, just as Lady Housden applied her eye to the keyhole, it changed.

"You just mentioned," said Redcliffe, "that you had something of the greatest importance to tell me."

"I have. Harold Forrester is at large."

"What? has he been dismissed?"

"Nay."

"Then the Headsman managed to release him?"

"He did not. I will tell you how he got out of prison."

Thereupon he told him of what Captain Coe had done, and the whole story of Harold's escape from Bellwood's house.

Of course the story had been told to his lordship by Bellwood, to whom he had gone on receipt of the letter.

The narrative astonished Redcliffe beyond measure.

It showed him not only that Harold Forrester was a daring and clever youth, but that he had clever friends behind his back.

Nevertheless, there was one thing that delighted him, and that was that Captain Coe had been killed.

"He worked with me a long while, said Redcliffe, "but he suddenly took it into his head that he did not receive a proper share, and then the fool set up on his own account. But do you know where Forrester is at the present moment?"

"Not at the present moment. But I know this—the Headsman, Master Duke, and one who is known as Don Fernando, are at the Tower, while the girl, Eveline is at Brixton."

"Brixton? Has she then left the duke's place?"

"She has, in company with a Jewess of the name of Moss—Lucy Moss."

"Can it be the daughter of old Abraham Moss?"

"It is."

"The man whom Sharpley murdered?"

"The same."

"But what do they want at Brixton? The mansion of the late duke and Brixton is as wide apart as the poles."

"You are right; but, if you have any

THE HEADSMAN OF OLD LONDON BRIDGE.

sense you will see the object of taking the girl to such an out-of-the-way place. It is to throw me and those I employ, entirely off the scent. But," he added, with a fiendish smile, "clever as they are, they cannot baffle me."

"You know the house to which she has been taken?"

"Yes, it is called Leathvale, and it is not far from the house built by Sir Walter Raleigh."

"Well, of course, all this throws out of gear all the plans I had formed. But I must admit that the coast is clearer than when you first spoke of the matter."

"Yes," replied Housden. "By midnight to-morrow this girl must be in my power. It is not my custom to talk of my love affairs to anyone, but I will tell you that I love this girl with all my soul. I *think* I love her well enough to make her my wife."

"But, my lord, remember you must first get rid of——"

Housden interrupted him with a wild laugh.

"My *lawful* wife?" he said. "Well, let me tell you that *she is not my wife*."

"Not?"

"Nay. We certainly went through a marriage ceremony, but it was false. I will tell you who the clergyman was—it was Sharpley."

Redcliffe stared hard for a few moments, and then he burst into a hearty fit of laughter.

The notion of Sharpley officiating as a clergyman was too much.

But what was the effect of Housden's statement on the lady who listened on the other side of that little door?

The unfortunate and deluded woman fairly reeled as the startling words fell upon her ears.

But for Jane, who remained close beside her, it is more than likely she would have fallen.

However, she quickly recovered herself, and, with set lips and a wildly-beating heart, she again listened.

"Your late secretary," said Redcliffe, "informed me that she was very beautiful."

"*Was?* She *is*. But what of that? I never loved her. It was her fortune I required."

"And you had it?"

"I had a part, and the rest—— But

what is all this to you?" Housden suddenly added, with a scowl. "How can a man of *your* class be interested in such matters?"

Redcliffe saw that he had gone far enough, so he made no reply to this.

"The first thing to be done," he said, "is to get possession of Eveline Duke. And I will set about it to-morrow night. But perhaps you have thought of a plan?"

"I have. Look—here is a letter written by her father, Launcelot Duke."

Redcliffe took and examined it.

"And here," continued Housden, "is an imitation of his handwriting."

"By Satan's own!" exclaimed Redcliffe, "it is perfect."

Housden smiled.

"Yes," he said, "as you say, the imitation is perfect. In most things Bellwood, who did that, is a fool, but when it comes to forgery, there is not a man in all London to touch him."

"He will go on until he gets his right hand cut off," said Redcliffe. "That is the punishment."

"In that case," answered Housden, "he would commit forgery again with his left. But read the letter aloud."

Redcliffe was by no means a good scholar, and it took him a considerable time to spell out the lines.

We give them without interruption.

"MY DEAREST DAUGHTER,

"Join us this evening at London Bridge. Master Vaughan will lend you his coach and two men. Take the road on the right of the church, and you will reach here without any danger of interruption. If you start at nine, you will arrive at the bridge soon after ten. I pray you convey my best wishes and thanks to Master Vaughan.

"This from your affectionate father,

"LAUNCELOT DUKE."

"Good!" said Redcliffe. "This should be effective."

"It *will* be; of that I am certain."

"But who will take it?"

"I have the proper man in readiness. He is one of Master Vaughan's servants —an ostler. He conveyed a message from Master Vaughan to Master Duke. I chanced to stop at an hostelry where he was, and I recognised him as a man who at one time had been in my employ, but at the time I saw him I had no idea who his new master was. He told me all, however, and when he produced the letter, you may imagine I was thunder-stricken.

"A good bribe caused him to place the letter in my hands. It was partly on business, but it mentioned that Eveline was well, and that she was happy with Lucy Moss.

"That is all I need tell you. You now know the hour and the place. Be there with half-a-dozen men, and the girl is certain to fall into your hands."

"No, no. I will take a dozen men, so as to make sure."

"As you please."

"Where shall I take her?"

"Bring her here."

"I will. And this ostler will take the forged letter?"

"Exactly."

"An excellent idea. He will say he brought it straight from Master Duke; and, of course, not the faintest suspicion that anything is wrong will be aroused."

"The girl in my power, I think I have a capital plan to get rid of Harold Forrester."

After a little more conversation Red-cliffe departed, and soon the front door was heard to close.

Lady Housden turned to Jane, to whom those few minutes had seemed like hours, and whispered—

"Take me from here."

At once Jane led her from the chamber.

"Come, my lady," she said; "not a moment is to be lost. We can leave the house by the back."

"Nay," was the steady reply, "I will leave it by the front."

"My lady! my lady! Consider the consequences."

"I have considered."

Jane reflected an instant.

To reach the street door they must pass the study.

Well, no doubt Housden would not leave it for some little time.

"Come, then," she said; "but I beg you to walk fast."

In a few seconds they had reached the study door.

Not the faintest idea had the devoted maid as to what her ladyship really intended to do.

Therefore she was astounded when Lady Housden paused at the study door, and said to her—

"Go, Jane, or stay. I must and *will* have a few words with this monster."

"My God! you *cannot* mean it?"

"I *do* mean it," replied her ladyship; and, the next instant, she threw the door open and entered the room.

Housden was just sealing up the forged letter.

When the door was thus suddenly opened, he sprang to his feet.

Thinking that it had been opened by a servant, he was about to launch forth a torrent of abuse; but when he recognised his wife, he stood as if spellbound.

For a few seconds he found himself unable to speak.

Then he said—

"*You?*"

"Ay," replied Lady Housden; "at last I am face to face with you—not in a filthy vault, but on your own ground. At last I am free——"

"Free!" thundered Housden, fiercely, as he advanced towards her; "you lie! You are not and *will* not be free. I have told you, again and again—and I repeat it now—that you go not hence until you are dead.

"Indeed I am not certain that you will go *then*. There is plenty of room for a burial in my own grounds. Go back to the vault, and there——"

"Stop! Listen to me. You have ever thought me a poor, weak fool—a worm on which you could tread and crush at any moment. I appeared to be weak, it is true; but what else could I do, guarded so strictly? But now a very different woman stands before you."

Housden forced a laugh.

"Indeed?" he sneered.

"Yes—a woman who is determined to at once seek the queen and place before her all that has occurred since you—liar that you are—professed to love me."

The reader will see that her ladyship did not say that she had overheard what had passed between Housden and Red-cliffe.

Nay, nor did she intend to.

She had already formed her plans.

"You fancy the queen would listen to you?" asked Housden.

"Ay, she would."

"Let me tell you you do not know

the queen. I should simply deny all you said, and she would believe me."

"Wait and see."

"But let this farce end. I will see you to the vault, and, by heaven! the old woman shall know the result of leaving you unguarded."

As he spoke he approached nearer to her ladyship, as if he would take her by the arm.

She drew back, and instantly plucked forth her dagger.

"Touch me, foul wretch," she said, "and I drive this deep into your black heart!"

She drew her fine figure erect as she said this, while her eyes flashed fire.

And now, indeed, Housden saw that he had a very different woman to deal with.

"After all," he considered, "this has happened for the best. The moment has come—I will slay her now. I will advance again, she will once more threaten me with the dagger, and I will plunge my sword into her heart.

"Money will silence the tongues of the servants—except one—and I can threaten her."

Aloud he said—

"Put down that weapon. Serious consequences may ensue."

"Serious consequences *will* ensue if you attempt to lay hands upon me. Stand where you are, for I have more to say to you. Then, when——"

She did not finish the sentence, for Housden, darting forward, drew his blade.

He made a movement as if to plunge it into her ladyship's heart, but, with wonderful swiftness, Lady Housden drew back; then suddenly she sprang upon Housden, and wounded him in the shoulder.

The wound was not a severe one, it is true, but the pain was sufficient to cause him to utter a bitter curse.

A moment he paused, then again rushing forward, he seized Lady Housden's wrist, and wrenched the dagger from her grasp.

And now, of course, he thought he had her at his mercy.

Again he shortened his sword, but, as he moved a pace forward, Lady Housden suddenly produced and pointed the pistol at him. From this he shrank.

Inexperienced though his wife was, it was scarcely possible for her to miss him at so short a distance.

Who had provided her with these weapons? Jane, no doubt.

His suspicions were fully confirmed in another second or two, for Jane pushed the door open and entered the room.

She had suddenly thought of an excellent plan, and resolved to put it into immediate execution.

"My lady," she said, as she placed a heavy cloak about her ladyship's shoulders, "come at once with me. My brother and the men he has brought with him are close to the house, and you will be safe." Housden started.

As for her ladyship, she, fortunately, immediately saw what was meant.

"I follow you," she said. "Keep your distance, Lord Housden, or I fire."

And she slowly backed out of the room.

Housden stood in the centre of the chamber, the point of his sword resting upon the floor.

"Let her but reach the hall," he thought; "I shall have her there."

He was grievously mistaken.

Lady Housden no sooner got without the room than, suddenly lowering her pistol, she seized the door, pulled it to, and turned the key!

Housden was thus completely baffled.

Before he could recover from his surprise, he heard the front door close.

"No matter," he muttered; "ere she has time to have an audience of the Queen, she will be again in my clutches. Fool that I was not to have disposed of her long ago.

"I should have done so, only I could not get her to attach her signature to the document which would place in my possession the other half of her fortune.

"As for that girl—by Satan! I will be even with her. Her brother and several men in waiting, eh? Is that the truth, or only a lie? Probably it is the truth. I know that she *has* a brother——a farrier.

"Well, without her, Lady Housden, as she fancies herself, would not have escaped. Some trick must have been played the old woman, for I believe she was true to me, in consideration of the sums I gave her."

He unlocked the door of the ante-room, and made his way below.

CHAPTER XLVI.

OF THE WAY HAROLD RESCUES THE STEWARD FROM THE CLUTCHES OF HIS PURSUERS.

AT a rapid pace, Lady Housden, with faithful Jane at her side, proceeded through the streets.

A few men were abroad, and, as they passed, they looked inquiringly, frequently insolently, into their faces, so that, at last, her ladyship was compelled to screen her beautiful face with the hood attached to the cloak.

Occasionally they paused to look anxiously behind.

But they were not pursued.

Had they been, her ladyship was determined to knock loudly at the door of the nearest house and ask for protection.

At last the grim, grey walls of the Tower came in sight.

Not a soul was to be seen here.

All was dark, and as silent as the grave.

But, passing through a narrow archway, which was a shorter cut, a tall, dark figure confronted them.

Both started back in terror, for they saw that the man was masked.

Where had he sprung from?

There were no houses near.

Lady Housden quickly recovered herself.

"Unless I am much mistaken," she said, "you are the Headsman."

She was correct, it certainly was he.

"You are quite right, madam," he said, in his well-known grave tones, "but how did you know?"

"Once seen, you are not easily forgotten. Yet it is some years since I saw you. Then, I always shuddered when I beheld you—but now, I am glad to have met you."

"Indeed, madam? your words sound mysterious. May I ask to whom I have the honour of speaking?"

"To one of the most miserable women on God's earth! Alas! that I should have to say it. My name, sir—but you will not believe me, I am afraid."

"I *shall* believe you, madam."

"My name, then is Lady Housden."

The Headsman started back with a cry of astonishment.

That was not to be wondered at.

"Lady Housden!" he said, "how can that be? Lord Housden is not married."

"He married me, and the marriage was kept a secret. I have but just escaped from his clutches, and I am here to warn you and Harold Forrester of what he intends to do with respect to Eveline Duke."

"You, then, were coming to the Tower?"

"I was—to seek an audience of the queen."

"My advice to you is, that you delay that for a few days. But I can conduct you into the Tower. My apartments are not elaborate, it is true, but you are welcome to stay for a time, so too is this lady."

Lady Housden naturally shuddered at the idea, but, when she considered that it might be better to remain inactive for a day or two, she accepted.

"If I make no sign," she thought, "he will think that I have abandoned my intention to seek an audience. But if he hears of me at the Tower, he will probably leave the country."

The Headsman led them to one of the smaller gates which led on to the green, and after a brief interview with the officer on duty, he was permitted to pass with Lady Housden and her maid.

In a few minutes they were passing along the corridor leading to the Headsman's chambers.

As they slowly followed the Headsman, who carried a lantern, they heard a most extraordinary noise, which seemed to come from the bowels of the earth.

They did not venture to ask what it was.

But they quickly found out, for presently they came upon a sort of pit.

Deep down a light was burning, and they made out a small figure seated at a grindstone, busily polishing the head of an axe.

It was Mat o' the Mist preparing the axes for the final touches of his master.

Then in another moment the Headsman threw open a door and bade his companions enter.

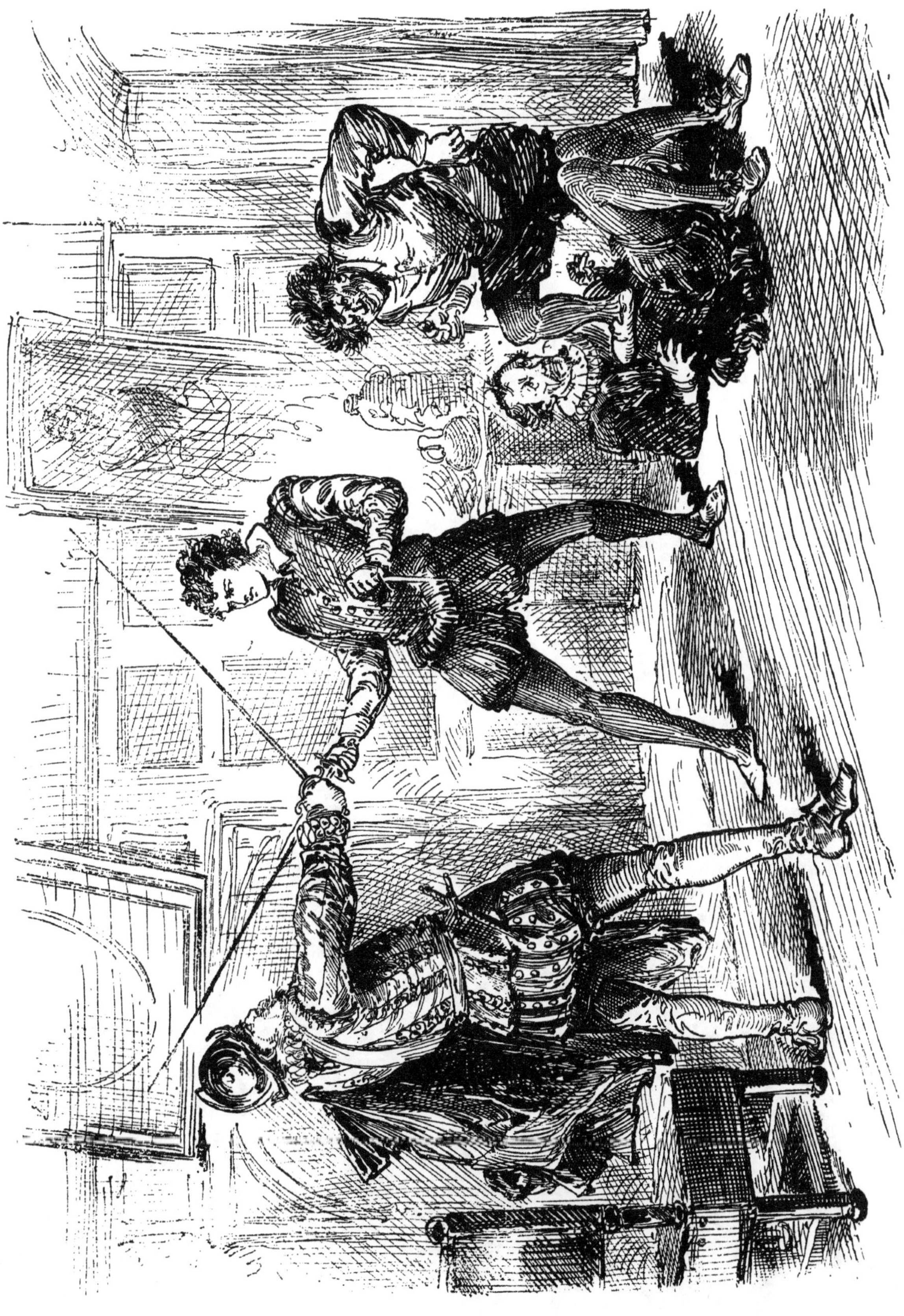

"'WRETCH!' CRIED HAROLD, 'WE ARE NOW ON EVEN TERMS.'"

No. 10.

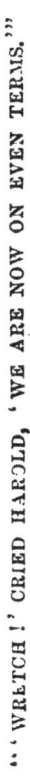

They found themselves in the presence of three persons.

These the Headsman introduced as Don Fernando, Master Duke, and our hero, Harold Forrester.

"And now, my friends," said the Headsman, "you wish to know who my companions are. Prepare yourselves for a surprise. This lady is the wife of Lord Housden, as he is pleased to call himself."

As may be supposed, the surprise was general.

"I will explain all," said Lady Housden; "but first let me ask what you mean by 'as he is pleased to call himself!'"

"The meaning is very simple," said the Headsman; "he is not Lord Housden at all. He is an impostor."

"Impossible!"

"You shall hear the story directly. But I may tell you at once that the real Lord Housden is here."

"Here?"

"Ay, here."

The Headsman pointed to Don Fernando.

"That," he said, "is Lord Housden, and this young gentleman — Harold Forrester, as he is called—is his son."

Overwhelmed with astonishment and indignation, Lady Housden could not speak for some few seconds.

But at last she commenced and finished her story.

Then Don Fernando repeated the story which is already familiar to our readers.

He concluded thus—

"From inquiries we have made we have learned that Housden—for it is better we continue to so call him for the present—was under the impression that his father, the steward, had fully repented of his shameful conduct, and that, if he contrived to get free, he would reveal all.

"So he made up his mind to kill him, and he went to where he was confined for that purpose. But, with the aid of a man called Sharpley, once Housden's tool, and who was killed, the steward had escaped.

"It seems that the landlord of the Orton Arms, also a tool of Lord Housden's, has been offered by Housden a large sum if he—or those he employed—succeeded in re-capturing the steward.

"He has employed three or four men, and, like bloodhounds, they are tracking the unfortunate man down. Probably they will be successful in tracing him, and, in that case, they will kill him.

"But as he has had a long start, I have no doubt he will have found time to write a full account of what he has done, and has got it witnessed.

"When you entered we were trying to hit upon a plan to baffle his pursuers, for, of course, it is of the utmost importance that we get the man as a witness.

"From what I have told you, my lady, you will see that your husband is a far greater villain than you thought him."

"But you now know that he is not my husband."

"If what he told this Redcliffe is correct, you certainly are not. But that is not *your* fault. So, until the end comes— and I certainly think it not far off—you will permit us to call you Lady Housden."

"I know this Redcliffe well," said the Headsman. "Sharpley was villain enough, but Redcliffe is a far greater one.

"Besides, he is surrounded by a swarm of ruffians. Lady Housden says he told Lord Housden that he would bring a dozen men with him.

"But it is more than likely he will bring a dozen and a half. However, let him bring them. We shall be more than a match for them."

"Let us consider," said Don Fernando, "we cannot expect Master Duke to be prepared to fight. There is Harold, the Headsman, me, and—what of Mat?"

"Mat?" said the Headsman; "he can fight well. That is but four of us, and it is not enough. Now, if I had been informed of this—but wait! An excellent thought. I have four friends staying at Kennington. If I could but communicate with them at once——"

"Why not?" interrupted Harold, "I am ready to set out immediately."

There was no reply to this for some few moments.

Each was considering; the hour had to be taken into consideration.

At last it was agreed that Harold should set out.

"Go to the 'Tower Arms,'" said the Headsman, and select the fleetest horse. Then set out at once for Kennington.

The friends I speak of are staying at the 'Three Swans,'—that is, they were there this morning. I know they are about to leave this country for France, but I do not think they have yet gone."

Sitting down he wrote a hasty note.

" Upon receipt of that," he said, " they will return with you, and they can be accommodated at the 'Tower Arms.' We will await your return. And you, my lady, with your maid, can retire, when you think fit, to this room."

Saying which he threw open a door and disclosed his bedchamber.

Poorly, though neatly furnished it was, it is true, but her ladyship was only too glad to avail herself of it.

Harold quickly prepared himself and, accompanied by Mat, who was to see him off at the ' Tower Arms,' he set out.

The host of the " Tower Arms " had the fleetest horse in the stable saddled ; and our hero rode away towards London Bridge.

This crossed, he rode at full speed towards Kennington.

From the Headsman's description he soon found the " Three Swans "—a hostelry which it was stated had been built in the reign of Henry IV.

He found the ostler just closing it, while the podgy host was stretching his fat legs on the threshold.

Dismounting, Harold asked him if all his visitors had retired, and he noticed that the host eyed him suspiciously.

" How do you know that I have any guests, young sir ? " he demanded.

" I know that this morning you had four gentlemen friends here."

" Well, that is correct. But they are not here now."

Harold's face clearly showed his disappointment.

" I am indeed, sorry," he said, not at all liking the look the landlord fixed upon him ; " for I have a most important message from the Tower."

And he threw back his cloak to produce the letter.

The host's demeanour instantly changed.

No man on earth could have been more respectful.

" Sir," he said, " I ask your pardon for my abruptness and apparent inhospitality, but, you see, men in my position have sometimes to be very careful. Step in-

side, sir, and if you desire it, I will place before you the finest bottle of wine my cellars contain."

He beckoned to the ostler to take the horse to the stables, and then led the way in.

Having closed the door, he said—

" First, sir, will you tell me, did you chance to see five horsemen on your way ? "

" Not one."

" Well, if— But, ah ! I am a fool. You came from the Tower, of course ? "

" Are they the gentlemen I seek ? "

" No. The four gentlemen for whom you have the message, and who have been with me a few days, are at the house of a friend—not far from here, and I expect them in an hour or so."

" Good ! I am overjoyed. Pray get the bottle of wine, and I will await them."

The wine being produced, the host said—

" It seems as if Providence has sent you here, sir, for if you like you can render an unfortunate man a great service."

Harold, of course, was astonished.

" Speak," he said.

" Some two hours back," said the host, " a man, almost in tatters and rags, rushed in here. I was in my parlour at the time, and you may guess how staggered I was when he opened the door, flung himself at my feet, and, clasping his hands, implored me in piteous tones to save him.

" At first I thought he must be a madman, but, after looking steadily at him, to my horror I recognised him as a man I had known years before, and whom I thought dead.

" He told me that he was being hunted by five men, who sought his life. For days they have chased him from place to place, and on many occasions he has narrowly escaped.

" He said the men were then not far off, and I have concealed him in an upstairs room. He has not yet told me the full story, but he said that he was on the way to the Tower."

" The Tower ? "

" Ay ; so you see, sir, that if you felt inclined you could do him a service."

" I am not sure. You see, you do not know why these men seek his life.

Perhaps they only seek to capture him, for he may have committed some crime for which the law wishes to lay hands upon him."

"It may be as you say," replied the host. "But perhaps you would like to see him?"

"I should. If I find him worthy of it, rest assured that I will give him my protection."

The host took a lantern, and asked Harold to follow him.

On the second landing—an exceedingly broad one, with three or four rooms—he opened a door and entered, closely followed by our hero.

"Tom," said the host, "come here."

There was no answer.

The host raised the lantern and advanced further into the room.

Harold was horror-stricken at what he saw.

There, in one corner of the room, curled up like a dog, was the figure of a man.

It looked like a skeleton clothed in rags.

The face was towards them, and our hero had never beheld a more awful expression.

Starvation and terror were plainly depicted upon it.

"Get up, Tom," said the landlord, kindly. "I have brought one who may be a friend to you."

"Yes, yes," said Harold, much moved at the terrible sight, "you may trust me."

The man slowly dragged himself to his feet.

He was a perfect wreck.

"Your friend the host," said Harold, "has told me something about you, and of your wish to get to the Tower. With that fortress I am connected in some way, and if I find you worthy of it, I will escort you there. What seek you at the Tower?"

"An audience of her gracious majesty."

"That you will find a difficult matter, unless you have powerful friends. But what is your name?"

"Thomas Ryder."

Harold could scarcely restrain a loud cry of wonder.

What! was it possible that his father's steward stood before him?

"Thomas Ryder!" he said. "Who is your son?"

The man hesitated.

Then he said—

"He is called Lord Housden."

"By the blessed Virgin!" cried Harold, "this is most wonderful. Listen to it," he proceeded, excitedly. "I am called Harold Forrester, but my father is the true 'Lord Housden.'"

"Impossible!"

"No, it is true. My father lives, and, at this very moment, he is in the Tower with a former friend—now the Headsman."

The steward seemed utterly dazed and confused.

"It is indeed marvellous," he said; "I can scarce believe it possible. But, of course, I never had any proof that he was dead. Yet, as he was not heard of, I took it for granted that he *was* dead."

"You then know the crime of which I was guilty?"

"I know all. But you can, if you choose, do a great deal towards retrieving the past. You are the chief witness that Lord Housden is an impostor."

"Ay, and if I live I *will* be the chief witness. I was about to endeavour to lay all before the queen."

He then told Harold of all that had occurred at the hut, and of the way he escaped.

"And for days," he concluded, "I have been chased by five men. They are, I know, employed by Housden, or by someone in his employ. They are, I am sure, in this very neighbourhood. At any moment they may——"

He was interrupted by a loud knock at the door, the effect of which was to cause the steward to fall upon his knees.

"I would not be surprised if that is them," said the host.

"Leave it to me," said Harold. "Quick! Give me your jacket and apron."

As he spoke, he threw off hat, cloak, and belt.

The host handed him his jacket and apron.

"Fasten yourselves in the room," said Harold. "Is the opposite room disengaged?"

"It is."

Downstairs went Harold and opened the front door.

A man who had just dismounted was at the threshold,

"Are you the host here?" he said.

"I am the son," was the reply.

"You will do. I am in search of a man who has escaped from justice, and I fancy he has taken refuge here."

"We have several guests," replied Harold, quietly. "Describe the man you are in search of."

The man described Thomas Ryder nearly accurately.

"Well," said Harold, "you have not made a mistake. The man you have described is here."

The horseman was so overjoyed with this information that he handed Harold a piece of money.

Of course our hero took it.

"Four of my companions will be here in a moment," said the man; "they are only making inquiries at the 'Load of Hay.'"

"Leave your horse there, then," said Harold; "he will be all right. You see," he said, confidentially, "if you go up and reason with the man, he may come down quietly with you. We don't want any disturbance in the house."

"True—true."

"I don't know whether the man is armed," continued Harold, "but you had better be prepared."

The man took a pistol from his belt, and cocked it.

Then Harold led the way upstairs.

Arrived at the room which was opposite to that in which was the host and Ryder, Harold paused and whispered—

"Get yourself ready."

"Good," replied the man, utterly unconscious that anything was wrong.

Harold opened the door, and the man eagerly entered.

But he had not taken six paces when Harold went behind him, suddenly placed his arms about his neck, and drew him backwards.

Taken thus entirely unawares, the man was unable to offer any resistance.

Harold snatched the pistol from his hand, and hurled him to the ground.

The host, hearing the noise, rushed out of the opposite room, lantern in hand.

"Hold this pistol to this man's head," said Harold, "and if I say fire—fire at once."

The man uttered a loud groan of despair.

He saw that this pit had been very neatly dug for him, and that he had blindly stumbled into it.

Harold took off the apron and folded it.

"I am about to gag you," he said, "and you will be kept for the present in this room. If you make any disturbance your arms will be tied behind your back. Do you understand that?"

"Yes, yes," replied the man, whose face was now as white as death; "but to whom am I speaking?"

"To one who will stand no nonsense. Now, before I gag you, tell me who employed you and your three companions."

"The host of the 'Orton Arms.'"

"He was trying to earn the reward offered by Lord Housden?"

The man started.

He saw that Harold knew all.

"Yes," he replied.

"Your name?"

"Andrews."

"It is as false as Hades!" cried the host. "I recognise him. This is Mark Skinner, one of the biggest rogues unhung!"

"He will meet with his deserts presently, or I am much mistaken," said Harold.

The landlord, then, did not know what was meant.

Having gagged the man, Harold took away his sword and dagger and locked the door upon him, but he left the key in the lock.

The host did not ask our hero what next he would do.

He saw that he was indeed a clever fellow, and a determined one.

Harold placed his sword and the pistol on the floor, where it could not be seen and yet be handy.

In less than ten minutes the other four men galloped up to the house.

By the way they demanded admittance, anyone would have fancied that at least they were queen's officers.

Harold descended.

But he was in no hurry, nor was he at all flurried.

"You are expected, gentlemen," he said, "a companion of yours has been here."

"Yes, where is he now?"

Harold saw that the ostler had removed the horse, which was fortunate for his plans.

"He first of all secured a prisoner——"

Harold was interrupted by loud chuckles of delight.

"Ha!" said one, "did I not say he would be found here? Well, he secured one man—where?"

"In an upstairs room, gentlemen. With my assistance he gagged him. Then, having locked the door upon him he went off to find you."

"He will be back directly, then."

"Enter, gentlemen," continued Harold.

The four dismounted and followed Harold into the house.

"Two bottles of the best," said one. "Then we will go up. Ha! we will take care that he don't escape us again."

Having conducted them inside, Harold left to get the wine.

But he paused just outside the door and listened.

"Now," said one, "you know what the host of the 'Orton Arms' said: 'Dead or alive, but better dead.' That will be all the easier for us, for if he is dead, we shall have no further trouble.

"We will kill him, and bribe the host here to take charge of the body, for, of course, the death of the man will have to be verified before we get the money.

"We will ascend, suddenly open the door, and fire upon him."

It was enough:

Harold fetched the wine—anything he could lay his hands upon—and again left the room to listen.

The four quickly swallowed the contents of the bottles.

Then the one who had acted as spokesman said—

"Skinner does not come."

By this Harold saw that the host was correct.

"No matter," said another. "We can do the job without him."

They called Harold, and directed him to lead the way upstairs.

"You will want a lantern," he said.

"No," was the reply, "we can do without it. We will wait on the landing until our friend comes."

Arrived on the landing, Harold showed them the door, and was then told he could descend, so as to admit the other man.

He went down the stairs as loudly as he could.

But he instantly reascended nearly to the top.

Only a few seconds did the four men pause.

Then one produced a tinder box and procured a light.

It was so faint, however, that scarcely anything could be seen.

So one called for a lantern.

Harold pretended not to hear him.

"No matter," said another, "we will make this do."

One then turned the key in the lock.

At once the man confined in the room rushed forward.

"Fire!" roared the man who had been the principal speaker."

Instantly four pistol shots rang out, and the man fell backwards into the room—dead.

The four ran in, and the light was brought to bear upon the fallen man.

Then a wild cry rang out.

"Mark Skinner, by——!" almost screamed one. "A trick has been played upon us. But by whom? By——"

"By me!" cried a loud voice.

The men simultaneously turned, drawing their blades as they did so.

They saw Harold standing in the doorway.

Behind him, lantern in hand, stood the host, now, it is true, somewhat alarmed at the extraordinary events which had just taken place.

The four men were about to rush forward, when Harold presented a pistol at the foremost.

Of course, he had to chance whether they had other pistols.

Fortunately they had not, and their spare ammunition was carried in their saddle bags.

"Attempt to quit this room," said Harold, "at your peril."

The men paused.

There was but one shot in that pistol, it is true, but neither cared to receive it.

"You will consider yourselves prisoners," continued Harold, "and here you will remain until placed in the hands of officers of justice.

"You would wish to know who I am. Well, I will simply tell you that I know by whom you are employed—the host of the 'Orton Arms,' who has taken his instructions from Lord Housden, or, as he is sometimes called, Alsdon.

"Now throw your swords here, and also your other arms."

The men hesitated. Then the first made a slight movement forward.

"Beware!" said Harold, sternly, "if you move again I will fire, so help me heaven! Host, get the two pistols from my belt."

The host stood the lantern down and speedily procured the weapons.

"We are done," said one of the men, as, with a curse, he hurled his sword, and then his dagger, to where Harold stood. "After all our pains we are baulked!"

The others at once followed his example, and the host took possession of the weapons.

The door was then closed and locked.

"Is the lock a safe one?" asked Harold.

"Yes, it is a new one."

"What of the window?"

"There are two strong bars on the outside."

"Nevertheless, let your ostler watch it from the yard."

The host left the house and gave the necessary instructions to the ostler.

It was fortunate he did so, for, in a few minutes, a loud crash was heard, and on inquiries being made, it was ascertained that one of the men had opened the window and looked out.

The instant his head appeared the active ostler hurled a brick at him.

It broke the glass and cut the man's face.

The steward, who had been nearly frightened to death at what had been taking place, was now escorted below, and the best part of a bottle of good wine given him.

"And now," said Harold, as he handed the host a sum of money, "look over your old clothes and see whether you have anything that will do for this unhappy man."

The host looked, but found nothing which would fit him.

"No matter," said Harold, as he took his own cloak and placed it over the steward's shoulders, "this will conceal his rags. I know one who will quickly provide him with some clothes."

The steward burst into tears.

"This kindness from the son of one I so deeply wronged overwhelms me," he said.

"I am afraid you were not wholly to blame."

"You are indeed correct."

"Did you, or your son, first suggest the plan which was to deprive my father of his just rights?"

"He who is called my son."

"Called?"

"Ay, he is not my son. The real truth is that I adopted him when quite a child. But I will tell all when I get to the Tower."

"Yes, you will be more composed then."

Turning to the host, Harold said—

"You had better engage a man to watch on the outside of the door, for you must not take the ostler from his post.

"Arrived at the Tower, I will inform one of what has occurred, and men will be sent to take charge of the prisoners.

"I will take particular care that they do not leave prison; so you need not fear they will molest you."

In another half-hour the four gentlemen to whom the Headsman had addressed the letter arrived, and were made acquainted with what had occurred during their absence, whereupon each regretted his absence.

They were loud in their expressions of approval of Harold's conduct, and warmly shook hands with him.

Fine fellows were these four friends—tall, soldierly, and gentlemanly; while their rich attire proclaimed them to be persons of wealth.

One read the letter aloud, after which he said—

"There you have it, my friends. An adventure, I'll be sworn."

"Yes," said Harold. "And I am afraid it may prove a dangerous one."

"So much the better. What did you say your name was?"

"Harold Forrester."

"Good. And now—do we set out at once for the Tower?"

"At once."

"Master host, bring your bill, and then, when we have settled it, saddle our horses."

"The steward can ride the dead man's horse," said Harold.

The animals were soon before the door and the party mounted and set off.

Reaching the "Tower Arms," the four

gentlemen entered, Harold assuring them that they would soon be joined by the Headsman.

Then, with the steward at his side, he proceeded to the Tower, where they were admitted by an officer to a large extent in the confidence of the Headsman.

The reader, of course, understands that Harold was simply smuggled in and out of the fortress.

Had the lieutenant been made aware that he was within the Tower, he would at once have ordered him under arrest as an escaped prisoner.

No sooner was the steward conducted before Don Fernando, than he threw himself upon his knees, and implored pardon.

All were shocked at his appearance.

It seemed certain that he could not live long.

"You shall have forgiveness in exchange for being a witness against Lord Housden as he calls himself," said Do Fernando.

"I accept—gratefully. But he is n my son."

"Not?"

"Nay, I adopted him when my ow child died. He it was who first suggested the plan which was carried into effect."

"Well, he will suffer for it soon. We will talk of this anon," he said to the Headsman. "But now we had better go to the 'Tower Arms' to make the necessary arrangements for to-morrow night."

CHAPTER XLVII.

HOW THE COACH WAS STOPPED, AND OF THE BATTLE FOUGHT ON THE BRIXTON ROAD.

THERE was not a prettier village in England than Brixton at the period of this romance.

It boasted many noble residences—the principal being that built by Sir Walter Raleigh, then new.

Elizabeth had frequently made a journey to it, and often remained many days to witness the various sports given in her honour, and which, though they did not vie with those at Kenilworth, nevertheless attracted thousands of persons of all ranks to the neighbourhood.

It was only on these occasions that Brixton thrived.

The hostelries then did a splendid business, and so did the shopkeepers of every class; they had to make in a few days what was to keep them for, perhaps, a few months, and, as in these days, they did not hesitate to "make" it.

Half-a-mile, or, perhaps a little further, from the wonderfully pretty oaken church, was the residence of Master Vaughan, an old and valued friend of Launcelot Duke.

It was small, but highly picturesque, while the grounds were the absolute perfection of prettiness.

Really, in the summer, it looked as if the house had been dropped in the centre of a garden of flowers,

And it was here that Eveline and Lucy Moss had been taken for safety, and it is needless to say it made both of them sigh for a life in the country.

On the morning after the interview between Housden and the blackguard Redcliffe, the ostler, who, as will be remembered, was intercepted by Housden, arrived at the house.

He found Master Vaughan, Eveline, and Lucy in the garden.

Eveline looked pale, careworn and thoughtful.

She was, indeed, thinking of Harold when the ostler handed her the forged note.

She read it and passed it to Master Vaughan.

Not the faintest suspicion of treachery had she.

She could have sworn that the writing was her father's.

Master Vaughan, too, who had had scores of letters from his old frien would not have questioned the docume for one moment.

"You saw Master Duke, then?" said.

"Oh, yes," was the lying reply; "he treated me kindly. He is a very nice gentleman."

"He treats everyone kindly. Well,

now go and tell Grayson that at nine he is to be ready with the coach; and you will go with him."

The ostler bowed and departed.

"So we have to take leave of each other," said Master Vaughan. "I am very sorry, indeed. As you know, we were making up our minds to receive Harold Forrester in a few days. However, I suppose your father finds that your presence is necessary while he is making up his accounts. Poor child! you are so pale, and look so ill! A few more days here would have done you a world of good."

"True. But I must obey my father's orders. Besides, I may see him whom I am so anxious about."

"I trust you may; and God grant he is rapidly getting out of all his difficulties."

Eveline and Lucy at once began to make preparations for their departure; and in this they were assisted by the three or four female servants, to whom, in the short time they had been there, they had endeared themselves.

*   *   *   *

"Captain" Redcliffe, in his own mind, was quite confident of success.

How could there be any danger in an enterprise, the particulars of which were absolutely unknown except to the plotters?

Nevertheless, he was resolved to be prepared for everything.

There *was* such a thing as a rescue by strangers.

That he had experienced more than once in his life.

With the assistance of his "right hand," Dick Ralston, he selected twelve of the youngest and strongest men from his vile associates.

He knew nearly all of them as men who were prepared to risk anything for a good reward.

The horses were picked animals—and we need scarcely add that not one was ever purchased.

When Redcliffe or his men required horses, they always "found" them.

Soon after the hour of seven they prepared to set out.

Dick Ralston provided each man with a small flask of spirits, while Redcliffe examined their arms, and supplied them with spare ammunition.

Then he despatched them two by two, so as not to attract attention.

They were to meet at a spot about one mile from Brixton.

They rode off in high spirits, feeling certain of a large reward and no trouble.

Certainly not the faintest idea had they that they were about to take part in a highly dangerous enterprise.

The flasks of spirits had been provided, so that the men should have no excuse for halting at any holsteries; nor did they.

But, nevertheless, it was nearly half-past eight when the last of them joined Redcliffe and Ralston at the appointed spot—a lonely lane a mile from the church.

"Now," said Redcliffe, "get ready. The coach, instead of going along the main road, will keep to the right. So, if we ride to the end of this lane, and cross a few fields, we shall be in the exact position. Follow."

Along the lane they went at a walk. The narrow road being heavy and wet, the tread of the horses was effectually deadened.

On either side of the lane were tall hedges; so that in most places, it was impossible to see into the adjoining fields.

Had Redcliffe, who, like Ralston, was keeping a sharp look out, chanced, when the centre of the lane was reached, to stand up in his stirrups, he would have seen something which would have thrown him into a state of the greatest terror.

Behind a clump of firs were no less than eight horsemen.

There they stood, as motionless as statues.

But the moment Redcliffe and his bravos had passed, one of them slipped from his saddle, scampered across the field, and peered through the hedge.

It was Mat o' the Mist.

Returning, he uttered a few words, and sprang into the saddle, his movements being as rapid and as quaint as a monkey's.

Then the whole party moved silently across the field in the direction taken by Redcliffe.

*   *   *   *

Shortly after the hour of nine, the coach, a huge, lumbering affair, drawn by four immense horses, drove up to the house.

Very seldom did Master Vaughan use this cumbersome affair; he, like the majority of people, preferred horseback.

Coaches were then only just coming into use, and the builders had but little notion of what ought to be suitable for the road.

So they built the coaches after the same fashion as the country waggons, the wheels and axles being of enormous weight.

Springs had not even been dreamt of, so the reader can perhaps guess what kind of comfort it was to ride in one of these coaches along rough, uneven roads.

In most instances it was simply torture, and it was for this reason that Elizabeth refused to retain the present of a superbly-decorated coach, given her by the afterwards celebrated carriage builders, Morgan and Loch.

Master Vaughan, when he *did* ride in a coach, never had more than two horses, and their average speed was six miles an hour.

But, so that Eveline should reach London Bridge as quickly as possible, he ordered four horses to be harnessed to it, and instructed the driver not to spare the whip.

The driver, a man named Grayson, was a very worthy fellow—a man who would not be guilty of an act of treachery for any amount.

He was just as true as the ostler, who was on the box beside him, was false.

The last farewell was said, tearfully on both sides. The servants stood respectfully aside, and the coach rolled off.

"Don't forget, Grayson," were Master Vaughan's last words, "the right road. Though," he muttered, as the coach disappeared in the darkness, "I cannot think why Master Duke should have selected that instead of the main road."

At first Grayson drove slowly, but when he had the horses well in hand, he made them go at their hardest.

On they went, the rapid beating of the horses' iron hoofs and the rumble of the broad wheels being heard a long way off.

Suddenly Grayson uttered an exclamation, and endeavoured to pull up his horses.

He thought he had made a mistake, and was about to plunge into the midst of a clump of trees.

But the semi-darkness deceived him.

In another instant he was horrified to see that it was not trees before him, but a number of mounted men.

No sooner was he convinced of this than he slashed his horses into a gallop, and tried to rush through the men.

But the next instant two shots rang out, and—not the coachman, but the villainous ostler fell dead.

Truly he had swiftly received a just reward for his treachery.

Again and again did Grayson, after calling to the ladies not to be alarmed, try to get his now nearly-maddened horses through the crowd of horsemen.

It was useless.

Three or four of them seized the heads of the leading horses, and threatened Grayson with instant death if he did not drop the reins.

The poor fellow, bathed in perspiration, and terrified at what would probably happen to the ladies, was forced to comply.

Redcliffe dashed to the coach door.

He was about to open it, when there was a tremendous shout.

At once turning his horse, he saw a number of men advancing at full gallop.

"A rescue, by heavens!" he cried, as he unsheathed his sword.

"Stand firm! stand firm!" he yelled, as he saw his bravos backing their horses.

Then, standing in his stirrups, he cried—

"Draw and fire!"

Before his astonished men could obey the order, several shots were fired by the advancing horsemen, and no less than four of Redcliffe's men rolled lifeless from their saddles.

Under cover of the smoke, and before it was possible for Redcliffe's men to take aim, Harold, with Don Fernando on his right and the Headsman on the left, dashed like a whirlwind into them, cutting them down right and left.

For some few minutes the fight continued with terrific fury, Harold being foremost in it.

Again and again he shouted that no mercy was to be shown—nor was it.

Meantime Grayson, though slightly wounded by a stray ball, waited his opportunity and, when it came, he snatched up the reins and lashed his horses.

The poor, frightened creatures wanted no whip, however.

They plunged forward, and more than once it looked as if the coach would be overturned, for the ponderous wheels rolled over more than one dead body.

At length they got clear of the spot, and Grayson quickly got them into a gallop.

Suddenly he heard a voice shouting—

"Hold! stop! It is I—Harold Forrester, who calls."

Grayson had heard Master Vaughan speak of Harold, and he at once pulled in.

Harold leapt from his saddle and pulled the coach door open, while Grayson, jumping from the box, took down one of the lanterns.

A cry of despair escaped both their lips, as they saw that the coach was occupied by one person only.

That was Lucy Moss.

There she was, huddled up in the opposite corner of the coach, her head leaning against the cushions.

Her pretty face was absolutely covered with blood, which flowed from a deep gash in her forehead.

The poor girl was totally unconscious.

Harold was nearly distracted.

What had become of Eveline?

"For God's sake!" he cried, "tell me —was not Mistress Duke in the coach?"

"Assuredly, sir," stammered the bewildered coachman.

"Then where is she now?"

"Heaven knows! I had not the faintest idea that she had left the coach. God help me! I am indeed a most unfortunate man."

"Her disappearance is not the result of your negligence, that I well know. But here, take this flask—try and bring the poor girl round while I return to my friends. Perhaps Mistress Duke ran from the coach, and is close handy."

He rejoined his friends, and found that the battle was over.

Seven of Redcliffe's men had been killed outright, three had been grievously wounded, including Dick Ralston, while the others had contrived to escape.

The first person Harold saw was Mat, who had been wounded in the head.

"Go to the coach yonder," said Harold "You are wanted there."

He then informed his friends of Eveline's disappearance.

Instantly a search was commenced, but no trace of her was discovered.

The reader must know the particulars. They are as follows.

When Harold and his friends fired their first volley, and the next moment dashed into the midst of the bravos, Redcliffe, after calling upon his men to stand firm, turned his horse, spurred him to the coach door, and dismounted.

Under cover of the smoke from the repeated discharges on both sides, and which was so dense, that the coachman could see nothing but indistinct forms around him, Redcliffe pulled open the door.

At once Lucy rushed forward to protect Eveline from any violence; and Redcliffe, with a bitter oath, dealt her a blow across the head with his sword. Then, as the girl fell back, he plunged into the coach and seized Eveline.

Despite the sounds of strife around her, Eveline retained full possession of her senses.

But, unfortunately, she was unarmed.

The "pockets" in the coach held no pistol, as was the case when Master Vaughan travelled.

It was a great pity, for Eveline would have been perfectly justified in using them.

"It is you I want," said Redcliffe, "and you I will have, in defiance of your friends, who, however, will all be killed. Come forth; and mind—if you utter one cry I will kill you. My orders are—dead or alive."

"Monster!" gasped Eveline, clinging to the woodwork, "you would not dare to kill me?"

"Not dare? By Satan, you are very much mistaken. If I take you alive I get a certain reward; if I fail I get nothing. But I would have my revenge, and would kill you. Come."

There was no help for it. Resistance was useless.

Redcliffe hurried her out of the coach, took her in his arms, raised her on to his saddle, and then mounting, rode away as fast as the horse could go.

It was a powerful animal, for, as a matter of course, Redcliffe always took care to have the first pick; and it did not appear to be at all troubled with its extra burden, a fact which caused Redcliffe to utter many a chuckle of satisfaction.

"Let them fight," he thought; "it does not suit *me* to do so.

"Who the devil are they but Harold Forrester and his friends? That I saw the Masked Headsman I am sure. By the holy rood! it was fortunate he did not reach me. I should have fallen as surely as that I am riding this horse.

"Everyone of my men will be killed, I'll warrant it. Well, what is the odds? I can get plenty more. Still, I hope Ralston will contrive to escape.

"Thunder and lightning! how did they *get* the information? Perhaps from one of Lord Housden's servants. We may have been overheard.

"Well, it is quite certain that I can't go to his house now, nor can I go to the "Parson's Retreat" direct. Then where *can* I go? Hang me if I know. If I could—but wait! I have it! I will take her to old Gabriel Everton. Good, good! Yes, she will be safe there. I will hasten to inform his lordship, get the money, and—well, there my responsibility ends.

"Captain Redcliffe, you have certainly come out of this in splendid fashion, and your reward is absolutely certain.

"Of course, when I return to the 'Retreat,' I shall be asked this and asked that, but I have my answers all ready.

"I shall say that I was bound to ride away on account of the girl. Then a hundred crowns among them, and I am once again a hero."

*　　*　　*　　*

The search for Eveline having proved unsuccessful, the bodies of the fallen men were examined.

It was hoped that the body of Redcliffe would be found among them.

When it was not, one of the four gentlemen who had so kindly lent their assistance, suggested that the absence of Redcliffe accounted for the disappearance of Eveline.

Dick Ralston, who, as we have said, was dangerously wounded, had been wearing a mask.

When this was removed, the Headsman recognised him.

"So, Dick Ralston," he said, "we meet once more!"

"Ay, and for the last time," groaned Ralston. "I shall never get over this."

"Where are you wounded?"

"Here," pointing to his forehead, "and here."

And he pointed to his breast.

"A blade has nearly passed through me," he said.

The Headsman rapidly examined him.

"Yes," he said, "I am afraid that you are fatally wounded."

"I am *sure* of it."

"You stopped to fight, you see, but your leader, Captain Redcliffe, took to his heels."

The ruse was effective.

Ralston opened wide his bloodshot eyes.

"No?" he said.

"I say yes. He ran away without crossing a blade, and no doubt he took the girl with him.

Ralston cursed him again and again.

"Ay, I see," he said. "He did not care for us. It is only the reward he seeks."

"From Lord Housden, you mean?"

"Yes."

"What was the amount?"

"A thousand crowns. But you say he has taken the girl with him?"

"No doubt of it. Now do you know where it is likely he will take her? Remember, he did not think of you. Answer me truly, and I swear that, if you should die, I will see that you are properly buried."

"You swear that?"

"I repeat—I swear it."

"Well, now that he knows you would be after him, he would not go to Lord Housden, nor would he return to the Retreat, at least, not with the girl. He would take her— But no. Let me think."

Impatiently did they await him.

At last he said—

"I would wager my life that he takes her to his father-in-law, old Gabriel Everton."

"Gabriel Everton? Not he of Cloth Fair?"

"The same."

"That man is really his father-in-law?"

"He is."

"Good. You hear, Harold?"

"Ay, ay; let the wretch wait."

At this moment Mat returned to them with the information that Lucy had recovered sufficiently to be able to speak.

Thereupon they adjourned to the coach, and their suspicions that Redcliffe had carried Eveline off were at once confirmed by Lucy.

"Listen," said Harold. "We will go to Cloth Fair and demand Eveline. If we would rescue her, it must be done at once."

"I agree with that," said the Headsman. "I know this Gabriel Everton. What we must do in the first place is this: we will return to the Tower and inform Master Duke that, in consequence of a slight illness, his daughter did not set out at all. Then we will go to Cloth Fair. Lucy I will place with a medical friend."

This was unanimously agreed to, and the Headsman continued—

"The coachman will return with the coach to Master Vaughan, and in order to account for the disappearance of the ostler, and the bullet holes in the woodwork, he will say that he was attacked when *returning* by robbers, who fancied the coach was occupied."

To this the coachman agreed.

Then the Headsman gave him the address of his medical man, and Mat, entering the vehicle, it was driven away.

Two of the gentlemen who had so kindly assisted them, remained to watch the bodies until the authorities could be communicated with.

With the exception of Harold and the Headsman, each had received one or more wounds, but they were not of a serious character.

Yet, had they not dashed upon the bravos like a whirlwind, and fired simultaneously as they came up with them, it is more than likely that two or three would have fallen to rise no more.

CHAPTER XLVIII.

OF WHAT OCCURRED AT THE " MONEY-CHANGER'S " AT CLOTH FAIR.

"CLOTH FAIR," then really what the name indicated, consisted of about a hundred wooden houses of various sizes, and all of them of great age, and they were divided by narrow alleys, which were never swept nor cleansed.

Of course, there were many businesses besides dealers in cloth—which came principally from abroad—and of these, one was that of a "money lender and changer," and the name of the proprietor was Gabriel Everton.

"Money lender and changer."

This was the announcement beneath the sign of his house—an anchor.

But, as a matter of fact, Gabriel did little business in the lending or money changing line.

It was no secret among the inhabitants of the rookery—for it was nothing else —that Gabriel Everton was a thorough rogue, and that he had exclusive dealings with the ruffians in London, who enriched themselves when the backs of honest men were turned, and, very frequently in a far more terrible fashion.

Nor was it much of a secret that " Captain " Redcliffe married one of his daughters, probably thinking that that might be the means—firstly of his being better treated by Gabriel, or, in other words, receiving more for what he might offer than if he were no relation, and, secondly, because he thought that, when the old man died, he would come in for a fair share of his ill-gotten gains.

It was close upon the hour of midnight when Gabriel's youngest daughter —the only one now with him, and the only person besides himself on the premises, heard a tap at the window.

Peering through a hole in the shutter, she made out the figure of a man, and also that he carried what looked like a bundle in his arms.

Nevertheless, she paid no attention to the knock, nor did she when it was repeated a second and third time.

She was waiting for something else.

It came in a moment.

The man commenced to whistle the chorus of a peculiar drinking song.

It was enough. Jane Everton left the window and opened the door.

" What ? " she said, opening her eyes in astonishment, " you ? "

" Why not ? " asked Redcliffe, for he it was, " why not, eh ? "

"What have you got?"

"A little lady, every inch of her," grinned Redcliffe.

"A woman?"

"No, a girl. But get out of the way, I want to take her in."

"Who gave you leave to bring her here?"

"No one. What leave do I require to bring anything or anybody to my father-in-law's house?"

"You will require the old man's leave to bring a woman here, at any rate."

"Why you—— But, ah! I see. Oh, oh! You are afraid that I may be forgetting your excellent sister. Do not fear, Janie. It is impossible that the beauty of any female could wean me from devoting all my attention to your *charming* sister."

"Let me have none of your foolery!" growled Jane. "Who *is* this creature?"

"A lady for whose capture I am to receive a certain sum. And, if you are good, and do exactly as I say, why I will not forget you."

Jane made way, though it was not with a very good grace; and Redcliffe carried his bundle into the dingy, foul-smelling parlour.

Poor Eveline!

For more than an hour now she had been unconscious.

For this Redcliffe had been thankful, since he had less difficulty with her, and no fear that she would shriek for assistance.

He laid her upon the couch, while Jane went to her father.

Gabriel soon made his appearance.

He was an Englishman, born in London, but he bore a striking resemblance to a Polish Jew.

He was very old, but he was still active; his hearing was good, and his eyesight excellent.

"So you are to have a reward for this lady?" he asked.

"I am."

"Much?"

"A considerable amount."

"Is she—— But she is unconscious."

"She is, and has been for some time now. But it is nothing serious."

"That is more than *you* know. It looks serious to me."

Redcliffe was alarmed.

"Do you really think so?" he asked.

"I do. You had better have a doctor at once."

"A doctor! Never."

"And why?"

"Her whereabouts must, for the present, be kept a profound secret."

"How is a doctor likely to recognise her?"

"She would tell him all. But why can't you attend to her? What of your boasts about your medical skill?"

"Well, well, don't get angry. I will see what I can do. But you had better carry her upstairs, Janie, and I will attend to her."

"I will if I am paid for it," said Jane.

"Pay yourself," said Redcliffe. "There is a pretty bracelet on her wrist, have that."

Once again taking Eveline in his arms, he carried her up the stairs and placed her on the bed in a chamber used by Jane.

"See what you can do, old man," he said, "while I go and find a place to put up my horse. And remember, that for what you do you will be paid."

"Yes, yes, I will remember."

"To be sure," grinned Jane. "Did you ever know him to forget?"

To give the old man his due, he was decidedly clever in simple cases requiring treatment, and it was not long before he was successful in restoring Eveline to consciousness.

"She is very beautiful," thought Jane. "Who can have employed Redcliffe?"

"Where am I?" were Eveline's first words, as her eyes wandered slowly around the miserable apartment.

"In my house," replied Gabriel.

"In what part of London?"

"Oh, a very pretty part—a wonderfully pretty part, my dear."

Whereat Jane burst into a loud laugh.

"Hush, hush," said Gabriel. "Your merriment distresses the young lady."

Then after a pause, during which our unfortunate heroine fixed her eyes upon Jane's peculiar face, as if trying to read her character," he said—

"What is your name?"

"My name is Eveline Duke," replied Eveline, without hesitation.

"And you live at——"

"London Bridge."

Gabriel opened wide his eyes.

"What," he asked, "are you——"

"Can't you see that your questions *distress* the young lady?" interrupted Jane, with a sneer.

"Be silent!" cried Gabriel, stamping his foot. "Tell me, young lady," he added, "the name of your father."

"Launcelot Duke."

"Soh!" muttered Gabriel, "this is really the diamond merchant's daughter. Hem!"

Before he could ask any more questions, Redcliffe was heard demanding re-admittance.

Jane opened the door.

"Well," he asked, "how is she now?"

"Better, much better."

"Good. Tell Gabriel to come here."

Gabriel quickly appeared.

"Look you," said Redcliffe, "I have changed my mind. I shall set off at once to see the gentleman interested in this girl."

"Very good — that is an excellent plan. There is nothing like striking the iron while it is hot. In other words, if you delay, the gentleman might take a fancy to another pretty face. Then you would have had all your work for nothing."

"Keep strict watch upon her."

"Don't fear as to that."

"And here are fifty crowns. Divide that amount between you. I shall, no doubt, bring the gentleman with me, and you may depend that he will give you a large sum."

"He is wealthy?"

"He rolls in riches."

Another few minutes and Redcliffe had set out on a journey to Housden.

It was about an hour after this that a man, attired very much like the rogues who assisted Redcliffe, walked up to the house and knocked upon the door.

There was no answer.

Gabriel heard the knock, however.

He was alone now, for Jane was up-stairs with Eveline, and we may add that she was torturing her with all sorts of questions, but she got no replies, for Eveline saw that she had fallen into the hands of vultures as bad as Redcliffe.

The knock being repeated with energy, Gabriel went to the door, placed a chair, and, mounting it, put his head out of the fanlight.

"Well, well?" he said, sharply, "what the devil is it, eh?"

"Ah! Gabriel," said the man, "is that you, eh? And how are you?"

When the reader is informed that the man was our hero cleverly disguised, he will admit that this was a pretty daring speech, for he had never seen Gabriel Everton in his life.

It was, however, partly effective.

"I don't know you," said Gabriel.

"You forget me, Gabriel, for it is long since I came this way. At one time, however, we did a good business together. I was then with poor old Sharpley."

This was only a random shot.

But Harold considered it more than likely that a man of this description had had dealings with Sharpley.

He quickly found that such was the case.

"Oh!" said Gabriel. "Well, what are you here for?"

Harold held up a small box.

"Something good," he whispered. "And I shan't be particular if you are quick. I have a good many miles to go, and if I hadn't been short of money, I would not have troubled you."

"Well, I will admit you. But the next time, don't forget the signal."

Harold was overjoyed.

But his joy quickly passed away.

"After all," he thought, "she may not be here. In that case, all our labours will have been in vain."

Gabriel opened the door and ushered Harold into a small room on the right.

Jane heard footsteps, and, being curious, she descended.

As she appeared on the threshold, Gabriel advanced.

"Fool!" he whispered, "why do you leave her?"

Though the whisper was low, Harold overheard it.

"Thank God!" he muttered, "she *is* here."

"I suppose I can come down when I like?" said Jane, fiercely.

"Go, go, girl, and think of the reward."

Jane, with a muttered oath and an eager look at our hero, slowly withdrew.

"Now," said Gabriel, closing the door, "now let me see what you have."

Harold, with the speed of lightning, snatched a pistol from beneath his cloak and presenting it at Gabriel's head, he said—

"One word, and I fire!"

"LADY HOUSDEN SUDDENLY PRODUCED A PISTOL."

Gabriel was so astounded and terrified that he staggered back and dropped into a chair, gasping for breath.

"I am not here to rob you," continued Harold, "but I am here to take charge of a young lady who has been brought here by a scoundrel in the pay of a certain nobleman."

Gabriel shook his head.

"You are mistaken," he said. "There is no young lady here."

"It is false. I just now overheard your whispered conversation with that young woman, and what you said confirmed my suspicions. You will remain in that chair, for it is my intention to lock the door upon you."

"No, no!" yelled Gabriel, leaping to his feet, "I will remain quiet. I——"

"I repeat that I shall lock the door upon you. And if I hear you call out, I will take care that you are severely punished. I am not alone, as I will convince you."

Gabriel, with a groan, resumed his seat.

Then Harold removed the key from the inside, locked the door upon him, and ascended the stairs.

When he reached the room in which Eveline had been placed, Jane was just coming out.

She had heard the whistles, and wondered what they could mean.

"By the Virgin!" she gasped, when she saw Harold, "what do you do here?"

"Stand aside," said Harold, sternly.

"Stand aside? I will see——"

"Stand *aside!*" thundered Harold, pushing her from him.

"Harold! Harold!" cried Eveline, rushing to the door.—"surely I cannot be mistaken—it is my Harold!"

"It is, indeed, my darling!" said Harold, as he folded Eveline to his breast. "I am here to save you. Come, let us leave this house——"

"*You* leave it," shrieked Jane, "but *she* does not. Attempt to take her at your peril."

"Attempt to stop us at *yours*, woman! Proceed, dear Eveline, I follow you."

Eveline, with a joyous cry, bounded down the stairs.

Harold followed her—backwards.

Arrived at the street door, he threw the key of the room in which Gabriel was confined into the passage.

"Take it," he said; "unlock the door, and tell Gabriel Everton that soon there will be a reckoning with him."

Jane did not attempt to pick up the key until the street door had closed.

Not likely!

She saw the butts of a couple of pistols in Harold's belt.

Though a woman, she was wise enough to know that force would undoubtedly be met *with* force.

Our hero placed his cloak about Eveline's head and shoulders.

Then taking her hand, he said—

"Come, my darling, the Headsman awaits us not far from here. Come quickly, for we have much to do."

They were hurrying through Smithfield, when suddenly, what at first seemed like a huge monkey, scrambled from a pole and dropped at their feet.

It was Mat o' the Mist.

"Ha!" said Harold, "how did you get here?"

"Oh, easily enough," laughed Mat. "I have a good pair of legs. Having placed Lucy in the charge of my master's medical friend, I was hurrying towards the Tower, when I stumbled across my master and Don Fernando at the foot of Holborn Hill, where they wait with a spare horse.

"They told me that you had gone on to Cloth Fair to endeavour to rescue Mistress Eveline—and you have, God bless her—and you," he added, doffing his cap—"and that, if I waited about Smithfield, I might see you. So, in order to command a view of all the paths, I perched myself up yonder."

"Good! Right glad are we to see you, faithful Mat."

"As we walk towards Holborn," said Mat, "I will tell you something of the very greatest importance. Ha, ha! Some people are sharp, but then, so is Mat."

"There is little doubt about that."

"You see," Mat continued, after leaving Lucy, I was crossing by the Fleet, when I saw a horseman coming towards me.

"I don't know how it was, but, fancying that I recognised him, I darted behind a post.

"Another moment and the horseman

passed. At once I recognised him. It was Redcliffe."

"Indeed! Are you sure?"

"Certain. He was then going slowly, but, as soon as he reached Fleet Street, he went on at a gallop."

"So you followed him?"

"Ay, that I did—every inch of the way. Though he went on at such a tremendous pace, I never lost sight of him. And where, think you, did he stop?"

"At the Manor House."

"Correct. And he was at once admitted. But this is not all."

"Not all?"

"No," said Mat, rubbing his hands together. "I have discovered that at least one of his servants will take a bribe.

"When I saw Redcliffe go in at the front, I went to the back; and, by the Virgin! I was nearly discovered, for I saw three females.

"Two were heavily muffled, but the third, I could see, was one of the servants.

"What was said I could not overhear; but I saw one of the ladies hand the servant a bag of money.

"Then, in another moment, they disappeared through a small door."

"What can be the meaning of that?"

"I know not. But it strikes me that his enemies are now fast closing around him. But here are my master and Don Fernando."

To them Mat repeated his story; and, after a brief consultation, the Headsman said—

"We must be careful and rapid now. If we do not proceed at once to the Manor House, Housden will have left with Redcliffe; for, of course, the villain has been to tell him that Eveline is safe at Cloth Fair.

"Mat must proceed at once to the Tower with Eveline, and having placed her in her father's arms, he must come at once to the Manor House with Thomas Ryder. You understand that, Mat?"

"Perfectly; and you may rely upon it that I shall not be long, for I can get horses at the 'Tower Arms.'"

"Adieu for the present, dear Eveline," said Harold, pressing a kiss upon her brow. "We shall shortly meet again,

when, I trust, we shall be able to say that our troubles have come to an end."

"Oh, Harold!" whispered Eveline, the tears welling into her eyes, "I fear that, if you go to the Manor House, something dreadful will happen."

"Fear not," smiled Harold; "I am well able to guard myself."

Having wrapped the cloak still more closely around her, Mat took her hand and led her away in the direction of the Tower, while our hero, the Headsman, and Don Fernando rode off towards Charing Cross.

* * * *

In the meantime, Redcliffe, having at once obtained admission to the Manor House, was, after a short delay, conducted to Housden.

"Idiot!" thundered his lordship, "you have blundered. The servant tells me that no lady accompanies you."

"True," replied Redcliffe, selecting and seating himself in the best chair the room contained: "but when you have heard my story, you will see the reason I have not brought her here."

"What—did you succeed in seizing her?"

"Ay, that did I, Master Alsdon," grinned Redcliffe. "Right out of the centre of a fierce fight."

"Where is she now?"

"At the house of my father-in-law at Cloth Fair—a place to which no one would think of going."

"Good! good! But the fight? A fierce fight, say you?"

"Ay, we were attacked by at least fifty men, and they were commanded by Harold Forrester, the Headsman, and others—at least, I have no doubt it was them.

"Heaven knows how they obtained the information. They rushed down upon us like a whirlwind, and just as we had stopped the coach.

"Of course, several of my men seemed paralyzed, for they had thought the job a very easy one. Had it not been for me, it would have been all over in an instant.

"Fortunately I did not lose my presence of mind. Having shot the coachman dead, I backed to the coach door, where I was at once surrounded by a swarm of men.

"But I soon showed them what I was

made of, for I cut them down right and left.

"Then, when I had cleared a space, I dismounted, tore open the coach door, seized the girl, placed her before me on the saddle, and rode away.

"I was followed for a long distance, shot after shot being fired at me; yet I escaped untouched."

Having delivered himself of this parcel of infamous lies, the ruffian coolly stretched forth his hand, took his lordship's silver goblet, containing wine, and drank the contents.

"How far your story is true," said Housden, "I should not like to guess; but——"

"True?" interrupted Redcliffe, affecting indignation; "every *word* is true."

"Well, as to the battle, whatever it was, I care not. But as to the girl, why I will set off and see her."

"At once?"

"As soon as I am ready."

"And the money?"

"I will place it in your hands as soon as I see that the girl is really at Cloth Fair."

Redcliffe scowled.

"I see," he said, "you doubt me."

"By no means."

"Then why do you not hand me the money as agreed? I have many to pay out of it."

"Would you buy a horse without you saw it?"

"I *never* buy horses."

"Nor I a pig in a poke!"

"Let me tell you this: I deserve double pay for what I have gone through in getting possession of this girl. Then look what I am answerable for. A round dozen of my men were, no doubt, slain."

"That is *their* business. The sum I agreed to give you I will pay, but neither more nor less. Now, will you await me, or will you go on to Cloth Fair?"

"I will go on, and await you at the gates. You know the place well?"

"Very well indeed."

Housden rang a bell and the servant appeared.

Housden looked hard at her.

He saw that she was very pale and looked scared.

"What ails *you*?" he asked, knitting his brows.

"My lord," stammered the woman, "her—— Nothing ails me."

"Do not tell me a falsehood. You are as white as death, and you tremble as though you had been confronted by a ghost."

"Yes, yes, my lord," said the woman, quickly. "I went down in the vaults to get some wood, and I saw something all in white——"

"Bah!" interrupted Housden, impatiently, "do not attempt to trifle with me. You saw nothing. There are no such things as ghosts. Go, and do not make a fool of yourself again. Here! see this gentleman to the door."

Redcliffe bowed and followed the woman.

Housden then seated himself to write, thinking no more of what the woman had said.

Ah! if he had known the real reason of her paleness.

The fact was that that very woman had just received from two ladies the sum of two hundred pounds to admit them into the house, and but five minutes before she answered Housden's call, she had conducted them into the anteroom.

Redcliffe, who, as may be supposed, was in no good humour, sprang into his saddle and rode off on his return to Cloth Fair.

He little thought that his movements were being closely watched by three persons, and that as he rode away one of them followed him.

Totally unconscious of danger, he rode straight on, looking neither to the right nor to the left.

He had reached a piece of land which adjoined St. Martin's Field's, when a horseman sprang before him.

So suddenly did he appear, that Redcliffe's horse, terrified, reared high into the air.

The moon was shining brilliantly at the time, and Redcliffe almost shouted aloud as he recognised—THE HEADSMAN OF OLD LONDON BRIDGE.

Yes, it was indeed that dreaded man who thus confronted him.

"So, Captain Redcliffe," he said, "we have met in a very nice spot, for here we shall not be interrupted."

"What do you mean?" gasped Redcliffe.

"Can you ask? For your share in the dastardly work at Brixton it is my intention to endeavour to punish you. Dismount!"

"No, no. I have important——"

"Dismount, I say, or as sure as yon moon shines upon both of us, I will blow your brains out. Dismount!"

Redcliffe scrambled from the saddle.

"Draw!" said the Headsman, sternly, as, dismounting, he drew his blade.

Redcliffe was forced to comply.

"Before we commence," continued the Headsman, "let me tell you that all your arrangements have been torn to pieces. At this moment Mistress Eveline Duke is safe in the Tower. As to your father-in-law, Gabriel Everton, he will suffer for his share in the transaction."

And now Redcliffe saw how completely baffled he had been.

So, like others of his class, he thought he would make an offer to the *other* side.

If he only got out of fighting with this man, who was known to be an experienced swordsman, it would be something.

"To-night," he said, "I am not in a fit condition to fight."

"Fool! what care I as to that? Fight you will, or I run you through as you stand!"

"Suppose I make you an offer to turn evidence against——"

"Your offer would not be accepted," interrupted the Headsman, and, without further ceremony, he attacked Redcliffe.

Now that the wretch saw that there was no help for it, and that he must fight, he used all his skill.

But it availed him not at all.

Before two minutes had passed his blade went flying from his nervous grasp, and the Headsman's sword passed through his heart.

He fell without so much as a groan.

"There lie!" muttered the Headsman, as he sheathed his sword, "until I can communicate with your villainous associates."

Remounting, he rejoined our hero and his father.

"He is dead," he said, grimly; "they will be wiped out one by one. Now, do you hold my horse while I go to the front. It is only by boldness and determination that we can accomplish our purpose."

"But would it not be better to emove your mask?" asked Harold.

"No; I will tell you why. Some time ago I suddenly appeared before a servant at a house I visited, and the effect of my mask and my general appearance had such an effect upon her that she could not speak.

"I hope my appearance will have the same effect on the woman who answers the door here."

"We will see to the horse," said Harold, "but the instant we see that you have gained admission, we will join you."

The Headsman nodded, and strode to the door, upon which he boldly knocked.

Had there been a wicket or spy-hole, through which the servant could have looked, it is a moral certainty that she would not have opened the door.

Thinking that perhaps it was her master's ruffianly visitor returned, she opened the door.

The effect mentioned by the Headsman was repeated here.

The servant uttered no cry, but started back, gasping for breath.

"Hish!" said the Headsman, hastily. "Make no noise, as you value your liberty. I am not here to harm you, nor anyone within this house, except your master. Justice claims him. Do you understand me?"

The woman shook her head.

Her terror was fearful.

As the Headsman uttered the last words, he was joined by Harold and Don Fernando.

Completely overawed, the woman promised that she would not cry out.

More, she indicated the room occupied by Housden, the door of which was ajar.

His "lordship" had finished writing, and was attending to his spurs.

"So well!" he muttered, as, having seen that his spurs were all right, he turned to the mirror over the mantel, and proceeded to adjust his hat and cloak, "the time has come for me to leave England for the present. With Redcliffe's aid I can secure a ship, and with pretty Eveline as my companion, make for the South of France.

"Then, should I tire of her, I can make my own terms with the diamond merchant to restore her to his arms. Ho! Harold Forrester—curse you!—I will yet have the laugh of you and your precious friends. As to the Headsman——"

As he said these words half aloud, he started back from the mirror as if a shot had just crashed into the glass, for the mirror reflected a well-remembered figure.

With a great cry he turned.

There, standing calmly against the table, was the Headsman.

"How came you here?" gasped Housden.

"Through the door," was the reply. "And I am here for satisfaction."

"Satisfaction?"

"Well, to hand you over to justice."

"Attempt to touch me," cried Housden, as he snatched his sword from its sheath, "and you will rue it!"

"Think you that that sword has any terrors for me? Be careful of it. Listen, my lord—as, for so long, you have called yourself—the game you have played has at last come to an end. I call upon you, Henry Ryder, to surrender!"

"Fool, you know not what you say."

"I *do* know, and I say that you are an impostor."

"I repeat that you are a fool, and I say—begone! I will seek the assistance of——"

As he spoke he advanced towards the door.

But the Headsman barred the way.

"You leave not this room," he said, sternly. "And if you attempt violence, it shall be *met* with violence. What ho!" he added, raising his voice; "this way."

At once Harold and Don Fernando made their appearance.

"A trap!" muttered Housden, slinking back like a baffled hound.

"Behold here," said the Headsman, pointing to Don Fernando, "the real Lord Housden. Of course, you cannot recognise him. But ample proofs will be forthcoming, and the queen will reinstate him in his former position."

"Idle words!" sneered Housden. "You do not know the queen so well as I do."

"In a few minutes you will be confronted by one who can prove all."

"Indeed! His name?"

"Thomas Ryder."

Housden—or, rather, Henry Ryder—cowered back still farther.

"Then, when you see that the net has indeed closed around you," continued the Headsman, "you will surrender."

"Never! never!"

"We shall see."

"Stand away from that door," shouted Ryder, suddenly rousing himself. "Stand away, I say!"

And, with his sword raised ready to strike, he dashed towards the door.

Harold immediately met him, seized him by the arm and swung him round.

Then he plucked his blade from its scabbard.

Neither the Headsman nor Don Fernando attempted to interfere.

In an instant Ryder, with a fearful oath, attacked Harold with fury.

But his mad plunges were met with calmness and determination.

One minute had not passed before Ryder received a severe wound in the left shoulder.

This only served to madden him the more.

A short pause only, and the fight was renewed.

Backwards and forwards went Ryder, followed closely by Harold.

Chairs, table, almost everything standing on the floor was knocked over, while the blades dashed off many a costly article from the sideboards.

In five minutes, or less, victory was declared in favour of our hero, who, watching his opportunity, sent his blade completely through Ryder's chest.

The villainous impostor and murderer staggered back, and fell with a crash to the ground. But not dead.

Nay, he was mortally wounded, but he had strength enough to curse Harold and those with him.

Suddenly horses' hoofs were heard, and, in a few seconds, Mat o' the Mist entered the room, followed by the steward, Thomas Ryder.

"There lies your precious adopted son!" said the Headsman. "He is dying, and yet, as you hear, he blasphemes with all his power.

"But, ere he dies, he shall know that Eveline Duke is with friends, and that the lady who for so long thought herself his wife is within the Tower, ready to lay her case before the queen——"

"A lie! a lie!" hissed Ryder, writhing in his agony. "A black lie!"

A sudden click was heard, the ante-room door was thrown open, and two ladies appeared.

The first uncovered her head, and was at once recognised as "Lady Housden."

The second hesitated a moment, then she also slowly threw back her hood.

A great cry of wonder and astonishment escaped the lips of all present, for the second lady was—

Queen Elizabeth!

At once Harold and his friends prostrated themselves.

"Rise!" said Elizabeth, kindly. "Do not let us stand upon ceremony here. While yonder false lord retains consciousness, let me tell him that I now know all.

"That here I acknowledge yonder gentleman to be the true Lord Housden, and this brave youth his son.

"This unfortunate lady, by an accident, came face to face with me in the Tower. I instantly recognised her, and charged her to tell me all. She did so, with the result that I determined to confront yonder wretch myself.

"But when I, by aid of a servant, entered that room, I had no idea what terrible events were about to take place.

"In fair fight this youth has slain him, but it is a pity, since he has escaped the hangman.

"My lord," she added, addressing "Don Fernando," "we will welcome you and your friends in the Tower to-morrow. Mistress Eveline Duke must also be present. A coach awaits us by St. Martin's Fields—let it be fetched."

Mat o' the Mist hurriedly left the house, found the coach, and the queen and Lady Housden, with Harold and his father as an escort, were driven back to the Tower.

It was not the first time that Elizabeth had thus left the fortress, and had been the means of seeing that speedy justice was done.

The Headsman waited until Ryder had breathed his last; then, leaving the steward in charge of the Manor, he mounted and rode thoughtfully to the Tower, followed, at a respectful distance, by brave, honest Mat.

*   *   *   *

The last act has been written, and we have now only to inform our readers, that the facts we have described in this romance, speedily flew over the country, and Lord Edward Housden was heartily welcomed by all his old friends, and congratulated by the public, who did not disguise their admiration for our hero's conduct; nor did the people forget to declare, in the most emphatic manner, that the Headsman had proved himself to be one of Nature's noblemen.

But the public had cause to express its astonishment and anxiety soon, for the Headsman mysteriously disappeared, and in a week or two, another was appointed in his place.

The fact was that the Headsman had thrown off his disguise, and had appeared once more as Athol Forrester, none but the queen and his immediate friends knowing the dread life he had led.

Mat and Lucy were presented with a cottage and grounds by Lord Housden, and with money by the Headsman: and on the day of their marriage, they took possession of it. The union proved a happy one.

But the grand denouement of all was the marriage of our hero to Eveline Duke, the diamond merchant's daughter.

Long in the annals of Old London Bridge was remembered that day, when flags were flying and trumpets braying, and a grand procession passed to the church of St. Saviour's, where the queen herself was present to grace the ceremony.

The happy fathers were accompanied by a tall, handsome man, dark and swarthy as from travel; but none knew that he was the one of whom so much had been said, and whose disappearance had caused such wonder.

We mean—

"The Headsman of Old London Bridge."